GEORGE TURNER

D0450971

Other AvoNova Books by
George Turner

BRAIN CHILD
THE DESTINY MAKERS

GENETIC SOLDIER

GEORGE TURNER

AVONOVA

AVON BOOKS • NEW YORK

GENETIC SOLDIER is an original publication of Avon Books. This work is a novel. Any similarity to actual persons or events is purely coincidental.

AVON BOOKS
A division of
The Hearst Corporation
1350 Avenue of the Americas
New York, New York 10019

Copyright © 1994 by George Turner
Published by arrangement with the author
Library of Congress Catalog Card Number: 94-619
ISBN: 0-380-72189-9

First AvoNova Printing: July 1995
First Morrow/AvoNova Hardcover Printing: July 1994

AVON TRADEMARK REG. U.S. PAT. OFF. AND IN OTHER COUNTRIES, MARCA REGISTRADA, HECHO EN U.S.A.

Printed in the U.S.A.

RA 10 9 8 7 6 5 4 3 2 1

For

Judith Buckrich

Oh, it's 'Tommy this' and 'Tommy that' and 'Tommy go away';
But it's, "Thank you, Mister Atkins", when the band begins to play.

RUDYARD KIPLING, *'Tommy Atkins'*

part I

A MEETING
OF AGES

1

THIS IS THE STORY OF SOLDIER, FATED to stand at the crossroads of history and there question everything he had been raised to believe and cherish. And, with only self-respect for a weapon, save his life. If he could.

The villagers called him "Soldier" but he was in fact registered as the Atkins's Thomas (he knew the sour joke implied); parents unknown; CB. CB stood for Carnival Birth.

At twenty-eight Soldier was, in the estimation of those qualified to speak, as hard and unyielding as he needed to be (which meant curiously different things in different circumstances) in a hard and unyielding profession. Some—though not the Jones's Johnno, a lifelong friend—would have been surprised to learn that Soldier thought himself quite otherwise.

He had been reared by Libary, the Celibate, without thereby embracing chastity for himself, and was in consequence a highly educated man within the limits of his time and culture, which accounted for his knowledge of the verses of the poet Kipling, dead some nine centuries. He considered himself a basically gentle man whose work could be endured only by those with a pragmatic understanding of necessity

3

and choice; the work itself had been finally dictated by his Genetic grouping. Libary, guardian and mentor of the teenager, could have interfered but did not; as an intellectual Libary held warfare in contempt but conceded that if there must be conflict, it should at least be conducted by competent minds, such as his Thomas's.

Soldier, who thought himself not much given to sentiment—at any rate, where it might be observed— never strayed far from Libary when his duties permitted. He had a great capacity for affection and gratitude.

So much for Soldier, marking time until time itself should question him.

The ambiguous attitude of the Forest Genetic, who made up the great mass of the civil population, no longer troubled him as it had once done. Soldiers grew accustomed to it and were able to joke about it without rancour.

Even the few Foresters who were fairly familiar with Thomas Atkins addressed him as "Soldier," partly from habit, partly because of their uneasy feeling that his profession was not wholly justifiable although practised in their defence. The paradox of preaching peace while being eternally ready for war was older than written history and defeated them as it had defeated their ancestors. It was too difficult for simple folk, and they called themselves "simple folk" when faced with hard questions.

They kept Soldier at symbolic arm's length by refusing his given name while affirming that he was really a good chap, not just any coarse fighting man. He's different, they would say, justifying both him and themselves; he's not just a trained killer, he's a nice bloke.

Behind his back they speculated on his procreative future. Twenty-eight was a late age for beginning a family, yet Soldier showed no sign of being caught in the sexual trap of Genetic Match, whereas most men had made their couple of false starts by twenty and begun fathering soon after.

No one doubted his sexual capacity; he joined actively, *very* actively, in the annual indecencies of Carnival and was known to have broken intercourse protocol in the privacy of forest assignations. There remained the possibility that his Genetic makeup was "unconforming", containing some rare "character" (the villagers knew nothing of genes and chromosomes) matchable only with a woman whose exotic "character" could accommodate his.

She would be a remarkable woman, they thought, who made Match with their Soldier and snatched him forever out of the license of Carnival.

(She existed and their meeting was imminent. And strange and disruptive and deadly. Yet there was little remarkable about her.)

And now something about Libary, the most senior of the Celibates who administered the great Book House on the hill. The villagers, respecting and a little fearing him, had christened him "Libary," which was a suitable name, given that the first "r" in "library"— a Late English word from the Last Culture—had been elided by time and carelessness.

Black Libary was over half a century old, a good age in an era when most of the clinical wisdom of the Last Culture had been lost. The Book House scholars found diseases and their cures described in the ancient, preserved books but they no longer possessed the means or the understanding to cope with them; Last Culture prescriptions might as well have been spells of the *caditcha* men or the lost memories of Dreamtime. They had developed an efficient plant-based pharmacopoeia of their own but the life span of a sturdy race had regressed to about fifty; infant mortality was high.

Why Libary had adopted and taught Soldier was his own affair, his secret, though the Ordinate scholars exchanged muttered opinions on the matter.

Soldier, clinging to Libary like an imprinted duckling, decided in early childhood that the old Koori was indeed his father. Discovering the meaning of celibacy was only a temporary setback because he soon found out, like any other sniggering twelve-year-old with the sap beginning to rise, the meaning of Carnival. Carnival was that one time of year when even the best-bred girls were liable to allow themselves a swallow or two more of strong country ale than propriety would sanction and so commit friendly errors against the Top-Ma's breeding programme.

When such errors were permitted to come to term the males were expected to accept parental responsibility and usually did so (though the occasional renegade faded from sight, for "administrative reasons") before the registration was made. The mothers were, on the whole, content to hand their deserted errors over to Public Patronage (not always; some screamed and clung while family reasoned, cursed, and struggled) because a girl had eventually to enslave with her sexual *rom* the right man in the right Genetic and he would not often care to be burdened with a Carnival by-blow who might not fit his occupational group.

Soldier, trained in Cadet School on the one hand and by Libary in Late English and History and Science on the other, began to research his own biological history in bathroom mirrors. Libary, shown in the record to have accepted Dedication at twenty-three, could have kicked up sexual heels in a few farewell years of Carnival before entry into professional purity. But it was a question which in "common decency"—that pestilent cover over truth and feeling—could not be asked; Libary, questioned, would have pretended not to hear and talked of something else.

The mirrors twinkled slyly at the boy's investigation. Libary was a full-blooded Koori; Soldier, lighter-coloured, was not so light that he could not be *nyoongan*, half-bred. There were resemblances which thirst for a parent exaggerated but they existed in, for example, the flared nostrils and wide mouth and slender bones. Blue eyes were a problem but could be blamed on the unknown mother; Libary's eyes were soft, Koori brown. To the boy, the general shaping of limbs and hands told their tale; Libary, had he not opted for Ordination, would certainly have been seen as Desert Genetic (from which the fighting soldiers were drawn).

Area General Atkins, Commander of the Yarra Valley Protective Force, was on an extended leave during a period of quiet in the regional animosities when The Comet made the first of its many orbits over southeastern Australia.

News travelled rapidly in the Twenty-eighth Century world, transmitted by the semaphore systems that ringed the planet. Islands like Australia suffered delay while the mail catamarans closed the sea gaps but Libary was not taken by surprise when the bright light rose overhead. Only the day before, word had been signalled down the coast from Nugini that a strange star had risen and sped through the night sky in many passages over many lands.

Over all lands, Libary thought, since its orbit was south to north, precessing as the Earth turned beneath it. He puzzled, though, over the rapidity with which it traversed the night; reports of dawn sightings indicated two complete circlings each day. He puzzled more when precession ceased on its east Australian orbit and it traced the same path, night after night, over the same area of the planet. Then he recalled the stories of *Search* and *Kiev* and instituted a headlong hunt for references by the crypt Ordinands; in hours he was able to surmise that a starship had come home.

As a wise man he kept that conviction to himself; he believed in proof before speech.

On the third night of orbital stability it rose again at the same time and place and careered through its six-hour path to zenith and vanishment below the midnight horizon.

Therefore it was no comet, despite the villagers' naming it so because of its wan, misty tail.

Libary sent for Thomas, went over with him what had been observed, but not what he had concluded, and asked what he thought of it all. Soldier, having no profound thought about a light in the sky, told him the village gossip.

Libary asked brutally, "What more did you expect from them?"

"Nothing, having no facts to argue over."

Whereupon Libary told this single most powerful authority for a hundred kils around that all his education had been wasted time, that his mind slept, that there were facts in plenty for any but the blind to wonder at and that he, General Atkins, should station himself at dusk on the crest of the neighbouring hill to the north and observe—with his eyes and then with his brain.

The Ordinands tut-tutted amongst themselves when Libary treated the General like a small boy, but they noted that the old man commonly marked his affection with challenges and that the General never failed to take them up.

Soldier climbed the hill, observed the rise of The Comet, its place and time, and made nothing of it. He knew little astronomy beyond the basics needed for march orientation—but enough, had he guessed what he was looking for.

Libary grunted, "Try again—if it will perform long enough for you to recognise it."

On the second night he was distracted by visitors to his hilltop and it was then, with only a part of his attention on the sky and the rest entertained by Johnno and his new beloved, that Soldier's brain delivered up common sense where cudgelling had only pawed over the rubble.

It was near the end of spring; day temperatures had risen to an average twenty-eight Centigrade. He took advantage of solitude and the little sundown breeze to strip and enjoy coolness with the UV radiation at minimum. He was dark enough to bear exposure with little risk of the skin evil but it was his professional business to be healthy and an example to his troopers, so he wore full dress by day, which the villagers thought eccentric.

From his grassy summit he looked across a saddle to the Library on its long ridge with, three hundred metres below, the village hidden under trees on the further side of the river bank. He would yet have to wait until near dark before The Comet rose, as before, over the left-hand corner of the building. Some flicker in his mind registered a clue there but he was immersed in the animal pleasure of cooling as sweat dried from the creases and hollows of his body.

Two figures emerged from the plantation of eucalypts on the lower slope. The stocky, overmuscled Johnno with his slightly bowlegged stride Soldier would have known at twice the distance; the companion, shorter but also broadly built, must be the matchwoman, brought for display and congratulation. She came from a village downriver and he had never seen her, but he had heard from those who had and his curiosity was whetted. He had shepherded Johnno through previous loves blighted by the veto of the Top-Ma and knew his friend's Genetically approved Match would be worth meeting.

(And what of his own Matching? He was in no hurry; there was pleasure in women, denied by the Match which would restrict him to one woman only. The Matched told him that the *rom* recognition was a sudden thing, a heaven-bolt that changed the world, but he was a thoughtful man who did not fancy restriction by lightning strike.)

As they climbed nearer he saw that she wore her hair at shoulder length, like the men, and that what he had taken for a very short skirt was a pair of men's thigh-length trousers. He sought a Late English word less damning than the local demotic speech and settled for "hoyden." It occurred to him to pull his own ankle-length trousers on as a gesture of respect, then decided against it. Johnno wouldn't give a damn and the sight of a lusty village siren, surely old enough to have survived a Carnival or two, going through the motions of coy avoidance of the obvious (without missing a detail) could be treasurable.

At closer sight it seemed that Johnno had excelled himself; he had always preferred wrestling partners and this one might well give him a fall or two. She was not at all bad looking for a workhorse of Forest Genetic and as sturdily built for her sex as Johnno for his. He fancied them bedding down like grappling grampuses, but what of that while they kept each other happy?

They stumped to a halt, not breathing very heavily from the climb, and Johnno introduced his woman as, "the Ridley's Bella," which seemed to match her no-nonsense solidity, and told her, "This is the Atkins's Tommy, but everybody calls him Soldier because that's what he is."

She looked him over with no pretence of modesty and said, "You've got a lot of Koori in you, haven't you?"

From some that would have been insolence, short of good manners though less than insult, but Soldier heard only the interest of a child with a novelty. (If the Genetics ever stopped to think about it, they all had "a lot of Koori" in them, the strong melanin that had made their racial persistence practicable in the Greenhouse light.) He caught Johnno's wink telling him that this was a blunt one and no mistake, so he gave back blunt for blunt: "Plenty but I don't know who from. I'm a Carnival get."

That would have set most strangers back into polite nothings but Bella said, "I know; Johnno told me. You're not what I expected."

"No?" Had she expected another ploughman's ox like Johnno?

"I've never seen a soldier close-to before."

So he was a showpiece, a curio. He answered with specious gravity, "Why should you? We don't advertise."

A gameplaying slyness in her eyes should have warned him not to be too easily amused. "You haven't got all that much to advertise."

That was close to breathtaking, even from the village hoyden, but he saw that matchstruck Johnno thought it a huge joke. Wounded pride assured him that it was not true, save that she would be comparing him with Johnno, whose endowment was a Carnival byword.

"Besides," said Bella, playing brashness to the hilt, "you're thin! Soldiers ought to be big men."

"They don't have to be."

"That's silly." She flexed a very respectable working muscle. "Why, I bet I'm stronger than you."

Soldier fell back on cool politeness, wondering was the girl possessed by some demented bush demon. "In some ways you may be."

Politeness was no defence against the total tomboy who rounded on her grinning lover to demand, "I can tough it with the men, can't I?"

Soldier smothered an ungenerous smile. Oh, Johnno, Johnno, do you deserve this hooligan lump of trouble?

He was unprepared for Bella's laughing attack, the launch of her seventy or so kilos on to his half-recumbent body. He was slammed smartly flat on his back while her knees ground into the biceps of both arms and a solid rump drove his stomach back to his spine.

He was instantly furious and as instantly controlled as he heard Johnno's shocked, "Bella!" No responsible person would goad a reflexive fighting machine into action. He lay still for a long moment, forcing a smile, and when he was ready lifted his legs from the hips with the coordinated smoothness built into the Desert Genetic and brought his bended knees round either side of her until he could plant his toes under her armpits and lift her away.

She went down solidly, sitting hard, surprised but still laughing and complaining delightedly to Johnno, "You never told me he could do that."

Johnno, between relief and embarrassment, said, "I told you not to try anything on him" and to Soldier, "Tommy, she arm wrestles with the boys in the beer-house."

The Match, Soldier decided, was more than merely mysterious; it addled the brain.

Bella became marginally respectful. "The other boys couldn't have done that lift."

"They could if they were practised in it." And if they were limber enough and fast enough, which most of her Genetic toughs were not.

"But you lifted me easy."

"Why not?"

"When you're so thin!"

By comparison, yes. "I'm just not thick."

She leaned over to slap at his calf muscle. "There's not enough there."

"There is, lass."

Johnno said, "The breeding's different, love. It's another sort of muscle."

That was a strange idea to her; like so many villagers she accepted Genetic variation without thought of the mechanisms within it. Her puzzlement brought out the eternal instructor in Soldier.

"There are two kinds of muscle fibre, Bella, for different jobs. Yours and Johnno's have a mostly crosswise grain, good for lifting weights and heavy work, but you get tired and have to take a break every so often. Mine have mostly a longwise grain for stamina, for fast moving over long distances, for doing lighter work without stopping or slowing down. A soldier has to go till the job is done, so he needs a body built to do that."

It was only a half explanation but enough for the purpose. Bella was doubtful. "Bend your leg," she ordered and pinched his calf and slid her hand down to the ankle, then felt her own bunchy leg muscle. "It's a different shape; yours goes right down along the bone."

"Extensors; tendons with lots of stretch."

"Um." She examined his arms, thin beside those

of the village men, something less than she would expect of a husband doing farm and forestry work between stints of factory loading and handling. "What if you have to lift something heavy?"

"Use two men."

Her approved man would grunt and strain to prove he could do the job alone. "Are all the soldiers like you?"

"More or less. We use some mixed-Genetics for special heavy duties."

"Mixed?" She was puzzled again at an idea outside her experience. "Do you mean they breed you like— like . . . "

Outspokenness had found its limit; one did not compare people with . . .

Soldier grinned at her. "Like farm animals? For fat or meat or hauling loads? Why not? It just happens that I'm a stray born of the right parents for soldiering but most come of parents deliberately Matched—like you to Johnno."

The Mas and Top-Mas were skilled in guiding like cautiously to like and in maintaining records to guard against inbreeding. And there was always Test Year to weed out social incompatibles. It was a fallible system but one that preserved a reasonable balance of types to fill essential niches. Bella seemed unaware of herself as a roughly designed end product; Johnno knew more because of his long association with Soldier but he knew also that in a basic-education community you keep special knowledge to yourself; nothing brings ostracism so fast as a hint of clever-clever.

Soldier said, "Anyway, I'm happy to meet you. Johnno has told me all about you." The lovelorn halfwit!

She simpered, an unnerving sight, and murmured, "We're starting Test Year."

"Best of luck to you."

In the macabre fascination of Bella he had missed the waning of the light. Now the corner of his eye caught the Moon clearing a cloud and a vagrant thought came to mind—of how it rose at a slightly more northerly point each night as the seasons changed. . . .

The evening breeze blew harder as the temperature dropped. It was nearing full dark and he began to pull on his clothes. Bending to lace his shoes, he almost missed the rise of brilliance.

The splendid silver-white spark lifted abruptly over the left-hand end of the Library, drawing its dim shaft of comet-tail after it like—

Like the comet-tail, he knew suddenly, that it was not.

The vagrant thought returned as revelation: If it rose in the same place each night, not shifting its orbit westward, then it was not "precessing." That was a word he had picked up from Libary, one that even the Ordinand translators of Late English encountered only rarely.

His mind, once stirred, made a web of connections and he knew, with an excited wonder, what it was. Old men in the beerhouses nattered of the folkloric Star People who might or might not have had an existence long ago, before the Twilight, but Soldier, reared in the very smell of history, knew the ancient reality.

Bella, with her back to it, had missed the not-comet's rising and was still earthbound. "Do soldiers always wear long trousers?" Her men might wear them for special tasks but not for sitting on hilltops.

A small part of Soldier's mind answered politely while the greater part cogitated and examined. "Mostly. We work in all sorts of conditions—mud, water, thorns, insects, snake country. We can't be changing into suitable gear all the time."

"Oh."

She probably thought the real reason was to hide his thin legs and he was suddenly tired of her. "I have to leave you; I must report back. I'll come down and see you both in your Test cottage."

He started downhill at speed, faster than they would try to follow, and heard Bella confide in her brass voice, "He's nice in his skinny way."

Well, he was not for the Bellas of this world, whatever virtues hid beneath her layers of muscle; Johnno was welcome to the hack work.

Above him the not-comet rose steadily, chasing and outstripping the lagging Moon. He stumbled more than once because he could not bear to take his eyes from the entrancing thing.

The barely literate villagers took pride in their Book House, visiting it on holidays, delighting in the ancient art works and the historical tales told by the Ordinands. Only a single storey high, but long and broad and deep in its underground rooms, it crouched on its high ridge as a dominant presence.

Soldier had ceased to be impressed by it while still a toddler; it was his place that he was used to. He nodded to the sentries at the outer end of the drawbridge and those under the war-door at the inner end; as he stopped for a moment to slow his breathing, he listened automatically for the creak of windlasses as the bridge rose and the war-door dropped, the quick bark of the sergeant's voice dismissing the outer guard now that the General was inside. Moat, drawbridge, and suspended war-door were not ornaments and the Library drew on his troops for its defence.

Libary, he knew, would be on the roof with his pride and darling, the small telescope he had designed and whose lenses had been ground and polished by workmen brought in from the villages of the Glassmaker Talent and driven to the edge of revolt by what they saw as finicking insistence on an unnatural precision. A high bargain would be exacted for any more such instruments!

Soldier had looked through the eyepiece and declared himself delighted by the craters on the Moon and the rather fuzzy rings of Saturn; in fact the life-pictures (in Late English, "photographs" and "illustrations") of these to be found in a number of the preserved books were clearer and more impressive. However, with Libary deep in designs for larger reflectors, enthusiasm was required of him and Soldier was willing, for affection's sake, and because the old brute's excitements tended to produce useful results. The Glassmakers had been more surly: We know, Sir, that two- and three-metre reflectors once existed; only find the means of their construction and they will exist again.

They had muttered among themselves, arguing impossibilities but already making tentative suggestions. Libary was confident that a step forward would be made but his present progress was limited to an eye glued to the small tube, rediscovering for himself the matters depicted in the illustrations.

At the top of the stairs Soldier changed into the fur-soled slippers worn on the roof to protect the thousands of glass panes through which the Sun lit the space below.

He saw Libary clearly in the moonlight, eye to the tube, following the splendour in orbit. Libary heard the loose shoes flap on glass and asked, "Thomas?"

"Yes, sir."

"Well?"

"The Jones's Johnno is Matched. Risking his life with this one, I'd say."

"I know that." Testy. The Top-Ma had probably

consulted with him on Genetic probity. "What else?"

"As with Johnno, nothing you do not already know."

"I'm not a fish; don't play me."

"Very well; your bright light is not a natural object but an artefact, guided and driven, or else it could not rise in the same place at the same time each night."

"That was obvious from the second sighting."

"To you. I am a soldier with a different expertise."

"Stop it, Thomas! This thing is not trivial. What is your conclusion?"

Soldier had to hope he was not about to make a thundering fool of himself. "A sky ship. A traveller between worlds."

Libary grunted, " 'Spaceship' was the term," and stepped back from the eyepiece. "This is donkey work. We need the secret of camera picturing. It will be somewhere amongst a million unread texts—and when found may be unintelligible." He rubbed his eyes. "So it's a spaceship, is it?"

"It fits the descriptions—a metal cabin reflecting sunlight, and a tail of fire."

"This tail of fire is pale stuff. Pictures of rockets show very bright tails of white fire, so perhaps this is not driven by a rocket. What then?"

"I don't know."

"There are mentions of a starship driven by ramjet. What might a ramjet be?"

"Again, I don't know."

"Nor does anybody." Bright teeth in the dark face showed him smiling in the night. "We ransack the past for useful knowledge and every discovery leads to a blank wall for lack of some simple information that a schoolboy of the time could have supplied."

Soldier guessed that something better than a schoolboy might have been needed to explain a spaceship but he said only, "Can you see it clearly?"

"No. I need a wider lens and a means of filtering sunlight and a method of stilling the twinkling and dimming of the air, but I can see well enough to tell you with certainty that this visitor is one of the ships that went into the sky before the Twilight. Tabulator Gerald found an illustration in a book in the crypts."

He gestured at the small table standing on padded legs by the telescope. On it stood a lamp, wick turned down to conserve precious oil—one of those called by its Late English name of "hurricane lamp," fashioned of thin, valuable copper after a dozen attempts and frustrations from illustrations in very old books indeed, dated two centuries or more before the Twilight. Soldier turned up the wick and a polished reflector at the back beat light onto the book. Libary had laid clear glass across the pages; only trained handlers were allowed to touch the easily damaged paper.

The ship was an extraordinary object, not the bullet shape to be expected for launching into the vast night but formed like two long trumpets joined end to end at the narrow point of their mouthpieces. The trumpet sides were not solid but a tracery, lattices of struts opening onto a huge bellmouth at each end, dwarfing the cabin set like a thick collar at the narrow point of join. The Last Culture had possessed extremely strong metals which were still found—resistant and unworkable—in ancient ruins and caches, so the lattice was too fine for the little telescope to break down into detail, but the outline was clear enough when he put his eye to the lens for comparison. The cabin, he remarked, seemed absurdly small.

"I think not, Thomas. How do we judge? How high in the sky is it? What can we compare it with? I have fifty Tabulators scouring the crypt shelves for detail and a few facts have appeared. For instance, that the crew and complement ran into hundreds. It must be larger than you guess."

The largest transocean catamarans carried crews of thirty or so and a few passengers; on the same scale this ship would be far larger than the Library itself. The Last Age had seen miracles before it crashed into history.

Soldier raised an objection. "Yet how can it be the same after seven hundred years? Those people worked their wonders but they did not live forever."

"Children and grandchildren, descendants growing and taking over. Leave that and ask rather what they do out there, circling the same course, doing what, and why?"

"That's in a soldier's bag of answers. They inspect, reconnoitre. They had vast telescopes; perhaps they see clear to the ground from up there."

"They had other instruments than telescopes. They could see a man from a height of hundreds of kils."

That was an eerie thought, a negation of all possible privacy, almost a confirmation of the concept of magic that still lingered in men's minds.

Libary's thought was nearer home. "What they see must puzzle them. They left a world of cities that towered to the clouds and people who crowded the Earth like ants; now they return to find a civilisation where people live with the land instead of merely on it."

Soldier, returning to realities, asked, "Were they supposed to return? The folklore speaks only of finding new worlds to settle."

"More than folklore, printed records; yet there's no certainty of what they set out to achieve. The facts will be somewhere available—if we ever find the texts among the millions waiting around the world."

"Common sense says they are deciding on a suitable place to set down. Get the semaphores working, sir; find out what other communities under the orbit path have seen. Perhaps, like our ocean catamarans, they carry lifeboats, small craft for landing reconnaissance parties. Somewhere, someone may already be in communication with them."

Libary grunted, "The semaphores have yammered incessantly for days and there is no news of a landing party."

"There will be. Then our questions will be answered."

Libary surveyed him sombrely. "And then?"

And the answers, Soldier thought a little grimly, *will set all your Ordinand knowledge running for cover and shivering in its ignorance.* For the sake of gentleness he rendered the thought with a smile. "And then there'll be trouble with all those manipulating politicians like yourself who will want to tell them how to behave in a changed world. On the other hand, they'll be able to explain all the mysteries in all the Libraries. You'll have to give and take."

Libary turned his back. He was offended but Soldier had in affection conceded as much blunting of truth as he felt necessary. In silence the older man covered the telescope with a sheet of expensive rubber, brought four thousand kils from Nugini by merchant catamaran.

When he had done he said, "You're not a fool, Thomas. You have stated the problem; now think about it."

2

AT ALTITUDE 2000 K, *SEARCH* CIRCLED
the homeworld, for which her complement had broken their oaths of service. Their clamour for return
had sunk from mutinous anger into a repressed hysteria they called "homesickness" as cover and comfort for pledge broken and duty deserted.

Now, with the planet radiant below—a vast plate
of blue and white—they snarled through the unbearable waiting while the Survey teams assessed this
strange new Earth and tried to settle on a suitable
Contact Area. In the Command Suite, Ship-Captain
Brookes sifted a chaos of information and conflicting
advice as he sought a responsible point of First Contact. First Contact of one's own people! That was a
joke of sorts and the major part of his indecision.

It may have been sheer exhaustion in the face of
imponderables that made him easy prey for the suggestion of Nugan Taylor, who offered at least an
opening gambit to the complex play of return to
Earth.

Nugan Taylor had trouble with time. She was forty-
eight years old in biological time and several centuries old in real time—whatever "real" time might be
and whatever the vagueness of "several centuries"
might represent when at relativistic speeds there was

22

more to be considered than the compression of time passing; the astrophysicists and mathematicians had been thrown into disorder when they found sections of space (high-gravity zones and some others less easily described) where distortions of geometry were matched by distortions of the flow of local time. Since the instrument findings were part of the general distortion, accurate definition of time and position had become matters of argument and approximation.

Being a practical woman, Nugan said to herself, *I am here and now, and that will have to do until I find a better way of thinking.*

She was a quarter-caste Koori/Australian with something but not noticeably much of the dark skin of her grandmother and the rather coarse Caucasian features of the white side of her family. Unmarried and intending to stay that way, she was proud of her eighteen-year-old daughter, Anne. She liked men and what pleasures they might offer but was not prepared to attach herself permanently to any of those available. After twenty-eight waking years aboard she knew them all too well.

Her appointment was Contact Officer, First Grade, and her work was physical survey of such planets as might be found on which human beings could dwell and flourish. As a High IQ Selectee she had been marked for social promotion at age ten and given the force-fed education which her test results and personal interests dictated; at age twenty, with knowledge and intellectual training that would have seemed magical to her ancestors of even a century earlier, she had been offered the position aboard *Search*, assigned by computer as a ninety-four percent job fit. She had accepted, partly because she saw Twenty-first Century Earth as a decaying slum which must soon rot away altogether and partly because oblique, unnoticed pressures from the Selection

Corps made it unlikely that she could refuse.

She went into space in the finest condition of body and mind that a technically brilliant culture could produce, superbly equipped for the work she was to do. That turned out a bitter disappointment.

Each of the three Wakings had a team of three Contact Officers, so Nugan was not unique in her training, but she was unique in one respect which had little to do with her professional preparation. Her black grandmother had been one of the shrinking number of full-blooded tribal people remaining in Australia and she had fired the little girl with her folktales and Dreaming lore; precocious Nugan had spoken the old lady's tribal tongue when she was three. Later, she had chosen Linguistics as an Optional during her training and had emerged with a thorough and probably useless understanding of the structure and evolution of language.

On the ship she was alone in her specialty; nobody aboard, least of all Nugan, could have guessed that a study "lodged with her useless" would one day find for Ship-Captain Brookes an answer to indecision. But, neither had anybody guessed that the complement of *Search* would eventually talk itself into homesickness.

Homesickness was not considered, not foreseen, by the administrative committees who assembled the complements and laid down the flight orders. Throughout history explorers had left home and country, turned their backs on family, and never returned. What was different here? Nobody asked the question because it did not arise.

Nugan might have foreseen the creeping illness if it had entered her mind but in fact she was devastatingly surprised by it. Yet she had set down its causes in her diary long before the muttering started. She was a compulsive diarist, not of events—there were few notable events in a starship where most of the personnel were in cryo-sleep at any given time—but of her private thoughts and observations:

"Contact Team dropping is an education in futility. The Electronic Mentors taught us what to check on a Contact Drop—not people, which were considered pretty unlikely phenomena, but atmosphere content and ratios, presence of chlorophyll, sunlight analysis, soil bacteria, edible protein, and so on through 101 criteria adding up to a planet's suitability for settlement.

"Settlement? Think about the parameters for human existence and the nature of the 'Earthlike planet' joke becomes clear.

"Atmosphere: Oxygen content, at Earth-normal pressure, should be not less than seventeen percent for rapid physical acclimatisation and not more than twenty-two percent to avoid overstimulation and rampaging bushfires. It doesn't seem much to ask until you remember that free oxygen is not automatically present in planetary atmospheres, that it has to emerge over millions of years in response to special circumstances—such as the presence of anaerobic life-forms that break down dioxides and sulphates—and that such a planet would have to be, counting from its final accretion, several thousands of millions of years old. That means that you have to arrive at just the right stage of its history. Which could be never; they don't all follow the Terran track to celestial adulthood.

"Temperature: To build a settlement you have to live and work mostly outside for at least a couple of generations. So the temperature range has to be suitable for physical activities—say, zero Centigrade at midwinter and not over forty-five at summer maximum. For this the planet must be at the right distance from its sun, in a reasonably near-circular orbit to avoid violent seasonal fluctuations and have not too much inclination to the ecliptic for the same reason. Planets of double suns are out of the question; the weather complications would be horrendous. And there are more damned double suns in this galaxy than you'd think possible.

"The sun: We can't stand too much UV without developing dangerous cancers—curable but not wanted in plague lots by labouring settlers. Then the infrared spectrum has to be considered in relation to cloud cover as a monitor of stable conditions. And there has to be an ozone layer, which turns out not to be automatically a part of planetary atmospheres.

"When you've got all that balanced out—which we never have found—there's gravity to think about, also inimical proteins, unassimilable airborne particles, poisonous vegetation and anything else you care to suggest. . . .

"So, you children of our pretty dim-looking future, the odds are loaded against locating suitable real estate by racing round the sky and dropping in on promising dirtballs. The fact is that we've done thirty-eight drops (I've been in thirteen of them) without finding a place fit to support anything but its own version of Hell."

The muttering may have begun as no more than a peevish outburst against life in a steel box, scouring the sky on a mission with no end in sight. It did not take long to reach a fever of conviction that the quest was a delusion.

The complaint did not affect Nugan greatly. Living in a steel box was not so qualitatively different from living in a family flat—more like a barracks—in a Twenty-first Century city, on a planet where all cities had taken on dreary sameness as population pressures forced disparate cultures to accept similar measures for coping. Little changed, little was better or worse than yesterday, little was surprising or unexpected.

Nugan, a very self-contained woman, was rarely bored except by the complainers; she had a daughter to raise in this crowded environment and that was a challenge as well as an absorbing interest. There were only ten children in all of the three Wakings, meaning that only ten out of a hundred and fifty women had, in the early years of the voyage, deliberately flouted common sense and given birth for their lovers of a moment. (There were a few permanent liaisons aboard, only a few.) That particular flouting of the sensible conventions of the voyage ended when Brookes threatened to dump the next baby into space. Nobody believed he would do it, but the threat made enthusiasts think twice. In Ship's Articles he had the power; his authority was absolute. In service pragmatism he was right to forbid birthing; there was simply no room for expansion. The ship carried several millions of viable, genetically designed cell clusters in cryo and they were the destined future, not the haphazard products of transient sex.

Nugan, when the muttering became mutinous discontent, was not prepared to desert duty. As she saw it, they had all taken oaths of service and accepted their orders and must carry on while capability lasted, not run for home when nostalgia raised its self-pitying head.

The idea of abandoning the search spread like a wet stain; it was a mutter, a complaint, and suddenly a demand. The ship's psychologists could do nothing for the simplest of reasons; they had nothing to offer but pep talk and hypnosis. The pep talk was hollow and the hypnosis failed quickly where no counter-neurotic atmosphere existed to sustain it.

The ship's log recorded it all for future generations—how Brookes ordered the whole fulminating Third Waking into cryo-sleep; how the virus of discontent was spread during the simple handing over of duties between Third Waking and its replacement; how discontent evolved into a strange species of mutiny, a sit-in strike wherein all but essential duties and maintenance were refused. Brookes knew the impossibility of disciplining an entire ship's complement and after a few months gave in with what dignity he could. At least no one was fool enough to attempt to depose him from command; that would have brought bloodshed.

The few who thought as Nugan did argued fruitlessly against the dereliction of the sworn duty embraced with Earthside fervour; they were brushed aside. Jack McCann, the Second Waking Dropmaster, friend and loud supporter of Nugan, was badly beaten by a group of women armed with billiard cues.

Search, then in the general area of Capella, was brought to a halt, which at her star-hopping speed took more than a year, and reversed for home.

Once on course for Earth, speculation about "home" began. A problem for the theorists was that they did not know just how long they had been in space; those fluctuations in time and geometry became the ground of fresh quarrels. The ship's mathematicians found too many approximations and unknowns to check any answer against a deceptive universe; they might have been in space for six centuries or eight or any figure between. The only certainties were that each had lived twenty-eight waking years in transit and perhaps an extra one in the ultraslow biological creep of cryo-sleep. These told nothing of the universe outside.

Debate became raging argument as people who had abandoned duty and now had none discovered animosities to fill their minds. Brookes put every possible body into cryo-sleep, but too many had to be kept operational for maintenance and emergency, and these formed camps and parties, arguing the possible outcomes of the Terran population crisis (which was most of the reason for the ship's existence), of the poor mineral resources that profligate waste had left for the new generations, of the persistence or non-persistence of the Greenhouse warming, of the ruthless culling of the seas as feeding the world battled with the preservation of essential species . . . There was even a hysterical group proving to its own satisfaction that an Ice Age had been due within a century or two of departure.

Nobody predicted the reality of the world to which *Search* came home.

The ship moved into a south–north orbit at 20,000 K, precession allowing a preliminary scan of most of the surface in a few days. What the instruments saw and relayed to the internal screens suggested more enigmas than answers. Brookes ordered the orbit dropped to 2000 K for close scanning.

What was seen amounted to this:

Search made sixty passages of the planet, covering continents and seas with cameras, radiation detectors, and direct observation, forming what Brookes realised was only a draft, something less than an outline, of the shape of the world below.

The planet was innocent of radio communication and artificially generated electrical activity of any kind. The population centres everywhere seemed to be small towns, actually large villages for the most part, mainly on the seacoasts but scattered sparsely in the interiors, where they hugged the rivers, surrounded always by broad farmlands into which obviously regulated forests speared green, geometrically husbanded fingers. The inland centres were smaller; the inhabited areas tended to thin out at frontiers of unbroken forest or desert or grass plain, as though demarcation proceeded on an ordered, controlled plan.

Of the vast cities of yesterday—London, New York, Moscow, Shanghai, and the rest—nothing habitable remained; their towers had fallen—or been blasted— and their sites buried under water or green canopy. If men and women lived like ghosts in the ruins, their presence was not detectable from orbit.

When night fell on Earth, darkness was almost absolute. North of the equator only faint shimmers marked centres large enough to glimmer palely. High resolution cameras picked up street lamps, probably gas lit, in a few of the larger towns; it was unlikely that much accessible oil remained in the looted ground.

They revealed communities laid out with buildings that could be small factories and, occasionally, clusters of larger structures that might be centres of administration and assembly. Road traffic seemed to be animal-drawn but the nature of the animals could not be determined with certainty from a vertical view; the consensus preferred horses. There appeared to be numbers of varied one-man vehicles based, at a guess, on the pedal-cycle.

All continents seemed to evince the same stage and type of development—all but Australia, which seemed even more sparsely settled though in much the same style. This uniformity suggested intercommunication on a considerable scale but the only discernible long-distance traffic seemed to be by way of large, oceangoing sail-powered catamarans which developed surprising speeds over long sea-lanes. High winds? Improved design? "Don't guess," Brookes told them. "Wait and see."

The climate seemed puzzlingly little changed from

that of the Twenty-first Century. Europe was green and fertile and the Russian wheat belt still skirted the edges of the marshes which had once been tundra. The huge once-desert belts of Africa had retained their Greenhouse fertility while the central plains of North America were recovering from the desertification caused by violent changes in ocean currents and seasonal winds. The equatorial zone was a vast jungle hiding God only knew what under impenetrable green.

The average global temperature had fallen a couple of degrees only and it seemed that the return to Twentieth Century stability was unexpectedly slow—or that other crises had arisen to maintain warming. Ocean temperatures were high and the ozone curiously patchy. Evil scenarios were plentiful and easy; only years of study would suggest what had slowed cooling.

One question concerned the complement urgently. The observers estimated a planetary population of no more than a few hundred millions, yet they had left behind them some eighteen billions jostling for food and unpolluted air. To the excitement of homecoming was added a desperate need to know what history had done to the shrunken breed or what humanity had done to itself, or what disasters sheer accident might have spawned. Knowing themselves and their time, they dreamed of war and pestilence.

That Brookes's advisers fixed on a spot in southeastern Australia for planetfall was no random choice. The island continent seemed demographically different from the others. It was more sparsely populated by groups of communes rather than townlets, few larger than a couple of thousand souls and with considerable distances—fifty or more K—between groups, like small states separated by huge stretches of forest. In terms of roads and inhabited areas it appeared something of a backwater in the larger world, though sea traffic was plentiful along the coasts.

In such an environment, the advisers reasoned, news would travel more slowly than on the busier continents and possible false steps on Contact would not endanger fresh attempts at other sites. After eight passes over the most-promising—that is, the most-isolated—regions, they settled on an area the maps had no specific name for but which Nugan remembered from a single childhood holiday at a townlet in the hills to the east of old Melbourne, a city partly drowned, mostly razed, and probably empty in a devastation hidden under green cover.

There were villages on the upper reaches of the Yarra (might that still be its name?) and a large building with a strange, brilliantly reflecting roof, on a hilltop. Its existence hinted at centrality and administrative minds more sophisticated than would be encountered in the farming areas. It was enough to make up Brookes's mind for him.

The Wakings clamoured for descent, urging that they had not come home to yearn at the world from space. Brookes told them briefly and coldly that the planet below was no home they knew and that reconnaissance was vital. Since control of all landing procedures was in the hands of technicians who, headed by the assaulted Jack McCann, stood by the Captain, Brookes had his way.

Rotation of duties had become close to religious observance aboard ship, so Second Waking Drop Team was notified for duty in its proper turn. Then Brookes considered again what he was doing and set the ship to useless circuits over the chosen zone while he wrestled with the problem of adequate briefing. The extent of change below was daunting and finally unguessable. How change had come about he did not conjecture but that the trauma of depopulation, divided and divided again, could have produced detours and fractures in social perception he was vividly aware.

The people below, meeting their own kind scattered down amongst them out of the sky (surely there would be legends, folktales, even written records to render the meeting intelligible) would have expectations of the strangers—cultural expectations solidified by time to the point where they would resent the newcomers behaving or thinking other than in the way that all right-thinking folk of Earth behaved. And what might that way be?

He did not know what to advise, other than caution, which is not enough of an operational order. After three decades the toxins of routine had invaded his thinking; he hesitated at a decision without precedent in history. He was a mathematician and a navigator but something less than a highly trained Commander.

Nugan's initial rejection of the return had faded into acceptance of the irreversible. Then, with the beautiful Earth rolling below, acceptance somersaulted out of all rationalising and the need for home swelled in her like a joy just born. Homesickness hit her as an explosion in the brain, the heart, the blood.

She watched the lovely planet in her cabin comvid, soaking up splendour as if it might seep through the skin into her soul.

Anne sat with her sometimes, willing but unable to understand, treating it all with a privately cynical forbearance. The ship's ten youngsters, of whom she was at eighteen the eldest, had been reared in a gush of unstoppable parental reminiscence of the "home" they had never seen, expected never to see, and in the end actively wished not to see or hear of. The memory-gossip of places and times had for them only the tedium of the inescapable. Now, with the impossible planet rotating below them, they refused to admit to more than a patiently cursory interest in what they called "just another damned world." Nugan, with fair insight into Anne's thinking, guessed that she was in two minds about actually landing on the planet and that the other youngsters probably shared her uncertainty.

That should have been expected. They had been born and raised in the ship, had never been out of the ship, had heard only despairing reports from the Contact Teams, who alone ventured beyond the universe of corridors and cabins and community halls. They had been grown in a cage, explored it thoroughly in their toddler years, and adapted their imaginations to the constraints of an unchanging reality. All outside the ship was fantasy. Even the vidplay library failed them eventually because its tales of Earth offered nothing they could experience as an anchor for belief; they lost interest.

They were not unhappy young people but they were overeducated, underexperienced, and in some ways permanently adolescent because they had had no environment in which to expand. The parents did a mostly inept and clumsy best for them, as if love could supply all that their stupid flouting of ship's convention had denied the young lives; but they had much to answer for, and knew it.

Anne, trying dutifully to share her mother's rapt attention, was little moved by a panorama viewed from a height that rendered people as doll figures moving incomprehensibly in a landscape of green on green. She said once in a burst of irritation, "It doesn't even look interesting. Just trees and water and the humps you call hills. There's more variety in our Eco-Deck forest."

Nugan knew that no credibility would be earned by chiding young boredom as ignorance of the facts. She said, "There will be activities; there will be difference."

"Difference?"

Nugan heard an undertone of uneasiness, a failure of sureness in Anne that she could deal with too much "difference." Aboard ship, "difference" appeared only in small matters; change tended to be resented in the hermetically sealed community. The kids would need guidance on an unknown, mysterious Earth, which secretly they distrusted.

Anne added with a glum sigh, "At least in your home country they'll speak our language."

Nugan, about to say, "They won't," halted the words at birth as suddenly she saw what should have been obvious from the moment the Drop Site was selected.

She said instead, "Leave me alone a while. I have to write a Command Submission. I'm going to make this Drop. Alone." Anne gazed on her mother with incomprehension while Nugan was so overcome by the excitement of her idea that she barely found the sense to tell her, "Be a good girl and keep that to yourself. Don't tell anybody. Not your best friend! If the other droppers find out, they'll try to block me." The girl was less than whelmed by this adult nonsense and visibly patient with her mother. Nugan grabbed her wrist to press the idea home. "Promise, Anne! Please. Nobody."

The girl answered coolly, "All right, if it's so important to you," and left the cabin.

Nugan scribbled her Submission, tore it up, rewrote it more intelligibly, and faxed it to the Command Suite before courage deserted her.

When within the hour she was sent for, her confidence and all her special arguments faded into brash overstatement. Alone on the Private Office's spread of worn carpet, facing Brookes, she felt more like hiding under his desk than arguing a case.

He sat like the riddling sphinx, rolling her Submission in a tube between his fingers, looking her over as if to discover values unnoticed in all their years on the ship, and asked, "Well, Taylor, what about it?"

All her justifications stampeded away from a suddenly empty head. Brookes's mouth formed the promise of a smile but he was offering no olive branch. Her case had better be solid.

She said desperately, "I'm an Australian and I have a special interest in this Drop."

"Why, so you are, Nugan. And so you have—and so has everybody else. Ethnicity isn't an argument. Sit down; take a minute to think it over." He waved the Submission like a minatory finger. "Make me believe in you."

Challenged, she sat through a little silence, studying his face. He was only marginally older than the majority of the complement but time had treated him less well; his command was no sinecure and the strain on his impartiality was incessant. Knowledge that only cold-blooded logic could earn a hearing rocked her back to sense, to laying out her reasoning curtly, without frills.

He did not answer at once but thought it over until he was prepared to say, "It really hinges on the language question, and you are trained in a specific area of linguistics. Give me an example of what you mean."

He wanted a demonstration of the development of language over a gap of centuries. That she could give.

"Chaucer. From the Fourteenth Century to our Twenty-first is roughly the same time lapse as we will meet down below. There's a very easy line in his *Can-*

terbury Tales: 'He was a verray parfit gentil knight.'
You can recognise the sound of every word, but how
would you render it in modern English?''

"Is there a trick in it? It sounds like, 'He was a very
perfect gentle knight.' "

"Meaning?"

"That he was a fine fellow, an ornament to the ar-
istocracy. How about that?''

"Chaucer would say you caught only the superficial aspect of what he conveyed and you didn't get
that quite right, either. And, believe me, sir, that line
is straightforward and simple compared with some
of the other stuff of the period."

"Go on."

"To begin, *verray* didn't mean 'very.' More like
'truly' and in this particular context, 'totally.' And
parfit was a past perfect, 'perfected,' meaning that he
was thoroughly schooled in all the arts of knight-
hood, from proficiency in arms and venery—that is,
hunting and falconry—to courtly protocol and address, common law and local justice, and the ability
to carry a tune or turn a verse. And *gentil* does not
translate as 'gentle' in the kindly or good-natured
sense; it means that he came of aristocratic lineage
and wasn't a newly created knight with his first quar-
tering, not a young upstart but an established land-
holder. You see, sir, translating on the matching of
like-sounding words doesn't give you a tenth of the
meaning the speaker is conveying while using what
sounds like your own language. And as I said, that
was a very simple example."

He took the point as seriously as she had hoped
and asked a few questions on the other claims in her
Submission—and at last agreed.

"You can go down alone. I'll call a meeting of the
Contact Teams." The promise of a smile reappeared.

"Second Waking won't take it well. It won't be easy for you."

In success she felt she could take on the three Wakings bare-knuckled.

The ship had made its tenth pass over the area when Brookes called the Contact conference in the Orders Room.

Nine of them, two men and one woman from each Waking, assembled in the chamber set up like a classroom, with dais and desks and screens. Eight of the nine whispered amongst themselves that the Old Man would do the sensible thing and drop the three groups in a single sweeping survey. The obvious thing! Sure, thought the ninth, if all you want is to get "home," even if the place is full of strangers and the houses have crumbled into shanties, and the comforts of civilised life have hardened into the primitive. You can't dismantle *Search* and take the comforts down with you.

Brookes wasted no time. He said, "Get it into your heads that we haven't returned to the planet we left six or seven centuries ago. This is in only a limited sense a homecoming. There will be few familiar scenes and a wholly unfamiliar population. I have decided, therefore, to vary the Contact system and not drop a complete Team. The circumstances argue against it."

They didn't like it. Brookes knew his decision would be fought with the spleen of outrage.

"You have been trained to deal with the wildly alien, to observe, learn, and grope for understanding in order to find avenues of approach to the unfamiliar. You have not been trained to deal with the unfamiliar in apparently familiar guise." They made blank-faced nothing of that. He paused but nobody spoke. He said bluntly, "I have spent a full day examining a Submission made by Contact Officer Taylor and have decided to drop her alone.''

He did not dare risk a smile as the reaction flared. Eight heads turned on Nugan in suspicious anger, smelling out double-dealing. Somebody muttered, ''Bloody Australian.''

A man from her own Team asked with undisguised fury, ''Why her? There's a roster of Drop Duties!''

Brookes knew his people and the power of conventional manners. He sat silent until the man got sheepishly to his feet in the normal courtesy of address to a senior officer. ''I beg your pardon, sir, but you took us by surprise.''

Nobody else stirred. Brookes nodded without answering. A small victory but enough to establish the decencies. They did not have the gutter touch of true rebellion.

''There may be greater surprises down there. Contact Officer Taylor has raised possibilities revealed by her specialised Terran studies in which I am not sufficiently schooled to have apprehended them for myself. She will outline to you what she presented to me.''

She thought, *This is being thrown in to sink or swim—or is it to the wolves?* She moved to the right of his desk and faced the assembly as he said quietly, ''Briefly, please.'' Meaning, Don't flounder among details for them to split hairs over.

She began too roughly, too loudly, ''The big problem down there may be language—'' and stopped, dismayed by her own defiant and abrasive voice.

She felt Brookes's patience like a cool cloud as he waited for her to recover. She took a long breath and said conversationally, ''We can depend on a form of English being spoken in Australia. Language persists locally, but it can change almost out of recognition in six or seven hundred years. It isn't likely that the

English spoken there today will be at once intelligible to us."

A voice said contemptuously, "So we can learn."

Brookes tapped quiet disapproval; Nugan pretended not to have heard. "If anyone asks proof of this I can show them the text of a poem, *Piers Plowman*, in the original Middle English, written at some time in the Fourteenth Century. It is difficult to read without tuition and nearly impossible to follow when spoken." It was indeed a much more formidable composition than the simple line she had offered Brookes, though almost contemporary with it. "The difficulty is that it sounds familiar though the meanings of the familiar-sounding words have changed, while syntax and grammar have made other subtle alterations to the sense. A danger down there will lie in feeling that we understand what is being said to us when in fact we will not. False interpretation could be disastrous if we tried to act on what we only think we understand. We don't know the history of these people or what they have become; we could get every little thing wrong, give them wholly wrong impressions of ourselves by thinking we understand attitudes of mind which may be totally foreign to us."

Brookes tapped impatiently. "The point is that CO Taylor is a trained linguist, the only one aboard."

For all the impression that made on eight frustrated longings he might as well have said "trained seal." Nugan felt she was grinding her way into rock.

"That doesn't mean only that I speak a number of languages, but that I have an informed knowledge of language structure and how and why changes take place over time—how vowels drift into other related sounds, consonants soften or mutate or disappear and word meanings take seemingly unreasonable leaps of association. It is a discipline that should allow me to move into the speech current down there with some sense of direction. I won't achieve immediate understanding, but I'll have a head start in comprehension and an idea of mistakes to avoid."

They didn't care; they would never forgive her the secret talent that gave her advantage over them.

"There's something more. The technological culture disintegrated after we left and the population declined. This could have involved the collapse of industry and a period of widespread starvation. If that was so, the Aboriginal tribes, accustomed to living with and off the land, may have fared much better than the mainly citified white inhabitants. To put it plainly, they may be the surviving rulers of the continent."

Here was a thing they had not thought of; hostility remained but they became more attentive.

"The people in this southeastern corner of the land were called Koori. I am one-quarter Koori by blood and as a child I was taught a great deal of my grandmother's culture, even to get along in several of the dialects. These things, with care and humility on my part, may be useful down there. Our culture can offer them a lot but we may need theirs simply to survive."

She stopped, not because there was no more to be said, but because the hostility was petrifying. They listened, perhaps they agreed, but they just did not care.

Brookes tapped loudly, turning their eyes to himself. "Therefore I have ordered CO Taylor to make a solo reconnaissance in a small area with which she is personally familiar in some degree, and to gather what knowledge of present circumstances we need in order to make ourselves acceptable to the people. When she returns we should be able to plan with more wisdom." He stared into the unforgiving silence and raised his voice slightly to emphasise command. "We have not come so far to fling ourselves pigheadedly into a clash of cultures." He let them digest that before he asked perfunctorily, "Questions or suggestions?"

He got what he expected, furious objections disguised as questions, barely disguised assertions of greater personal suitability and minimising of Nugan's. At length he asked, "Are there any *constructive* suggestions?" and they knew they had not been listened to.

In the end, down on Earth, all Nugan's arguments proved correct but irrelevant, yet the decision to send her alone proved arguably the right one. Or perhaps it made no difference.

3

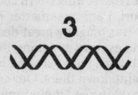

ANNE ASSISTED HER MOTHER IN DRESSing for her Drops, calling it "learning the job," stifling an instinctive fear of "outside" in the hope of one day succeeding to the single interesting occupation in the ship. So she was there at the end of the thirteenth circuit with Nugan timed to make planetfall near the village a couple of hours after dawn.

The Drops were made from a module on the outer hull. The rotation of Quarters, which provided the "gravity" necessary to bone marrow and general fitness, had to be stopped for the operation; slowing the rotation occupied a full circuit of the orbit. Nugan kept to her cabin until the centrifuge stopped, knowing that on the community decks she would get no greeting.

When the module was in position and at rest, Jack McCann, as Drop Operator, opened the access door from within. Anne and Nugan stepped through.

Jack worried over the Drop, giving them only a gesture of welcome without interrupting the delicate balancing act he called "calibrating." The Contact group trusted him absolutely. During the last orbit the ship's altitude had been lowered to 100 K and her speed reduced to approximately 1.8 K-seconds, allowing her to hover, with the assistance of side thrust, directly over the Drop Point. Exact positioning of the mass was almost impossible with the controls used to manage the brute power of ramjets geared to relativistic speeds, but the Flight Crew had trimmed the orbit to the limit of their capacity, then Jack had taken over with his battery of microtubes that drained only tiny amounts from the main jet, fining down the hover position by sight and delicate touch.

His wall screen showed the Drop Point enlarged to vague haziness, flickering and shaking, jumping off-screen and back again as he overshot and corrected, narrowing in; his ideal was to hold the Drop Point central for a full minute for the final touchdown. Team Two claimed that he had never missed yet.

Nugan hauled her dropsuit from the locker and spread it out while Anne indulged the teenage entertainment of making a nuisance of herself to Jack by leaning over him (he was one of the few adults she was prepared to accept as equally human with herself) and ruffling his hair simply because he disliked it.

"Are you going to make a perfect Drop for Mother, Operator Jack?" The little girl stuff grated and she knew it.

He told her through gritted teeth, "The bestest and perfectest on record. Now go away."

"Promise?"

"You'll have my belt round your arse if you bother me."

That was not quite a joke; he had given her one thumping a couple of years before, to make her understand once and for all that his work was demanding and his concentration extreme. What had cemented the lesson had been Nugan's refusal to interfere.

Anne turned to her role as assistant dresser. The dropsuit was a soft, flexible overall of cross-linked carbon and silicon chains, baggy and bat-shaped, with gloves at the "wingtips" allowing the hands to be withdrawn to operate internal controls. It was a complex product requiring a point check at every stage of dressing—boots, ankle seals, and heating batteries—air pressure tank and controls—particle, gas, and toxin filters—internal temperature regulation—helmet transparency modulation, visual, and UV—emergency signals and radio—cameras and sound recorders—concentrated ration packs and medical kit . . . and a hundred more. Last of all, the armament—violent, lethal, and sited for instant use though almost indetectable from the outside. Energy weapons could not be tested inside the ship but they had to be lifted out, stripped, examined, and reassembled. They had been used only once in all the voyage's Drops, when the First Waking had landed in a field of large "boulders" that rolled around them, opening like clamshells. The suit could maintain its wearer for several days although no Drop in all the years of alien planetfall had stretched beyond a few disappointing hours.

Suited up, all but the helmet, Nugan checked the screen. Jack had neared the end of his juggling and steadying but still the picture shook so badly that she made out only a green patch in an expanse of deeper green and an occasional flash of light on a ribbon of water that ducked in and out of the edges of the screen.

She was shaken by a surge of the homesickness she had tried to put aside, a longing for clear air and grass and trees, telling herself furiously to damp it down, forget it, concentrate only on the work ahead. She was a city dweller, a walker in the canyons; aside from the one childhood visit she had seen little of the countryside, so the longing, she told herself, was sheer sentimentality—with tears threatening while Anne watched her with an infuriating I-know-a-secret smile.

Jack said, "Got it, love." So he had; the view rocked gently about a suddenly clear Drop Centre. "Meadow—well, looks like grass from here—with forest round it. There's a village a half-K or so over to the east, hidden by the trees. Hills to the north, across the river, and a long rectangular building atop one of them. Sound right to you?"

"Spot on."

"I'll drop you into the meadow." She heard the grin in his voice as he suggested, "Put you down in the village if you want to enter with drama."

"You mean drop me through somebody's roof."

"Ah, love, you don't trust me. After all the times I've dropped you!"

"And all the shit you've dropped me into. I'll take the meadow."

Nonsense eased the touch of strain always present in walking outside to the empty fall.

Anne said suddenly, "I wish I could go." She watched the screen with a frowning concentration Nugan knew well; she had let slip what could not be recalled and now wished to treat as unimportant, forgettable.

Nugan needled a little at the pretence. "Has boring old Earth got to you at last?"

The girl was offhand, unwilling to admit feeling. "Not just Earth. Anywhere would do." Then, as if her tongue helplessly betrayed her, "You weren't brought up in a closed box."

My fault, Nugan admitted silently; *my fault for deliberate defiance and contraceptive carelessness, though she has never thrown it up at me.* She said as lightly as she could manage, "With luck we'll all go down once I've had a look around. Then you'll get homesick for the comfortable ship."

"Is that a joke?" Anne was angry, feeling herself not taken seriously. "Knowing there is a place outside . . . we that were born in here . . . " She let it slide away as though the emotion were too complex for expression. Perhaps it was.

Jack, trying to be jovial, said a foolish thing, "Mice in a cage, eh?"

Anne loosed a little unaccustomed savagery. "No. Minds in body bags, blind and deaf and only waiting to be zipped up."

They had nothing to say to that.

Jack gave first warning in his edgy operational voice, "Holding, Nugan," meaning that he was ready and couldn't hold it forever. Nugan pushed her chin over the neck ring and pecked Anne on the forehead. "I may be a few days but don't worry. I'll call you every night."

"Few days" was something she had never been able to say before on a Drop.

With the internal control she brought the helmet out of its concertina ruff and over her head in a seamless, transparent bowl. Anne checked the outer seal and placed a kiss on the bowl.

Nugan's last act of readiness was to darken the helmet to near blackness; once through the module's sally port she would be in full sunlight. Jack opened the air lock; she passed in and closed it behind her. As the sally port opened ahead of her she glimpsed the sun over to the east, still fairly low to the planet, too bright for direct vision even through the helmet's protection. Under her feet a short launch platform thrust itself forward, carrying her with it. The air lock closed and she was alone in space.

There was no feeling quite like the first moment with a planet spread out below her in a sheet of light. The Earth filled all downward vision, sea and land and floating cloud all monochrome-soft through the filter. To the west the knife-edge of departing night raced away from the dawn.

She could not make out the Drop Point though she knew it was directly below her booted toes, but the coastline was as clear as a map. Port Phillip Bay and Western Port were sharply etched while to the north and east long morning shadows pinpointed Mount Baw Baw and the Dandenongs. In there, sheltered among foothills, lay the target, a village, one of those along the upper reaches of the river where, centuries ago, the satellite suburbs of a huge and sprawling city had struggled to contain the swelling human load. It would now be some two hours after dawn; people would be astir and at work.

The suit made a flutter of tiny jumps as Jack fed power to his beam magnet, taking hold of the suit's monopoles and bouncing her lightly to confirm his control. He muttered in her ear, "Testing."

"OK, Jack. Ready to drop."

She set herself for the first plummeting fall. He lifted her clear and withdrew the launch platform. "Right?"

Instead of the usual *Go!* she said, "Send me home, Jack."

At the touch of reversed polarity she was tossed violently down, reaching four thousand metres a second in crushing moments. *Search* shrank into the stars like a toy overhead. There was always an instant of shock at being flung through space, flung at a vast, hard target with only Jack's manipulation between life and death.

That passed and her breathing slowed. It seemed an age before the approaching Earth swelled perceptibly, moving away on all sides from the invisible central point of the Drop. Passage should take eight minutes, but time speeded up with the sense of approach and she was taken by surprise when the first faint hiss of air penetrated her earphones, and again when the disc of the planet made its inversion to become a bowl open to receive her. There was a moment of engulfment and emergence from a high cloud.

The country expanded with dramatic speed, then slowed as Jack began deceleration.

She cleared the helmet to full transparency and the homeworld blazed into colour. Training routines took over from her gasp of excitement and she used the last minute to form an outline map in her head— square fields amid hectares of trees, a winding river between roads and low buildings, hills and one special hill with the long, square-cornered structure on its ridged crest, its roof afire with what could only be sunlight on glass. Life and safety could depend on knowing precisely where she was in a strange environment.

Then it was over; all downward motion stopped and she swayed in air, five metres above the grassy meadow of the Drop Point. Her pendulum swing narrowed to a shivering hold, as nearly still as miraculous Jack could make it.

He said tightly, "Over to you, Nugan."

"Taking over, Jack." She eased downward with the belt control until her feet brushed the tips of the thick grass. "Let go!"

At that moment she was peripherally aware of being observed, of a figure gazing, stock-still, hands to mouth.

Jack cut his magnet and Nugan, poised to fall a handsbreadth, tumbled a good half metre into deceptively long grass that reached her knees. She sprawled, off-balance, on hidden unevenness in the ground, got up, tripped again and swore at the pain of a wrenched ankle.

Her greeting to Earth was a drawn-out, "Oh shit!" while the watching figure turned and ran, scuttling into the shadow of a grove of palms and vanishing.

Resting on one knee and taking her weight on her hands, she tried to stand. And sat down abruptly. The ankle was too painful to carry her.

She hoped the pain might be temporary. Calling Jack to lift her out would be a humiliating end to her protestations and pretensions; the Wakings would never let her forget it. She would stay until staying became impossible.

Would there be time to remove the boot and bind the ankle? Probably not. The fleeing figure predicated an inspection party and she could not risk being caught with air seals open if a fast departure was needed.

She said, "I'm down, Jack, Anne. In the meadow. Let me just look for a while. Then I'll tell you what it's like."

"Be careful, Mother." And Jack, "Take your time, love."

She saw the horses fifty metres away and had a moment of caught breath before scrambling memory brought recognition of their probable tameness. In her past life she had seen few animals larger than pet cats and dogs and the rats endemic to the cities; identification of the horses rested on remembered illustrations. Or was she confusing them with cows? In either case they were reputed harmless and seemed uninterested in her.

Not that she needed to fear attack—the heavy gloves could spit death along levelled fingers—but she had never killed a peaceable organism and did not want the experience. Her business was to smooth the way for a welcome, not to alienate with a display of strength.

The air sampler clicked and she glanced at the wrist display. Earth's air was, expectably, similar to Ship Standard with the addition of traces of inert gases. She tripped the helmet seal, the dome folded back into the neck ruff and—she took her first full breath of home.

It was like—

—like nothing in her memory of people and cities—

—a little like entering the Eco-Deck on the ship—

—yet not like that, milder and less overpowering in this meadow, where everything was not crowded into a minimum cultivation space.

The smell of greenery contained unfamiliar scents and the warmness of dry ground; absent was the sharpness of fertiliser from the hydroponic tanks and sour mulch from the grass and fern plantations. The air itself was strangely dry, as when ship's air had been completely scrubbed after cleaning the filters. Constant recycling did not save the crowded Quarters from a pervasive human stench and this was, above all, clean air. Nothing in her past compared with a single breath of the world that had endured a half-death of man-made spoliation and rebuilt itself into a condition of trees and beasts and small centres of humanity, with no vast exhausts of poisons and chemical dusts in a planetary slum.

For a while she simply breathed, less excited than pensive, aware of the starship years as an enormous loss of living and being.

She discovered a nervous foreboding that this new Earth could be a stranger organism than logic could foresee or history suggest, that she had no qualification at all for grappling with what her world might have become—linguistics, native heritage now as meaningless as radio in a world without electronics. Even those horses could carry new plagues deadly to unprotected blood. . . .

Stop it!

Take hold!

Disease we can deal with, any disease. And the small pretensions to special knowledge can be useful if I keep my head. This is home, not some ball of mud out by Capella. . . .

It was not home. It was an undiscovered country.

She forced herself to catalogue all she could see—nameless trees and shrubs—a thumb-sized, grey, ratlike, furry thing with a pointed nose scuttling away from her boot—some flitting insects and a tiny brown spider throwing a web between spikes of long grass . . .

Behind the nameless palms, hills undulated into the distance, on one of them the square-cornered building that had clinched this meadow as the Drop Site. Beyond it the sky was a blue roof yet no roof at all, confusing with its threat of pressing inexorably down while receding into an endless faraway.

For God's sake let something happen before my senses are overloaded!

Something happened.

They came out of the trees, at their head a tall and slender woman in a black dress, rather a robe than a dress, enhancing dignity though it fell only a hands-breadth below her knees. Her white headdress, stiff as cloth starched and folded in some immemorial descent from the nursing tradition, was held at the neck by something that glittered in sunlight, probably a brooch. She seemed elderly but even at that distance had presence marking her out from the rabble of her escort.

Lady mayoress? Village witch? Not one to take lightly.

She clutched another woman, squat and thick-built, by the arm, dragging her forward; Nugan recognised the grey trousers that had fled from her touchdown. Grey Trousers pointed and planted herself firmly in a no-further pose. Madam-in-Black called to someone behind her and a man came forward.

He wore only the shortest of short shorts, little more than a gesture at sexual privacy. He listened to Madam-in-Black, looked steadily at Nugan and back to the woman, then strode through the long grass with a very male combination of wariness and cocky swagger.

Nugan remained perfectly still.

Twenty metres from her he stopped, sniffing the air.

His skin was dark, not Aboriginal or Negroid but deeply copper-toned. He was little taller than Nugan but deep-chested and broad and heavily muscular, like a—she sought a comparison from the past—like a rugby scrum-half. His face was widemouthed and craggy-featured. *Macho Australian*, she thought, *as the men always fancied themselves but rarely were.*

Then . . . *If I were a free agent . . . not bound by*

duty. . . . The arousal surprised her like a malicious grin. This one was very much a man, a sudden and needed change from the too-familiar, unaltering masculinity of *Search*. And the shorts disguised nothing.

For the second time she commanded herself to call on intelligence and ignore emotion: *I haven't come light-years to bed the first available man in a horse paddock.*

4

JOHNNO ROSE IN DARKNESS ON THE morning of the advent of Flighty's Angel and stole out of the Long Dormitory of the single men to spend an extra hour on thatching the cottage which Bella would share with him through the Test Year. And forever after, he thought, stretching his muscles in lover's euphoria and conceding that he was no end of a successful fellow.

The cottage ceiling was completed, caulked and rainproof; the great sheaves of thatching lay on the floored, finished rooms but he had still to cut the roof beams. Like most of his Genetic he could manage the elements of the domestic trades and could cut a roof as well as a master carpenter; first light was glowing as he took his sack of tools and climbed to the bare top of the cottage. Balanced easily on a rafter and fumbling in the sack for tape and T-square, he was the first that morning to see The Comet (which Thomas had said was no comet at all and then refused to say what he thought it was) rise with startling speed in the still-dark south.

Johnno had seen it cross by night and reappear each morning to flicker and vanish in the sunlight, but this time it blazed like white fire, far brighter than it had ever been before and many times larger, so large that almost he could discern a shape to it; even the hazy tail shone pale yellow against the fading stars. It rose quickly, as Sun and Moon did while low in the sky, slowing as it mounted and losing its brilliance as the daystar overwhelmed it, but this time he was able to see it long after it would normally have been swallowed by sunlight.

There would be activity in the Book House, a mole-scurry of scholars and pedants searching their books for clues to this new manifestation while Soldier Thomas ate breakfast undisturbed and waited for their conclusions. Nothing disturbed friend Tommy; he was comfortable to have by, undemonstrative but dependable. Later in the day Johnno would ask him again what The Comet really was; for the present he calculated, measured, laid out, and began cutting the beams for his roof.

When he saw the other men moving in the street he collected his tools, shinned down to the ground, and moved to the bottling plant, where he would help with the extra workload imposed by the ripening of the banana crop. If he had stayed aloft a few minutes longer and turned his eyes overshoulder, he might have glimpsed the clumsy finish of Nugan Taylor's Drop.

Flighty alone saw the landing and then only because the whoosh in the air made her swing around, stare in surprise and then in fright, clap hands to mouth, and finally turn and run, making little mouse squeaks as she fled.

"Flighty," in the village speech, meant something like the Late English "scatterbrained" and it was more often used (though not to her face) than her family name, which was the Robinson's Hello-Mary, a far descendant of Ave Maria. She owned the bottling plant on the village side of the banana plantation by the horse paddock, left to her by a doting father; this made her a woman of consequence in the village but not, therefore, a figure of respect. Genetic Matching weeded its misfits but its occasional failures had to be endured with the kindness and good manners of a people who reckoned class by propriety of behaviour.

The bottling shed crew were a good-humoured lot, prepared to tolerate Flighty's crotchets, but her pantings and hoots and gestures so early on a workday morning would have tried the patience of the Top-Ma herself. They left her to Johnno, for whom she cherished a harmless affection and to whose protection she fled anyhow; his patience took the load off the bored forbearance of the others.

Johnno rocked her gently and whispered that the men were watching and she must remember dignity. "Dignity" was one of the few imperatives to which she reacted; she feared the anger of the other village women when she forgot herself in front of the men.

Johnno set her down on one of the low benches and tried to make sense of her stuttering; the other men stayed at their work while listening keenly.

She had no clear idea of what she had seen. It had "whooshed" down from the sky, all bright silver, and dropped down and bounced and dropped again and hissed at her and she had run for her life through the banana palms, fallen over twice, and stumbled into the shed in disrepair.

"What was it like, Miss Mary? What shape?"

She only shook her head distractedly and said she couldn't tell but it bounced.

"Like a ball?"

"No. Like a—" She fluttered her hands. "—I don't know what."

Some sort of animal, Johnno decided, but what animal bounced? Kangaroo she would recognise. And what hissed, besides a snake? Flighty was silly but not given to hallucination; she had seen something. His first thought was to look for himself, his second, that if the apparition turned out to be some simple thing, it would make a beerhouse laughingstock of Flighty, not for the first time; better that the matter stay with the womenfolk. He called to one of the workmen to fetch the Low-Ma.

Low-Ma came without delay, knowing that Johnno would not send lightly, but by the time she arrived Flighty was over the worst of her distress and striving for sense.

"There was I, counting hands of bananas for squeegeeing into baby pap, when I heard it go 'whoosh' and I saw it floating in the paddock."

"Floating?" asked Low-Ma and Johnno together. This was new information.

"In the air. Over the grass."

Low-Ma, who knew enough to make connections beyond Johnno's capacity, asked, "What shape was it? Like a bat?"

"A bit." Also like something else she couldn't quite think of. She moved on to safer ground. "It fell down and bounced and hissed at me and I ran off."

"Hissed at you, Mary? Like a snake?"

"Like ssshi-i-i-i-t!" She began to cry in returning helplessness.

"Hello-Mary, try to be calm." Low-Ma lowered her voice. "The men are watching."

The men had in fact politely turned their eyes

away from tears but Flighty drew herself up in own-
erly dignity over a quivering lip.

"Now, what did it look like?"

Flighty tried hard. "Like a bag. All silver. With
legs. And a glass pot on top." In a burst of relief she
found her memory and her mental bearings. "Like
the pictures in the Book House. In the stories part.
You know, where the angels go up? Well, like the
angels."

Low-Ma knew, no matter what the villagers preferred to believe, that the pictures on the Library wall
did not represent angels. Her startled and apprehensive thought leapt to include The Comet which Libary had privately told the Mas was no comet, and
might have been disentangled as, *Why here? Why us?
With all the world to fall on, why bring trouble here,
to us?*

"Johnno, ask Top-Ma if she can spare a moment to
visit the bottling shed." That was for pointing ears;
privately she gave him the sign for urgency.

Top-Ma listened to Johnno, asked no questions and
came to the shed, without evident haste but without
wasting time, and listened to Flighty's renewed stam-
merings . . . and said, as though visitations were no
matter for consternation, "We will examine the thing.
Six men will come with me in case their strength is
needed."

She was not given to fear but she was prudent; a
muscular entourage could discourage danger before
it moved into action. The village men were a Genetically powerful lot and also a superstitious lot but
they made the conventional show of courage when
the women claimed protection. On Johnno's lead
they took up their choppers and mashing-clubs and
looked grim and only one muttered that there should
be a duty soldier for this sort of thing. Johnno shut
him up. They were not sure of themselves; man-to-

man could be blood-warming when village honour was called out but man-to-whatisit had queasy overtones. They agreed with Low-Ma's prim admonition, "There could be danger."

Top-Ma said drily, "There could be greater danger if we do not investigate. Lead the way, Hello-Mary."

Flighty was on the instant thoroughly terrified and ready to swear that she hadn't really seen anything, but Top-Ma took her arm and urged her firmly through the banana grove.

Perhaps, Flighty suggested, it had gone away; perhaps it had bounced again and kept on going up and up.

It had not gone anywhere. It remained seated in the long grass on the far side of the paddock. It had taken the glass off its head and revealed the cropped hair of a man.

"A man," Top-Ma murmured crossly to herself, thinking like the politician which at heart she was. A man, not an ordinary man but one in the panoply of the Library "angels," could be as troublesome as any monster Flighty's confusions could dream up. Matriarchy was a historical development, not an evolutionary given, and she knew perfectly well what had dropped into the paddock.

The horses, she noticed, munched about their business, undisturbed by a fallen angel.

The male escort, puzzled by a man in a bag but relieved to face nothing worse, grinned and winked at each other, enjoying the sight of authority at a loss. They had been brought up to revere women, even during orgasmic Carnival, but the reverence was more habit and cultural convention than reality; the old girl had better make a decision before somebody made it for her.

The very practical old girl knew better than to hesitate too long. She called to Johnno, "Walk up to him—carefully—and observe him."

Ma and man exchanged bland stares, each knowing that even Top-Ma had no power to order a man into possible danger.

She said, "Take no chances, Johnno." It was a plea and both knew it. He stared her down and when her eyes averted moved smoothly forward, as though challenge had not entered his mind.

Johnno feared no human being (but would have thought twice before risking himself against the fighting methods of the soldiers) and he had noted the indifference of the horses, so he walked steadily, swaggering a little for the benefit of the other men. The man in the silver bag raised his head and stared but made no other motion.

A whiff of breeze crossed the paddock and Johnno sniffed what it might tell him. He was forest bred and Genetically capable in sensitivities which in his ancient ancestors (so Libary said) had become atrophied; his sense of smell was extremely keen. What he sniffed for was the trace of sharpish, slightly sour odour which warned of fear or anger and consequently danger; what he detected was something else altogether.

He shouted back to the others, "It's a bloody woman!" He was resentful; the angel-thing should have been a man, a gender hero, not another damned female! Johnno's intelligence was better than average but his heart was as sexist as any bossy woman's.

A faint, residual *rom* aura had taken his attention, not so much "come on" as background to the personality. He knew of women about whom it seemed to linger permanently, like a small fire waiting to be lit; perhaps this was one such. He was not so gender-macho as to see himself as the immediate cause and focus; besides, cropped hair and narrow features and an unwinking gaze were not his idea of desirable womanhood.

He went slowly forward, careful not to offend with manners her community might consider outlandish, and at an arm's length from her inclined his head politely and smiled. The woman smiled in return and spoke a single word that sounded like "H'lo" but meant nothing to him.

He bent to rest on his haunches and said, "You aren't really an angel."

She plainly did not understand him. He knew there were other languages than Angloo; the black Murri in the north had a secret language as old as history and Thomas said there were dozens of tongues spoken round the world.

She spoke again, unintelligibly. (Thomas was able to tell him, later, that she had said in Late English, "I haven't a clue, handsome.")

If there could be no communication it was a matter for Top-Ma to handle—if she could. He shouted back, "She's peaceable. Come on!"

The whole party came, the men slightly in advance, and spread themselves in a half circle round the "angel," with Top-Ma in the centre and Flighty peering cautiously from behind her.

Top-Ma bent close over the bland brown eyes, observing the hints of Koori blood in the almost white face and disapproving the mannishness of the close-cropped hair. A woman's hair should be worn as long as she could grow it. Still, the woman was behaving very properly, observing the position of requesting-welcome as was expected of a member of a distant community. This placed the issue of acceptance on Top-Ma, who knew that the distance of this one's community could be measured only in historical terms and that acceptance must be in restricted form, almost minimal until more was known. An open welcome was far from called for.

The village Mas did not learn Late English as a discipline, not being Erudites, but commonly picked up a reading knowledge of it during their training years with the Ordinands, so Top-Ma gathered her small store to say as clearly as she could, "You are welcome to visit."

That committed the community to nothing.

The angel's face lit in wonder. "You speak English!"

"I have small Late Angloo. Not many words. I am Top-Ma here."

"I am Nugan. You are Tupmaheer? Have I got it right?"

"Top-Ma in this place, not a name. You would call—" She fumbled for the ancient title. "—Mother Superior."

"A nun!"

Top-Ma had never encountered the word (which was wildly wide of the mark). Best to ignore it; she did not want conversation. What she wanted, urgently, was to get this problem woman off her hands.

Now the woman was talking, pointing upwards. "I come from the Starship."

So it sounded. She spoke with what seemed to Senior Mother a coarse accent, as if a villager mouthed the words; the vowels were blurred. "Yes. We know stairsheep."

The angel listened intently and repeated, "Stairsheep," in excellent imitation of the Ma's cultured accent. Then, with a lift of the voice, "We are not forgotten?"

That was difficult to answer with exactness. Top-Ma contented herself with, "Old tales. Pictures in Library." The angel would have spoken again, excitedly, but the Ma talked over her: "We go to village. Near. Walk."

"Walk!" The woman who called herself Nugan began a lumbering effort to rise to her feet. Johnno made what he considered a polite gesture in taking her silver arm but she pushed him away, complaining in the secret tongue (Thomas's Late Angloo?) which Top-Ma seemed to understand.

Top-Ma said, "Leave her alone, Johnno. She has twisted her ankle. The men can carry her to the shed." To Nugan she said, brusquely enough to warn off protest, "No more talk now. You talk to proper one after. To Libary. Now the men carry."

"Carry" meant two husky males with wrists clasped under her with her arms around their shoulders, lifting her and her suit without effort and moving at a half-trot through the grass and down the avenue of palms.

Johnno, watching her face as they started off, noted her appreciation of the physiques of the carriers. The Forest Genetic were a solid, hardy crew and the woman seemed to make no effort to conceal her roused *rom*.

He had caught the word "starship" and from Thomas knew its meaning; he would look for Thomas at the first opportunity.

5

BANANAS, NUGAN THOUGHT. *THAT'S what they are, bananas.* So something of the Greenhouse heat persisted yet, so far south. The dropsuit maintained an even temperature within itself but she had been too taken up with the new and strange to notice the heat on her face. *I'll take sunburn and itch like the devil.*

She should have no time for such personal trifles but the eruption of English speech had given her a sense of familiarity and acceptance which she must deliberately keep at bay. The Top-Ma's final words had conveyed an irritability which inevitably must involve herself; she should not take amity for granted. The woman had, after all, said "visit," a limiting term. There were no wide open arms here, only a sharp curiosity with little in the way of wonderment.

She was to meet "Libary," whoever he/she might be, presumably someone of authority. Meanwhile, observe . . .

The carriers took her to a large, thatched shed where more men worked at vats and tables and, at the direction of the one whom the Top-Ma had addressed as "Johnno," sat her on a bench by a table well away from the working area. The workers looked curiously once then turned their eyes away.

Not quite away, she decided, catching the oblique glances of people too well mannered for outright staring.

Nugan had no such reservation. Staring, cataloguing, evaluating was her business.

The twenty-two men in the shed were—and this was puzzling—an unnaturally homogeneous lot. They were, to a man, strongly built in the manner of Johnno and her carriers and their heights varied by no more than a couple of centimetres; they were brown-skinned like Johnno though with some variation of shade and in every face was a tinge, though not always the same tinge, of Koori blood. Her speculation on the ship concerning persistence of the Aboriginal component was here justified. There should, however, be more variation in physique. The diversity of features and a lack of common abnormalities ruled out massive inbreeding, yet the similarities of build were intriguing. It was something to be investigated.

She felt that in their carefully uninterested way they were discussing her in quiet voices. Why not? She would have loved to discuss with them. (Johnno, if he had had Late English, could have told her they made highly personal bawdy remarks about the pervasive *rom* titillation.)

Top-Ma knew what they discussed and in what fashion; she wanted the troublesome female out of her village and up the hill.

She called on Johnno, who could be trusted to carry a message without garbling, to make his best speed up the hill to announce the angel to Libary. "Angel," she thought, would be interpreted correctly by that sapient man. That suited Johnno well; he would be able to reach Thomas before all others and perhaps discover meanings the Top-Ma kept to herself. Thomas, intimate of Libary, knew more secrets than a dozen domineering Top-Mas; he set off happily on the gruelling run.

The Top-Ma, Nugan thought, was making herself busier about the shed than need be, unwilling to talk with her visitant. *Afraid of saying the wrong thing in half-baked English and making a fool of herself.*

The Top-Ma had not, however, forgotten sympathy and hospitality. From somewhere outside came a young woman, a pleasant-faced, dark, stocky version of the menfolk, bringing a basin of water to bathe the twisted ankle once Nugan had deciphered the signs asking her to remove the heavy boot.

The water was very cold, from the mountain stream.

Unlike the men, the girl was frankly curious but made no attempt to speak. She laughed at Nugan's basin crop and displayed her own waist-length hair coiled in thick plaits. She shook her head over the clumsy suit, the huge boots, and the thick gloves whose fingers carried deadliness her innocence would not dream of.

She uncovered a jar of thick yellow grease for massage into the ankle and produced a strong bandage of unbleached cloth to swathe ankle and instep, tightly and expertly.

The Top-Ma, passing by, vouchsafed a sentence, "Girl is nurse, very good."

"Thank you, Top-Ma."

Then she was left alone to wonder, *What now?* and, *Am I being treated with reserve or simply frozen out?*

A cardinal rule of Contact was, Don't invent expectations; wait and see.

She applied herself to observation. The place appeared to be a bottling plant. Bananas were trimmed rapidly by men who tossed the skins into refuse bins and the fruit into close-woven baskets. Filled baskets were passed to other men at a delivery chute of free-turning wooden rollers emerging from the wall at the end of the shed; down the chute came an endless supply of glass jars, moving of their own weight on the gentle gradient. The men crammed each jar with bananas and pulped the soft flesh with plungers to fill them tightly. Last, before applying a glass cap, they added a pinch of some noisome green dust (Preservative? Bacteriophage? Why not?) and the jar exited through another slot in the wall, moving gently down its gravity path.

Labour-intensive, of course, and unproductively expensive but in a simple society better than dole queues.

But who said this society was simple? A factory, however primitive, suggested complex social activity and interaction. Wait and see, Nugan; wait and see.

Top-Ma called loudly and the nurse girl appeared with a bunch of bananas. "You eat?"

Nugan hesitated between common sense and the risk of insult. She did not care to chance local foods before setting up a test kit; enzymes and once harmless proteins could alter radically over time. Her biochemistry was hazy but she preferred to play safe. She shook her head, smiling to disarm the refusal, and said, "I have rations."

She dug out her pack of concentrated ration and swallowed a tablet before an uncomprehending Top-Ma, who frowned but made no comment. After a moment Top-Ma said, "You wait in this place," and left her.

Nugan waited. No one took the least notice of her—or so it seemed. She took up her empty right boot and pulled the thick but loose insulation layer out of it.

At once notice was taken. Nobody stopped work but heads turned sufficiently to see what she did and turned back again. Could they have heard the slither of a fabric as soft as fine wool being lifted out of its fitting? She pulled the emptied boot over the bandages and found it roomy enough. Again the heads turned, noted the movement, and turned away, satisfied. (About what? That she did nothing that should be prevented?)

She recalled Johnno sniffing at a distance and deciding that he could safely approach. (But what had he smelt?) A community of highly sensitive ears and noses could be an embarrassment; every movement would destroy privacy, offer account of everything save thought. Selection, aided by the more acute senses of the interbreeding Aboriginals, might have achieved a return to primitively sharpened senses in twenty or thirty generations in the wilderness, where existence hung on the essential equation of the fine-tuned and the dead.

The really surprising thing about these people was their lack of fuss after the initial wariness.

So I came home and nobody gave a damn. Not true; her ankle had been efficiently attended to—but coolly, as of a conventional obligation observed. The throbbing had ceased. Did the yellow grease contain a local anaesthetic? There would be a herbal pharmacopoeia of sorts.

Wait and see, Nugan; wait and see.

Three-quarters of an hour had passed when Johnno returned, sweat-runnelled, gulping breath as if he had taken his message at the run in both directions. (She discovered later that he had run better than a K uphill and back.) He staggered into the bottling shed, leaned with both hands on a workbench, and gulped words in the accent that made phonemes unrecognisable. At once four men laid down their work and left the shed.

Then Top-Ma appeared and shooed him away, literally shooed him away, with a rap of fingers on the rump. Johnno's face sharpened with quick resentment but he took his place at the worktables and did not look back.

Top-Ma searched her little store of words, "The men make a—a carry. To lift—to carry to Libary."

"Thank you, Top-Ma."

The boot was noticed. "The foot not hurt more?"

"No, it does not hurt."

"Good, that."

Then the men Johnno had sent out came with their "carry," the simplest of litters, layers of coarse cloth slung on two poles. A wooden crossbar spread it at each end and somebody had added a headrest of long grass tied in a bundle. They held the litter level with the edge of the table and Nugan eased herself onto it. The four pleasantly bulky men took it on their shoulders and Top-Ma murmured, "Top-Ma good-byes you."

"Good-bye, Top-Ma, and thank you."

In a moment she was out of the shed and swinging along a broad track between small, trim, thatched houses. She noted an absence of people—one woman only, hurrying, balancing a bundle on her head and bearing a small child, papooselike, on her back. *Work begins early and fills the day*, Nugan thought; *socialising comes later*.

They moved down the slope of a riverbank. Craning, she saw a footbridge of narrow duckboards slung on a webbed rope base, the whole supported by thickly woven hawsers at waist height. Its hundred or so metres of length was no mean structure for a community working with limited materials. Or did specialised tradesmen build bridges while others made roads or stuffed pulp into bottles?

The duckboards were too narrow for four bearers; the crossing was made with one man at each end of the litter, walking as rapidly as before. The bridge swayed breathtakingly to their footsteps but they carried her with ease over the river and to the top of the farther bank. There they stopped and the other two carriers assisted in lowering the litter until it was suspended at their arms' length.

Nugan found herself looking up into the face of a very different kind of man.

His skin was a shade of the universal dark copper but his features were long, narrow, and fleshless despite the traces of Koori in his ancestry, the lips and flared nose that looked back over millennia of breeding. Unlike the near-naked others he was fully dressed, but the homespun shirt did not hide the true Koori body, with its deep chest and strong shoulders and slender hunter's hips.

She silently bet with herself that the slenderness extended to flat, long-muscled flanks and long-muscled calves under the grey trousers, which were caught by a band under the soles of strong shoes. Yet with his blue eyes he could have been of a different race and culture.

She asked, "Are you Libary?"

He flashed brilliant teeth. "Alas, no. I am only Socher. And Johnno says your name is Nugan. Have I it right?"

6

SOLDIER WAS OUTSIDE THE LIBRARY
when Johnno trotted doggedly up the hillside a half
kil below him. As Johnno was not one to run for a
cause less than urgent, Soldier jogged down to meet
him.

Johnno's panting halt, chest heaving, and face
streaming sweat, did not disguise his happy urgency.
"The message is for Libary, Thomas, but you can receive it—I think."

"I'll hear it, then decide, eh?"

Johnno tipped his head with sly expectation. "Tell
me about the angels on the wall painting."

"Nothing for nothing, is it? You know they aren't
angels."

"Real people, Thomas? Flying up to—something
like a comet?"

"We think so. Who have you been talking to?"

"You, mainly. And using my brains. I think about
what you tell me."

"That's why I tell you. Spit it out."

"Want to meet an angel?"

Soldier felt that his heart had stopped, paralysed
with excitement. "Here, Jo? In the village? Here?"

Johnno grabbed his hand and pulled him down.
"Sit a minute, Tommy."

With Soldier staring like an astonished boy,

70

Johnno told what he had seen and sensed and heard, Soldier interjecting gasped words and white-hot questions.

"A woman! Hurt? Hurt how?... Damn your woman-hunting nose; the *rom* doesn't matter.... The Top-Ma spoke to her? Late English, then!"

Johnno spread a hand like a food dish on his friend's bony knee, wondering not for the first time about the Genetic mysteries, far back in time, which had packed so much strength and stamina into a patently frail body. "This is a big thing, Tommy. I saw the Top-Ma's face!"

Soldier's face shadowed and cleared. "Too big. We aren't ready. Nobody anywhere is ready. And only one comes when we thought of a horde, who could have landed anywhere in the world yet chose this place!"

"Does that matter?"

"It matters to us. It leaves us decisions to make."

"Decisions?"

Soldier shook his head. "Forget that. Tell nobody."

"All right, but you'll have to tell me later on."

"When I know what there is to be told."

Johnno stood. "I have to give Libary the message."

"Forget Libary; I'll see him for you. Go back and tell the Top-Ma that Libary says the wounded angel is to be brought to the Book House at once."

Johnno would have trusted Thomas before a dozen Libarys; he trotted off down the hill.

Soldier, thinking of Libary's capacity for making mystery while keeping his counsel, decided that Libary could for once wait while he saw the "angel" for himself. An hour would make no difference to colliding centuries.

He strolled casually downhill, weighing in his mind Libary's reservations as to how these people should be received—and concluding that after the lapse of generations all speculation must be point-

less. At the bottom, by the riverbank, he waited for
the stretcher party to appear on the swinging bridge;
there was a sturdy footbridge lower down but village
pride could be depended on to make a display of carrying prowess for the stranger.

He stared down into the face, which was the only part
of her visible outside the enveloping suit of silvery
material like a metallic cloth. She would be, he
thought, no older than himself, neither pretty nor unpleasantly plain, probably a little on the plump side,
and staring back at him with lively interest brightening her brown eyes.

He noted the unmistakable Aboriginal traces in her
features, surprised that the racial mingling had taken
place so long ago and showed so clearly after twenty-
five or thirty generations. So, when had the Genetic
Plan been originated? She might know that. And
much, much more.

While he looked and pondered, she spoke before
him, asking, "Are you Libary?" then blushing in an
apparent confusion.

Did she think her words would not be understood?
The vowels were pushed forward behind her teeth
and the accent dully flat but the language was clear.
He cut off his staring to remember good manners and
smile a welcome as he denied, "Alas, no. I am only
Socher. And Johnno says your name is Nugan. Have
I it right?"

He stumbled a little on his Late English and felt
that the last construction was questionable but she
nodded and replied, "I am Nugan Taylor."

Was there a correct formal answer to that? Some
lost convention of greeting that he knew nothing of?
He said, a little desperately, "We would say you are
the Taylor's Nugan. That is the way now."

"But you speak English!"

"Late English," he corrected pedantically. "It is a tongue for scholars. Libary taught me. You will meet him—" He gestured at the square building partly visible through the trees. "—up there." He thought rapidly before embarking on a more difficult speech. "That is the Library where he is the king—no, the headman. In charge. The village people call him Libary because it is easier to say so. His Ordinand name is Papa Melchizedech but nobody says—calls him that. I am sorry that my speech is not very good."

She smiled up at him. "But it is very good. I did not catch your name properly. Did you say Socher?"

"That is how the village people say it. You would say Soldier." He pronounced it with three clearly separated vowels.

The woman, Nugan, shook her head. "We say Sohljer. In English, sound and spelling are not always the same."

Soldier nodded gravely, accepting and storing the lesson. The woman continued, "But is that really your name? Soldiering is a profession."

Strangely, he felt at ease chatting trifles with a woman who had plummeted from an orbiting ship. "It is the name they give me because soldiering is my profession. My given—my registered name is the Atkins's Thomas."

The look in her eyes was amused incredulity; she spluttered with laughter and caught herself up to apologise. "I beg your pardon, Mister Atkins, but Soldier Thomas Atkins is a queer combination to meet in this time and place." He could scarcely credit that she knew the jest of his christening but she quoted at him, " 'Oh, it's Tommy this 'an Tommy that 'an Tommy go away—' Fancy old Kipling being remembered! I shall like this world!"

Silently he doubted that but the words recalled

him to what must be done. "We will go on now to the Library."

He signed to the carriers to continue uphill while he ran ahead of them to warn Libary of the apparition whose education included the joke of Thomas's orphan name. How trivial an exchange at the crossroads of histories . . .

He recalled as he ran that at some point in his outpouring of news Johnno had said, "But you should smell her! She stinks of sex! It gets stronger when she looks at you. She's right for a Carnival, that one."

The sharpening of the *rom* awareness was a fundamental part of the manipulation by those forgotten Wizards of the Last Culture who—or so the tradition held—had designed the new men for the new world. Soldier had been conscious of the Nugan *rom* but had not been roused; she was not near enough to his Genetic type to rouse him. Besides, he had read some of the puzzling "romances" of the Last Culture and gained from them an impression that they had observed no sexual season but lived in a continual readiness. Theirs must have been a time of complex, highly tensioned relationships that allowed no emotional peace. Little wonder that such straining against nature had brought them down in ruin.

He found Libary at one of the semaphore stands on the roof, coding a complex message into the simple groupings that cut signalling time by two-thirds and passing the completed slates to the signaller, who worked the black-and-white-striped arms in rapid clacking. The next stand of three was on a hill fifty kil distant; the signaller, worked with his eyes at a powerful binocular (a toy instrument beside Libary's joyous telescope) to catch the answering *Understoods* and *Repeats* from the receiving operator. A fairly long message could be relayed a thousand kil in a couple of hours.

Libary had been sending and receiving for days, recording the exchanges in his diaries and saying nothing of what they contained to Soldier or to any other. The operators, highly skilled Ordinands vowed to silence (a vow enforceable by powerful social pressures) were not to be coerced even by a Regional General, and Libary himself sponged the slates clean as each message was passed.

The exchange, Soldier guessed, was worldwide, of starship matters to which he was not privy. It was easy to imagine the network of pedants in intellectual uproar, less easy to guess what lay at the heart of the argument.

He said without preamble, enjoying his little bombshell, "The village is in ferment, the Top-Ma is at a loss and Johnno has come running full of news—" Libary looked up from his encoding, impatient and scowling. "—and an angel has tumbled down in Flighty's horse paddock."

The older man straightened in shock. A gesturing hand holding the slate struck the writing table and the slate broke into pieces. "Here, Thomas? Here?"

"Here. We are favoured by a messenger from heaven."

The operator heard and turned to focus Soldier with wide eyes; he knew about "angels." Libary recovered his dignity, unwilling to be caught in mental disarray; he kicked the broken slate under the table and said to the operator, "Send *Wait Urgent*. Then rest." The huge arms clacked in a double swing that set the receiving station stand on *Wait*. "Only one angel, Thomas?"

"Only one. There might be others elsewhere."

"Have him brought here at once."

"She is on her way."

"She?"

"A woman and young for such an ambassadorship."

"You have seen her?"

"Yes. She should be here in twenty minutes."

"Tell me—before I forget my dignity and yours and take unbecoming action."

"Well, now—she is wearing what I take to be an airtight travelling garment; she has sprained an ankle and so is being carried; her hair is cropped like a man's; she shows strong traces of Koori interbreeding—which I think sets our ideas of the racial mixing back a century or two—and she speaks Late English with a bland, front-of-mouth accent which is quite understandable. I would estimate her age in the late twenties."

"What does she want here?"

A pedant's question. What in the name of Genetic Destiny did he damned well think she would want? Libary's mind was not always easy to follow. "I asked no questions because a clumsy question may give as much information as its answer—and I thought you would wish to frame careful enquiries for yourself. Your activities over the last few days howl aloud of secrets."

Libary was not to be baited. "She is to be brought directly to me, speaking to no one else. See to it." Then, remembering that even Papa Melchizedech could exert no direct authority over a soldier: "Would you look to it yourself, Thomas, for my sake?"

Save your false humility; I want to be involved. "The private office?"

"Naturally." He took a fresh slate and began coding thoughtfully, then looked up to say, "I shall need an amanuensis for the interview. I hope you will be willing?"

"Of course, sir." *Oh, but I am rewarded handsomely!* "The woman's name is Nugan Taylor and she is familiar with Kipling." Libary's stare was unbelieving. "We are on first name terms—'Tommy this an' Tommy that.'"

Libary handed the slate to the operator. "Save that. Now, Thomas, tell me everything said in your session of intimate gossip."

7

A CURVE IN THE PATH HAD TAKEN THE soldier out of Nugan's sight among trees. *I come home after thirty years—or is it thirty generations?— and talk nothings with a stranger on a bush track. There is nothing unusual under heaven.*

Oh, but there was. There was a quartet of sturdy males carrying her shoulder-high like tribal bearers in ancient Darkest Africa, and there was the square-cornered building glimpsed through the trees, with spires of smoke rising from points on its roof. (Fires? In this heat?) The belt of trees ended suddenly, neatly sliced by some art of forestry, revealing the hill covered with the same sun-scorched grass as the horse paddock and at its top the building, immense when seen entire. Ahead of her Soldier ran a zigzag uphill path, already a good three hundred metres ahead and gaining steadily.

She fumbled telelens spectacles from her pouch. The bearers at her shoulders glanced and glanced away; they were probably familiar with eyeglasses, which had been invented . . . Sixteenth Century? Seventeenth? At any rate, before the onset of galloping technology. Historical detail was not her strength.

Her contact with the ship was permanently open and she wondered what the listening ears on *Search* had made of the exchanges of speech so far. Analysts would theorise in a crossfire of speculation but no one would ask her a question until she signalled a need for conference or they diagnosed emergency— in which case Jack would be reaching down for her with magnetic fingers.

In the telelenses the walls of the Library seemed formed of irregular bluestone boulders cased in weathered cement, showing black against the bright sky. (Cement? Historically late? No, the Romans had used it.) Windows were regularly spaced but narrow and deeply sunk; otherwise the building was as featureless as a warehouse.

Looking about, she recognised sheep, belly-deep in the heat-faded grass, knowing them from the pictures in *Search's* Embryological Section, where the cryo-preserved cell clusters were identified by hologram and description. There were yellow flowers in the grass (she guessed wildly at giant dandelions) and butterflies amongst them, otherwise only unidentifiable trees. *How little we city dwellers knew of the real world outside.*

Soldier reached the Library in an astonishingly short time, rounded a corner, and vanished. Nugan's bearers took twenty minutes to cover the same distance.

She saw then that the Library was only a single storey high but some three hundred metres long and surrounded by a broad, stone-lined moat; as she watched, a blue-scaled fish surfaced and splashed down again.

The bearers rounded the near corner to move along the western face and she found herself in the Middle Ages. In the centre of the wall a drawbridge led to a high doorway guarded by the vertical tines of a half-raised portcullis. Close-to, the effect was less medieval than practical, like the goods entrance to an institution that needed a grating against bandits. There was one touch of romance detail—a man sat on the edge of the drawbridge in a faintly monkish robe, fishing with rod and line.

Soldier Thomas appeared on the drawbridge, pushing a wheelchair that caused her to mutter, "Oh, no!" because it was a sophisticated artefact from a dead age.

He called cheerfully, "Perhaps you will walk tomorrow, but not today." As he stopped beside her the carriers dropped the stretcher to arm's length and the slim Soldier lifted her off without any great effort and deposited her in the chair. (Nugan wondered at his physical characteristics; she and her suit weighed ninety kilos.) She touched the metal wheel rims, plastic tyres, and steel spokes, all unmistakably factory produced. Only, what should have been the material of seat and backrest had been replaced by white, furred leather which she guessed to be sheepskin; the rest was pristine Twenty-first Century. Or earlier.

"Where on earth did you get this?"

"On Earth," Soldier agreed. "It was found in a sealed museum cellar—basement? A place where samples of furnishings were stored with air . . . withdrawn. To preserve them."

A historic crypt, laid down for the future by people who knew their time was over. . . . Later than the departure of the ships . . . Nugan could not envision the circumstances of the breakdown of hope.

Soldier was saying something about other gases.

. . . Helium, she thought, or argon, inert and long-lasting. "But the seals failed. Buildings fell or were broken by men to recover the metals which they needed. Or perhaps the ground shifted and air entered. Leather and cloth rotted away." He slapped the fleecy backrest. "Those we replaced." After a moment he added, "Libary was angry."

"Why?"

"For our stealing. He said we should make lists and drawings and seal up again. For the future. But I said we cannot make such things so well as this and it is useful for people who are hurt. And for him when he is very old. He was offended."

If his English halted and faltered, it was for lack of constant practice; he had been well taught. "Libary is an artist?"

"Not that. He is a philosopher, a historian, a scientist, a teacher. He raised me and taught me."

"Your father?"

"You must not suggest that; he is a Celibate. I know nothing about my parents."

His tone, suddenly dark and measured, warned of treacherous ground. She would have to be alert for taboos and social circumlocutions; the local mores, conventions, and superstitions could be minefields. It was as well that ears in orbit were listening and dissecting; there would be a deal of discussion when she found herself alone to whisper at the microphone.

As they crossed the drawbridge the monkishly clad man pulled in one of the blue-scaled fish and dropped it, flapping and struggling, on the planks. The simple life, Nugan thought, might be a mass of built-in contradictions.

She looked up at the portcullis as they passed under it. "Does the Library have enemies?"

Soldier laughed. "Perhaps jealous friends. That is

a long matter to discuss. Perhaps afterwards."

That sounded like politics, which Nugan regarded as the most pernicious of human inventions.

The portcullis guarded a passage rather than a doorway, a passage a good seven metres deep and opening into a huge roofed court occupying the entire vast interior space and surrounded by large alcoves or, rather, rooms with no fourth wall. The whole court was roofed in small glass panes, tinted against the strong sun and set in square frames that looked like iron. (No metal in the bottling plant but metal in abundance here.) Strong timber masts, connected by carpentered architraves and themselves consisting apparently of entire stripped tree trunks, continued downwards through the floor and probably supported it also. The floor itself was another structure of thick glass panes, untinted but not of high clarity. Below it, Nugan gained only an impression of a maze of rooms and passages, of people in motion and occasional lights; it was like looking into a termitary.

Soldier pushed the chair rapidly but in one of the doorless rooms she glimpsed a man in a grey gown, standing at a lectern on which rested a book very much of her own time in appearance. In the moment of her passing he turned a page and she saw that he wore light gloves for the handling. An old book, handled with preserver's reverence. Surviving books must be precious.

She caught herself shivering slightly; it was cooler in the court than outside. The very thick walls, of course. But—sunlight struck through the glass overhead and yet there was a mild but definite current of air carrying coolness. Conditioning? No mean feat, she thought, in a structure of such size.

She asked, at a reasonable venture, "Do you have a great many books here? Old books, I mean, from before the—'' The what? She did not know.

Soldier spoke over her head. "The Downfall? The Collapse? There are many names for a time of which we know not much. There was the Last Culture and then a Twilight when only a few books were written and most of them lost. Not preserved because they did not anymore know how. But the big libraries were sealed with the gases. Not all of them but some big ones. Melbourne Public Library was one. More than four million books! We have all of them here, down below.''

She was amazed. "Such a hoard!''

He laughed. "So much knowledge, you think? We have not read one tenth of them. The Tabulators have not even finished making the—the word for listings?''

"Catalogues.''

"Thank you—catalogues. Every day a new treasure and a new excitement for secrecy.''

Nugan noted the last word for future questioning. A different association of ideas suggested safer ground. "And is the air kept dry to preserve the books?''

"Most surely. They are precious beyond men's lives. The furnaces never go out. The, er . . . humidity . . . is kept very low. It is cool here but in the cellars it is dry and warm.''

Warm air, passed through water, perhaps, to cool it, then chemically scrubbed? Difficult on a large scale but not impossible. Nugan suspected that labour for great projects might be no problem and she began to entertain a considerable respect for these resourceful people. A quotation rose unbidden out of memory: "The past is a foreign country: they do things differently there.''

This world, though a part of her present, reeked of the preindustrial past. She shuddered in a sharp attack of confusion. Past and future here were one.

Soldier said, in a tone she had not heard from him, soft, deep in the throat, soothing but wholly artificial, "There is nothing to fear, Taylor's Nugan."

Suspecting mockery, Nugan reacted with anger, forgetting objectivity. "I am not afraid of anything!"

"Taylor's Nugan, you are a little afraid. Do not be. Here a soldier is not only a man for fighting; he is also a protector."

Now she felt, unreasonably, that he babied her along, like a dentist's nurse. "Why do you use that stupid voice? Is it for soothing brats?"

He stopped pushing and moved round to face her. "I beg pardon of you." His expression was more puzzled than contrite; he had erred and was seeking the right reaction. "The calming voice is a—er—a conventional thing, a social gesture, an assurance. It is, maybe, a manner of doing that you do not have."

She took a long moment to put anger aside and say, "I'm sorry, Thomas; we were at cross-purposes."

He went back behind the chair and said as he pushed again, "That will happen often, I think."

"I suppose it must. Everything I see is in a sense familiar, but I look again and it is not familiar at all."

"So, too, when I consider you."

Of course! It had to be that each would recognise yet not recognise.

But she puzzled over his detection of the little uncertainty in her. Then she recalled the men in the bottling shed, and Johnno's sniffing, and felt herself in a most alien land indeed.

She became aware of quiet, not quite silence but quiet imposed like a weight on the few small sounds of voices in the open rooms; the huge space swallowed and drowned them. She became aware also of people, a very few lone men and women hurrying along the narrow brick causeway that surrounded the expanse of glass floor in a protective frame; the few who crossed the glass wore shoes soled with sheep's fleece that would not scratch. It seemed that Library life scurried mostly underground.

"Where does the iron come from, Thomas, the iron rims that hold the glass frames?"

He chuckled gently. "Like the chair, stolen. The great city buildings had steel skeletons, so our fathers stole the skeletons and let the buildings fall. Metal is not easy to find. There are iron mines in the western part of the continent but the metal must be—um—refined? It was cheaper to steal, but little remains now for scavengers. We have stolen most of the useful rubbish—litter? debris? of the older world."

"You melt down the metals and remould them?"

"We remould all the things that are scarce. Even wood is used afresh where that is possible. Now, Nugan, here is another stolen thing." He halted the chair where a stretch of wall separated two rooms. "See how the Top-Ma knew where you came from."

The mural was some ten metres wide by four high and the sight of it was a startling moment of home. She looked closely for signs of ageing in the paint, for crackling and light damage, but the preservative techniques of the painter had carried his picture unharmed across ages. Had much worthwhile art survived, she wondered, or did this lowest denominator spread of decorative dross serve to represent the painting of her time?

Second-rate or not, it brought a pang of recognition. Against a matt, nonreflecting background of blackness spangled with stars, the silver bat figures, arms outspread and heads thrown dramatically back, rose above the pale aureole atmosphere of a tiny Earth and soared, conquering, into an endless sky. It was little better than tossed-off advertising art but it had caught the cheap yearning of an age in need of fantasy.

She said, "It's melodramatic stuff, but people liked it. You could have found better work to preserve."

"We did, Nugan, we did, but this was brought here a hundred years ago and it is a historical document, is it not? The labour of removing and transporting it makes a tale of dedication and ingenuity. The Forest Genetic has ballads about it."

Forest Genetic? A vagrant idea about biology commenced to form. It would have to wait.

"So much work for such a poor thing! It was in the entrance hall of an entertainment centre."

Soldier was silent through a long beat before he said, "You would have had copies of it in your starship?"

"Heavens, no! I saw the thing when it was first displayed. At a charity concert. A lot of silly oohing and aahing—"

She stopped dead, realising what for him must be the implications of what she had said. Behind her Soldier was silent. She craned back to look at him and saw the absorption of a man dealing with the wholly intractable.

He nodded, whether to his own incomprehension or in recognition of a marvel, she could not tell. "You were there to see it? That is what you said?"

Timidly, knowing that she was about to deliver a monstrous fact, she reached over shoulder to lay a hand on his. His hand was rock steady. "Thomas, the crew of the ship are not the descendants of those who left Earth. They are the same people. It is not magic or miracle. It is a simple thing, when you know how it comes about."

He smiled, a touch grimly, she thought. "I believe because I must. You will explain to Libary and we will listen together."

He pushed the chair round the end of the mural and into a room much larger than the others they had passed, halted before a wide and cluttered desk, and said, "Libary, this is the Taylor's Nugan, from the starship. Nugan, this man is Libary, the Librarian. He is also Papa Melchizedech, but that is a formal name for ritual."

A thin man of middle stature and late middle age came forward to examine her with soft brown eyes set in a lined face. A white shirt sparkled over wide-cut grey shorts. He was barefooted. He was a full-blooded Koori, the only one she had ever seen with the single exception of her black grandmother.

He said, with an unexceptionable pronunciation though with the slightly throaty accent of his time, "Libary welcomes you to the Library, Nugan Star-woman."

He extended a dark hand and she took it with a return of the eerie feeling of meeting across centuries.

8

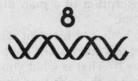

SOLDIER KNEW THE WOMAN HAD NOT lied. The reading of body language was a basic element of military policing investigations, taught over years of meticulous training, and Nugan appeared to have only the most superficial techniques of restraint; she was as readable as a child. She had stated an impossibility, but she had not lied.

When she took Libary's hand Soldier read the un-

certainty in the movement; Libary would be aware
but able to disguise his perception. (Libary could be
curiously inept, could lay disguise over disguise and
yet in an emotional moment betray himself utterly.)
The woman's outward calm did not cheat an eye
which interpreted the tightening of throat muscles,
the tension in shoulders, the barest hesitation in
handshake, the too calm pitch of voice as she asked,
"How do you do, sir?"

How did he do what? It sounded inane but might
be a formality of her period, its meaning lost.

Libary seemed unsurprised as he replied, "You
should address me as Libary. The people do so."

As he crossed to the small secretarial desk to take
up ink stylus and a pad of stiff paper, Soldier
watched her make instant appreciation of the room.
She showed practical interest in the ceiling glass
which allowed good light while cutting the fierce ul-
traviolet radiation of the coming summer and the
shining, enamel white walls and floor which made
optimum use of light. *We earn a mark for efficiency.*
Her eyes lingered on the floor mats and the inset designs reminiscent of and developed from the Koori
patterns known in her time. Her swift appraisal of
Libary's desk, its woodwork as fine as anything those
ancient centuries of hers could have produced, was
knowledgeable and approving.

All this in seconds. She was a competent observer
but unaware that her body spoke loudly and contin-
uously of her thinking. She would be unable to lie
convincingly in this world and Soldier suspected
that there would be much ambiguity and indirection
on Libary's part. Nugan would find no friend in that
secretive brain.

Her first remark was unexpected. (A technique of
obliquity? It would achieve little with Libary.) "This

fine building is very different from the timber and thatch of the village."

Libary gave her more answer than she could have bargained for. "For the preservation of knowledge we build palaces, but where your great councils sat in vast and gilded chambers, ours argue their decisions under trees."

It was a direct statement of philosophic and intellectual differences, of traps of misunderstanding lying in wait.

Nugan smiled, nodded acceptance of the message and took another tangent. "What is Mister Atkins doing?"

Soldier said, "I am making a record of our talk for transmission round the world."

To her uncomprehending frown he explained, "Transmission by semaphore. Slow by comparison with the lost art of your radio but fast enough for simpler needs. This is an important meeting; a record is necessary."

"But you cannot write as fast as we speak!"

"Your people with recording machines forgot their own arts. Two generations ago Pitman's Shorthand manuals were rediscovered and the making of verbatim records began again. It is a system of writing complete sounds instead of single letters."

She was suitably amazed but he felt that nothing of real import was being said. He dropped his small bomb.

"Nugan has told me that her starship people are not the heirs of the Last Culture, but are of the Culture itself, that the crew are those who left Earth at the end of the Twenty-first Century."

Libary's muted reaction told Soldier that he was taken aback and rapidly reassessing his attitude toward the interview. While he wondered what new thinking the information had sparked, Nugan rushed in to explain away the incredible.

"It is true but it is easily understood. We have visited many of the nearer stars." Then she saw her explanation as not so simple after all and said, seeking an entry, "The distances travelled are enormous."

Libary's smoothness might never have faltered as he came to her rescue. "We have read your astronomical works—those we can understand. We know what a lightyear is and that light travels at an unimaginable 300,000 kils in a second." He smiled thinly. "I had not expected the information ever to be of use to me."

Soldier diagnosed a moment of confusion in Nugan, a useless guessing at what this age might or might not know, but she put doubts aside to concentrate on explanation. "Decades pass in the passage between stars and there is no reason to keep three hundred people unproductively awake. A handful maintain the ship in flight. The rest sleep in the cryo—special freezing chambers."

"Cryogenic," Libary said. "The word appears in Last Culture books."

She was impressed by this grasp of the past. "Most of us slept during the entire flight, waking only when our special skills were required. I was in waking mode for only twenty-six years in the centuries of travel and there is almost no ageing in the cryo vaults, perhaps one-tenth of one percent."

She looked doubtfully at Libary as if unsure whether to attempt further difficulties, then made up her mind. "There are other effects. When a ship reaches eighty-seven percent of the speed of light, the perception of time is halved. It is an effect of relativity."

She expected incomprehension but Libary was before her. "I have read of relativity but do not understand such consequences. Nor do I feel that I would gain by understanding them. A question remains: I can conceive that time has been in some sense evaded, but to what extent? What is your age in physical, waking years?"

"I was twenty-two when we left Earth. I am almost fifty now. There is a small uncertainty because of quantum—er, of fundamental disturbances in space-time."

Libary, determined to maintain charge of the exchange, preserved a bland face. "Thomas is twenty-eight; I had judged you much the same. Did the people of the Last Culture retain youth longer than we have suspected?"

"No, oh, no! The gene surgeons operated on us before we started out. It was expected that the voyage would take hundreds of years and at the end we would need youth and strength to establish a settlement. They altered our metabolisms so that we age slowly."

Soldier expected the next question to concern the passing on of longevity to the children but Libary turned his attention abruptly elsewhere.

He asked bluntly, "Why were *Search* and *Kiev* sent into the sky?"

Nugan answered at once, too quickly, "To find planets on which humans could live."

"That is nonsense."

"You asked a short question; you received a short answer. The whole answer is more complex."

Soldier hid his smile; Libary would not cow this one with terseness as he sometimes cowed the Ordinands. He guessed that the old man would change tack rather than risk withdrawal or impasse—and so he did.

"You must pardon me, Taylor's Nugan, if I hurry to the heart of things. Your eruption into a quiet Earth must be discussed across five continents and I must know accurately what I am to tell. Unless, of course, there are other ambassadors descended into other areas of the planet?"

"No others. I am alone in reconnoitering my own country to see what changes have taken place and report back. We would not drop three hundred people without first knowing what they will find."

Soldier recorded her words impassively. The population of a small village. That her scouting was solitary was a fact of enormous value but Libary moved at once away from it, bringing her back to the point— his point.

"And the reason for seeking new planets?"

Nugan spoke slowly, carefully, "We still argue about that. Earth was impossibly overcrowded. The seas were polluted as well as the land. People—"

Libary interrupted her. "We have records of your period, here and in other countries—thousands of tonnes of paper, unguessable millions of words. We know the problem. We know, too, that even your gulping of resources could not have produced ships enough to carry away the yearly increase of population. Yet the real reasons for assaulting the stars remain unanswered—save, perhaps, in some document we have not yet uncovered."

Nugan bit her lips and clasped her hands. *She cannot think without betraying that she grapples with thought.*

She said at last, "Competitiveness and dreams— and maybe bread and circuses to keep brooding turned away from despair. I think that at bottom those were the impulses. The most powerful nations had formed a secret group to practice genocide on the remainder. It was to be the ultimate solution to the problem of overpopulation."

She fell silent, waiting for reaction. If she expected horror she was denied it.

Libary was dismissive. "We know of that. It is recorded. Mankind has survived other crises since then and we know what human beings can do to their own kind; we are not shocked by realities, nor do we sit in judgment on monstrous solutions to monstrous problems. Your time's necessity is not ours and to preach the sanctity of life would be vulgar cant."

The neutral tone, Soldier thought, was subtly encouraging, an invitation to call vileness by its right name in this sophisticated company.

Nugan said hurriedly, "A politician, in Melbourne, revealed the plan in a fit of mental imbalance—"

"The Premier, Beltane. That story, too, is known."*

"The plan had to be abandoned for fear of global war but the revelation split the whole race into hostile, suspicious factions—national, religious, philosophic—roughly, the English-speaking people beleaguered by the rest. A result was resurgence of national prides and religious fervours; sleeping rivalries awoke, with nations and enclaves attempting to assert themselves in nearly insane ways. Even among the anglophones there was rivalry expressing itself in grandiose, ultimately useless projects. The search for new planets was one of many; giving Mars an atmosphere was another and there was a brainless plan for terraforming Venus. It was a time of suppressed hysteria. People no longer looked at reality on a planet that had become a slum; it was easier to look at the heavens and dream. The ships were built not because they were necessary but simply because it could be done. They were a huge gesture of attain-

---

*See *The Destiny Makers*, Avon Books, New York, 1993, for the story of Beltane and the genocide plot.

ment. Man in decline could still reach for the stars! It was nonsense, but nonsense to keep hearts alive. We crew trainees saw our voyage almost in terms of religion, in mystical fashion. We were years in flight before common sense broke out and we saw ourselves alone and forgotten, thrown away to divert the attention of the slum dwellers. You see, there were no new worlds for conquest."

Libary allowed himself mild incredulity. "Do you mean that no other stars have planets?"

Nugan made an indescribable, bitter sound in her throat. "More stars with planets than without. Planets too hot, too cold, too poisonous, too drenched in radiation. I have stood on a dozen planets and we could not have lived a day unarmoured on any one of them."

Libary gave no sign that the information held interest for him. "So you returned to Earth; the dream of Man amongst the stars could not maintain its mystique." He might have been speaking of failure to keep a social engagement.

Nugan laughed aloud, unhappily. "It began to look damned silly."

"And so, disillusioned and disheartened, you returned."

"They called it homesickness."

"They?"

"Some of us wanted to go on but we were voted down. In fact, howled down. A good friend of mine was savagely beaten—by women—for opposing the return."

"But you—some of you—would have continued the search?"

"Yes, but we have come home."

Soldier noted the minimal hardening of Libary's eyes, contradicting the deliberate assumption of reasonableness—the reasonableness of a hunting snake, Soldier thought—as he said, like one explaining gently to a child, "But this is not your home."

Nugan, angry and dismayed, fell into the trap of mollifying. "Oh, we know that the world has changed, that our time is dead and that we will have to cope with utterly altered conditions, that we will have to behave with circumspection and not make unwelcome nuisances of ourselves."

The black face inspected her with smiling interest; white teeth gleamed through slightly parted lips. *He has decided*, Soldier thought, *that he is dealing with a fool; these Celibates lose touch in their solitudes of learning.*

Nugan hurried on with words. "We can be of great use to you, to your people. We can teach, pass on our knowledge, once we see what materials are available and what you need. Medicines, for instance . . . all sorts of things."

Libary said, still smiling, "I look around me and see little that we greatly need; what is required, we will develop in time."

Now, that is a deliberate lie. Soldier recorded it with heavy strokes as a deviousness to be questioned later.

Nugan replied (Soldier could have slapped her for the foolishness), "You don't know yet what we have to give."

Libary shrugged. "We know what we do not want." He added, with no change of tone, "You should remain here for several days, should you not, to observe all that your superiors will expect of you? Will your absence alarm them?"

"No. A Contact Officer takes what time is needed. I can send a signal at any time to assure that 'All's well' or to say, 'Lift me away.' "

Soldier took down the words impassively. *You*

*must never lie, Nugan, even by indirection. You cry
aloud that you say one thing and hide another.*

Whatever Libary thought, he gave no sign but said,
"I must confer with others in other places. Not all
will be in agreement."

Nugan was puzzled. "About what?"

"About the nature of your reception. You must
know, Taylor's Nugan, that there are many people in
many lands. When a great thing happens, and this is
a great thing, there must be agreement. You will realise that?"

*Observe, Nugan, how an artist tells his lie! He even
obliges you to agree with him.* And indeed she was
saying, "I know there is much to be discussed—
among my people also. I will help in every way I
can."

"You help with every word you speak."

*An error, Libary; contempt for the intellect of oth-
ers is a scholar's blind spot.* Nugan's reaction, instantly suppressed, agreed with him. The Celibate
said, "We will meet in a day or two. I may by then
have information for your people."

Nugan seemed unbelieving. "You are dismissing
me? We have hardly begun discussion!"

Libary allowed his smile to widen, to become gentle and intimate as he spread his hands in depreca-
tion of his clumsiness. He could exert charm at will
but Soldier thought he had left it too late. "We have
discussed the subject that matters, Taylor's Nugan.
Your people wish to live on Earth and those who now
live on Earth must be told so. It may be that many
views must be heard."

"As to where we may land, who will have us, and
who might refuse?"

The charm faded a little. "Those things among others."

"But there is so much I need to ask!"

"Ask Thomas. He knows more of the real world than a recluse like myself. He is a soldier on leave, with time for conversation, and he will be happy to practice his Late English. And he is a notable squire of dames." He stood and bowed slightly. "Until our next meeting, Taylor's Nugan."

She did not answer him, anger gagging on the implication that her presence could be dealt with as a matter of office routine, an everyday complication to be passed through channels until somewhere a form was stamped and a permission granted.

Soldier drew her out of the room. He disapproved of Libary's careless revelation of his contempt and was a little sorry for Nugan, who would not have read as much into the exchange as he had done. Out in the court and moving along the brick walkway, he was aware of her unrest under painful control. When she spoke it was deliberately of a side issue.

" 'Squire of dames!' Where would he have learned such an expression?"

"In some old book. He prides himself on his use of rare idioms."

"And fits you with a reputation."

"Alas, undeserved."

She could not know that the phrase had been a communication to Soldier, a direction to him to follow a course of action in search of truth. She asked him, "Where are you taking me?"

"To guest quarters. You must have a private place to retire into." He wanted her out of sight before stray Ordinands recognised an alien presence and came flocking.

"That old man dislikes me."

Not you but what you represent. "That old man is little more aged than yourself. He is . . . reserved in his manner . . . because he does not know what to do for the best."

"Thomas, we are not an invasion of demons!"

"Perhaps not, but think of this: What follows if your people land here and find themselves isolated among demons? You do not know what we are."

She was silent. He had made her, at last, aware of possibilities beyond the obvious.

He waited until eventually she said, with some uncertainty, "I have been treated with courtesy and kindness here. Even that old man can be excused; he is a politician, using words as screens. I have seen no demons."

"Are not your people courteous and kindly?"

"On the whole, yes."

"On the whole. Until?"

"Until aroused or interfered with."

"And then?"

"There can be violence. You know this; you have read our books."

"A few only. What came of violence in those days?"

"Perhaps nothing—a flaring up and a dying down. Perhaps rioting, to be halted by the police."

"And when great countries were roused?"

"Sometimes war."

"Fought by soldiers?"

"Of course."

"I am a soldier, a General with an army at my call. Why do you think my profession exists? To quell the tiny quarrels of the courteous and kindly? Or of demons?"

She was quiet, recognising a vast ignorance.

At the far end of the great court a row of empty rooms stretched the entire width of the building. Soldier steered her into the nearest and loosed a cord by the entrance; a blind woven of reeds slithered to the floor.

"Privacy. None will enter unless you wish."

Sunlight through ceiling tiles gave sufficient light. The furnishings were simple—a table, two chairs, an empty bookcase, a doorless cupboard with hooks for hanging clothes, and the flat, bare tray of a bed.

"Wait here. I will withdraw bedding and necessities from the store and return very soon."

"Thank you, Soldier."

He pulled back the edge of the blind to slip outside and walk fifty metres before he turned back to listen at the blind and smile privately at the murmur of Nugan's voice, pitched low and speaking rapidly. He did not wait or try to hear; her reporting, so soon and with so little knowledge, would be unimportant. In any case he had known that she suppressed truth about "signalling." He returned with a pushcart holding bedding, a round bath of caulked wooden staves, towels, a cup, and a jug.

He had thought that she would remove the silver suit while he was away but she had taken off only the heavy boots. Could she be naked beneath the suit's protection? He thought that unlikely.

He placed the bath where two ancient brass taps protruded from the wall. "More stolen treasure," he told her cheerfully. "The old buildings were temples of cleanliness and we have stores filled with the plunder of bathrooms." As Nugan said nothing, he continued, "Hot water pumped from the furnace room; cold water pumped from the river, stage by stage! The Last Culture left gifts for its distant children."

He saw that only part of her mind was on furnishings and was ready for her when she said, "Tell me about your profession."

"Why, I am a trained, skilled murderer."

It was a minuscule part of the truth but he had thought to shock her. She only asked, blandly, "Do you take pleasure in your work?"

"Yes, or I would not do it."

"So nothing has changed."

"A great deal has changed." He perched on the little table, leaning over her, watching her face. "The purpose of soldiering is peace. A paradox? Nugan, do you imagine that soldiers ever enjoyed killing save in moments of unbalanced rage or thought-blinding excitement? A soldier does what he must, or be himself killed. He operates in fear; if he says differently, he lies. There are men who have no fear but they are less than wholly sane and do not make good soldiers; we get rid of them because they can be a reckless danger to their own. I have read training manuals of your day and seen that the instructors laid most emphasis on self-protection, on remaining alive. Do you know that with the bullet-firer you called a rifle, only two lessons in twenty taught aiming and firing? All the rest were about cleaning and maintaining in order that the man should be always ready to defend himself. Yet I said 'murderer' and your thought agreed instantly."

At once she argued, "Armoured tanks and huge guns killed at a distance and bombs flew thousands of K to their civilian targets. Soldiers murdered not each other but the unarmed and helpless."

"I know it, Nugan. The books, the pictures have been found and studied. In our thinking these were not the acts of soldiers, who are men, but of huge, maleficent states, enslaved by the pragmatism of self-preservation and its brother, the instilling of hate. They planned in safety and passed their orders to those who must carry them out or be punished. Men became counters on a gameboard, no longer soldiers. Murder was done at a distance and so lost the immediacy of agony. That cannot happen today because there are no huge, maleficent states."

"None?" The tone was startlement.

"In the whole world, none. There are communes, there are groups of villages with interests causing each to depend on the welfare of the others, and there are large tracts where communities share usage in common. There are also loose—federations—" He hesitated. "A wrong word, I think. I need a word saying that the communities work together and are friendly but do not share each others' social ways and local laws."

She appeared scarcely to believe him. "A world of villages and self-supporting communities! It seems hardly possible."

"If self-supporting means living only on what they produce, it is not so. Every community depends in some sense on every other. Trade and exchange are essential, or no one could live. I mean only that there are no masses of villages bound under a ruler and calling themselves a nation or an empire. There are no rulers in the manner in which the word had meaning for you."

Nugan protested, "But there must be someone in charge. Otherwise who declares law or justice, who decides quarrels or makes decisions about shared questions, such as roads between different communities?"

Soldier had gone further than he had intended and her question edged on matters whose explanations he was not wholly sure of. He knew the local ways and the theories of social behaviour, but the total philosophic web—the underlying scheme of beliefs and guidances that held the whole together—hung on a balance of ideas and forces whose exposition he had rarely considered.

He said, grudgingly because his omniscience had been undercut, "You had best go to the Top-Ma for that. She has been reared to deal with such affairs."

Nugan took the opening. "In the village she

showed authority. Do those women rule?"

She could not see Soldier's grin, urchin wicked. "They think so. They have the authority that the men and wives allow to the Ordinand-trained, but it is not unquestioned. They preserve authority by being fit to hold it, not otherwise. I said that no one rules, but some bear the burden of making wise decisions for others."

"In that case, who needs professional soldiers?"

With a few words plucked out of the air almost at random he showed her an underside to the pastoral world. "The homeless, the starving, the dissatisfied—and now and then a Top-Ma in trouble."

She considered that unlikely list and asked (from his point of view) the wrong question, "How can a village such as the one on the river below, or even a group like it, support an army? If there is no state, no nation, no organisation big enough—"

"Many villages support us as we support them. My army consists of a thousand men and is responsible for scores of Yarra Valley communities. They feed us and supply other needs. In return, we assist in harvesting and forestry and we have many specialised artisans on whom villagers can call to practice their skills and teach them to the growing young ones. We are often what you would call a police force. We arbitrate in matters of violence and suppress it where necessary. The villagers find us an essential arm of social stability and so they support us."

She seemed taken aback. He reflected that to her this version of soldiering must appear naive measured against memories of global uproar. "You judge quarrels and deal out punishment to lawbreakers?"

"Punishment is not our business. I said only that where necessary we suppress violence. Punishment is a community matter; men and women are judged by their peers, not by uninvolved, uncaring strangers."

"And if a person is continually violent or a thief or a troublemaker—a criminal? What then? Who punishes?"

"Such may be killed by their exasperated neighbours. It does not happen often, once folk make their feelings known. The certainty of death or maiming is a strong deterrent. We do not interfere in internal affairs."

The movement of her shoulders told that she found this appalling. There was a cynical jest in the queasiness of one whose culture had slaughtered millions in brute expediency.

It was time to direct her interest to other truths. With a village girl he would have used the soothing mode, but with this one he had no ready-made social approach and must stalk the defences like a cautious scout. He asked with a disinterested courtesy, "Do you need assistance to remove your silver armour?"

"Yes, I do. Usually my daughter locks and unlocks me."

Daughter? "I had not thought of you as one with a daughter."

The advance was tentative, a manouevre from afar, but it paid with unexpected speed.

"Why not, Thomas? I don't need a man pawing me when I dress for work."

If the tone was dismissive, the undertone was not. It was as if, almost unknown to herself, she played a double game. She was certainly aware of him as a male; the denial of a need covered an opposite implication. No village woman would have given so complex a response; he would have known at once whether or not he was wanted.

Unsure, he shrugged, smiled and said, "Luckless man!"

"Do you think so, squire of dames?"

Now he was quite sure. The mockery revealed, taunted and dared. Did these people of the past approach sex as a ritual game, as children might tempt each other with sweets? He did not know the rules.

"Well," she said, "I have no daughter here and am imprisoned in armour." She held up a small implement like a pocket knife with a blunt, rounded blade. "Here is the key. Unlock me, squire."

He examined the thing, seeing nothing keylike about it. Nugan indicated a dark line in the silver material, a circle just below the metal collar, leading over the shoulders, and took the key from him. She set the rounded end on the dark line and drew the key along it. The material parted.

"So. Just draw it completely round."

He did so, following the mark over the shoulder, across her back and round to meet the starting point. The silver fabric parted. Nugan lifted the collar and helmet-shawl clear and laid them on the floor. He fingered the exposed edge, unsure whether it was woven metal or textile fibre or some amalgam of both.

"Now you must help me stand."

She struggled out of the chair and onto one leg while he supported her.

"Now open the line down the back."

The second line stretched from shoulder, down between buttocks, to crotch. As the key opened it the loose material sagged forward. Nugan shrugged her arms loose and the upper section of the dropsuit fell forward onto the floor. Soldier was not prepared for the thud of heavy metal as the gloves struck the bricks; he promised himself a close inspection of those harmless-seeming accessories.

She was covered in a tightly clinging woven costume, a single-piece garment like, he thought, the nightsuit of a scout patrol, but blue rather than black.

He held her, both hands under her armpits, as she lifted her legs and feet from the dropsuit and, still supporting her, stood a short pace back to scan her body. His hands on her ribs told him and the little lift in her breathing confirmed that he was, however inadvertently, playing her culture's sexual game correctly. The *rom* increased perceptibly.

He said without reserve, "You have a fine body, Nugan. You would make a wife for the Mixed Genetic."

A compliment? "I don't want to be anyone's wife."

Yet she had a daughter . . . A dead husband, perhaps? "Pleasure without the burden?"

That must be plain enough. He had never given himself to a woman old enough to be his mother, but he was a soldier and this seduction was demanded of him. He turned her gently about to see that age had not troubled her body at all; he disliked the cropped hair, for he had a mild fetish for long hair to wind around his arms and throat, but all else of her was what a squire of dames would seek and be thankful for—without the complication of lightning strike.

His quick fingers opened the studs of the body stocking and he wished, as the thing fell to the floor, that he could be a little less cold-blooded in the lovemaking to come. He comforted himself with an excuse, that the woman was tense with the battened down fear of exotic circumstances and needed an explosive relief—a therapy.

When she lifted her mouth to him and set her hands to work on the buttons of his shirt there was nothing for it but to begin the task of moulding her need for emotional release into trust and dependence. That, he had decided, was what Libary wanted of him. His cool soldier's soul had no moral qualm over a tactical conquest; she was, after all, an attractive enough woman and was not she also using him to her own purpose and need? Still . . . only a lifetime's debt to Libary made it possible for him to prostitute an act of intimacy in cold blood.

Any of his troopers would have said, Go to it, Tommy! It beats fighting, any time!

9

TO HIS BARED BODY, LEAN, AS A MAR-athon runner's is muscularly lean but effortless in movement, Nugan was wholly receptive, while her mind lay in wary waiting.

As he knelt for a moment between her knees, searching her face with a smile at once alight with anticipation and strangely knowing, as if he read more of her than she wished any man to read, she thought: *He knew I was attracted though I showed nothing; he knew he needed only to touch and grip and I would move to meet him. How? I am not a schoolgirl without screens or defences.*

Then he stretched himself along her body as smoothly as a gliding snake and took her in his arms. Like a snake's tongue, too, his kiss lighted on her breast, flickering and darting, to settle at last on her lips. It was, she felt, the practised but rousing kiss of the consummate hunter—and her body rose to it. A soldier's whore! And why not, for once?

Into the lovemaking entered other ideas, not too coherent in the press of heat and movement, illuminating her response in flashes of immediately dimmed sense. Dismaying. *He has no real interest in this . . . he applies the instruments of passion, one by one, testing and employing . . . the machine proficiency of doing what he feels is required of him . . . but, oh, how he does it with art and power . . . he plays me like . . . ah . . . ah, ahhhh.*

She lay still. *Did I cry out? I think I did. I felt the cry rising.*

His voice chuckled in her ear. "Consider the poor celibate Ordinands, ruffled in their stronghold by the sound of passionate encounter, hoping perhaps it was only that you knocked your injured ankle against a chair."

Celibates? So they had had their pleasure in the equivalent of a monastery! She felt momentarily like a naughty child flouting the grown-ups' rules. Like a naughty child she giggled, "Would they set me a penance?"

"A punishment? Oh, no, but they would be horrified—at least in a fair pretence of being horrified—and would gossip like cockatoos in a cornfield. Within the hour it would be known throughout the crypts and cellars; by sundown the village would be aware."

"That the woman from the stars lay with the first man who offered?"

He rolled aside and lay on one hip, head arched over her, faint smile alive with knowledge she needed to share. "That would interest them, Nugan, but the core of talk in the beerhouse would be that Soldier had declared private Carnival. Any man will do so—given safe opportunity—but it makes a scandal when it is found out. And the more prominent the sinners, the more heinous the sin."

This made no sense at all. "Are you telling me that casual sex is socially taboo?"

"Taboo? Oh, yes—'forbidden.' Not punishable unless there is violence, but disapproved." His smile widened. "There was no violence but we two are exceptional people and therefore exceptionally at fault."

"How extraordinary."

"You might think so. Your books suggest that in the Last Culture you were able to indulge yourselves throughout the year, without restriction of season."

She echoed, "Season?" not sure that she understood him.

"Was it so?"

"Yes, of course. Why not? It was always so, throughout history."

Soldier lay on his back and contemplated the soft sunlight of the ceiling. "Then there may be truth in the tales of the Genetic Wizards."

Nugan wanted to shake him to stop his musing. Her linguist's instinct for mutation and change insisted that here might be the key to the behaviour of this new world. "Thomas, who were the Genetic Wizards?"

"Their names? We do not know, or if they really existed. The story goes like this: After the Collapse, in the period we call the Twilight because we know only dimly what took place for a space of at least two hundred years, the race of men took on a new social form, in some ways a new physical form also. The religions were still strong in those days and some said this was the providence of a merciful God and some the laughter of a devil called Satan. In time order appeared again, and the recovery of books, and there were references which nobody could understand and still can only half understand, to something called genetic engineering."

Nugan sat up abruptly. "Thomas! Are you saying that the gene surgeons redesigned the race?"

"I do not know what a gene surgeon might be."

She simplified rapidly, "He is a special kind of biologist—you know of biology? He treats sperm and ova to produce offspring with special characteristics. Instead of breeding over generations to produce a— oh, say a grey and brown horse—he changes the birth plasm to achieve it in a single move."

Soldier was not much astonished; his reading of the Library's books, themselves replete with the miraculous, had inoculated him against amazement at the past. "That is interesting but does not answer all questions. I will tell you what we have been able to discover. Remember that I am not a historian, only a man who reads."

"Tell me."

He nodded at the crumpled dropsuit lying halfway across the room. "Should you not make some record of what I say? Your superiors will be interested."

She suspected mockery but could not pin it to his voice; she hesitated over how much to tell him, then thought that the suit's activities would become apparent soon enough, anyway. "It can hear us."

"One should have a care—as when making love-play."

They laughed together because she had forgotten the suit listening to their ardours.

"Do you not care about their knowing, Nugan?"

"No. Let them talk if they want to." But she thought uneasily of Anne and took comfort from the certainty that Jack, dependable Jack, would have been routing the suit's output to Contact Supervision.

Soldier asked curiously, "Will your husband not care?"

"I have no husband."

"Yet you have a daughter."

"Yes."

Soldier considered it. "That would cause—" He

hesitated. "—discussion. Best not to speak of it here. The Top-Mas would be upset."

"Do they exert moral coercion?"

"Some. Let me tell you the history and it will become plain. Or perhaps not. There are few facts and much guessing."

He swung away from her to sit on the edge of the bed, facing the dropsuit as though he wished his words heard and remembered. (More accurately, she thought, heard, dissected, and deconstructed on *Search* until a dozen gutted meanings lay ready for evaluation.) The overhead light flowed over his brown skin like a thin lacquer and she saw, with fresh unease, how when he spoke only his mouth moved and his voice contained only what he allowed there; no small body movements added the peripheral life that makes the difference between utterance and communication. Libary also had spoken so, with only the occasional studied gesture.

Soldier said, "We use the word 'genetic' to mean the manner in which traits can be bred into or out of a strain. As in dogs or cattle or—" He turned his head briefly. "—human beings."

How little he knew. "That will do well enough."

"Thank you, Nugan. So the Last Culture did have its Genetic Wizards."

"Not wizards, Thomas. Chemists, surgeons, biologists, even genetic physicists. Scientists, not wizards."

"I know only what is handed down. A time came when the pressure of population became unbearable. I cannot imagine such numbers—an infestation—but the lore tells that many animals and birds died out for lack of places to breed, that the soil died of poisons and people starved and even the sea was polluted. Was it so?"

"It was under control when we left, but we knew

that it might happen. Side effects were becoming unmanageable."

"The fight for living space did not begin at once. The foolish Beltane had put fear of massacre into the world, but it began when its time had come. People died; whole nations died. But it was not carnage enough. There is a limit to the life this Earth can support; we think now that eventually one thousand million men and women, placed with care to balance with forest and meadow and all creatures, will be enough."

Nugan frowned. "More than that, surely. Three or four times more."

"Why, yes, Nugan, if only humanity counts and all other life must make way."

Good sense told her to shut up. She was walking the edge of a basic belief and should beware of a primitive conservation theory.

Soldier said, "You would say, I think, that human numbers will always grow because human power can sweep all other life from its path, and so the crowding and the starving and the culling must happen again and again. Eh?"

She said unwillingly, "Perhaps so. Probably."

"Not so, Nugan. You forget the Wizards. When killing had exhausted itself, still too many remained and it was then that the Wizards intervened. Or it may have been a miracle, life crying out against its habitat raped and pillaged by an unstoppable marauder. But we suspect the Wizards. Barrenness descended on the women of the world. For a long time—some say as many as two hundred years—only a few women in small enclaves in particular parts of the world gave birth. The rest grew old and died and left no young behind them. The cities died also and the machines rusted, but the oceans cleansed themselves and forgotten life returned to the wild as the new forests spread across the scarred world."

He turned to her to ask, "Could your genetic scientists have caused that? Were they wizards enough?"

She said automatically, "I don't know," but her mind raced down channels of possibility and the improbable shook down into the possible: A virus inserted into the DNA chain (into the X chromosome?) the action spreading through sexual congress from generation to generation, at first slowly and then in rapid multiplication, with soon only a few remaining uncontaminated (or in some manner immune) while the vast remainder lived out their sterile lives and died. And the virus? Could its span have been calculated by the implanters—so many passages before it mutated into a harmless form and became recessive?

She said slowly, "It is not impossible. It could have been done by determined, ruthless technicians with dedication to the future. Restriction groups flourished when we left Earth, but all the solutions involved genocide in one degree or another. A virus could have been spread without immediate detection. If the Collapse came soon after, no science would have been available to counteract it. It could have been done."

On *Search* the biologists, ears assaulted, would be already shouting at each other.

Soldier said, "We like to think that predatory Man solved the world's problem at his own cost."

Not *our* problem but *the world's* problem. These people thought very differently from hers. Her mind leapt to to the side issues that had hovered all the morning at its edges. "The Koori women were immune to the barrenness? They gave birth and their numbers grew?"

Soldier smiled as at a gifted child. "You think quickly, Nugan. Indeed the Koori and Murri and the other regional groups spread across Australia again with their knowledge of living in harmony with forest and desert and seashore. They taught the remaining white people also how to live with the land side by side with tree and beast."

"Then there was intermarriage?"

"How else survive?"

"And now there is only the new race without Koori or white man?"

"There are a few pure-blooded Koori and many Murri in the north. Libary is Koori. Many of them are Ordinands. I have never seen a pure-blooded white man. He would be a curiosity."

"And the rest of the world—outside Australia?"

"There are brown people and olive-skinned people and even white people, I am told, in Europe and America. But there are no separate races as you knew them—no emperors, no nations, no tribes. Only people."

And Celibates and Top-Mas and soldiers and no such simplicity as you toss at me. "People, yes. Including women, which is where we began. You were offering an explanation, Thomas."

His smile came and went as at a private joke. "A man to explain women? You jest, Nugan. I will tell you what the women expect us men to believe. Through many generations there were barren women and a very few fertile women and the barren stock died out and the small fertile stock repopulated the world. Now, the fertile stock claimed to be different from the women of the Last Culture. They claimed to be able to regulate their fertility, to breed or not breed at will and to be ready or unready to accept a man, also at will. The second is certainly true. A man knows when a woman is ready; there is a . . . not quite a scent but a tingling in the nose and the taste buds at the back of the mouth. We call it *rom*. With each woman it is a distinct and personal thing.''

Nugan was fascinated. ''A pheromone!'' That was the trick of Johnno's sniffing and knowing!

''I do not know that word, Nugan.''

''It is a—a sort of sexual signal, common in insects where males converge on females from great distances. It is true of animals and birds also. Humans of my time had lost awareness of the scent, the signal.''

Soldier was silent for a while. Then he said, ''There is a puzzle here. I will risk foolishness by guessing that in the closeness of your numbers you lost the ability to recognise the tingling signal because it was closely around you at all times. A scent becomes indetectable when it is always present. Or perhaps the sense withered with time. I cannot know; no one has thought to study such a thing. But this I can tell, that you display the signal—not strongly but a little, rising and falling with your mood and your awareness of a male. How else could I have known that you would receive me?''

Smelt out like a bitch in heat. She was in immediate dismay at an invasion of privacy which could be neither controlled nor denied. Then came angry understanding of his cool knowledge that he had only to project his wanting with certainty of acceptance by a ready whore. *Never again, Thomas; not ever again.* In this world women would be slaves to the male sexual whim . . . without escape . . .

Common sense took over. He had said, ''ready or unready to accept a man, at will . . .'' They *controlled* the flood of pheromone.

''And so,'' she said, ''the women have you on a string. To the unready woman a man does not exist! So you dance to their tune.''

He eyed her gravely, trying, she thought, to assess the small feminine triumph she could not repress. He said, "A woman will make herself ready when she chooses a man. That is her real power, the ability to choose."

"A man can force a woman."

"Did that happen in your time? It is a rare crime in this day. The enforcer might not live long. And what point would there be in seeking response from the equivalent of a block of wood?"

A doubtful point for lynch law, but a point. "That does not explain the authority of the Top-Ma."

"That is another matter. Men do men's work and women do women's work."

"Nothing changes!" With the words still hanging in the air, Nugan saw in a flash of insight that Soldier had spoken literally and that she had interpreted from a point of view centuries dead. He watched, as though he saw the working of her mind and waited patiently on the outcome. "No! Of course everything changes. Your men do the physical work of a nearly machineless world, the logging and ploughing and fighting, while the women bear the next generation and preserve the social conditions under which the sexes live together. The men work the world and the women keep it running."

Soldier stood, long and slender and copper brown. "You are quick to see, but that is only a beginning. I told you the women *think* they run the world; add that the men *think* they let the women run the world—so long as it suits the men to allow it so. Both are right and wrong. I am a soldier whose business is to look for truth behind the appearance of truth so that I may apply pressure to the depths men and women are not totally aware of. You have begun shrewdly but this world is more complex than we can unravel in a bedside conversation."

He bent and would have kissed her but she turned her head away, saying, "No, that's over."

He was not offended but thoughtful. "With us, Nugan, the last kiss is the acknowledgment between friends that the excitement of the encounter is pleasantly over."

"Encounter!" *If you mean fuck, say fuck.* She fought for control of a too easy anger. "I'm sorry, Thomas; I see everything through the eyes of a dead culture."

He made no comment but began to dress and to speak of other things. "There are a few female scholars here. I will ask them for suitable garments for your stay." He kicked at the discarded body stocking. "I will bring clothing quickly; you need not put that on again."

"Thank you, Thomas." She had wondered how to manage with the sweat-soaked thing.

His dressing occupied no more than a minute; he looked down on her, smart as a trooper ready for parade. "I have answered your questions, Nugan. Now you owe a reply to mine."

"That's fair."

"Now that your ship has returned to the home that shows itself to be no home at all, what will your people do?"

She said readily, "Make the best of it. It won't be easy dropping back through time to a preindustrial age but we'll have to adjust ourselves to new ways and new needs. It's a big world with more room in it than we ever knew; there will be a place for us once we learn how to approach each other. And we can pay our way in social terms. There is a lot we can give you, do for you—"

He broke in. "Nugan! Be careful of saying such things until you know more. Why should you walk

into a stranger's house with gifts and demand a welcome?''

She sat up, furious. ''For God's sake, man, you
aren't warning us off our own world, are you?''

''Calmly, little Nugan, calmly! I listen and consider
because I am Soldier and that is my work; others may
judge without listening. I am as yet the only person
you may allow to see into your heart's desire. Be an
observer. That is your role. Play it until you see with
understanding.''

He slipped round the edge of the reed blind and
disappeared.

Nugan shivered in the warm air, then reached out
to grasp the arm of the dropsuit and drag it across the
floor. She lifted the body until her mouth was level
with the microphone and whispered, ''There's activity buried and bad here. Like something in the dark.''

The suit whispered back, ''Our reading is that you
are in no danger. You have made a friend in this soldier, a powerful friend, it seems. Use him.''

Soldier wondered at his warning to her. It had surprised him from depths below conscious thinking, as
if from concerns he had not until now lifted into the
light. Like the Genetics, he had tended to accept his
world without querying its working; it could be time
for him to examine his own warning.

10

SOLDIER KNEW BETTER THAN TO TAKE his request to any of the Trainee women who would become the Mas and Top-Mas of a later day. "Clothing for whom? What manner of woman and where from? If she has no garments of her own, why so?" Refused answers, they would have been affronted and set out to see for themselves. Soldier with a woman in the Library precinct! Who and what is she?

He went instead to the laundry at the back of the furnace room where Johnno's mother soaped and rinsed and wrung and dried for four days each week, and begged from her underwear, shirts, and a grey robe from the common store. "Tell Johnno you've given me these things and he will tell you about the woman—who is not my playgirl."

"Soldiers are practised liars," said Mem Jones, "What's she like?"

"Pleasant enough. Johnno will tell you that. And you must tell nobody about these borrowed clothes."

"If I do tell?"

"Then the Trainees will drive you mad with questions and refuse to believe that you don't know the answers."

"Those titless wonders!" she grunted and provided all he asked for, if only for the satisfaction of a secret.

Soldier found Nugan asleep, naked under a sheet.

117

He did not wake her but noted that she had dragged her silver suit close so that the front of the metal collar was handy to her mouth. It seemed logical that the communication equipment would be located there.

Then he went to Libary's office to transcribe the shorthand notes he had made earlier.

The Koori asked, "No information of note, Thomas? No rush of confidences extracted by martial virility?"

"You are not usually given to carnal gossip."

"Nor am I usually frightened to the point of grasping at indecencies."

That was uncharacteristic, something of a confession, but Soldier had perceived the man's state of mind while he interrogated Nugan and had been disturbed by it.

"There were no indecencies. There was an encounter between willing persons and I think your talk is lip service to your celibacy. You were not born celibate."

He had never before ventured so close to insulting his foster father. He looked down at his papers, looked up again to say, "I will not apologise for that. What are you afraid of?"

Libary said frankly, "Of that thing circling overhead. I do not ask for apology, rather I beg your pardon for forgetting that you are not a boy at my knee. Now that we feel uncomfortable with ourselves and each other, tell me what this Nugan had to say."

"Nothing new, but she repeated it more urgently. She asked once was I trying to deny her people's right to live on their own world. She knows in her head that this is not the world she left but her heart and blood and longing refuse to believe that time is a barrier. Those aboard the ship, those who beat her friend for opposing the return, will I think be more deluded than she. They have had time to set their intention firm in a hysteria of purpose. They will come, welcomed or not."

"And then?"

"There will be problems but none that good brains and goodwill cannot solve. Goodwill," he suggested, "may be the sticking point. Nugan knows you dislike her."

"I did not pretend to be pleased. To me she is not a person; she is an omen, a forerunner."

"Of wickedness? Why that? Their medicines, their knowledge, their ability to prolong youth . . . these may be worth a little upheaval of custom and convention."

Libary let anger show. "That is the road back to the Last Culture! You're no philosopher, Thomas. Have a mind to your own affairs!"

Soldier bowed slightly, in silence; Libary would make amends when his private harassments subsided.

For the moment, however, the Celibate said only, "Your talents may be called upon."

That was nonsense. "Will you ask me to conduct a campaign against the armaments of the Last Culture?"

"I am not stupid, Thomas! This is not the world of the Collapse and the true end of all your training is not vulgar bloodletting."

Soldier asked bluntly, "Then what are you talking about?"

"Ends and means. We will discuss them when the time comes—if I am given permission."

That was an extraordinary qualification; Soldier had never thought of Libary as a man with superiors who gave or witheld permission to act. He knew that Senior Celibates met in occasional Conclave and that these meetings were inviolably private; now he supposed there must be a hierarchy amongst them, a graded authority. But—authority exercised to what end? How little he—or anybody—knew of Ordinand desires and goals . . .

"Permission? From whom?"

Libary ignored that. "The woman must remain here for six days; I rely on you to see to it. On the fifth night there will be a Senior Conclave. Afterwards we will tell her what message to take to her people."

Soldier said gently, "You misunderstand. She speaks to them all the time. What she sees and hears is an ongoing message. The old word was radio."

Libary gestured that aside. "She sees and hears surfaces. What she learns does not matter so long as you tell her nothing about the Libraries and their work. I will see to it that no other does so."

Soldier let his impatience be seen. "All my life I have shared your heart but never your mind. I know nothing of any work of the Libraries. You constitute yourselves a secret society and create mysteries to impress the commons and build a mystique, but if you have work to do, I know nothing about it."

"We are neither poseurs nor mountebanks. If you are called on you will be told."

"As you'd tell a little boy? As much as is good for him to know!"

"If that is how you care to phrase it, yes."

Soldier shrugged and left him. He knew from experience that he would pry nothing from behind the dark face.

part II

INDRA'S NET

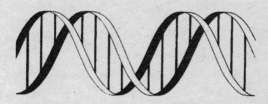

1

NUGAN KEPT HER PROMISE TO CALL Anne each night and afterwards talked to the Data Group, filling in the actions accompanying the disembodied words they had heard and recorded. She had avoided using a camera chip until she felt it safe to tell people they were being observed; she did not want to be discovered accidentally as a peeper.

Thank God you didn't wake me. I slept like a log for five hours. Ship's routine is out of kilter with daylight here so my wakings may be haphazard for a day or two. Jet lag! I woke up starving, ate two tablets, and filled my stomach with water to pretend there was food in it.

I must send some local stuff up for analysis. Tablets are punishment when there's real tucker available.

Thomas found me some clothing, so now I have a shirt, underwear, and short cotton trousers. The material is rough stuff but I suppose it is sweated out by women over handlooms, so I mustn't complain. Also a grey cloak like a dressing gown with a cowl, close-woven of a fine, strong yarn which he says is wool yet is as light as spider-silk and as strong; the sheep that grew it have been got at genetically by someone, somewhen.

I dressed and went out into the court. There was

nobody about but I found a staircase leading to the roof and went up to look around. The sun was within minutes of setting.

The flat roof seems huge when you come onto it but it is not bare. There are small enclosures holding I don't know what, but the main structures are four huge banks of semaphores, each bank facing a different direction and each equipped with three separate transmitters. Away at the other end of the roof someone was sending a message and one pair of arms was clacking like an animal snapping its teeth.

I looked for a receiver and spotted a pale answering flash on a hill way over on the horizon, I can't guess how many K distant. One bank was near me, so I saw that there is a small binocular telescope beside each pair of arms. I uncapped one and found a magnification good enough for the distance. The instrument is plainly handcrafted but the fitting and tolerances seem to be of high accuracy.

Thomas came looking for me and talking about food, so I had to explain my problem about foreign proteins and plant mutation. (I am just beginning to realise how much mutation has been accomplished in a few centuries. Suspiciously much.) He was concerned and helpful and agreed to supply sample foods for me to send up for analysis. I'll have a parcel ready for you by morning.

There's no knowing what will excite the curiosity of these people. Old Libary, who seems to be a pig of the first water, wants to know what "Nugan" means. It appears that he has written some erudite work on the derivation of names and is unable to trace mine.

Of course he can't because it isn't a real name; it comes from a child's attempt at difficult words. My names are Kathleen Rebecca but my Koori grandmother, who came from a South Australian tribe, used to call me her little *nguyonawi*, which really means cousin but was her attempt to combine the blood relationship with the distancing effect of the white admixture. My two-year-old's attempt to repeat this Koori mouthful of a word came out as "Nugan." It caught on, as such things mysteriously do in families, and Nugan I have been ever since.

Thomas says the old devil will be most interested. I hope he chokes trying to say *nguyonawi*. The native languages have probably died out.

Thomas brought me bananas and apples, some slices of beef and mutton, a bottle of milk, a small bag of coffee beans and an assortment of cooked vegetables.

He was fascinated when I pulled out the carbon-silicon strip and opened it out into a bag big enough to hold a body; he could not believe that anything so flimsy would not rip at a touch. I let him try to tear it. It would have been hopeless to try explaining molecular cross-linkage so he had to be content with his amazement. (Not that he showed a great deal of it; these Library folk seem to specialise in emotional repression.)

I sealed it with the seam-knife and balked again at explaining how the same instrument filled two opposed functions. Thomas smiled his faint Thomas smile and accepted one more paradox. Then I had to bind the monopole band around it and affix the activator. I made a despairing attempt to describe monopolar magnetism and then felt ashamed of my previous condescension (because that's what it was) when he caught on very smartly.

Just after dawn we laid a large white cloth (courtesy Thomas, as usual) on the grass beyond the drawbridge, placed the package in the middle of it and waited for the ship to come over.

When the time came I gave Jack his direction where to look and powered the activator as soon as he said, "Got it!" The parcel whizzed up and away and Thomas said—

No, he didn't exclaim in amazement; nothing amazes him. What he said was what you have a record of him saying, "I see the jewel in your ear, Nugan, and I think you hear the ship through it. But where is the jewel through which you speak to it?"

He doesn't miss much. I showed him the chip I had taken from the dropsuit and lodged inside the left septum of my nose.

He inspected, nodded some message to himself and asked, "Is it awkward when you have a cold?"

What do you do with a man like that? Particularly when his question involves you in trying to explain genetic protection against viral agents and why our ship people don't get colds.

Genetic change he understands; he says the folklore is full of it. Viruses were something else; we settled for microscopic insects in the blood, which worked well enough; he knew about insect-borne disease. I have a feeling that he could repeat my crazy lecture flawlessly without understanding half of it. These people have capacities that we do not, capacities so commonplace to them that they don't think to emphasise or discuss them.

Oh, beautiful lab report! When I told Thomas, he produced a banana from his pocket as though he had kept it ready for my private celebration of food. Then he went away and collected a whole solid meal for me. After two days of concentrates I fell on it like a brat at a party.

The meat was soft and white, the flesh of some small animal rather larger than a rat. "Rabbit," said Thomas.

I recalled vaguely that once they had been a rural nuisance in Australia, proliferating as vermin and denuding the grasslands. The biologists had wiped them out before I was born.

"Not quite," said Thomas. "They are still with us but have an altered characteristic. They drop only a single pup twice a year. We breed them for food and skins."

No species forsakes its evolutionary advantage—which for the rabbit was its gushing fertility—without gaining some complementary advantage, but I can't see that the rabbits gained anything. The Genetic Wizards again? Providing easy food for a failing future? More and more I wonder about them and their influence on history. And not only on history; there have been social changes, too, but I can't make much sense of them yet.

I wonder, also, how these preindustrial villagers cut and shaped the steel from the shattered skyscrapers. How, in fact, did they knock them down in the first place? Must keep it in mind to ask Thomas.

He has promised to take me to the village tomorrow and says there will be surprises for me.

The first and least pleasant surprise was my physical unfitness for the climb down the mountain. Either my sprain was minor or the local herbal is miraculous but I had no ankle trouble. What I did have was a realisation that gym exercise, even with centrifugally simulated gravity, is no real preparation for Earthly conditions.

But descending a mile on a rough track slippery with morning dew, spattered with stones and pebbles that rolled underfoot, and pocked with ruts and holes and wandering roots was no jog-trot at all. I fell twice simply through not being accustomed to watching where I placed my feet. I barked both knees and Thomas offered no knightly aid to a damsel in distress but said in his practical, soldierly way that I must learn to manage my body under Earthly circumstances.

Then there was the damned bridge. It is one thing to drop a few hundred K with the monopoles holding you up, quite another to navigate a swinging, jumping, creaking plank ten metres above the water while you hold the side-ropes with both hands and feel rampaging seasickness coming on. The Terrestrial boondocks are no place for a civilised lady.

I sat down for a minute on the far side, waiting for my calf muscles to stop quivering, while Thomas pretended he wasn't laughing. It just happened that I looked back up the hill in time to see, through a break in the trees, what I took to be two enormous birds with huge, unflapping wings, that glided out of sight in a matter of seconds.

Thomas said, "Gliders. My men."

"Hang gliders!"

"Yes." I must have worn my all too common dropped chin of surprise because he added, "How else could I maintain surveillance of five million hectares of country?"

How else, indeed? About a fifth of the state of Victoria! "Another theft from the past?"

"Books don't care who reads them, Nugan. Your era hid its secrets in tapes and chips, whatever chips may be, but the Twentieth Century provided manuals and diagrams, and we have good craftsmen who seek out substitutes for what materials are no longer available."

But you heard all that.

2

YES, IN *SEARCH* THEY HEARD ALL THAT
as the satellites spotted round the orbit picked up
Nugan's continuous broadcast and relayed it to the
ship.

The hang glider reconnaissance caused a minor
flurry and a hurried visual sweep of the area which
picked up scouts circling over the hills and road-
ways.

They listened to Thomas's prim and careful English and learned more of the capabilities of these
people, as when Nugan suggested that navigation of
hang gliders was a chancy project considering their
dependence on weather, temperature, updraughts,
and a dozen other variables.

Thomas agreed that exact navigation was nearly
impossible but: "We have used gliders for more than
a hundred years, Nugan, and we have mapped the
territories in many combinations of weather conditions. My fliers study the weather, the winds and
temperatures and their relation to the—the shape of
the land. Topography? Thank you. Given many decades of comparative records, they know where to
seek out winds and calms and updraughts and down-
draughts, where eddies will form and where conditions cannot be predicted. Experienced scouts cover
their areas with great efficiency."

"What do they look for? Enemies?"

"You think with ancient ideas, Nugan. We need no scouts to warn of an enemy; the whole countryside tells when soldiers are in movement. It is difficult to surprise people who live with the land, harder still to deceive the birds and animals. Word races through the forests with the speed of ill news."

Aboard *Search* the Data Chief said, "There's that 'with the land' idiom again. He's used it half a dozen times. It has to mean something. Get her to ask about it."

The Contact Supervisor told him, "That's been done. She says she'll ask at the right time. She's got ideas about what she can ask and what might start a clam-up."

Nugan's voice asked, "So what are they looking for?" and Thomas answered, "For the approach of summer. This is the fourth year of the cycle, so the country will soon be dry and all that long grass will be tinder. You will have noticed that it is cut short all round the Library. When the fires begin there will be people who need help and that is a soldier's business."

"El Niño still operating!" said the Chief as if welcoming an old friend.

The Supervisor said, "Those blokes need a union. They have to double as soldiers, police, and fire brigade as well as help with harvesting and forestry."

The Chief pointed out that if the system worked, it should be studied: "We may have to live with it." He knew better than to break in on Nugan when she was not alone but he muttered through his teeth, "Push the questions, girl; push the questions!"

But Nugan's attention had been diverted. She was saying, "Thomas, tell me about these men."

The Supervisor shook his head. "That's our Nugan. She's got an eye on the local beef."

3

THE VILLAGE IS A SINGLE STREET ABOUT
2 K long, lined with houses—and only with houses;
I saw no shops. The ancillary buildings, such as the
bottling shed, seem to be sited behind. The houses
are all of lapped weatherboard, like the ancient
houses I remember still standing in the oldest suburbs—hell-hot in summer and frigid in winter—but
with thatched roofs, all very olde worlde and unin-
viting to a child of the tenements who likes her windows glazed rather than shuttered. All that glass in
the Library and not a pane in sight down here; metal
and air-conditioning in the Library and take-what-
you-find down here. History hasn't solved the class
distinction bit; only changed the description.

On the plus side, I see no poverty in the village;
everything is spick-and-span, as though the house-
wives live in permanent competition. The houses are
of different shapes and sizes, with even a couple of
double-storeys in evidence, but the common building style makes them all look like modules from the
same mass production catalogue in spite of plenty of
individual colour and decoration.

Every house stands in the middle of its own vege-
table garden with a smug look of self-sufficiency
through the whole vitamin range plus trace elements.
I muttered to Thomas that in my time householders

grew flowers in their front gardens and vegetables out of sight around the back.

Says Thomas (and I'm not sure whether he was genuine or merely keeping a straight face), "Why grow flowers? The forest is full of them."

There were very few people in the street. "You will see them soon when they stop work and come to their homes for the midday meal."

The few in sight were all dressed in the denimlike cloth I had seen earlier, in shades of grey and blue. The men wore skimpy shorts and sandals and little else save for an occasional straw hat and shirt on a few with fairer, less Koori-tinged skins. Some women wore shorts, some a loose miniskirt and halter, with, again, a shirt and hat for the lighter skinned—UV conscious, I suppose.

And, like the men at the bottling plant . . . I said, "They look as if they are all blood relations."

Thomas showed the minimum flicker of concern which probably meant that he was quite taken aback. Did I really think so? Let me be assured that they are not. The Top-Mas keep strict account of genealogy records and use heavy persuasion to ensure cross-fertilisation.

This explained much about the Top-Mas' authority. I couldn't resist asking, "As in a stud farm?"

The Top-Mas, he told me seriously, would never follow animal stud procedures wherein grandfather might be mated to granddaughter to preserve a specific coat colour or odour sensitivity or fat deposit, as with dogs and cattle. Such close breeding weakened other characteristics.

Still, a dozen or more people of shortish stature with heavy shoulders, thick necks, slightly bowed legs, and the muscles of idiot bodybuilders was cause for wonder. More fool me! I had to explain what bodybuilders were and why I rated them as idiots.

(Having grown their gym-and-steroid muscles, what use did they make of them? None, that I ever saw.)

Thomas pulled me down beside him on a bench that someone had built for no obvious reason on the side of the street. Two or three people passed us as we sat there and showed no sign of seeing us; I was sure they were aware and curious but too well mannered to stop and stare. A camouflage-clad soldier and a crop-haired woman in an Ordinand's robe can't have been an everyday sight.

Thomas said, "We must speak again now of the Genetic Wizards. The folklore tells that they laid down the breeding tables."

Well, you have it all recorded up there and may have nutted out some answers by now, but to me it seemed to mean (remembering that to Thomas it all seemed to hover between folklore and crumbs of history distorted by time and passage through too many imaginative mouths) that in the years after we left Earth there were people who previewed the slide to disaster and set themselves to generating a differently oriented race that would make a better fist of managing their planet than we did. (We can't complain if we smell bad in the noses of those who had to pick up life amongst our leavings.)

There would have been different choices in specific areas of the planet but in Australia they seem to have settled on the black Aborigines as the most apt physical type for dealing with a rigorous existence in a destroyed world and, by means we can only guess at, arranged their immunity to the antifertility virus (if a virus was indeed the vector).

What they gave them in lieu of the hypothetical virus was female control of fertility and sexual readiness. (Would it be possible to design a mutation series that would work out its minor changes over generations until a stable form emerged?) There was

the Collapse and then the Twilight and from that
emerged the Genetics who, Thomas assures me, pop-
ulate the whole Earth today.

The Forest Genetic has developed powerful bodies
for heavy work under heavy conditions; the Desert
Genetic is designed for hunter-gatherer regions and
has incidentally spawned the beautifully adapted
soldiers; a Mixed Genetic shares something of the capacities of the other two without such extremes of
physical development and turns a hand to anything
not requiring the extreme adaptations of the other
two. They crew the oceangoing catamarans and are
the expert artisans in wood, metal, glass, papermak-
ing, and so on.

It sounds pretty distasteful to our ideas of individ-
ualism. A place for everything and everything in its
place! Aaaaagh!

To which Thomas pointed out that when you finished the day's work you were socially designed for,
you could do whatever pleased you. His mate,
Johnno, for instance, is an expert house carpenter
(Mixed Genetic work) as a useful sideline and as a
hobby makes tapestry pictures which are prized by
Libraries throughout the land. The thought of that
great ape absorbed in needlework was nearly too
much for my self-control; I shut up.

So where do the Ordinands come from?

From everywhere. There will always be the odd
mutant, the breeding throwback, the unmatched pair
of lovers who evade the Top-Mas' listings and produce an unclassifiable by-blow. The best laid plans
o' mice and men . . . They could be trained as Junior
Ordinands. The best brains, however, appeared
among those of all Genetics who chose the Celibate
life and dedicated themselves to learning and the
philosophic mysteries.

I asked, "Is no one ever dissatisfied with his lot?" and he answered, "Have you ever known anyone truly satisfied with his lot? All strivings compensate each other to form Indra's Net."

"What's that?"

You heard his answer but you could not hear my silent conviction that for once he told me less than the truth when he said, "It is a saying of the people to express eternity and infinity. Its origin is lost in time."

Thomas, I think, never lies but the soldier in him exercises evasion as a professional tactic. He did not say he doesn't know.

Indra was a Hindu god of some sort, wasn't he?

Then something happened, as something always does, to divert my attention. The street began to fill with people, mostly men but with a fair sprinkling of sturdy women obviously homing from work of some sort, looking for a wash and brushup and a meal.

"Midday," Thomas said.

They came from both sides, from the buildings on the outskirts, walking through each other's gardens (there are no fences) to the street. One or two spoke to Thomas but pretended I wasn't there. There must be some ritual of formal introduction before you officially exist. With so much similarity of physique and clothing they were a drab lot but Thomas, as he so often did, seemed to know what I was thinking.

"See them in the evening or on holiday, Nugan, in all the colour you could desire."

The social format caters to every need. Too neatly.

4

THE DATA CHIEF WANTED TO KNOW, "Anybody ever heard of Indra's Net?"

Nobody had. A hopeful voice suggested, "If it's to do with gods, there's a *Larousse Encyclopedia of Mythology* in Data Library."

"There is?" The Chief made it sound like a personal affront. "Why? What do we want with mythology? And how do you know about it?"

"The kids dug it out. They like that stuff; it serves instead of fairy tales. We never thought of having kids' books in Data."

"We did, for the cryo-generations, but not magic and hellfire stuff. There's an approved selection of ethical tales and easy-learning stories for the new generation."

"You don't know much about kids," said the Assistant, who had a teenager of his own to bedevil his free time. "They don't like self-righteous garbage after age six. Anyway, mythology is a useful guide to the evolution of philosophy."

"Thank you for bugger all. That doesn't tell me who or what Indra was."

The Assistant said, "Get young Annie Taylor to chase it up. She's getting to be a useful researcher, and with her mother involved she'll do a proper job."

5

THOMAS HAD DECIDED THAT I MUST meet his friend Johnno, who, it seemed, would be at the very end of the village street, where he was building a new house for himself and a muscular beloved.

We found him sitting on the doorstep with a great lump of cheese in one hand and what looked like half a loaf of dark wholemeal bread in the other. Ploughman's lunch!

At sight of Thomas he placed his food carefully on a large cabbage leaf and came to greet him, ostentatiously not seeing me in spite of our being, after a fashion, acquainted. They passed a minute or so in rapid-fire dialogue, then Thomas introduced us formally.

You have it on chip so you don't need a rehash of our efforts at establishing verbal contact. I cursed myself for not dismounting the camera chip from the dropsuit helmet and making a record of the village. I'll do it tomorrow.

Johnno turned out to be anything but the shambling ape with muscles to spare and hands like shovels. He was very much nature's gentleman, very much in love with his lass from the next village downstream, and very proud of his brand-new house, into which he will usher her two days from now. We are invited to the wedding party. At least I think it's a wedding though their ideas about marriage seem more practical than ours ever did.

We spent the next hour exchanging languages while Thomas took down every word in his rapid shorthand. When Johnno had to go back to work, Thomas rewrote the whole stumbling conversation in village English and our present speech, which he calls Late English.

Once I could see the versions side by side, the whole apparatus of vowel shift and consonant elision and phasing in and out of meanings became reasonably plain. Johnno's English is complicated by local idiom and careless, slurred pronunciation, and that had tricked my ears quite a bit, but when Thomas showed me the key it became . . . well, not simple but more manageable than I had feared.

Thomas proposes to speak only village English to me for the next two days, so I should be able at least to compliment the bride and groom at the wedding.

6

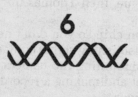

THE JOB ANNE TAYLOR DID ON *LA-rousse* was as good as could have been expected of total ignorance of the subject as a starting point. The trouble with the *Larousse* was its self-containment; it explained in detail but included no references to other works or sources of information, no indications of how to follow up queries. She found a short article, two useless illustrations, and twenty textual references to Indra but not a word of Indra's Net.

She ran off six copies of the major article, dropped the side references as uninformative—except one. The Data Group read the transcripts hungrily, paying no attention to her sitting by the door and hoping to be at least thanked for her trouble. She probably wouldn't be; the specialists tended to regard the youngsters as good for little but running messages.

"What it boils down to," the Chief decided, "is that Indra represented the sun—and so did half a dozen others in the Hindu pantheon or whatever they called the collection. He was also lord of rain and lightning, making him a fertility god and the link between Heaven and Earth. That would make him a good deity for a pastoral people. Covers everything—drought, storm, bushfires, rain, new growth, the lot. The other thing is that he was a brawler and a drunkard, the only one of his kind in the Hindu heaven; all the others were strictly business. So Indra was the common man's god, who forgot himself in public and got into drunken brawls, the sort of god a man could get along with. Perhaps the Koori imported him from Asia. But what about the Net? Not a bloody word."

"Something else," the Assistant reminded him. "This Thomas feller said the people don't have a religion."

"Helpful, aren't you?" said the Chief, then noticed Anne waiting by the door. "All right, kid, you did your best. Thanks."

Anne had little respect for any of this lot who had in any case no authority over her. She said, "You've missed something—that side reference."

The Chief glanced at the abstract. "The caste system? What about it?"

"The Hindus imported it from Persia and the Middle East, which was all desert country like the western half of Australia. It might have seemed suitable to a desert people. The three basic castes, it says, were the common people, the soldiers, and the ruler/priests. That fits pretty well with what's down there, doesn't it?"

The Chief was indulgent. "Nice work, kid, but how does it help?"

She shrugged. "It might give you a line on how they think. The psychs might have some ideas."

"It's a thought."

He turned away, shutting her out of the discussion. She left.

Jack said, "She's ready for sleep, I think; Thomas just left her. Talk to her if you like."

"Privately, Jack. You can listen but I don't want it on the public screens."

He cut the intercom connection. "There now."

"Mother! Are you awake, Mother?"

"Yes, darling. Something up?"

"Nothing wrong, but I've got news for you. About Indra."

"You *have* been busy. Did you find out what the Net is?"

"No, but there's a lot of other stuff. I'll read it out."

Nugan agreed that it was interesting. "But somehow I don't see this peculiar culture descending from ancient India. Still, you could ask Jean Sengupta about it."

"I don't know her, Mother."

"Neither do I, but I know she is a social scientist in the First Waking and that she is of Hindu descent."

Miss Sengupta, very small and brown and patient, was Indian born but not Hindu in her beliefs; she belonged to one of the quasi-Christian sects that had fragmented the spiritual thinking of the late Twenty-first Century. She had, however, been sufficiently interested in her father's beliefs and in her mother's vague Buddhism to research their religions before choosing her own.

"Is this important to you, Miss Taylor?" She noted the girl's nervous urgency and thought she was old enough to behave in more adult fashion—and followed with the further thought that these "ship children" shared a common failure (or was it a common reluctance?) to grow up. They made little effort to find common cause with their elders or for that matter with their own parents, but secreted themselves in a tight little communion to which adults were not admitted. *This is our fault*, she admitted to herself; *we have not considered their position properly; we are all specialists and they are nothing in particular and we have done little to make anything useful of them.*

"It could be important to my mother. She is down there alone, trying to understand strange people."

At least the girl had proper filial feeling. "Indra's Net is an allegory, but it does not belong to Hinduism. It is a Buddhist allegory, one of their ways of reducing difficult concepts to visual images simple people can comprehend. They often took ideas from pagan literature to explain their own teaching."

Anne lapsed into drooping disappointment. "I'll have to research Buddhism, then. It's big, so there'll be great Ks of it. I don't know where to start looking."

"Do not despair so easily. Tell me again what the soldier said to your mother. Can you repeat it exactly?"

"Yes, word for word. He said, 'Have you ever known anyone truly satisfied with his lot? All strivings compensate each other to make the whole of Indra's Net.' When Mother asked him what he meant, he said, 'It is a saying of the people to express eternity and infinity.' Mother thought he was being evasive."

The small brown woman smiled gently. "I do not think so. He was parroting words taught him without thought of their meaning, just as Christians in the old-style churches parroted responses, sometimes in Latin, without ever considering the implications of what they said. Words becoming too familiar become also meaningless."

"But you know what the Net is?"

"I am not sure of its significance. We may be able to unravel it. Tell me what you found out about Indra."

Miss Sengupta was patient in sorting the jumble of information that poured over her without form or sequence.

"Now," she said, "we know his attributes. All the rest, the battles and wivings and magical tales, do not matter. We know that he was the father of the gods. We know that in drunkenness and brawling he displayed affinity with fallible man. We know that he was the sun, and so responsible for drought and famine as well as rain and fertility and the night-time of healing sleep. We know that he was personified as the lightning, which was not only a heavenly weapon but also the contact between himself as Heavenly Father and the ground as Earth Mother. Put all that together and what have we?"

Anne shrugged. "Just about everything. He becomes responsible for everybody and everything that happens."

"Not quite, Miss Taylor. Not 'responsible' but aware and capable of interfering. You might say that he could fling the net of his consciousness around all creation."

"Religion!" The idea depressed her. "They thought he was pretty important; their old books, the Purana, had more prayers to Indra than to all the other gods put together, the *Larousse* article says."

"Religion or perhaps philosophy," Miss Sengupta told her. "The difference is what your perception makes it. The Buddhist allegory of Indra's Net was that all people are suspended in it, so that all history exists in an eternal now. It was a metaphor for the wholeness of space and time. There was possibly more to it than that but I did not pursue the image very far."

The girl was silent.

"Have I disappointed you, Miss Taylor?"

"You've told me a lot but I can't honestly see how it helps."

"Perhaps you should tell the Data Section."

"I suppose I ought to, but then they'll come bothering you."

"If we learn, that does not matter."

The Chief listened, whistled through his teeth as vague implications suggested themselves, and took Anne to the Chief Intelligence Officer, who listened intently and ordered a search of every relevant sound and word from Nugan and the people she had spoken to on Earth.

Because he did not know precisely what he was looking for, and so could not lay out a programme, the search was recorded on printouts for individual scrutiny, but words and suggestions commenced to fall raggedly into place.

In reply to his enquiry, the Observer teams told him that the planet was covered by a close network of semaphore batteries which seemed to be in continuous operation throughout the daylight hours and, under powerful reflectors, much of the night. They could make no sense of the messages which seemed not to be encrypted but reduced to a form of arbitrary phrase compression which the computers could not decode for lack of key relationships. It might take weeks . . .

To himself the CIO said, *They aren't human.* But they were human—simply not his kind of human. The species had been reconstructed, but what had been introduced and what discarded?

He should ask Nugan to investigate but hesitated; she had freedom of movement so far, but an unwary moment of too much insight might place her in jeopardy. He took seriously her distrust of Libary. He could have her brought back now but—

—he wanted better information; the I Section could not work on half-facts. Besides, he was humanly curious to know what went on down there.

7

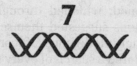

SOLDIER AWAKENED NUGAN BEFORE dawn. "I am called to duty. I have work with my men." In the lamplight his face was stark and bony.

She came swiftly to alarm. "Fighting?"

"No, no!" His amusement denied and soothed. "A soldier fights when he must, not when he sees a buttock for kicking. He will try to convince the other that a settlement without violence is possible; if it is not, he will consider force."

"So in the end nothing changes—death and more death."

"What wasteful folk yours were! A dead man needs only burial but a wounded man is a nuisance to his companions and a charge on his community until he recovers or dies, perhaps many weeks later. Twenty wounded men can make the most successful engagement a communal disaster."

Nugan sat up, pulling the blanket over her breasts then letting it fall because his interest was plainly not in her body. "Are you saying that you deliberately don't kill?"

"We kill if we must. No, I will be honest—we kill if it seems expedient, but we would rather not."

"Expedient is a bitter word."

"Expediency is a bitter business. You will have seen that I am not a sentimental man; I do what must be done."

Indeed so. He had shown no sexual interest in her since the first day and she had concluded, with some ruefulness, that the one occasion had been dictated by a perceived necessity to untangle her confused emotional response to the new Earth and ease her down to a level of cool seeing. Once over her anger at the expedient taking, she had seen that it placed them now on a footing of intimacy that neither cloyed nor demanded.

"And what is your unsentimental purpose today?"

"To observe what is happening on the grass plains beyond these hills."

"What can happen?"

"The sun can shine—as it does. The rains can stop—as over wide hectares they have done. The grass can fade into yellow stalks and the grain wither on the ground and men and animals can starve. Then communities may raid their neighbours for food, with their local soldiery in advance to clear away opposition, for soldiers are beholden to their villagers for much of their food upkeep. It happens in drought years. This may be a drought year."

"Surely food stores can be established against drought."

Thomas said, a trifle brusquely, "That is no simple matter. The Yarra villages supply hundreds of mouths in this building, send payment in food to my soldiers, and pay in food for imports from manufacturing communes." Nugan was no economist; she had not considered the logistical problems inherent in small communities with no mass transport. Thomas said, "Now I must go. I expect to return on the second morning from this."

That would be the day of Libary's meeting of . . . Librarians? Nugan said, "What can I do? I had wanted to see Johnno's wedding."

"So you shall. Go alone. Johnno expects you and no one will molest or question you. I will send a message ahead of you to Top-Ma; then the village will expect you and be very interested in you while making well-mannered pretence of not embarrassing a stranger by quizzing her."

"Thank you, Thomas. It would be dreary here in the Library. Will the Top-Ma find me somewhere to stay?"

"You will stay in Johnno's house."

"You're not serious!"

"Why am I not?"

"Stay in a man's house on the night of his wedding? What will the village think? And his bride?"

Thomas stood, ready to go, smiling down on her. "They will think nothing at all. This is not Carnival, when the girls are free with their . . . what did you call it? Pheromone? Then you might choose among the men who favoured you, but at this time it will not be thought of."

"Not by his Bella? You know I can't control the pheromone; you've said yourself that it is with me all the time. I will feel like someone with an unpleasant smell."

He bent suddenly and kissed her, swiftly but hard. "You will not get even that down there. Not every woman appeals to every man and Johnno's nose and gullet respond to a tang far different from yours. He is besotted with Bella, whose smallest release will bring him like a puppy to the tit. No man will attempt you out of Carnival time—unless you make secret rendezvous, which could cause unpleasantness for the man if it were detected."

"Such a serious matter! Yet you had no hesitation on this bed."

He frowned on an issue he felt to be indelicate, and answered gravely, "I am Soldier. I do what needs to be done."

"I've gathered as much. It's no compliment."

At the raised blind he stopped to look back at her. "You are mistaken, Nugan. Our togethering was the greatest compliment in my power to pay."

He was gone and the precise nature of the compliment was obscure but all at once she was pleased with herself and looking forward to the day.

She said to the air, "And what do you think of that, you snoops?"

The voice at her ear replied, "You're doing all right, Delilah. Samson sounds like a nice bloke with a plum in his mouth."

"Don't depend on that. He's duty-conscious and every move has a motive."

With Thomas gone Nugan had no one to turn to for company. Anyone she addressed would bow a polite head, smile, and pass silently on. Thomas had toured the Library with her, showing her the ingenuities of the air-conditioning system, the housekeeping areas with their staffs of villagers, and the labyrinth of the book crypts where endless rows of volumes filled featureless corridors and near-naked Ordinands went about their hallowed task of tabulating recovered knowledge.

She had asked him directly, "Is no one allowed to speak to me?" and he had paused for thought by a vast, sweating kitchen. She had noticed that only working villagers were within earshot; none would understand Late English.

He had said at last, "No one is forbidden for no one has authority to forbid. Each can do as he or she pleases but each knows that it is hoped that none in the Library will speak with you and that to . . . fail that expectation could cause . . . reactions."

Nugan felt that he stumbled over the precise expression of an imprecise matter.

"If no one forbids, how do they know?"

"An attitude is perceived. Knowledge spreads. A small community's instincts absorb rapidly."

"I think you mean that Libary has expressed a hope and his hope is accepted as law."

"As a social preference . . . as the best way to behave until the difficulties of your presence are resolved."

"What difficulties?"

"Nugan, in ancient days, before your own time, men with knowledge and power sailed to the countries of the ignorant and weak and destroyed them in the name of bringing the gifts of civilisation. This Earth has risen out of the barbarism inflicted on it and will not be destroyed a second time."

She shied away from that argument; whatever she said could return, misapprehended, to plague her.

"But anyone who speaks to me may suffer for it?"

"By ritual punishment? No. The person might be moved to where the . . . transgression . . . could not be committed again. That is social common sense—

the removal of opportunity, of temptation."

It sounds, she thought, like freedom to do as you please in the lion's mouth.

Soldier seemed, as he so often did, to penetrate her thinking. "I have read of your system of incarceration, where the unfortunate and the evil were thrust away together until both became the damned. We see that as a system without pity or dignity."

Again she rejected argument as incautious. She pointed out instead: "Yet I have talked with your friend, Johnno."

"And will again, Nugan. The villagers cannot argue cultural philosophy with you. We have been speaking only of the Ordinands."

So nobody gave a damn what the plebs said and did, but the intellectual classes should not be polluted by new thoughts until the answers were prepared.

8

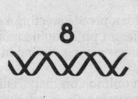

ABOARD *SEARCH*, DUVAL, THE SENIOR Intelligence Officer, spoke to Captain Brookes. "It seems to be a totalitarian system with nobody in charge, if you can imagine it. It's as though everybody knows what's expected of him, is raised to do the right thing, and does it under threat of social disapproval for breaking what are effectively unwritten laws. It sounds fragile but apparently is not."

Brookes, who had learned a great deal about social

pressures during his captaincy, said, "It sounds like a system that has shaken itself down over generations, has become accepted without question, is taught to each child as being the shape of the world, and is accepted because it works."

"Until maybe somebody suggests an improvement and discontent sets in."

"Suggesting improvement would be like trying to reform one of the Christian churches from within. You could only suggest reforms that fitted the established framework; anything beyond that would be bloody revolution. And those libraries—the planet seems infested with them—are seminaries where talk of reform would never be heard outside the walls. The Top-Mas keep the Genetics in order, Libary and his kind keep the Ordinands in order, and I suppose the world's Thomases keep their own lot in order. Who mentioned a place for everything and everything in its place?"

"Nugan. But how did it get that way? It's not a natural evolution."

"It might be for a people erecting a social structure on a totally different philosophic foundation. I keep thinking of Thomas saying, 'living in harmony with forest and desert.' "

Duval had an opinion on that. "That's the Aboriginal input, expressing their relationship with the land which could be lived on but not owned. The Twentieth Century Greenies were getting round to something like it; it was still strong when we left. Perhaps it dominated thinking after Thomas's 'Collapse' threw them all in a starving heap."

"It should have done."

9

WORKING TO INSTRUCTIONS DELIVERED softly from the ship, Nugan extracted a camera chip from its bedding in the helmet of the dropsuit and placed it carefully in the centre of her forehead, just above the nose, and hoped that its blue diamond capsule would allow it to pass for a jewel. Feeling vaguely like an old-time nautch girl wearing her jewellery in unexpected places, she left the room and proceeded towards the Library exit. Two male Ordinands and a woman who was probably training to become a Ma acknowledged her presence with a bowing of the head but did not speak.

Approaching Libary's office, she thought there was no reason not to ask him the question sitting like a word game in her mind. He could only refuse to answer. His reed curtain was rolled up and he was at his desk, leaning back and staring into the sunlit ceiling. Perhaps it was his pose for cogitation.

"Libary!"

He did not move but said, "Enter," and, as she neared the desk, "Thomas is absent. Have you a need?"

"A question."

He sat up to the desk, his dark face expressionless in what might have been boredom if she had not believed that he was more interested in her than he pretended. "Could you not have asked Thomas?"

"I did. He gave me only half an answer."

"Saying he knew no more?"

"Not saying so but allowing me to think so."

She thought the brown eyes lit fractionally. "That is unlike Thomas. The question?"

"What is Indra's Net?"

"It is a loose expression for the oneness of creation."

"So he said. I was able to find out more from my ship but not much more."

His interest quickened. "Please sit down." She sat on the bench by his desk. "Yours is the anglophone ship. I would not have expected a Buddhist aboard it."

The arrival of *Search* must have precipitated a pillaging of old material; every useful detail had been on public record. She did not bother to explain Miss Sengupta. "We have a vast library in micro form, the equivalent of several million books. A few references were found, telling us only that the Net is, as you implied, a Buddhist allegory."

Libary stood and moved to the centre of the room. Today he wore only a grey loincloth which he stripped off and dropped on the floor, not looking at her but upwards to the sunlight. He had the archetypal body of the desert people, deep-chested and long-limbed, flat-flanked over narrow calves.

He said, "This is a matter of great significance. I offer you knowledge because a half-truth is an intended lie and even an intruder deserves better. Thomas told you truly what he knows but his knowledge is laic and limited and his soldier's mind has no interest in pursuing it."

The term that remained with her was "intruder"; now she had a word for his view of her and hers.

Libary knelt to sit on his heels with eyes closed and

head thrown back, straining at the sun, arms raised
in a gesture she at first saw as religious supplication,
then recognised as awe at the wonder of an inward
vision. He spoke in a voice robbed of its coldness,
infused with humility and warmth.

"Indra's Net is the gathering of all space and time
into the single mind of the universe. The warp of the
Net is Space, which is a single dimension from emergence to extinction, unchanging and containing all
change within its infinitude. The weft of the Net is
Time, which is not then or now or later but *is*, always
and unchanging. These form the Net, unchanging
and containing all things which in our perception
have the appearance of change."

What was this? Incantation? A confused babble of
space-time theory handed down from illiterate shaman to brainwashed believer? *But he believes, he believes.*

"Wherever weft crosses warp hangs a node of life—
a tree, an insect, a fish, a beast, a woman, or a man—
expressed as a mirror-drop of heavenly liquid,
eternal and brilliant, each drop reflecting every other
in the bounded but infinite Net and by reflection containing the image of the Net and its own self. The
universe of the Net is many but one, the parts and
the whole aware of the whole and the parts because
the whole is one and forever."

It was like the rhetoric of a self-hypnotised
mystic—until in the visual image she glimpsed a
reminiscence of quantum relationship, of the inter-
dependence of particles of a universe wherein every
point of matter and energy depended on every other
and space-time itself shrank to a metaphor for an unchanging instant, the representation of a total mind.
Hadn't one of the old astronomers said that with each
new discovery the universe assumed ever more the
semblance of "a gigantic thought"?

No intellectual response was remotely possible. With an instinct that might have been drawn from some Koori mystic in her ancestry she stood, folded her hands across her breasts, genuflected, and bowed low.

It was the right response. As she lifted her head, Libary stood and regarded her with a reserved approval, as though he had not counted on a proper respect for his revelation. The expression faded instantly and he asked, "Do you feel that you understand?"

"Not yet. It will need thought."

"Not thought, which is self-referent, but vision." Without change of tone he asked, "What is the jewel on your forehead? You have not worn it before."

"It is a camera."

"I have imagined a camera as a box with a lens. But this . . . so tiny a picture!"

"It does not take pictures. It records—" There was no possibility of explaining recording at the molecular level. "Think of Thomas's shorthand. Think then of a system of compressing vision into symbols which can be recovered later and restored to their full form."

Libary smiled faintly. "No, I will not; I have more urgent thinking to trouble me. Thomas tells me you are to visit the village."

"For Johnno's wedding."

"Tell him and his Bella that Libary dwells with them."

Said the Data Chief, "I'm glad she's got the camera on-line, but if Libary's a sample of the local folk, we've got some pretty bizarre neighbours."

Duval disagreed. "We've just heard him speaking from the heart—for the first time. He believes every word of that rigmarole. Make printouts and I'll get the big brains on Captain's Council to beat their lobes on it. It might even mean something."

"It means a view of the universe," Anne said. Her willingness to run messages had established her on her unofficial bench by the door. "All life is one life—a description of the God idea if you like."

The Chief argued, "According to Thomas they don't have a religion, so God's out of it. What, then? Some desired state of mind?"

Anne suggested, "Perhaps it ties in with the 'living in harmony' stuff."

"The ultimate conservation philosophy? Could be."

Duval was not satisfied. "Too simple. It's a Buddhist thing. Anne, ask Miss Sengupta what it means."

All Miss Sengupta could tell her was that the original Net had garnered human souls only; the people below seemed to have expanded it to include all living things, even insentient plants. She offered no interpretation.

10

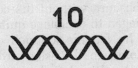

ALL YOU HEARD WAS AN HOUR OF background noises with me panting and stumbling my way down the hill, and then a lot of stuff that must have been mostly meaningless, so I'll fill you in.

I had timed myself to arrive approximately at Johnno's lunchtime break but walked into a sort of procession in the village street—two ancient and whiskery pure-blooded Aborigines carried on litters by Forest Genetic men and another, younger pure blood marching solemnly behind them. They looked neither right nor left and the passersby played the polite game of pretending not to notice them. The same passersby did, however, acknowledge aquaintances among the bearers. Manners—or a caste system?

Not having the local talent for observing without being caught at it, I gawked like a bumpkin, feeling that my behaviour was deprecated with a silent shrug for the out-of-towner who knew no better.

Johnno appeared as if by appointment and called out, "Hullo, Nugan!" two words he had learned from me and which set heads twitching in our direction. Johnno is not much taller than I but about thirty kilos heavier and you know I'm no fairy lightweight; being escorted across the street to his new house meant being lugged bodily by a grinning gorilla while he showed off his newly acquired Late English.

It would be hopeless to go through all our talk. You will have caught about half of the meaning, but much must remain obscure without the context and gestures. We managed to exchange quite a lot of information while he fed me a lunch of nutty-tasting porridge and some small roasted bird, possibly a pigeon, but it was hard work for both of us. I'll give you a précis of the useful bits.

The three pure-bloods were, he told me, on their way up the hill to meet with Libary, who is to hold some kind of Council in a day or two. It will be quite a big affair. Some visitors will be "old wise men" and others "young wise men" (that was his expression) coming from distances of up to 1000 K (they say "kils" but the distance is much the same) on horseback. He didn't know what the Council was about, nobody was likely to tell him and he didn't care anyway; it was "caditcha" business.

The word rang a bell. Questioning showed it to be a slightly changed form of *kurdaitcha*, a term from the Murri people of the north of Australia, meaning something like "medicine man" and something like "magician," according to context. There are probably ancillary meanings like "elder" or "wise man." Their meeting will be about us.

I said as much to Johnno, who thought it likely.

And what would they be talking about?

Probably about telling us to go away.

But why?

His surprised eyebrows asked was I really so stupid? Because they didn't want competition, of course. If we had this ship that Soldier Tommy said could fly to the stars, we must know a lot more than the Ordinands and the Readers of Books, and that wouldn't suit them at all. They would lose face, lose respect, lose authority.

I replied that Thomas had told me they had no real authority, no right to give orders.

The gist of Johnno's answer was that Tommy had plenty of respect from everybody and could stand up against the will of the Readers and make them think twice about trying to push him where he didn't want to go. But the village people were tied to custom and the Genetic system supervised by the Mas and Ordinands, and could be brought into line by manipulating social pressure. There could be a pretence of no suitable marriage partner being found, for example, and a man childless at thirty was an object of derision, unfit to continue his Genetic.

Rule by unspoken threats of personal ignominy and sexual deprivation! Witch doctor stuff, but more sophisticated.

I asked did no one ever object or say this was wrong.

His reply was complicated; at bottom it meant that Thomas had told him to answer my questions truthfully but that it must be understood that I did not discuss with other villagers what Johnno told me.

This was Thomas telling me: You may have the truth but you may not cause trouble for Johnno. I was amazed that he trusted me so far and said so. Johnno's answer to that was a small revelation. He said: Tommy talks to you and listens to you and watches you move and soon knows how far you can be trusted; people are Tommy's business. How could he guide and guard all his big territory if he could not manipulate people to his will and their good?

"Then why," I asked, "does he say the villagers are not truly friendly to soldiers?"

It seems that this is because the Desert Genetic from which the soldiers are drawn is capable of physical activities which are beyond the powerful (but muscle-bound) Foresters. Also they think differently, being capable of savagery with weapons which no villager would use in a quarrel; soldiers are hard men, just but without pity.

I felt like crying out, For God's sake, who really runs this show? Instead, I asked him did no villager ever try to change the system.

He looked straight at me and asked, "What system?"

It was blatant blocking. I'm afraid I played an unfair move; I said I did not believe that the man Thomas chose for his best friend could not know what I meant, or that Thomas would choose a friend with no brain.

His reply made me jump a little, as much at his irritable disgruntlement as because of his opening statement, which was, in essence:

We hang in Indra's Net, if you call that a system. The Readers strive to understand the meaning of the Net and Man's place in the universe, while we Genetics maintain the world and all the life in it against the day when the meaning will become clear. They think; we work. The meaning makes no difference to us yet.

But did he really believe that?

A shrug. I think that almost any belief will suit Johnno so long as life is secure and pleasant. He is careful and nobody's fool.

"Does Thomas believe in it, Johnno?"

"Ask Thomas, Nugan; that is treacherous ground."

So I stopped asking.

11

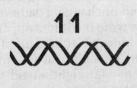

BELLA ARRIVED AT NIGHTFALL, A stubby girl with a good-natured face, shot-putter's muscles, and her wedding gown folded in a bag of woven reeds. After a single searching survey she paid little attention to me but chattered like a monkey at her adoring Johnno, who listened, answered little, and wore a slavish grin.

"Beautiful!" he said to me when the girl went to dress. I nodded enthusiastically; I could scarcely do less.

The wedding dress was a simple, body-fitting, knee-length white skirt which gave Bella the general appearance of a friendly barrel, but few of the village women would look any better. My interest rose with a jerk when I saw the green drape, a sort of huge shawl which she spread across her shoulders, wrapped round her body, and pulled into a cowl over her head.

It was a great square of openwork lace some three metres on a side, intricately knotted and decorated with what I took at first to be tiny trinkets. I asked permission to examine it closely and Bella was proud that a sky visitor admired a village girl's possession. Through Johnno she explained that it had been worn by four generations of brides and would pass to her own daughter.

The lace was in fact a web of small squares with at each junction a miniature, finely carved and coloured bone figure—in order: a fish, a tree, a lizard, a flower, a bird, a cat, a bee, and a woman, repeated throughout in an unchanging pattern. It was brutally heavy but Bella wore it without apparent discomfort. It made sense; Indra's Net held all of life.

The ceremony took place at sundown, in the open street, where anyone might attend who wished to, and it seemed that most of the village did, bringing not bridal gifts but food and drink. Johnno introduced me to half a dozen neighbours whose averted eyes swung at once to smiling attention, with offers of food and complicated attempts at questioning by gesture and by speaking slowly and loudly. Everybody knew who and what I was and wanted to know more.

Torches were produced, great resinous flares on long poles jammed into the earth. The Top-Ma arrived and an approximation of quiet fell on the crowd; she offered me a so-you're-still-here expression and called Johnno and Bella to order like unruly children. The ceremony was short, a routine of symbolic bows, handclasps, and chaste kisses which the Top-Ma ordered like a drill sergeant. There was no exchange of vows or presentation of a ring.

Afterwards the Top-Ma stopped by me to say with unexpected friendliness, in her slow Late English, "Soldier makes you a friend. Help you if you be careful." She smiled and nodded at Bella. "Not like her, pregnant before wedding. Still, good breed stock for Johnno."

Casks of beer appeared. Mugs were pressed on me and dreadful stuff it was, mule-kick powerful but sour and flat. I made a mental note to research ale brewing and bring the village some genuine cheer. I got mildly drunk (so I thought) and was glad to find a bed on a mattress on the newlyweds' floor. I passed out.

Listen to this; it could be important. I woke with a filthy hangover; God only knows what's in that beer besides alcohol. Johnno and Bella were up before me, merry as larks over my thick head and having a day off work in honour of a wedding which seems to have been about four months overdue. Thomas had made the cohabitation rules plain but there seems to be some honouring in the breach rather than the observance. (So what's new?)

They fed me bananas and porridge, the local staples, and carried on a noisy discussion while I forced myself to eat.

Johnno said Bella was insisting that he tell me to visit them as often as possible, and that he was in full agreement. I felt that my Contact techniques were doing well until it emerged that my visit lent considerable cachet to their standing in the village and that even the Top-Ma had complimented them on the capture.

The next bit was less pleasant. It seems that I'm to visit as often as possible "before the old men send me away." Johnno was reluctant to say this but she pestered him. Naturally I asked why the old men—presumably senior Ordinands—should try to push me out.

I got a different explanation this time and the lack of vocabulary made things difficult, as well as Johnno's inability to find firm words for philosophic ideas he had probably never really thought about. (How much sense would any of us make if asked for instant declarations of our ideas about God, or the problem of good and evil, or the meaning of morality?) What it boiled down to was that we from the Last Culture had gone one way and they who stayed home had gone another. We were in another part of the Net and, though all things were one thing, the Net was not yet complete and our presence would "spoil the weaving, make wrong knots, block the road Earth's people take to Nirvana." He actually used that word, Nirvana, which ties in with the Buddhist connection.

But Thomas, he said, had his own thinking and did not always follow the teachings in his heart. He told Bella that as a wife she must know what he knew but must not repeat it to others. She accepted the order submissively.

So it seems that a certain amount of free-thinking goes on despite the tight swaddle of custom and social pressure; this was different from his talk of jealousy and losing face. Both versions could be true.

As I climbed back up the hill (suffering) I saw that even in the few days I have been here the long grass has lost more of its colour and taken on that dirty yellow tinge that means the rains are very late or finished. Thomas had mentioned drought, and under a hot sun the grass could dry to brown stalks in a week or two.

At the drawbridge I found the three *kurdaitcha* (if

that is how they think of themselves) fishing placidly in the moat, stark naked and gossiping like the old women that men really are when they get together. You couldn't imagine more harmless people.

They heard my footsteps on the planks and turned to see who came. When they saw, they stared in a hard silence and one of them spat from deep in his throat into the water. There was nothing harmless about that.

But they can hardly force us out if we find ourselves a vacant lot and settle in to stay, grit our teeth, and refuse to be shifted.

12

SOMEONE HAD ENTERED HER ROOM IN her absence. On the pillow lay a book and a pair of gloves. Remembering the reader at the lectern on her first day, she drew the gloves on before picking up the book.

Her reaction to the title was a mental double take, the equivalent of a deprecating, Really, you can't expect me—

A voice from the ship, silent all morning, murmured in her ear, "That just might give us a new line on the Net business. Read it, Nugan. I'll read with you and make a copy for study."

"But it's rubbish. The idea was dumped early in our century."

"Old ideas sometimes surface in unexpected

places; even Lysenko turned out not wholly wrong. Somebody wants you to read it, so why not?"

She opened it gingerly but the binding glue had been softened, presumably by some crypt Ordinand, and it spread without cracking. The acid-free paper was white and soft and only the faintest smell of mildew remained from whatever treatment had been given it.

"OK," she said. "Prepare to be bored out of your cross-referencing mind."

Despite herself she became interested—unconvinced but interested. Overhead they studied the printout and speculated on why someone, probably Libary, had set it there for her.

Soldier returned on the following morning and went directly to Libary to say tiredly, "There will be an attack on the Library, disguised as a drought-driven food raid."

Libary was not disturbed; he placed great faith in Soldier.

"Soon?"

"Perhaps within the month, perhaps later."

"By whom?"

"The Murray Valley soldiery, under pressure from the Librarians of the Plains. They accuse you of concealing valuable community knowledge."

Libary was dismissive. "The excuse is outworn."

Soldier pressed him. "You do hide discoveries; you do keep useful information undisbursed."

"That's not your business. Are you justifying them?"

"I am pointing out that you bring this upon yourself—and that is my business."

Libary lay back in his chair, relaxed, unimpressed—but his fingers were too long in settling and his eyes a trifle too theatrically averted. He was furious and not good at the body language game. "I evaluate the documents of this Library for distribution. Much is inconsistent or of doubtful provenance, needing to be considered, probed, and decided upon. It would be only too easy to plunge the world of Libraries into wasteful factional argument when a little delving will weed out the useless."

"They claim that their powers of assessment are as great as . . . as others."

"And you agree?"

"My agreement is neither here nor there, but I must have a truthful argument to hand when the time comes for peaceful resolution of complaints."

"A defeated force is resolution enough."

Soldier shed a little of his weariness, beginning to enjoy cornering the old devil. "So much for the intellectual approach! What if it is I who am defeated and suing instead of dictating?"

"Then I shall have wasted my time rearing a beaten soldier and my world may well rot." Having extricated himself by declaring an end, he asked, "Am I to be told what has occurred?"

What had occurred was in outline so simple that it gave little hint of the speed, precision, and expertise of Soldier's operation. His glider scouts had spied movement in the grain fields to the north of the central range and counted three advance reconnaissance patrols working the tree line of the foothills. They had agreed that the pattern of movement indicated a search for fresh approaches for surprise penetration of the Yarra Valley.

Why? The grain country was in fair condition, with water channels still above the safety marks; the area food supplies were known to be sufficient to tide over a bad year, and commanders did not order track reconnaissance a year or more in advance of an action. Soldier took forty men, with no sleeping gear because there would be no sleeping. With more than enough men to outnumber any resistance he might encounter, he made a day and night foray across the hills to the nearest enemy party, covering nearly seventy kils in twenty hours and surprising a group of eight as they sat in conference. Outnumbered, they made no resistance. He was able to move directly into questioning of their Patrol Leader, a belligerent lad who covered his deficiencies with defiance.

"Like yourself," said Soldier, without mercy, "he could not play the body language game well. Badly trained. He signalled every answer he tried not to give."

"And?"

"And nothing. I shall evaluate the information and act on it. You need not be concerned."

"I am not concerned for the future, Thomas, but your throat is bruised and your voice strained."

Soldier said unwillingly, "He attacked me. He knew his concealments had failed, so he tried to kill me."

"And?"

"He was armed and very strong, stronger than I. I was forced to kill him." That was enough; he did not confess that after breaking the man's neck he went into the trees to be physically ill and to ponder, not for the first time, the questions of ends and means, necessities and actions, and the value to be placed on life—another's life. He had elected for the soldiery when a boy, fascinated by the romance of responsibility for the well-being of others; he had become a fighting machine of the highest capacity before his first serious encounter told him he was no killer and by then he was beyond any change of mind. There was no place in his world for a man who deserted his choice so late in life; he was trained for nothing else.

He did not linger with Libary; he had covered 140

kils on foot, in rough country, in two days and nights and needed sleep. He felt, however, that he should spend a moment with Nugan, who might be solitary and depressed with no one in the building to speak with.

In the Data Room Anne had grown tired of reading, over her mother's shoulder as it were, a book on a subject whose argument made little sense. It seemed to be drawing a parallel between a subtle form of communication between human intellects and the so-called "mutual awareness" of particles on the quantum level—between a micro/macro-condition and an unprovable metaphysical input.

She was musing on the overmuscled Bella and the pleasant but physically unattractive Johnno— nobody remotely like either of them figured in the ship's complement of citified specialists—when she heard Nugan cry, "Thomas!" and returned her attention to the screen.

He was utterly different from her cursory imagining of him, unlike Libary or the villagers or any of the intense but nondescript Ordinands. It was not possible to guess his height but an allover slenderness made him appear tall. He was dressed in what old military photographs told her was a camouflage suit of shirt and trousers whose dappling flowed in a nonstop mirage of forest colours as he moved under the sunlight; in the green-brown Australian scrub he would be a shadow among shadows.

He said, in his accented English, "I have only now returned," and came forward to sit on the edge of Nugan's bed. His face filled half the screen.

His features had something of the same quasi-Aboriginal cast as her mother's, and in lesser degree her own, but his fleshlessness gave him prominent cheekbones and a narrow jaw, unlike anyone she had

ever seen. His skin was darker than her own and lacquer smooth. His blue eyes were alive and warm; his
wide mouth smiled and the smile was real, a friend
greeting a friend.

The Chief cried in mock wonderment, "So lookit
the soldier boy at last! The new Anzac breed! Our
Nugan knows how to sort wheat and chaff."

Then he remembered Anne's presence and shut
up; she scarcely heard him and forgot immediately.
She was examining the first product of Earth to touch
her imagination with the mystery of the exotic and
new.

"Your throat's bruised. What have you been doing?"

He had thought to pass the marks off as the result
of clumsiness on a training exercise, saving himself
the endless explanation necessary for one with no
experience of military affairs. Now his instinct for
truth rebelled as the face of the dead, foolish young
man sickened his memory; she and her people
should know what manner of world they coveted—
different from theirs and gentler but in its own fashion as merciless in its logic.

Explaining movements and motives took much
longer than his brief account to Libary. And at the
end Nugan said, "So you fooled this poor brute who's
expertise was inferior to your own, and then killed
him."

This seemed to him so grossly unfair a summation,
ignoring every other aspect, that he had no answer.

She continued, with an anger he failed to understand, "Such things happened in the slum streets of
our cities. The Swill classes grappled and killed each
other in the public gutters but they did not call themselves soldiers worshipping duty."

A gutter brawl? Her conception of war was that of
the civilian uninvolved, watching a colourful screen

as armadas raided, cities were laid in rubble, and dramatic explosions filled the view, removing the human element, taking the blood out of the spectacle.

Today's experience of war was at firsthand only; there was no monstrous entertainment for onlookers.

He asked, subduing anger, "Should I have let him kill me? He had a knife; I was unarmed."

She was not to be trapped in a moral question. "You could have had your men secure him."

"He attacked me, not my men."

"That made it personal? A matter of honour?"

He listened to the waspishness, subtly at variance with a hesitancy in her expression, and made a stab-in-the-dark diagnosis of personal pacifism at odds with a fear that her moral stance might be untenable. He said slowly, "Not honour or even self-respect. Self-preservation only."

"But your men . . . "

"They would have done as I ordered . . . and behind my back rated me as one who delegated his difficulties to others. My soldiers are not the automata of your ancient mass-trained armies; they are individuals who value their ability to resolve their own adversities. This is not your day of mass murder, when devastation numbed response but blood spilt in a brawl roused horror."

Confused, Nugan tried to make peace. "Thomas, like any clear-thinking person, I cannot understand why human beings set up organisations designed for murder. You see it differently. Let it go at that, please."

"No." He would not let her withdraw with prejudice intact. "I have told you we kill only when we must. My army—your floods of men and machines would laugh at my small force—seeks to protect, to save lives by leaving the villages in peace and resolving the problems—the politics, if you wish—for them, and so leaving them to work out their destinies in peace. What, do you think, would be the outcome if those very physical villagers fought their own wars in time of drought or natural disaster? Then you would see brutes in the gutter, Nugan, wars carried out on the doorstep, not in the sky over some distant land—wars which might grow and spread until whole communities were wiped out, food fields trampled into starvation dearth, and the homes of generations levelled with the ground. We prefer small wars, Nugan, contained wars where combat is the last resort and every leader's training is in logical discussion. We are the world's policemen. You had armies of police in your cities, did you not? And your records tell that you called them corrupt, using their power to take profit from those they were paid to suppress. My men are not corrupt. No soldier is corrupt, because after one such lapse he is no longer a soldier but an outlaw with no village, a forager for food. If it were otherwise, this world would collapse in ruin as yours did, neighbour against neighbour. In ten years not a Library would be left standing as the jealousies flared, all looted and gutted by the stupid who imagine that destruction of the other man's treasure is the stair to power. In a decade or two we would be back in the Twilight, when men fought each other for the privilege of living. My men fight, and that not often, so that others need never attack each other like starving beasts.''

He startled himself with his own unprepared defence of his world and his profession; he had not been sure when he began where the argument would lead because his professional life was so familiar a thing that he rarely thought of it in depth. His personal revulsions were another matter. He was simply one who had chosen a career unwisely, but the career itself he believed to be honourable and necessary.

Nugan's attitude he found difficult to fathom. Surely these star roamers, erupting out of wholesale slaughter and unceasing brutality, should be inured to murder and grim death. Their culture had finally denied the right to life, yet she preached a pacificism and tolerance she could never have experienced.

She said, "You make it sound sensible and rational but my common sense says it is not. I just do not understand this society."

"Nor I yours, Nugan."

"My people won't understand."

"Those?" He had forgotten the ship. "Are they listening?"

"Always. Watching, too, now." She touched the bright jewel on her forehead.

"Through that?" He refused to be impressed by one more exhibition of anachronistic magic but raised a hand in mock salute. "A good day to you, eavesdroppers!"

Said the Chief, "Quite a boy, isn't he? He believes all that stuff, like a Holy Joe at a revival meeting. You can see it trickling out like molasses. It can't work that way; human nature hasn't changed that much."

"You don't think so?" Duval had been brooding over the intake from Earth. "I get the feeling that something more than genetic fiddling went on back ... back whenever it was. Some other seed was planted, but I don't know what or how. We were out of the way by then."

Anne, born in space, had never seen humanity in a ferment of violence; even the revolt that brought *Search* home had seemed to the youngsters a cackling of hens and roosters which they tried to ignore. Now she thought this Data crew were absorbed in nonsense; the social duty Soldier had outlined seemed to her wholly rational. He spoke like a man who knew precisely what he did and had no doubt of himself or his responsibility. A man to be depended on. There were none like him in the ship. Except, perhaps, familiar and dependable Jack; but Jack was old and did not count.

"Are we quarrelling, Nugan?"

"If we are, we must not. Pax, Thomas!"

"Pax, Nugan." He extended a finger to touch the book on her lap. "From the crypts?"

"Apparently. Libary must have sent it to me."

He picked it up to see the title. "*Morphic Resonance*. Some mystery of your time? I have never heard of it."

"Some nonsense of our time. An idea that all intelligent forms exist in a sea of thought though not consciously aware of it, that all mental operations exist in recoverable form in a universal reservoir, and that individuals often unwittingly draw on it. They used it to explain how two persons, unknown to each other and in separate locations, could hit upon the same theory or novel concept at almost the same time, each drawing unwittingly on the contribution of the other. The history of science is full of such coincidences. The concept never came to anything; it wasn't susceptible to proof."

Soldier knew at once why the book had been given to her. It was a preparation. "It is an idea that appears and reappears in different forms, Nugan. Your psychologists wrote of a collective unconscious."

"No, no, that was quite different. That referred to attitudes and instincts common to all thinking structures. But where would you have stumbled across it?"

"Not stumbled, pursued. We have read the works of your psychologists ever since the recovery of books began. We have taken from them what we needed and ignored what seemed controversial or too difficult. How else do you think we have learned to control a diverse world with so little overt governing? The collective unconscious is an expression of Indra's Net."

She resisted. "You pile metaphysics on a mythic allegory and try to make a creed of them."

He was so tired that he felt more like finishing the conversation by shaking her than by gentle exposition; he was sure she would prove impossible to convince. For himself, he neither believed nor disbelieved in the collective unconscious or the Net, but harboured no disrespect for those who based their philosophies on them. As he saw it, belief in a metaphysical existence only placed constraints on one's capacity to act in this one.

He said abruptly, "I am close to physical exhaustion. I must leave you. Read the book. Understand it, whether you believe or not. It should help you tonight."

"Why tonight? What happens tonight?"

Soldier needed a small release of anger. "That damned old man tells nothing, does nothing, and expects the world to arrange itself for him! Tonight the Readers will decide your case. You are expected to be present."

He went quickly, leaving her resentful that a group of semimystics in a peculiar byway of human history took it on themselves to decide the destinies of others and to order her presence as if she were a servant.

What in hell, she thought, did they have to decide? Did they imagine they could give their thirty-or-so-times great-grandparents orders? And make them stick?

*   *   *

They sent Anne to search the data files and she found the pickings meagre.

"It began," she told them, "with a learning experiment. A group of people were given a word puzzle involving recognition of strange words and association lists, and they were timed in solving it. Later, another group of similar composition was given the same test and solved it much faster. A third group solved it faster still, so they decided that a thing once learned went into some sort of universal store and filtered into the minds of others, so that the more people learned it the easier it became for others. They tried it on rats running mazes and got the same results; the second group of rats did it faster than the first and the third faster again, and so on."

"And then," said the Chief, "the rats all hung themselves on their hooks in Indra's Net and congratulated each other on their contribution to the culture of ratkind. It's a bit thin, isn't it?"

Anne didn't care what they thought. She was looking forward to the mysterious meeting of Readers and thinking that Thomas would surely be there to support her mother.

13

LATE IN THE NIGHT SOLDIER ACCOMpanied Nugan to the roof. *Search* was past its zenith while the Moon rode high amongst stars in clear air.

"What will this council do, Thomas?"

"They will sit in a circle and claim that they communicate. Perhaps they do."

"You have seen this before?"

"In small fashion. Three or four Readers in session."

"And you think there is some form of silent communion?"

She held up her lamp to catch one of his rare displays of readable expression, a puzzled indecision. "I neither believe nor disbelieve. Something happens but it is not seen or heard. This I can tell you, that there is a form of communication other than the semaphore and it is practised by the Readers, in groups. Perhaps over long distances, but this I have not seen. Tonight's group will be the largest I have heard of, thirty-eight Readers."

Nugan asked, almost angrily, "Are you talking about telepathy? That's an impossibility."

"I do not know the word."

"It means mind speaking to mind in words. Only charlatans claimed it and the brain structure offers no mechanism for it. Also, people don't think in words or even in mutually compatible analogues and visualisations."

Soldier marvelled quietly that a history so productive of mystics should have produced also such committed materialists. "When the Readers make claims I often doubt them but I am wary of the word 'impossible.' The Readers meet in silence and something happens."

Behind them Libary said, "Indeed something happens and tonight you will see proof of it. Thirty-eight in Council make an engine of power."

Nugan turned to him. "What will I see?"

"That I cannot tell. There will be consensus and we will observe it."

"You sent me a book."

"In preparation. It might be that if you could relate tonight's Council to the theorising of your own age, the experience could be rendered more pertinent to you."

"The ideas of that old book were discredited long ago."

"Were they indeed?"

She caught a quick surge of emotion in the dark features, a flicker of contempt. It frightened her. In her ear a tiny ship's voice chuckled, "Curiouser and curiouser! Witch doctor stuff, eh? A coven of shamans, no less. Should we beam down a jar of holy water?"

She slapped hard at the receiver behind her ear. The joker would be assaulted by a shellburst; it might preempt a continuing barrage of iconoclast's wit.

Libary brushed past her, moving over the moonlit glass as if he walked the surface of a pale lake. He was naked, and few other than dancers can stride gracefully without the disguise of draped clothing and heeled shoes. His discomfiting aura shrank and crumbled in the movement, reminding her that he was human, no dark wizard.

In immediate contradiction a silent stream of naked figures flowed from behind her, dividing round her and drifting past like ghosts drawing substance from the moonlight. Each turned a head, to peer momentarily into her face as though to capture her in memory, and moved soundlessly on. Most were black, full-blooded Koori—or perhaps from other tribal areas—but many were of mixed breeding and two were startlingly white. Many were women.

Their scrutiny was blank, impersonal, recording without assessment—save for one man, whose eyes blazed for a moment of rage before retreating into a statue's blindness. He was the old man who had spat into the moat as she passed; she shivered under a directed hate.

The silence shrank her voice as she whispered to Soldier, "Some of them are women!"

"Why not?"

"I had felt . . . with Libary . . . and the village Mas being so much lesser . . . "

"They are Readers."

"Do the men, the Librarians, elect them?"

"Nobody elects a Reader. Readers declare themselves and are recognised."

"How?"

"I do not know. I am Genetic, Nugan; those transcend the Genetics."

The usual trickery; creating mystery round themselves and preying on credulity.

She did not quite believe it. The two blazing eyes had been a warning of dangerous reality.

Soldier divined her shaken confidence and placed an arm around her shoulders. "Fear nothing. Whatever the communication, they will not harm you." He allowed feeling in his voice because she needed comfort and he said with a touch of sarcasm, "Readers never make the mistake of taking action. They cozen soldiers into that. And so they are never at fault."

"Are they fakes, Thomas? Mystic con men?"

He was slow to answer. At last he said, "Not fakes. Mystics? I think so. Is the Net mysticism or is it only allegory? As for con men, I do not know the term."

"Never mind. You think they are genuine?"

He laughed gently. "They are real and I think they believe they are genuine. Strange things happen and it is sure that in some fashion they communicate. Not in words. Feeling, understanding are shared and consensus achieved."

"As in drawing on the knowledge available in the morphic field?"

"You do not believe in that."

"I am trying to keep an open mind."

"That is best; then you will not twist what you see with prejudice."

The moving figures merged in a dark mass midway along the roof, were still during an extended moment of waiting, then separated to spread from their centre and form two circles, inner and outer. In a single action they seated themselves and were still.

Nugan counted them, an activity to defuse the unease which Soldier's warm presence could not hold completely at bay—thirteen in the inner circle and twenty-five in the outer, with a gap in the outer circle where one more could fit.

A man stood and looked back at her. It was Libary. He beckoned.

"I don't want to do this, Thomas."

"Do not fear."

"I'm not afraid, I'm . . . revolted."

He squeezed her gently. "I have observed this thing before. You are to share their received will. It is, I think, a very great compliment."

In fact he thought it more like a contemptuous condescension, designed to impress and overawe, but it was best that she accept the experience and have done with it.

Libary beckoned again.

Soldier plucked the habit from Nugan's shoulders. She gasped, "Does he want me naked? Why?"

"It is the custom. Perhaps it has meaning. You are a communicant, Nugan, not a sacrifice. Courage!"

She shivered. "Very well. Courage!"

She slipped off her fleecy sandals, let the shorts fall round her ankles and stepped out of them.

Libary motioned to the gap in the circle, then sat

down and took no more notice of her, as if he did not care whether she joined or not.

She joined them and sat, crossing her legs before her as she saw the others had done.

The night was warm; the nakedness ceased to trouble her; there was no prudery in her. She mused that this lack of sexual self-consciousness might have been the trigger for her sexual defiance aboard ship, where privacy was minimal and the habit of personal reserve had become endemic, save among the rebel few. Only ten children in all that time! Into her mind crept a sense of disapproval, as though someone nudged a corner of her mind, reminding her of . . . Duty? Obligation? Obligation to do what? With the question came realisation that it had not risen in her mind, that it was a demand, a caution from outside. A woolgathering child was being silently told to pay attention, to quiet her extraneous noise.

I am imagining . . .

She glanced around the motionless circles. No one moved or met her eye but she knew she was being told to behave herself, to stop disrupting . . . to become part of the circle, not sit without joining.

She tried to empty her mind; instead of emptiness she encountered disordered strands of thought and then a sudden panic at her inability to make her mind behave.

Reflexively, reaching for a friend, a reassurance, she turned her head, looking for Thomas. He was there, a few paces behind her, a still column in the moonlight. He made a sharp gesture ordering her back into participation and she obeyed, almost in fear of his displeasure.

She stared into the heart of the circles and tried to relax. There came a sensation of her thought being patted, massaged, gentled—and she gazed into an intense blackness where the only intrusion was a knowledge of waiting for thought to enter.

The feeling of outside influence vanished. She was quite alone, not part of a menacing coven but alone with a private darkness that would in time be filled.

And in time something appeared. A form emerged from its private place, slipped out of its own darkness to show itself to her. It was for a moment amorphous, shapeless and transparent, then it was swiftly solid and meaningful.

What she saw was the figure of a man, as black as the people of the central desert, not entering her thought but separate as of another mental fabric, not glowing but in itself visible. It grew swiftly to giant height, to the stature of three men, and she saw— without shock or curiosity or any simple feeling— that it was not a man at all. It was a human form, naked, neither distinguishably male nor female, devoid of sexual identity; where genitals should have flowered smooth flesh flowed unbroken into the hairless crotch. Its face was unclear because unfinished; suggestions of shape flickered, fluid, never coalescing.

Only the eyes were formed, black orbs glittering without whites or irises or lashes, and they gazed implacably down at her, asking nothing, offering nothing, contemplating.

It raised its head and searched across the sky, for suddenly sky was there, to the shining star that was *Search* sinking to the horizon. The flowing features gathered themselves like the coming together of a decision, into a face of brilliant anger, the face of the Koori who had spat into the moat.

The likeness lasted only a moment. The expression vanished, the features lost shape, the head turned and only the black eyes looked down on Nugan, expressionless, contemplating.

Without warning, in a fraction of a second, the figure dwindled, collapsed, and returned to its darkness.

Nugan fainted.

She opened her eyes on sky and stars. Thomas's hand supported her shoulder; her head rested on his thigh, hard, muscular, offering a resting place but no sense of affectionate comfort. She strained back to take in his face (pushing away the black thing her memory was not ready for) and saw that he looked not at her but into some inner infinity while automatically caring for the fallen.

She said, "You don't give a damn, do you?"

His eyes returned to seeing. "For you, Nugan?"

"For anybody. You are Soldier, bound to holy duty without sentiment or favour."

He said only, "You have recovered sufficiently to sit up."

She jerked angrily free of him and sat clutching her knees. The congregation of Readers was gone; they were alone on the roof. Her head swam briefly and steadied as she resolutely put away the implacable black eyes of the giant while a deep unreason rocked back to sanity.

Soldier said, in a meditative mode at odds with his unfailing sureness, "You may be correct, Nugan. I was raised without love; Libary inspired in me trust and respect, even affection, but not sentiment."

"Christ, but you're cold-blooded!" Her mind recovered rapidly as she shed her disturbance on Soldier; almost she could look again into the black thing's eyes.

Soldier placed his hands under her armpits and stood up in a fluid movement, raising her with him. "Stand, Nugan! You are not a little girl fearing darkness. And I am not cold-blooded, merely rational."

To himself that sounded less than satisfactory; he was not merely a bland solver of problems. He said quickly, "You have experienced . . . what you have experienced. Face it."

Comfort ration withdrawn, she thought, and stepped away from him. As for facing . . . a figure of darkness . . . soulless eyes without pity, with only a maniac rage, instantly repressed, and a return to still contemplation of her intrusion into its world . . .

With hardy control she said, "They created a vision for me, not a real thing."

"Is not a vision a real thing, with meaning?"

Oh, yes, it had had meaning. "It represented the collective will. Is that right?"

"I imagine so, Nugan. I saw nothing. I was outside the circle."

"Nothing!" She called it a vision but it had seemed to have texture, bulk, solidity. It had been created to impress her and it had done its work. "They resent us. They don't want us here, any of them."

Soldier was silent.

She said tiredly, "I suppose it was a miracle of sorts. An apparition representing consensus. I saw what I was meant to see. Hypnotism on the grandest scale."

Jack McCann's voice said softly in her ear, "This is wickedness. Come back to the ship, love. They're dangerous."

She murmured, "I must talk first with Libary, find out the exact meaning of this Council. Then I'll come. I don't want to stay longer." Despite herself she sobbed on two choking breaths and Soldier's arm curled comfortingly round her. "They've frightened me but I have to finish the job. I don't think they'll actually harm me but I've had a monstrous shock."

"What did you see?"

She told him in inadequate words, unable to convey the darkness, the vastness, the illusion of reality. "It's hard to believe the camera didn't see it."

"What our cameras saw was two circles of naked flesh behaving like a cult demonstration and then collapsing in what looked like physical exhaustion."

"Psychic exhaustion, Jack."

"Whatever. Finish up and get back here."

"I will. They don't want us here."

"Maybe so but it may come to, Who cares what they want?" His tone lightened. "Get some sleep. Say hello to your cold fish soldier for me; he seems all right."

"Good night, Jack." She turned to Soldier. "He sent you greeting. He appreciates your looking after me."

"I am honoured. It is a pity we cannot meet."

Almost she said, *Don't bet on that*, but held the words back. Let trouble arrive in its own time. She said instead, "Your Readers have given us a display of power."

Soldier laughed, an unexpected sound. "Power, Nugan? Mental mummery to awe and mystify. A moment of energy ending in the collapse of the exhausted generators! I have told you that the Readers do not involve themselves in physical action. If you need a figure of fear, fear Soldier and his planning."

He was smiling but the moonlight falsified the planes and angles of his features; if his voice sounded honest, even light, his mouth seemed sardonic and shadowed with warning.

Nugan said, "You're serious. You mean that!"

"I have never lied to you or hidden necessary knowledge from you." He took her arm to lead her back to her room. "I am the most dangerous weapon you will meet."

As she prepared for sleep, Nugan mused on his calling himself a weapon rather than a man. He was one who chose his words with exactness.

14

LIBARY ROSE LATE. THE SUN WAS HIGH before he entered his office and would have been higher had he not forced down weariness in order to confront the woman who must be dealt with while dismay was still strong in her. His face was drawn and his eyes dull; the beckoning inertia of psychic exhaustion warned him of his limitations.

Thomas's complaining presence made tired body and mind no more bearable under the accusation of, "Mummery. Trickery. Carnival show."

Libary rested on his weariness to preserve calm. "Less tawdry in presentation, I think."

"But to the same end: to seduce the suggestible. But Nugan is no villager to be overawed by a phantom."

"Phantom?" Libary was astonished. "You saw?"

"What Nugan saw? No. I saw nothing but I was aware of a happening amongst you. You claim to tap a repository of the world's minds, I think; but I think also that you Readers delude yourselves that a belief is a truth. Now—"

Libary cut across him. "You have doubted me? And said nothing?"

"I grew up and claimed the right to private thinking."

Libary smiled his understanding and acceptance, while Soldier read the affronted anger behind it. "I have been careless, Thomas, not noticing enough. We grow apart. You were about to finish your statement."

"Now I think you folk have developed a technique allied to hypnosis. I know the working of hysteria in crowds and I can imagine you secretive people developing control of group weakness to impress your wishes on obedient others."

Libary was satisfied that Thomas had no inkling of the facts. "Confusion, Thomas, confusion. You speak of hypnosis and then of group psyche as though they were the same thing. You have not thought properly."

"In time, I will. A soldier's responsibility is to all men; it is my duty to probe chicanery when I detect it."

Libary's weariness fled before the totally unexpected. With loud, defensive disbelief he cried out, "Are you threatening the Ordinands?"

Soldier had not intended confrontation. He had spoken from an area of compulsion unsuspected in his mind until it tangled his words. He said with care, "I am reminding you that it was you who taught me that duty comes before sentiment and a clear duty must be carried out against all personal inclination. I am bound to you by affection but also by your teaching."

"There is a conflict?" Libary's expression suggested that it could be easily resolved.

"Not yet. I understand what you did last night but not why. You tried to frighten and you succeeded— in some degree—but you gave Nugan no understanding, only an emotion which may recoil on you. The ship people are not genetically driven to accept without question."

Libary saw no need for further acting; he could say truthfully, "The understanding will be given. When will the woman come?"

"Shortly. She is dressing for return to the ship."

*   *   *

Nugan came in her dropsuit, face set to reveal nothing, pretending to herself that her attitude was businesslike and unemotional, and on a deeper level not believing it. Soldier smiled at her, gestured her in, and retired to his table, where pens and paper were laid out.

It was plain that Libary was tired, which might mean tetchy, but he bared his teeth in forced welcome, said, "Good morning, Taylor's Nugan," and indicated the chair by his desk. She sat. He had placed her with her back to Soldier and now said, "You are dressed for departure."

"I have been here long enough. I hope to carry a definitive message from you to my Captain." Best, she thought, to keep the exchange on a formal level.

"You will have told him what you saw last night, the expression of a will, a consensus?"

"Not in such terms."

Libary clasped his hands under his chin and said without emphasis, "The message should be clear: We wish that you will leave this world and not return. There is no welcome for you here."

That was blunt but expected. She asked calmly, "By what right do you speak for the world?"

"By consensus. You were present."

"The world was not."

"Its decision was present. It may prove impossible to convince one who is certain that the concept of universal consciousness was discredited before she was born."

"Do you mean morphic resonance?"

"Perhaps. That was, I think, the beginning of understanding. Only the beginning."

Nugan fell quiet. Soldier, observing the slight movement of her neck, as if halting a lifting of her head, knew she listened to a voice instructing her from the ship. She said, "Leave argument aside for the moment, Libary. Convince me that the world knows who we are and why we are here."

Libary's expression became one of hard dislike of this person who, he thought, pursued trivia as a delaying tactic. "Let Thomas convince you. You know him for a concise and accurate teacher."

Nugan heard Soldier, behind her, tear off a fresh sheet of paper as he began, "The semaphore system, Nugan, còvers the planet. It transmits the most complex messages by a visual shorthand over thousands of kils in a day. Even with short catamaran passages between connecting islands, the semaphores can reach England and China in a hundred hours, operating night and day."

"Passed like mouth-to-mouth messages—mis-sent, garbled, mistaken, and misread!"

"There is an inbuilt checking system, Nugan, which detects errors and demands correction."

She was determined on finding fault. "And South America, across the ocean? Don't tell me racing catamarans devour distance."

"I will not. Messages cross the Bering Strait to North America and thread that network in two days. South America counts for little; few live there."

"Very well. I accept that they know, but the ends of the Earth cannot confer and formulate answers and return them in less than ten or twelve days, and this is only my seventh day here."

"No answers were asked for, Nugan. A message was promulgated, telling that your ship was in the sky and that its people proposed to make their home on Earth. Reactions to the message were automatic. Senior Ordinands and their equivalents in other communities—" He groped for a suitable expression. "—drew these *reactions* from the Net—or so I am given to understand."

She leapt on that. "What Net? Indra's Net? Is that what you are talking about?"

Libary's gaze was fixed on her with an expression in which scorn and impatience made an unpleasant mixture. Behind her Soldier said, "In a sense, yes. The Net is allegory but it is also an expression of universal consciousness. More than that I cannot tell you; I offer only the received explanation of the swift response."

Again he was aware of her listening. In a moment she said, "Why was the initial message not sent by the Net?"

"As I understand it—and that is not well—" (Nugan thought, *There's no mystic in him; he doesn't believe this.*) "—the Net is not an instrument for talk. It holds knowledge which the Ordinands in concert can . . . obtain from it."

Libary said sharply, "Leave that!"

Soldier continued across him, "Libraries exist across the planet, so the history of the Collapse is known everywhere, as is the existence of the two starships. No more was needed than to say, They are here."

"You mean that all around the world the message went out: *The wreckers have returned. Fear them!*"

"No, Nugan; the fact of the return only. What the communes thought was for them to agree on."

"And we got thumbs-down from the whole damned planet!"

Soldier did not answer.

Libary said, "Yes."

"And is that all the message you have for us?"

Libary settled back in his chair, relaxing, confident, ready now to complete the destruction of arrogance as this woman, and through her the complement of *Search*, were brought to see themselves through other, saner eyes. "No, not all. It is for me to speak for the Earth, to explain why you cannot remain here.''

"Cannot?''

He replied frostily to challenge, "Must not. Let me spell out what I am sure you have already thought for yourself.''

Nugan, resentful of the self-possession worn like a skin of conscious superiority, said furiously, "Let me spell out what your vanity sees and never questions! You see us as representatives of a culture that destroyed its habitat and itself and went down in universal misery, as a disease to devastate your bucolic self-satisfaction by reinfecting you with the ideas of the past. That is all you see!''

Libary said again, "Not all."

Soldier recognised Nugan's effort to master an angry tongue; he imagined faceless listeners overhead counselling, exhorting, and calming. Take hold, Nugan! This is all our futures, not just yours. Keep your temper. Don't let that black twister get to you!

Nugan said in a conciliatory tone, "Please remember that our crumbling culture found time and willingness to create yours. Your existence is our act of recognition that the planet should be handed on to those better fitted to survive.''

Soldier approved, on the whole, but she sounded too much like a dealer from a distant commune preparing to bargain. However good a choice she might be for an exploratory contact, she was far out of her depth here.

Libary was placid. "History is deficient in facts, but the act of recognition would seem to have been the project of a sighted few rather than of the self-serving many. The sighted few did what they felt they must and died unsung—but they do not seem to have predicted this situation. They saw an end to their culture, not its reincarnation.''

Nugan did not try to argue but said, "We have much to offer."

"So it comes to that? Expectably." Libary inclined his head in the briefest of concessions. "What have you that we need?"

"Obvious things, such as communication equipment."

"The radio we read of? Endless chatter in the air? You saw last night that we have a sufficient means."

Nugan answered with deliberate gentleness, "I saw the capacity of certain highly trained, privileged persons. But a radio-telephone can be the property of every family in every village. Communal isolation can be opened up to an intimate perception of the whole world."

"Indeed so—if isolation were their perception of their condition. You have not seen enough to discover that each village, each commune, behaves as an extended family. An intimacy of five hundred or a thousand people bound by commonality of interest and emotion makes for as full a life as most humans can aspire to. Extend the bounds and intimacy disappears; the necessity to treat the vast surplus of acquaintances as strangers becomes paramount. Experience becomes externalised rather than ingested and considered. Your own writers noted more than once that the loneliest place on Earth was a great city. Why turn the world again into a vast mental slum?"

Nugan had never encountered such a point of view. "Small is beautiful" had in her time been a gibe at the artily pretentious and she could not imagine a limited community offering a full life experience. The boredoms and petty feuds of *Search* were example enough. To her, Libary's world picture was a vision of a conditioned, hidebound, custom-controlled folk unable to realise that a wider, freer existence was possible. The gift of freedom of experience . . .

In her ear a voice said urgently, "Don't argue with him. He's on his own ground. You'll lose."

So she listened as Libary set about destroying her culture. "It can be argued that rapid communication was the most significant factor in the self-destruction of the Last Culture. With instant conversation and dissemination of news, political interference with each other's internal affairs, backed by very rapid transport of explosives, became possible. What was possible became immediate fact among powermongers. Not until the age of instant communication did wars involve tens of millions in nations of every continent. There is value in distance and a lapse of time; they encourage second thoughts and discourage automatic reaction to pressures."

Nugan said, a little doggedly, "That becomes a matter of intelligence—of how you use your abilities, of restraint and common sense."

A voice, Brookes's now, muttered, "Stop it, Nugan!" while Libary shot a glance at Soldier, who said, "Nugan, there is no common sense with dangerous toys, only an urge to instant solutions."

Brookes urged, "Health, Nugan! Talk health!"

Nugan conceded that a sensible people would covet only what was useful to them, using words to cover thought until she could begin slowly, "There are general and personal benefits that we can provide. I have learned that your average life span is about fifty years as against ninety in my time. There is a huge bank of medical knowledge available and a pharmacopoeia to deal with nearly every known illness."

Libary was not tempted. "We are a healthy people though many die in the vulnerable early years. We suspect that our unknown Wizards—very well, scientists—provided us with resistance against the most common ailments and that the weakest are weeded out. Your books describe malaria and measles and syphilis and a hundred more infections which we cannot relate to anything we know and which we do not wish to see re-created amongst us."

"Your life expectancy suggests that you are vulnerable to cancers and the degenerative diseases of middle age and die of them because you cannot treat them. Fifty is too soon for death. We can change that, give you the good years of late life when knowledge and experience combine in an informed enjoyment of the world."

Libary laughed. "You have that at second hand. You know nothing about age or its pleasures—if they exist. As for extending the life span, you should have found time to query Thomas about it. Inform her, Thomas."

Soldier said quietly, "Extending life span to ninety years would increase the population by more than half in a single generation. Population is a matter of concern to us, of ensuring that each communal area can support those living in it without squeezing the life rights of the animals and growing things. Much depends on balance, on water usage, soil fertility, drought subsistence, availability of metals and minerals . . . All that is the province of the Mas. Growth in population is not discouraged but it is closely watched. The race must not cripple itself again by overgrowth. The planet you left us is one whose resources are not seen as inexhaustible; they must suffice for the life of the race, which may be measured in millions of years. The animal at the head of the food chain is responsible for the whole."

Libary took up the lesson. "We have doctors and chemists in special university communes who examine the questions of health and disease. Gradually, over generations, the great panaceas will be rediscovered and applied with careful monitoring of results. We do not reach for immortality; disease serves its purpose in preserving the balance of life."

She tried once more, "You surely know that your system of genetic control, preserving selected traits, will eventually restrict the gene pools. You will end up preserving the characteristics you want and also the weaknesses bound with them, which you don't want. Mutation and adaptation are essential to survival."

"Is that a sample of the wisdom you can bring? We are aware of the obvious and of how to guard against it. We waste time while you offer poisoned gifts instead of telling outright what your people want. What is it that they are prepared to pay for in the treasure of their science and techniques? What are we expected to give?"

"A place where three hundred people may live."

Libary smiled, not pleasantly. "A small place?"

Nugan put a hand to her ear and dislodged the receiver, irritated and confused by the sudden babble of instruction and suggestion from the ship. Holding the polished housing of the chip in her glove, she affirmed, "An isolated place. You want no contact with us and in honesty I have to say that we are unlikely to find your culture appealing except as a study. But who knows that we may not learn unsuspected things from each other? Yet I feel we would prefer not to intermingle. Natural social contact would find its own eventual level but we would want to keep to ourselves at first, adjusting to life on Earth and settling our own new social system free from the constraint of a steel box."

Libary said again, flatly, "A small place."

"Your Earth is not short of room. You heard Thomas say that South America is sparsely settled."

"That is not what he said. That continent was ravaged in the genocidal wars of the Collapse. The land is seeded with decaying armaments and ruined power plants; the rivers are poisoned by your invisible weapon of radioactivity. Those unable to curb their homesickness would be welcome to die there—fairly quickly."

For a moment Nugan was quiet under the insult. Then she said, "We have not earned that. We have goodwill for your people."

"Yet you lied."

"I? No!"

"You suggested three hundred persons."

"That is the complement of the ship."

"That we know." Libary stood, leaning forward to look down at her. "Did Thomas not tell you that we have full descriptions of your ship in the records? We know what is aboard there—three hundred men and women and six millions of pre-embryos in cold suspension. How much land do you ask for those? A few hectares—or perhaps a continent? Just an isolated foothold where the new growth may breed and breed and destroy a world we have laboured for centuries to bring into harmony?"

Nugan struggled to her feet, shamed and shaking. "It isn't for me to argue. I don't control anything. You must talk to my Captain."

"Why? He will have the same answer. Tell him to find another world. This one belongs to its builders."

While she fought for words, for some way of ending the interview with dignity, Libary stepped around the desk and without looking at her again left the office.

Miserably she turned to Soldier, who gazed after Libary, for once not hiding an expression of thoughtful disapproval. "Oh, Thomas, I've made a foul mess of it."

He came to her, at once friendly and ready to assist. "So would have any other, Nugan; that was foreordained. Now it is time to go while *Search* is in the sky and your Jack can still find you. Shall I come with you to say good-bye?"

They went, hand in glove, out of the building, the slim soldier of a forming world and the woman out of his far past, like a shambling ape in her dropsuit.

15

A GREAT QUIET HAD FALLEN ON THE Library. "A silence of waiting," Soldier observed. "A decision has been given; the reaction is awaited."

Nugan said, "I made a fool of myself, with my people listening. Now you see me as a liar."

"I have not judged you."

"Not?" She was incredulous.

He said, choosing his words, "I heard no concealment in your voice. Yet you forgot the embryos, if only for the moment. Six million is a considerable feat of forgetfulness."

"But I had forgotten—for the moment. That cryounit has been with us, silent and untouched, from the beginning. No one speaks of it because there is no need. It waits on the future, of no immediate importance or even interest. It affects no one. Those cell clusters have lain there, out of mind, from the beginning. The only imperative in my mind was the need of my three hundred for a landing. I was racking my brain for arguments for them and worried about the anger I will face on *Search*—for they'll blame me. They'll find a way to make it my fault; that's the blindness of their need. When Libary spoke of the embryos I was ashamed of being caught so stupidly. All I could think of was that I had earned his contempt—and yours—and that no excuses could make sense. So I didn't offer any."

"I would not easily forgive your lapse in a soldier but I would understand it in a villager, for the villagers think with less discipline. I knew you did not lie with deception in mind and I was puzzled."

"I was simply incompetent."

"Yes."

Soldier Thomas was not one to kiss the spot and make it better.

At the drawbridge nobody lounged or fished. Two camouflage-suited sentries stood guard under the portcullis but they made no move to recognise their General. Looking for a change of subject, Nugan said, "I thought sentries had to salute their officers."

Soldier asked, "What is 'salute?'"

She explained, supplying an inept demonstration.

"You are saying, Nugan, that they must be reminded of their inferior status. That is to insult them."

Another question of point of view. "I think it was a form of discipline, enforcing alertness."

They stepped from the drawbridge to the grass. "Alertness for what? They know me, I know them; no recognition is needed. For intruders? Those are their ongoing duty; they would hardly salute such."

Crossing the road, they moved into the area of cut grass; over a few days it had dried visibly. She said clearly, "Jack! Jack McCann!" The ship would be approaching the morning vertical; he should find her easily.

"Here, Nugan. Coming up?"

"Yes, Jack. I'm at the west end of the Library, out on the hillside."

"Calibrating. I'll call you."

"Yes." She checked the dropsuit seals and instruments.

Soldier continued his theme: "Your age did not breed soldiers; you had to teach them, train them. So they needed constant reminding—as with salutes."

Nugan had a flash of insight. "Your folk are born to this or that manner of life but not to be adaptable to other ways of existence."

He thought about it. "That is not easy to consider. Other continents do things differently but in the end they are the same things."

"You could not live our lives, Thomas."

"Nor is there a niche for you in ours."

"There might be. We were born to be adaptable."

He said cautiously, "That could be a virtue in those seeking a new world."

"Or returning to an old one."

"Speak plainly, Nugan."

"The ship will not accept an expulsion order. It will be ignored, Thomas. They want a place in their world."

"We have agreed that this is no longer their world. I think you warn me."

"They will come down. I am sure of it."

He nodded, shaded his eyes and looked up at the sky as if he might see them. "Argue against it, Nugan."

"Why should I?"

He looked down at the ground and then at her face with a greater seriousness than she had seen in him, a total lack of all feeling, all meaning. She felt that she saw him for the first time, not Thomas but Soldier. When he spoke she had no doubt of the menace.

"To avoid confrontation, Nugan. We will not let them stay; we will force them out."

"Force? Look!"

Soldier had examined the heavy gloves but had made no sense of their bland, seemingly solid metal components. Now Nugan stretched an index finger at the grass between them and the ground smoked, grew red and, swiftly, blinding white.

She switched off at once and joined Soldier in stamping out the little ring of burning grass.

He grinned at her like a boy and was Thomas again, shaking a finger in her face. "If you carry a weapon you must command its uses! Left alone you might have burned the hillside. Amateur, Nugan!"

He kicked dirt over the smoking spot of ground.

Jack said, "I saw a flash. Did you fire?"

"Yes. Forget it; it was nothing."

"OK. I'm getting you steady. Sealed up?"

"Not quite."

"Give you two minutes."

"OK."

Soldier waited politely for them to finish before he said, "Do not depend on weapons, Nugan. There is more to war than noise and death."

She said, "I may never see you again. Or I may. In either case, thank you for your goodness. Remember me."

"Oh, I shall, I shall."

She fingered a control and the helmet rose out of its folds to cover her head in a seamless bowl. She increased the internal air pressure, listened for a hiss of leakage, and shut it off.

"Ready, Jack?"

"Got you."

He bounced her gently to test the monopole grip and asked, "Right to lift?"

She raised a hand to Soldier and said, "Lift, Jack."

He took her up and away. The figure of Soldier dwindled and vanished, the Library shrank, the sky turned black and she was alone in space, climbing fast.

16

SOLDIER WATCHED THE SILVER SUIT rise and glitter, shrink and vanish, while he thought: *They will come down with their hot, bright weapons—and what then? I hope she does not come with them; I don't wish to be enemy to a friend.*

He went directly to Libary's sleeping quarters, sure that the depleted man would have returned to bed. Libary lifted his head from the pillow, sighed venomously and said, "I don't need commentary, Thomas; I need sleep."

Soldier seated himself on the side of the bed. "Your Readers should have done better."

Libary, however tired, had had his way too long for temporising. "Are you saying *you* would have done better?"

"I would not have declared war."

"Nor did I."

"Every ploy and intonation declared it. You command people to keep clear of what they consider their own and expect them not to spit in your face? They will come down. They will defy you to shift them."

Libary settled back and closed his eyes. "Three

hundred cannot defeat a planet, no matter what their weapons."

"History tells that a few hundreds destroyed the old empire of Mexico."

"They toppled superstitious, priest-ridden cultures with the aid of disaffected natives."

"Here the priests call themselves Ordinands and Readers and practise hypnotic coercion and speak on mysteries, such as Indra's Net. The minds up there will find chinks in your philosophy and preach a new dispensation to the villagers, one attractive with gifts to the common people—medicines and simple machines."

Libary's eyes remained closed. "If they come—and I say *if* they come—they will not corrupt the people."

"You will prevent it? How?"

"You will prevent it."

Soldier thought of boiling ground and fire flickering in grass. "Nothing changes, eh, old man? The villagers do the world's work, the soldiers keep them in order, and the psychic elite pursues its plans of—of what? in the safety of its soldier-guarded isolation! You dealt less than wisely with the Taylor's Nugan and you look to Soldier Thomas to avert the consequences."

Libary's eyes opened wide. "Are you taken with this woman?"

"I am partial to many women and taken with none. I am the product of your pragmatic teaching—a pragmatic man, governed by the imperative of duty."

"You are what you were born for."

"What I was fashioned as. But times change and it is said that we change with them; I have discovered ideas outside my prescribed ruts. Now, have your sleep."

He strode off, satisfied that Libary's sleep would be restless. He would never learn to hate the old mountebank but he was determined to see straightly past the swaddle of affection. As for the ship people, he was in no way daunted by what powers they might display but he did not wish to be forced to a determination.

17

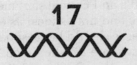

THE SUIT DROPPED TO THE FLOOR IN A heap and Nugan hugged the daughter who wanted to know at once, "Was it all as beautiful as you remembered?"

"Of course it was. Air and trees and running water and the things ship's weather can't give—breezes and morning mist and dawn and twilight."

But no rain. She had hoped but there had been no rain.

McCann cleared his operation board and switched off. "Something to tell you, Nugan. We kept it from you so as not to confuse your thinking down there."

"It got confused enough at the end."

"Forget that; it can't be undone. What's new is a message from *Kiev*."

"The Ukrainer? Hailing us after seven hundred years?"

"Not us. Their message was beamed at Earth but there was only *Search* here to receive it. They've found a planet. It isn't perfect but it seems practicable."

Nugan sat on the floor and hugged her knees.

"Well, well, after all this—a brand new world! Where?"

"Fifth planet of a star called Postvorta. Ever heard of it?"

All the promising stars in a fifty-light-year radius were indelibly in her memory. "In Virgo and not too far out—thirty-two lights. Not in *Search*'s contact area."

Jack said, "It's an FO-type star, meaning that it's a bloody hot one and not as ideal as a G-type, but the radiation patterns should be reasonable."

"Then that's where we should go."

"I agree, but will anybody else?"

Nugan threw up her hands. "We won't go of course. Forty years more travelling when there's a green world here for the grabbing? Greed beats thinking any day."

"That's how it is. Preparations are being made to drop a hundred—lots drawn from each Waking."

"I'll try to talk them out of it. We'd be a pestilence down there."

They had forgotten Anne. She said, "You mustn't! They won't listen to you, anyway. I've been watching through your camera and hearing you talk to Thomas and Johnno, and I want to see it all for myself."

"Anne, they don't want us!"

Anne gathered up the suit and dragged it across to the locker; when Nugan tried to help, she snapped that she could do it. Stretching it across the clamps, she spoke over her shoulder, striving for offhandedness without the demeaning overtones of young rebellion. "We ship's kids have talked about it and we say it isn't our fault that you all ran away into space and left our world to others. It's the one you've all talked about as long as we can remember and if it's all that wonderful, that's the one we want. Who gives a damn about some only maybe practicable lump of dirt round a not so suitable star? We don't want to live forever in a flying box, either! And we're sick of all your arguments. If Earth is our home, we want to see it, and anybody who wants Postvorta is welcome to it. On their own."

part III

SOLDIER PROFESSIONAL

1

THE GLIDER PATROLS INFORMED SOL-
dier, in his forest training camp, within half an hour
of the arrival of the starship people. The troops called
them the Searchers.

They dropped in groups of twelve, silver in the
morning sky, pausing a handsbreadth above the
ground and dropping the last few inches to become
discrete figures shedding dropsuits and donning
wide-brimmed hats to begin at once their reinfesta-
tion of the planet. Containers of supplies and
machinery floated down and were swarmed over in
orgiastic opening and gutting. A small village of
white tents sprang up.

Soldier had foretold, following his own line of reasoning, that the drop would be made in this area
rather than any other part of the planet and their
choice of a particular spot confirmed his estimate of
their logic. They chose the hill next to the Library
ridge, the vantage from which he had puzzled over
"The Comet." It was some fifty metres lower than the
Library crest and planted on the lower slopes with
tall, bare-trunked gum trees rising out of a cover of
long grass. The eucalypts were effectively drought-
proof, their taproots deep in the soil, but the grass
had died into a rusty fur over the ground.

A hilltop was, of course, a sensible tactical position—if you knew how to use it, and he thought that unlikely. There were, he concluded, two probabilities: Either they thought to make social or diplomatic contact by their nearness or they were intimating, Here we are and now do your damnedest. Perhaps a little of each.

Libary would be bottling rage behind his black features lest he be observed in less than placid self-command. The landing would be for him a nose-thumbing, open insult. He would expect Soldier Thomas to come running, all belligerence and ingenious plans. Let him expect. Soldier Thomas had indeed some plans which were militarily imperative but not at all designed to soothe the Librarian's bile. He sent a fast messenger to the General of the Murray Valley and followed it, on horseback and without concealment, with an unarmed "peace" escort.

The Generals met, considered and agreed.

He returned several days later to a squall of angry messages from a simmering Libary. It was time now for him to see the old man and direct him to useful action, also to view the Searcher encampment for himself.

Before entering the Library he looked down on the lower hill, seeing that his gliderscouts' descriptions erred only in underestimation. Their first sketches had shown a cluster of tents on the hilltop, huddling for comfort against the unknown, forming a circle into which supply containers dropped each day from the ship, invisibly overhead. The miraculous levitation became customary.

Machinery whose purpose was a mystery had reared itself in the centre of the encampment and on the third day of the General's absence a column of water had gushed, white and sparkling, a hundred metres into the air, to be immediately quenched and not seen again.

Then, overnight, the whole Searcher "encroachment" (a nice word, Soldier thought, which the scouts had evolved for themselves) had been covered in a single vast, flat, black roof supported some four or five metres above the ground on metal struts. It must, the Scout Captain suggested, be infernally hot under such a cover. His General doubted this but kept the thought to himself; he knew enough physics to imagine the solar heat in some way gathered and used.

The Searchers, they reported, seemed occupied in the heart of their "encroachment" and ventured into the open only late in the afternoon, dressed from head to toe and wearing their wide hats. "They are white-skinned," the General told them, "and afraid of sun sores." *Poor buggers*, was the reaction of the troops, whose loyalties did not involve beating up meaningless hatred against a putative enemy as human as themselves, *they'll swelter*.

Soldier surveyed the black supertent through binoculars and saw little but the tent itself. The space under the huge cover was lit by lamps glowing more powerfully than any he had ever known, but whatever proceeded there took place beyond his vision.

He watched for a long time, seeing his scouts glide over at a considerable height, as ordered, attempting nothing beyond accustoming the Searchers to their harmless presence. He had ordered five passes a day, irregularly spaced. He was not yet certain what he might gain by this beyond allowing the Searchers to form the habit of not noticing—on the understanding that all habits are bad and lead to carelessness.

When he had watched fruitlessly for an hour he asked himself why he continued, and decided, with a twitch of surprise, that he watched in the hope of not seeing Nugan, of satisfying himself that she was not there.

He harboured no erotic interest in her, only a

friendly tenderness for someone out of a strange oth-
erwhen, who had bared her thinking to him more
completely than she knew because she had had little
other company. She had been a kitten loose and
mewing in a strange terrain; he did not want the guilt
of evicting a friend from a fool's paradise. *Because,
when I see how it is to be done, I will sweep you all
back into your lonely sky.*

He went in to Libary—

who received him with self-discipline rather than
smooth temper. "You should send word when you
are going away."

Soldier leaned comfortably against the amanuensis
desk. He had expected the complaint and decided
against soothing; Libary must bear with the parting
of mental ways. "I was about military business."

"No doubt, but you should—"

"Why should I?" He could not recall that he had
ever cut the old man off before. "I am the General
commanding this area; I am responsible to no superior, only to the requirements of duty and to my
men."

Libary regarded him with a surly summation as
though that might disguise emotional shock from
Soldier's reading of him, knowing that it would not.
He said, with love and anger at war in him, "There
was once a bond of affection."

"There is still, but it cannot interfere with my decisions. The matter of the Searchers takes precedence
over simpler loyalties."

"What difference would have been made—"

"If I had told you what I had in mind? You would
have raised a hundred Libary-oriented considera-
tions to throw logical denials around my ideas and I
would have had to waste time cutting them away."

"You are telling me that my mental capacity does
not extend to sociomilitary problems?"

"Capacity you have but no basic knowledge to back

it—any more than I have the knowledge to criticise your metaphysical forays into contact with the Net."

That had been a long shot into deep dark, but he knew at once that he had divined correctly the nature of the communication seances. And why not? He had spent the days on horseback mulling over that night on the roof.

Libary took refuge in stillness. After a while he said, "That is not for general discussion."

"How could it be? I have my expertise and you, yours. I am a soldier, not a shaman." He did not use the word contemptuously; he knew it as meaning "one in contact with minor psychic powers" and it seemed a suitable term. "What we discuss across each other's boundaries is for our tongues only."

"Thomas, am I to know where you have been?"

"I went north to meet the Grady's Benito, General of the Murray Valley communes. He has agreed to persuade his Librarians that this is no time for Library-raiding. They will listen to him because they can achieve nothing without him, so there will be no danger at least until the Searchers have gone. He has agreed also to provide additional manpower if I call for it; he recognises that this is not a merely local problem."

"What does he want in return?"

"Nothing. This is between soldiers, a recognition of necessity."

"A week's absence well spent."

It seemed the old man thought he still patted a small boy. "There is more. I sent runners to the Store and Mining communes to the west of Old Melbourne. I have placed orders for quantities of sulphur and saltpetre and have received word that they will be filled. The stuff can be portered upriver to the village."

"For a price?"

"Naturally; they want eucalyptus timber, sawn and cured for building, and three tonnes of river fish, preserved. The Mas can find fish among the villages downriver."

"It sounds very expensive gunpowder."

Soldier was not surprised that the old man recognised the mixture. "The price is for urgent speed of delivery and for the large quantities. I need enough to make two tonnes of explosive. I will teach Johnno how to prepare the charcoal and mix the powder and provide a few men to work with him."

Libary was silent a while. At last he said, "Two tonnes!" and seemed troubled.

"Enough, I think."

"What do you intend to blow up? Or may a philosophic web-spinner not ask?"

"Explosions are dangerous to life and I have no intention of killing anyone. To unnecessarily damage a few Searchers might stir the sort of trouble that would end only with our having to kill the lot of them—if they didn't kill us first."

Libary was disdainful. "A shipload cannot murder a planet."

Soldier, grinning, tossed him an idea: "They might drop their ship, vent down with fuel blazing, over village after village."

Libary was horrified. "I am happy that I cannot think like a soldier!"

"An idea only; I doubt they could do it. The ship was built in orbit and if it could land it would do so instead of sending a small party to prepare the way. We will simply make life uncomfortable for them until they realise that this is not their home and never can be."

"How? Ah, very well—I may not ask."

"Not yet knowing, I cannot answer. Come to the

roof and let me use those large semaphore binoculars."

The more powerful glasses showed him nothing he
had not evaluated through his own. The black cover
looming over the tents like a monstrous pall was either a textile stretched tight and supported on mul-
tiple standards or some light, strong material that
held its shape. But what material displayed that dull,
absorptive blackness? He could make nothing of it.

He asked Libary about those who came out at sun-
set to enjoy light and air.

"They do nothing in particular; it is a toolsdown
time. They talk and carry out exercises and play
games and look up at the Library—and see no more
of us than we of them." He added slyly, "Your Nugan
is among them."

"She is not my Nugan." Her presence rankled.

After a little time Libary asked, "Why, do you
think, they set up their camp there? In their place I
would have attempted other continents in hope of a
better welcome."

"They have been told that a better welcome is not
to be had."

"And have accepted it without question?"

"Yes."

"So, why did they choose that site?"

"Because you wished them away and made yourself so objectionable that they have felt it necessary
to insult you to your face."

"Childish!"

"Human. A better reason is that they have famil-
iarised themselves with this region through their instruments and have seen how they may
accommodate themselves to it. A third will be that
they are curious about the history of the past, and
much of that can be discovered in your Library. It is
a satisfaction you should afford them."

Libary turned his face away and leaned on the parapet, his eyes on the black encroachment.

He asked coldly, "Is it part of your strategy that I should lull them into feeling that we have reconsidered our position?"

"I have no strategy yet; ideas, yes, but no strategy. Why not let them have their history and a little freedom of movement—until I am ready to shift them? Why be inimical? Why not treat them as guests whose time is limited but who may exercise the rights due to their ancestry? I feel they have some."

"Chivalry! Do you expect me to exchange small talk with them?"

"It would be an opportunity to learn something of your distant forbears. Let them know that their time is limited and that they will be told when their liberty is over. Don't lull them, just put them on notice. They are our own kind and that much honesty is due them. Also, I will not be ready to move for several weeks and there is no reason why they should not fill the time to their intellectual profit."

"You laugh at me!"

Soldier took his arm gently. "Come and sit down. It is time for the classroom. You have forgotten what it is like to be a simple man away from the odours of secrecy and intellect. I must reteach you what you have forgotten, what it is like to be an ordinary man."

2

IN THE MORNING SOLDIER RETURNED TO Libary to ask, "What have you decided?"

The old man continued writing at his desk, not looking up, as he answered, "I am not an ordinary man and I have decided against your soldierly advice."

Soldier, expecting the refusal, had decided on a simple strategy. "Not soldierly, political. Consultation is an essential prelude to both war and peace. It would be appropriate if you made the first advance."

"I will not." He laid down his pen and leaned back in his regular pretence of disinterested exchange of views. "In the first place, I distrust my temper in dealing with interlopers." *That*, thought Soldier, *is true but little to the point.* "Secondly, I see no gain in offering concessions." *So much for my argument for buying time.* "Also, I have played your tactical game of putting myself in the enemy's place and deducing his action. I have no desire to find myself held hostage among strangers."

"You have deduced what *you* would do rather than what they might do. They will be hoping for conciliation, not confrontation."

Libary said flatly, "We differ."

That was no argument; he was simply afraid of the risk and not open to persuasion. Soldier read it in the blunt refusal of reason, and thought no less of the old man for that. Every soldier knows fear (only dangerous nuisances do not) and the necessity to work with it and against it, but Libary's wars had been fought on an intellectual plane where spiritual agonies (possibly as forbidding in their fashion) took the place of fleshly dread.

He said, "They remain under cover and make no move. Contact must be made."

Libary took up his pen. "Go yourself if it is so necessary." He turned his attention to the papers under his eyes.

Soldier had toyed with the idea of using Johnno as the bearer of a written message but now, stung, he said, "I will. Today."

Libary did not look up. "And leave your force with its leader in the hands of the enemy?"

"They will not see themselves as enemy. Perhaps as suppliants. As for hostage taking, they are not the fools you try to think them."

He turned to leave and Libary called after him, angrily harsh, "Don't dare implement your idea of allowing them access to the crypts!"

Soldier paused, considering the tone of a reply that would wound, no matter how expressed, telling the old man once and for all that his accustomed influence was no more than an incidental product of a pattern to which he was as strictly bound as any villager. He said, over his shoulder, "Papa Melchizedech, you have placed the negotiation in my hands; I now control communication with the Searchers. Now I *give* orders, not discuss them."

He knew what would come—the slapping down of the pen, the scraping of the chair, the slur of sandals on the mats, and the voice at the edge of breaking, "Thomas!"

He turned back, ready to soothe but still shocked by the imminence of tears in the brown eyes and the

power of his answering emotion. It had been a lifetime . . . He hugged the old man lightly and kissed
him gently on the cheek, the ritual assurance of en-
during respect, and said, "You reared me; see now
the outcome and don't grieve over it. This crisis of
Searchers will pass."

The General returned to camp to inform his lieuten-
ants what he intended and to plan his approach to
the black canopy. The General brooded over the matter of dress, but it was adventuring Soldier who
stripped down to shorts and soft shoes and set out,
bare-chested and bare-legged, without weapons.

Early in the afternoon he stood midway up the hill,
hearing the sound of axes round the farther curve and
pleased that the Top-Ma had acted so swiftly on a
request given only the previous evening. Johnno
would be there; he was always the Ma's choice for
ganger in emergency calls. West Old Melbourne
would see its timber floating downriver very soon.

He climbed quickly past the tree line and halted
where the rise melted gently into the crest. A hundred metres from the black roof he stood motionless;
no Searcher was in sight but he was sure that their
artificial eyes saw him and passed their visions to
observers within.

Time passed. He guessed that they argued: What to
do with the sightseer? enemy? spy? And who should
be sent to examine him? If their social intelligence
equalled their technological expertise, they would
send—

Nugan!

She came swinging down the slope, at ease now
with rough ground, calling, "Thomas, soldier
Tommy! You can't imagine what a rumpus you've
caused, showing up here!"

She hugged him and he kissed her, a little formally,

on the forehead. "Are you not wary of your enemy?"

She laughed delightedly. "You can see that I'm ter-rified. Everybody here wants to meet you!"

He had more or less expected it but had not taken his reading of these people as a certainty. He had thought deeply over the facts and clues gleaned from Nugan and come to a number of conclusions about Searcher psychology; now he wondered if their minds were not even more disorderly than he had dared hope.

"Nugan, you've not been fool enough to tell them I might be sympathetic!"

She sobered at once. "No, I told them that you had described yourself as the most dangerous weapon to be faced. Some actually heard you say it. But this is Earth, their Earth!"

She hurried across his, "It is not, Nugan, not," to tell him that they saw him as someone who would listen and see without prejudice, "Not like your damned old Libary with his automatic fount of hate."

He wondered at this homesickness that could blind the mind to facts. "Not hate but fear manifesting as anger and implacability."

"I know, I know, but nobody will listen to warn-ings. You can't know how the sight of Earth enchants after the cooped-up years. They call the ship a tomb and talk of setting it free to find the end of space alone."

May sanity forbid such nonsense. "I grant that I cannot imagine it. I have never left home."

"The Captain had to approve this landing, to let them take their chance, or there would have been blood in the corridors."

He nodded understanding of hysteria if not of its causes. "Yet for eight days they sit here and make no overture."

"Trying to outwait you, to force you or Libary or anybody to make the first move."

"Thinking to put us at a moral disadvantage? Well, here I am—with nothing to offer. I should speak with your Captain. Is he listening?"

"No, I'm not wired."

"Can you take me to him?"

"He wants you no closer than the edge of the canopy."

"A careful man. But will he come so far?"

"Of course."

They went up the slope together. There was little sound to tell of the activities of a hundred people. She said, laughing a little, "They are waiting, on edge." The most persistent sound on the hill was the bite of axes and, as they walked, the single splintering crash of a falling tree. "What's that noise, Thomas?"

"Foresters felling logs to be bartered." That was a most precise truth. He asked, "Do you really believe you will be permitted to stay on Earth?"

She did not answer but he heard the slight intake of breath, felt the tiny tension of fingers and the touch of her arm as a momentarily incautious step brushed her against him. "No, you do not believe it."

"They didn't see the Net figure. I did."

Interesting that she should name it so; there would have been much discussion up there in the skyway.

As they approached the canopy a pervasive *rom* made itself apparent. It had been a background in his mind for some time; now, as they drew near, it became obtrusive. "The *rom*—the pheromone you called it—is most strong. I don't understand how your men can be unaware of it."

It lay like a heavy breath, part scent, part taste, across his throat and nares. It was like the eve of Carnival when in the villages the first tremors of readiness rose with the eager stars. It invested the canopy, impossible to ignore but not rousing in its undifferentiated fog, allowing no one personality to reach out and beckon. Nugan, close by him, he could recognise and ignore since she was not for him a matching partner but the rest made only a "noise" in his senses.

"Poor Thomas. Fifty women!"

He said, almost prudishly, "Sexual recognition is selective, not haphazard. Thomas is safe . . . thus far."

From the edge of the canopy he saw into the interior. Tents stood in straight, soulless lines lit by brilliant globes on standards. The narrow passageways were uncluttered, void of rubbish or fittings, the streets of people to whom clear access was second nature; they had brought the ways of the ship down with them.

"I see no one."

"They have been told to stay out of sight until Captain Brookes has spoken with you. A sort of protocol, I suppose."

"That is natural." Protocol he understood, having been all his life immersed in what might and might not be done, by whom and where and when.

So suddenly as to shake his self-control to its limits he was assailed by a *rom* intense with eager readiness, a surge that cut through the female cloud in a flood biting his receptors. He turned his face quickly away from Nugan, for once resorting to camouflage for his stricken self. It was a matter only of a second before he turned back, but in the instant he had detected the source as unerringly as in the following of a silken cord, had seen the peering head of the girl who watched him from the entry of a tent thirty metres away.

Schooling his voice to a lightness he did not trust, he said, "Protocol is breached. We are observed," but his mind reeled under receptors brutally overloaded.

Nugan, following his gaze, cried out, "Really, Anne! You've been told—" The head vanished into the tent. "Our kids are hopelessly undisciplined. Our own fault, really. We let them do much as they please."

As she spoke he became aware of his erection. It would have caused no comment among his own people (perhaps a sympathetic private smile) where every man sooner or later was caught by the sudden strike of his definitive sexual mate, in the public street as like as not. But here, in a sea of unsleeping sexuality, what mores might rule? His instinct was for concealment until he knew what reactions to expect.

With his shoulder half-turned to Nugan he risked a smile that threatened to freeze the muscles of his face. "Was that the daughter you told me of? I think so. You are born again in her." Summoning words was an effort.

"Are we so alike? Others have said so. We mustn't blame her for being curious; she saw you on the screens when I began using the camera. The kids are all dying to meet the General—and to avoid Libary."

"I must not be too friendly. There has to be a parting."

It was as though a cold squall swept between them. Nugan said hurriedly, "I'll get Captain Brookes," and went off down the rows of tents.

Soldier stood stock-still under the bombardment of his senses, unable to think what the implications of this encounter might be, unable to think clearly at all. In all his controlled, sexually cool and deliberate life he had never come so powerfully under assault or been so conscious of the limits of his resistance.

He looked again. She had emerged from the tent to stand and gaze, taking in each line and aspect of him.

She took a step forward and with a leaden arm Soldier raised a warning hand as if he would push her back. She halted, wondering at him and he said, in a quiet voice that cracked with strain, "Not yet!"

He could not imagine a stranger declaration, but she understood. She raised her hands to her breasts, smiled in the fleeting fashion of a lightning strike, nodded her head slowly, and retreated into the tent.

The emanation was no less powerful with her out of sight but he could take command of his tattered wits. Yet his most urgent thought was, *In the name of all powers, I have made her a promise and she has accepted me.*

Gently the *rom* receded as Anne's excitement calmed. Soldier's body relaxed, grateful for release while it cried out for the touch of her.

A shortish, heavy man in severely cut white jacket and trousers and stiff-peaked cap came striding between the tents in a self-consciously military manner. Nugan was not with him.

With a rending effort of will Soldier tore his mind from Anne to concentrate on what he must say to this man. He knew he could not shake free of her disturbance; it was a physical thing, no more to be ignored than pain. He wished he could call out to her to put distance between them, to leave him in peace for the time needed to deal with a soldier's business. A prickle of sweat stung his forehead and his armpits ran moist; he felt like a drunkard gathering himself to stand straight.

The newcomer came to a stiff halt two metres away, swung his arm in a half circle to bring his fingers to the peak of his cap and said, "General Atkins, I am Ship-Captain Brookes."

At a loss, General Atkins bowed from the waist as the only compliment he could summon and said,

"Would it not be best if we waive formal mien and speak in simple terms? In formality my command of Late English may display deficiencies. There could be misunderstanding."

He saw little of the serviceman in Brookes. The drill-square bearing was an assumption, a memory of training long ago. Even a Catamaran Captain, commonly a cross between Forest and Desert Genetics, was capable of gruelling physical work and of leading a fighting group (piracy was a peril beyond the shallow coastal waters) but this short, overweight man could surely do neither; the uncared-for body mocked the authoritative bearing. On what ground did these lost people, innocent of Genetic selection, choose their professional leaders? Had the Last Culture been an undifferentiated human stew wherein random gobbets floated up to decision and command?

"You sound all right to me," Brookes said, the words rapid and slightly slurred after Nugan's deliberate precision and not at all the careful words of a commander dealing with a commander.

The Anne *rom*, Soldier recognised with relief, was fading. It would not flicker out entirely while she remained near but he was able to suppress his reaction. The initial chaos had been nearly unbearable; he had not believed that contact with a matching *rom* could strike with such power. He now knew something of Johnno's helplessness when his Bella called.

"Your Nugan Taylor found me pedantic, but that is the manner of speech my tutor's training has given me."

"So she told me. I'll be plain with you." Plainness seemed to reside in speaking slowly and a little too loudly, but it served.

"On this Earth of ours, Captain Brookes—" Soldier laid a faint stress on "ours" and saw that Brookes took the point, resented it, and swallowed anger; there was no body language training in him. "—we sit on the ground to confer. It is an old custom originating in the thought that seated men will not so easily come to blows as standing men." His eyes played over the close fit of the Captain's jacket. "I speak, of course, of unarmed men."

Brookes lost composure momentarily, allowed himself an embarrassed laugh, opened his jacket and slipped a short, black tube from his belt. Without looking he tossed it behind him. It disappeared in the corridor of tents.

"You're sharp-eyed, General."

"I am a soldier." He could scarcely be one without being the other.

"Which I am not. I am a mathematician and a navigational engineer."

Soldier allowed a dash of puzzlement to be seen. "I do not understand. Do your guard troops operate under a separate command?"

The question was crude and he neither expected nor required a reply in words. Brookes frowned, recognising an enquiry he should divert, cogitated rapidly and said, "We find it works well enough."

The signals of a lie were unmissable. There were no troops. He had reasoned from his first days with Nugan that this might be the case, that the ship carried only settlers, scientists, and maintenance crew. In theory, settlers looked to their own defence. He changed tack to gesture after the discarded weapon: "I trust you were not thinking that I might assault you—" Brookes shook his head, cold-eyed. "—or that it might be expedient to hold me hostage."

"It would be peculiar if that had not occurred to me."

An inexperienced tactician, thinking in terms of action rather than outcome. "There must, *must* not be hostile action on either side. Were we to provoke you, you might unleash killing powers whose existence we suspect but do not wish to face. Should you take action to harm any of us, you would find a whole world your enemy."

"Isn't it already?"

At the direct question Soldier's regard for truth hesitated. He decided on an answer which did not commit him to a lie: "The matter has been discussed on every continent and consensus achieved. The complement of *Search* is to be regarded as having the status of visiting envoys until such time as you leave. You will be treated with a consideration balanced against such consideration as you give. No one will raise a hand against you save in self-defence."

"Self-defence is easy to arrange and claim."

Soldier let the insult pass. This man was neither fighter nor diplomat; by what right or talent did he lead?

"In any case," Brookes added, "we have no thought of leaving."

"Visitors do not outstay a welcome."

"Where's the welcome?"

Soldier said quickly, "That will appear when we agree on simple requirements." He turned, walked a dozen paces away from the black canopy and in a fluid motion sat down in the dry grass, legs crossed, facing Brookes.

The Captain followed him. "Conference begins, does it?" He lowered himself cumbersomely into the unaccustomed position, leaving a man's length between them. "Now, what do you want?"

"As the Atkins's Thomas, which is the correct form of my name, I want to see what I may of an unfamiliar culture and to greet occasionally my good friend, Miss Nugan Taylor. As General of the Protective Force of the Yarra Valley I wish to liaise with you, to discover your attitudes, and to offer what information you may need."

"Also to spy out our defences."

"How else should a soldier behave?"

"There are no defences."

"So I have surmised, but you are not individually weaponless or incapable of inflicting harm."

"That's as may be."

"Your reserve is natural. We must cease to speak of weapons; violence is too easily talked into existence. Let us speak briefly of water."

"We have water."

"Quite so. You drilled a well and pumped a fine fountain into the air. I will not enquire the method of such rapid drilling and sheathing because I would not understand the answer, but I must ask the depth of the well."

Brookes studied him. "Do you want to poison it? All right, all right, but don't blame me for being suspicious. I can't give you the depth in metres but it takes from the aquifer below the level of that little river down there."

"Your hundred people use many thousands of litres each day."

"Maybe seventy, eighty thousand. It's hot weather."

"Do you know, Captain, how long it takes to replenish a depleted water table by seepage through rock and clay? Many years."

Brookes had not thought of it and felt guiltily that he should have. He said defensively, "You've got the river; you aren't short of water."

"Not yet, but the villagers of the river soon may be—and there are many villages. This is the end of the cycle of summers and the first year of a drought which may extend into a second year and possibly a third."

"Goddamned El Niño! Still operating!"

"I do not know the term but I do know that water must be conserved against the time when the rivers fall and the water for growing food must be drawn from wells fed by the aquifer which your wastage is depleting."

The vast aquifer would in fact outlast any inroads the encroachment might make, but understanding of mutual rights was essential to Soldier's planning.

Brookes was silent. Soldier decided that a basically good and fair man wavered between doing what he should or losing face by admitting wrong and taking a step back from his position of unyielding occupancy. He was not surprised when the leader accepted fault and the good man made concession.

"OK, General, I'll get the ship to supply us. There are big lakes water can be scooped out of." He made a large gesture, regaining status by asserting fresh capability: "Or we could bring you a chunk of iceberg from the Antarctic. How would that be?"

"Impressive, sir." And he was indeed impressed. "I have never seen an iceberg and our villages do not need one. There are tested systems for living through times of scarcity; they work very well so long as they are not overloaded."

He had allowed himself a touch of sharpness, sufficient for Brookes to appreciate that his casual assertion of power had been less well received than the backdown which prompted it.

"Are you telling me, General, to observe local ways and not make unwanted offers?"

"I am pointing out, sir, that we have no urgent needs. If it appears that you can do us a service, we will ask it of you and discuss proper payment."

"Puts the boot on the other foot, doesn't it? What can you pay that we might need? I can't think of anything."

"Perhaps, knowledge?"

Brookes was silent. He had been thinking in terms of trade and barter of objects while the General conducted the conference, he saw now, on his own terms.

"Captain, your ship goes to found a colony. A colony must have a past before it can have a future; it must know its roots and how it grew, in order to know its abilities. You left Earth too soon to know the end of your people's cultural errors; you need to know it so that repetition may be avoided. You find here a culture you do not understand; surely you must wish to know how such a world grew from your fallen one. This knowledge can be made available." Brookes screwed his neck to look away and up to the Library on the nearby ridge. "Your people must be eaten with desire to handle our books and find out how the Last Culture collapsed into Twilight."

Brookes made no ceremony of his acceptance. "They're dying to know and so am I. Nugan has brought us puzzles and we're almost sick with the need of answers."

"It can be arranged. There will be . . . um, policies to be followed."

"Protocol?"

"Precautions. It will be very difficult to convince Papa Melchizedech that this should be done."

"Who's he?"

"You know him as Libary. You have seen him on your picturing machines—screens? He has great influence."

"The Koori that gave Nugan a smart round of the kitchen?"

"Thank you for that interesting phrase. He has no love for you and yours; you are intruders, troublemakers, creators of problems which must be solved.

He wishes no truck with any of you. He will insist that whatever is done shall be by my contrivance." That was a loose construction of the fact but Brookes, he thought, must be impressed that General Atkins would be in full control and cognisant of all that transpired. Later he might realise it as a strategy, a holding operation while planning proceeded against him. Later.

Brookes felt that progress was being made, but— "My people will appreciate this, General, but in what coin do we pay for the privilege?"

"We do not use coinage as you conceive of it and knowledge is your hereditary right, not a product for bargaining. You will accept this access, I hope, as the hospitality due to visitors."

The navigator, mathematician, and administrator had found little need to develop the sense of timing necessary for verbal web spinning; it seemed to him that the *Search* position must be emphasised, left unambiguous. He said, too harshly, "Let me make it clear that we are not visitors. Here we are, here we stay!"

"Those are not proper words of conference," Soldier said and rose to his feet in a single movement Brookes could not emulate. He lumbered upright with a sense of playing a game outside his compass.

"For plain words," said General Atkins, "I return plainness. You are visitors, unwanted but entitled to a certain standard of forbearance. When your welcome is outstayed you will be told to go."

"And when we refuse?"

"I shall evict you."

"You? With bows and arrows or whatever you fight with?"

"Evict, Captain, not fight."

"How?"

"That will appear. You have my promise, never broken, that when I tell you to go you will become only too willing to do so. Meanwhile, I shall attend you in the morning to see what arrangements you desire. I suggest Library parties of no more than six persons in one day."

He turned his back and strode rapidly down the hill. He forgot Brookes at once. The vision of Anne, slender, beautiful even in the shapeless shirt and trousers that could not disguise youth and its power, shone across his brain. In his mind a cyclone of astonishment circled a still centre, astonishment that the logical, pragmatic defences of sexual Soldier had dissolved in a revealing instant, leaving him helpless to the storm.

On the surface rode a lesser but dazzling amazement that he had in the flash of recognition divined, surrendered, and raised his hand in conspiracy to tell her, "Not yet." And she had understood, had withdrawn in the knowledge that this was only the moment of plighting and that soon they would meet. The suddenness of the encounter had come close to unnerving him. The wash of the sexual *rom*, swelling as she saw and wanted him, had been overpowering; it seemed barely credible that these ancient people's deadened senses had no knowledge of what cried out from Earth to Heaven.

There was more to the moment than the assault of the *rom*; there was the indescribable recognition that Johnno had tried often to convey to him when he had laid his dizzy heart at the feet of Bella, and which had made only nonsense to the never-conquered Soldier, the instantaneous knowledge of acceptance and possession as union was made before the first touch of flesh.

Because he was Soldier and had been reared to be what he was, all reality did not desert him; he knew that he had fallen into a trap of impossibility: *She cannot stay and I cannot go.* But the idiot confidence of the lover cried out, *There will be a way. We are Matched!*

Nugan said to her daughter, "Now you've seen the great General, what do you think of him? A heartthrob?"

Anne had expected the question. She looked up from her book, shrugged, and was offhand. "All right if that's what you like. He looked bigger on the screen; he's not much taller than me."

She could not remember when she had last acted an elaborate lie to her mother. But he had said, "Not yet," making the lie necessary to this wholly private adventure.

Nugan could not remember either but was not altogether deceived. Nor was she much concerned; *Search*'s youngsters were in a teenage flux of crushes and sexual experiment and the new and strange must have its attraction. The excitement of strangeness would wear off as Soldier's unfailing politeness rendered him ultimately a bore; fascination would dwindle before the impenetrable.

3

NEXT MORNING, SOLDIER CONSIDERED the reflexes of his *rom*-excited body and the consequences of Nugan or any of the Searchers realising his condition. He had concealed his physical response from Nugan but he could not turn his back on people at every strike of the *rom*.

Eventually he adopted a stratagem demeaning in its crude simplicity: with a long roll of field dressing he bound his penis to his inner thigh. He had no idea what physical pain under pressure—and he expected pain—might torment him but he could think of no other disguise.

He paid his first call to Libary. Prepared for eruption, knowing he could not afford to be affectionate Thomas, he told the old man bluntly that he had promised the Searchers access to the Library crypt. He bore with the storm of anger until it threatened to become hysterical, then cut it short: "Papa Melchizedech!"

The extreme formality, tantamount to insult, set them at bay with each other.

Libary whispered, "You dare!" His instinct, Soldier saw, was to treat rebellion as the act of his teenage ward, as though intelligence and emotional attachment could never condone flouting of innate authority.

"What do I dare? I warned you that in leaving me to act alone you reduced this affair of the Searchers to a purely military operation."

The black face became a mask over thought and decision. "I spoke incautiously and you took advantage. Unworthy!"

"Only sooner than later. If you call on my ingrained duty to rid the world of these people, you must defer to my analysis and planning. I must have total trust."

"Analysis! This is not a question of rioting villagers. It is outside your experience."

"And yours. It is my advantage that I am not driven

by fear of a philosophic mysticism being exposed and questioned."

That was a challenge and perhaps unwise but Libary said quickly, "That is not your business," brushing it aside.

Soldier, whether as responsible General or surrogate son Thomas, had already decided that it must become his business once the present emergency was done with. The smell of secrecy was rank.

"My business," he said, "is to preserve social balance. Commonly that entails reconciling the Genetics but it does not exclude managing the Ordinands; the jealousies of Librarians have caused trouble enough in the past."

Libary was close to spitting at him. "Your right is recognised. Stay within it."

Libary, like most Ordinands, paid little attention to the villagers and nursed a cordial scorn for the physical activities of the army. The thought of his Library violated by strangers was to him the desecration of a shrine, and desecration was what the General proposed.

Soldier was coolly practical. "It is essential that the minds of the Searchers be totally engaged during the weeks necessary to prepare their eviction. I have suggested to them that they satisfy a natural desire to discover the circumstances of the end of their culture; the materials available here should occupy them for the time I need. There will be six each day examining the archive. To prevent friction between Ordinands and Searchers I propose to move all of you—excepting a few crypt Tabulators to assist the Searchers—to village accommodation until the encroachment is over."

Libary, trapped in his dependence on the General to effect an end he could not begin to achieve for himself, could not contain dismay. "This is their home, Thomas! This place is all their lives! You cannot simply turn them out among the common demos!"

"I can and it will do them no harm. They also are people and it may be time for them to remember it."

He was perhaps more brutal than he knew; he had only a superficial idea of how the Ordinands, and particularly the very senior Readers, thought of themselves, their dignity, and their role in the world. He did not, in fact, know what such a role might be.

Libary asked, stricken, "Must I be sent out also?"

Soldier became Thomas, and gentle. "They will need you with them; you are the focus of their work and discipline. Besides," and he smiled in an attempt to reestablish intimacy, "your temper might not survive contact with Captain Brookes. He is a coarse-grained man, neither diplomat nor intellectual—but not therefore a fool or one to face opposition placidly. I will advise the Top-Mas of the villages to receive all of you."

The dam broke. He was confronted by a black madman howling like some Dreamtime beast from the deserts of the heart. The drawn-out misery ceased only with gasping for breath, to be followed by revilement and cursing, of Thomas, of the Searchers, of the Last Culture, of the threat to everything pursued and planned through generations—

The last phrase entered Soldier's mind as through a window suddenly opened. And Libary, as if finally aware of his voice and what it told, fell silent. He threw himself on the younger man's chest to hug him and weep, but Soldier recognised camouflage; unwise revelation was to be smothered in diversion. He was to be, in that ancient word taught him by Nugan, "conned."

There was noise outside, the slap of sandals on the

walkway and a crowding of Ordinands at the doorway, alarmed by the long howling.

None of them spoke; the Librarian was not one to
be questioned until he signalled permission.

Libary lifted his head and gestured at them. "Later.
There are grave matters but later will be time
enough."

They melted away, muttering but obedient.

Libary said, "Bring soldiers, Thomas. Those out-
casts will thieve and secrete and deceive, but I'll not
have one book taken! They must be watched every
moment."

"They will be."

It was enough; Libary knew better than to insist
beyond the given word. He reverted to sentiment:
"You are most surely the result of my inept upbring-
ing. I was not a fit person to raise a boy; my mind
was too much elsewhere."

"On 'everything pursued and planned through
generations'?"

Libary pushed him petulantly away and returned
to his desk. "Have you imagined that all our study is
aimless, a piling of knowledge for sheer information's sake?"

"Until recently I had not thought about it at all.
Now I wonder do you—Ordinands, Readers, Librarians, Mas—seek, touch by touch and pressure by
pressure, to mould the whole Earth as you would
have it?"

Libary leaned back in his chair, master of himself
and assuming tranquillity. "Get about your business,
Thomas. Don't meddle." Then, to Soldier's departing
back, "And don't talk loosely about your guesswork."

"Not while it remains guesswork. But you and I,
later on . . . "

He was gone.

*   *   *

Libary dwelt in dismay on Thomas's unfinished phrase: "you and I, later on . . . " *will discuss the reasons for the existence of the Ordinands and their researches . . . ?*

His accusation of "moulding the Earth" had been, then, no bubble of irritation but the outcome of suspicion and reason. Such thinking, offered to the gabbling Genetics, lapped up by minds intrigued by gossip of their intellectual betters, argued in the lamplit homes by night, coloured and distorted by loose imaginations unable to distinguish between surmise and fantasy, batted from tongue to tongue until it tattled itself into monstrous suspicion and falsehood, should not be set loose in the communes.

Libary's mind, half raging, half aching with love, fastened on the bitch, Nugan, as the poisoner. In setting Thomas as guardian over her he had not foreseen what communication might pass from the woman's strangeness to the man's exploring, reaching mind— talk of a time when every common matter was handled in the fashion of another culture, of exotic directions of ancient thought oddly logical to a hungry brain, of social systems where empty, puff-in-the-wind terms like "liberty" and "human right" and "equal opportunity" struck home to the startled mind.

Libary anguished, Papa Melchizedech feared. Knowledge of what should be done was refused by a lifetime's proud affection. The cowardice of love needed the support of colder minds; duty was not solely the province of the soldiery.

The coded question went out from clacking semaphore arms and by morning the replies were with him: *The man must be placed in Silence.*

It was the expected, only possible judgment. But not yet . . . Thomas had said, "Later on," so let it rest until subversion was openly spoken. He would withhold the blow until no alternative remained.

* * *

Thomas was in no hurry; the black canopy would not fold up and vanish because he took his time idling down one hill and up the other. He had much to think about.

Familiar from earliest perception with the stratified society of Genetics, to the fitting of man and woman to a productive pursuit in his or her birth setting, he had not before questioned the arrangement of his world, but Nugan's questions and misunderstandings had stirred in him the possibility of other patterns.

When as a schoolboy he learned that the stratification had been in some sense designed by Wizards centuries dead, he had accepted the fact with no more than a mild contentment that someone, at some time, had devised an Earth that meshed so well. It was not a perfect Earth; there was violence in the form of piracy on the seas and raiding bands in the forests, as well as the communal tumults arising from the differences in individual needs and desires, but the disposition of work and rewards seemed satisfactory. Crime and violence were roughnesses in a society he had been trained to understand and control; his close involvement—and perhaps his pride in personal expertise—had effectively prevented him from questioning values. In its loose fashion, the world ran smoothly; why pry into its working?

Now the world was not running smoothly and his lazy microcosm, the Yarra Valley, was the focus of attention of every continent. The system—if there was indeed a system—was under challenge by three hundred people who had, in all reason, no right to exist in this time, and Libary and his peers from thousands of kils around had taken the first step towards eliminating their presence.

That step had been, for Soldier, a revelation. Like

everybody else, he had known, with the indifference of the uninvolved, that the Readers indulged in a semimystical form of communication, real or pretended, between themselves, but to the Genetics this was affectation and the subject of jokes. Now he knew that it was real and terrible. He had seen nothing that night on the roof, but what Nugan had seen and described to him had been a demonstration of power hinting at greater powers.

Libary's unwillingness to discuss it roused suspicion of manipulation; Nugan's talk of societies which despite their tragic endings had persisted through millennia, had turned his mind's eyes at last on his own.

He saw a world of small communities watched over and in some sense managed by a soldiery whose business was peace rather than violence, with both groups separated by a gap of ignorance from the Ordinands who lived reclusive lives in pursuit of excellences they kept to themselves.

In some manner this pursuit was bound up with the belief? postulate? fairy tale? called Indra's Net. And there were powers abroad that could challenge the easy satisfactions of the common man.

He, Soldier, did not think of himself as a common man. There was information among these intrusive Searchers and it could be tapped. He would get nowhere questioning Libary; he needed the penetration of the differently furnished wits from the Last Culture.

That was not all he needed.

He needed Anne, ragingly, insupportably. The thought of her quickened his pace.

He began to stumble and sweat as his approach to the canopy drove other thought out of reach. He was forced to stop, cool down, take hold of common sense while brain and body vied for command.

When he stood waiting to be noticed he was again a man carrying out courteous duties with a calm face covering physical pain that could not be stilled.

Brookes came quickly, not in uniform but in loose shirt and shorts and looking, in Soldier's fastidious vision, shabby and loutish, unlike a commander of men. Round, bare arms accentuated his tubbiness to the point whereat Soldier wondered whether or not he dealt with a sick man. Superfluous weight was a rare condition among the Genetics, usually a metabolic problem and viewed askance by the Mas guarding genealogy; Brookes would never gain breeding approval. It was hard to credit that this shambles of a man, aged apparently in his thirties, was a preserve of more than twice soldier's own years.

What Brookes saw was a slender man of middle height, deeply tanned. The light bones and deep chest belonged to a distance runner carrying perhaps a little more muscle than a trainer would wish to see, while the narrow face contained a suggestion of the Koori flared nostrils and wide mouth present in Nugan Taylor. The erect carriage belonged to the soldier Brookes could never be; the extraordinarily impassive face, breaking just now and then into a flash of feeling as though a window rapidly opened and closed, suggested someone a chromosome or two removed from Brookes's own humanity.

Standing at the canopy's edge, Brookes saw a glider slip through the valley between this hill and the Library ridge, catch an updraft, and begin to circle lazily towards him. At the same moment another came from the rear, over the canopy, moving to meet the first. As their courses converged the pilots waved to each other and passed on.

He stepped into the sunlight, shading his eyes to

watch after them and calling to Soldier, "What are they up to? They're over here a dozen times a day."

"Five times a day, Captain. Aerial reconnaissance is necessary for oversight of a very large region. Twenty gliders are in the air at all times and this hill is a crossing point of one flight pattern. It is routine."

True; it had become routine the day the Searchers landed.

"They must be highly skilled. Well, come inside and meet my Intelligence group." As Soldier hesitated he said, "Not thinking we'll hold you captive or some such, are you?"

"No; that would gain you nothing. I am surprised that you have decided so quickly to trust me in your—" for "encroachment" he substituted a diplomatic "—area."

Brookes laughed (a social ploy, Soldier decided, with no amusement in it) and said, "I trust you as far as I could throw you—not far—but fair's fair. We go into your place, you come into ours."

A smile was required; Soldier produced it and walked under the canopy—and halted. As he moved under the black edge a mild tingling had flicked his skin when he crossed the boundary between hot sun and cool shade. He had expected fans, or the enclosure would have been oven hot, but the air was as still as in a room, and gently cool. Curious, he took the pace back into sunlight and again into shade, feeling the tingling each time. He looked enquiringly at Brookes.

"It's a static curtain, General; it behaves like a wall holding out air and heat. I'd have to think a while to explain it in terms you'd . . . er, be familiar with."

Soldier nodded, satisfied that if his people with ingenuity and effort air-conditioned the Library, these technological superiors should manage as much with less display. He could appreciate their miracles; he did not have to be overwhelmed by them.

Brookes led the way under glowing lights. The few men and women in the "streets" stared at Soldier with none of the polite concealment a villager would have pretended. Fascinated, he surveyed them as openly.

He had never seen such a mixed collection of humanity or imagined that so varied a group could exist. It was as though each formed his or her own Genetic and no one guided their breeding. Tall, short, thin, fat, muscular, spindly, dark-haired, blonde, clear-skinned, strangely olive-skinned, and a few as brown-dark as himself—this, he imagined was a microcosm of the Last Culture and the image of its ungovernable failure. Add to it the lack of a controlled sexual pattern and the whole of their history seemed explicable as an undisciplined descent into ruin. (Yet, he reminded himself, they had risen from barbarism to the stars. Much remained to be understood).

The *rom* of the women was strong, there being so many of them, but he detected no distinctive presence of Anne. She was not nearby, or not in arousal, or he would have located her with point precision. For the moment that was as well; he could not afford distraction.

They came, he reckoned, close to the heart of the canopied area, to a cleared space fifty metres across with at its centre, a cluster of thin pipes rising from a circular metal housing and arching overhead to feed the tents. A faint, regular sound identified this as their pump and well.

Brookes interpreted his interest. "We're still pumping water but the ship will begin supplying us tomorrow."

It was a proper moment for a pretence of generosity. "Continue to use the well, Captain. I exaggerated the possibility of drought. It was a test of your willingness to confer reasonably."

Brookes muttered like a suppressed explosion, "You have your damned little ways, don't you! I prefer straight dealing."

Soldier thought this was probably true; Brookes, like Nugan, was incapable of a concealed deviousness and all the Searchers might be the same.

He offered the smile of a friendly man suspending cross-play in the interest of cooperation. "We have tested each other and ended with truth. We can speak openly." Brookes had tested nothing, but no matter.

The Captain muttered that he hoped so and led the way around the wellhead to six male Searchers who, in various states of near undress, waited on small stools. Soldier was unsure whether or not the universal lack of smart dress implied a slight, a statement that they thought him of no account, but decided to bury reaction until he knew their habits better. His own shorts were immaculate and freshly pressed.

The six were as physically varied as six separate Genetics; they were alike only in their appearance of being all within a few years of the same age and reasonably coeval with himself. That he knew better was more disturbing than any spectacle of wonders.

Brookes named them in order and each stood to extend a hand. As the first offered, Soldier made his natural move to lay the palm of his hand on the other's forearm, remembered at the last moment that Nugan had told him at some time of the clasped-hands greeting, and fumbled it with limp fingers and a touch of surprise at feeling his hand firmly squeezed.

Ceremony done, Brookes told him that these were the six who would visit the Library on the following day.

Six men and no women? Muscular differences between the sexes were, he had noticed, more marked than among his own people. So—an all-male squad to test the ambience in case of physical disturbance and encounter? He could guarantee there would be none.

He said, "Captain Brookes, you see that I carry no weapon and no notepad. Could you supply me with a written list of your men's names? In case of problems—say, of communication—I must know to whom to refer."

Brookes produced a small pad and a short, black stick like a slate pencil. "You might like to write them yourself. I bet you won't spell them as we do."

That was certain; some surnames in the Library's books had defeated his attempts at pronunciation and his spelling would be phonetic. The peculiar writing stick was a quarter of a centimetre thick, tapered to a point at each end and seemed to be a solid light metal. It left a clear, soft black mark on the paper.

He wrote down the names as the owners spoke them and handed pad and writing stick back to Brookes, who said, "Keep the stylus. It will last your lifetime and your children's."

Tempted, he turned the thing in his fingers. "It is a curio. I would like to keep it, but the consensus of the world is against acceptance of your technology. I return it with regret."

Brookes took it back. "Then you're refusing much that could be good for you. What time tomorrow?"

"I will meet your men outside here at sunrise, Captain. An hour's travel each way, perhaps a little more, will still leave time to make the most of a long summer day."

A very blonde man (he glanced at the list . . . Sargesson) spoke. "We're going to need more than six on the job. Nugan Taylor says there's millions of books not even sorted yet."

"True, but let us move slowly. You will be working with Tabulators—trained cataloguers—who speak a little Late English and may be of assistance. That will depend on relations between yourselves and them. If there is no friction, then we shall see."

"Friction?" That was Brookes.

"It is possible, though the Ordinands will be instructed to engage in no argument without reference to my Lieutenant-General, who will be present. Please remember that your encroachment is unwelcome and that very simple misunderstandings could fire resentments—on either side."

Sargesson persisted, "That's understood; we aren't stupid. Still, we'd like one extra with us tomorrow. Not a researcher, but for liaison."

"With Captain Brookes?"

"If need be, but actually with our own library computer system. It's no good us turning over loads of stuff that looks promising and finding that half of it's already in our data banks. Besides, if we find something interesting that our computers don't know about, they can check relevant subject holdings and suggest the sort of related stuff we should try to locate."

"The machines can do that?"

"Sure; that's what they're for. The important thing is for us to keep information going back to our library so no time is wasted. For that we need someone to do nothing but keep contact and pass messages."

"One of you—"

"We don't want to waste researchers. We've got someone does odd jobs for Data Section and would be useful there. Very fast and accurate."

To be rigid or to be amenable? "This man would

communicate as Nugan did, with the chip at her nostril?"

"That's right, but she's a girl."

"Girl" he had said, not "woman," and there were only ten youngsters among their three Wakings. He signed to Brookes for pencil and pad. "Her name?"

"Anne Taylor. You know her mother."

For a blistering moment it was as though she was all around him, conjured by the speaking of her name. Sure that face and body betrayed him, he stared at the ground between his feet.

He said shortly, "Bring her. But no others."

He listened to questions and comments and gave mechanical answers while his heart cried out that his intelligent Anne had moved while he still pondered opportunity.

4

IN THE MORNING HE DID NOT GO TO THE encroachment to lead the Library party. He could not face the prospect of guiding them along the hill paths with the *rom*, the cloud of her close and urgent and he in agony in the presence of all of them. He sent his second-in-command with a scribbled note excusing himself on the ground of other duty. Even that essential untruth offended the sense of honesty encouraged from childhood.

He told the Stathos's Allie, his 2i/c what was to be done. "Send eight troopers direct to the Library. I'll be with them by the time you get the Searchers there.''

Allie was efficient, also older than his General, avuncular and companionable. "Thomas, you've the reek of a marriage bed. Get your mind off her. She'll keep another night."

Soldier did not attempt to hide body truth from a reader whose adeptness matched his own. "Is it so bad?"

"Reeking at twenty paces! May I ask who?"

"No, Allie. Not yet."

"She is not being kind? You want but she does not match? Never mind, Thomas, there's Carnival in forty days."

Carnival freedoms did not apply. Nothing rational applied. Yet Anne had indicated opportunity by contriving her attachment to the party and it was for him to act. His urgency could not be stemmed for thirty days.

He began to speak of training programmes, of special gunpowder pouches to be manufactured, of glider troops accustoming themselves to the different draught patterns of night patrolling.

Allie left after ten minutes, satisfied that his General's reek was damped down against the mocking indecencies of his troops.

Soldier saw him out of sight before he started for the same hill, to a point lower on the slope and hidden from the canopy's unsleeping artificial eyes, where the first axes were already ringing in the sunrise. He needed to unburden himself; he needed Johnno. There was little the two did not know about each other.

He jogged gently across the broad spur that carried most of the plantation, following the top line of trees. The Forest axemen were fifty metres lower down, where they would not catch the reek he could not

entirely suppress save when urgent matters engaged
his mind. Coming to a halt, he funnelled his hands
round his mouth and gave the identifying two-note
cooee which Johnno would recognise and answer if
he were within a mile or so.

He was much closer. The answer came at once and
the man a minute after it.

"Haven't seen you in a week, Tommy. And heigh,
but you reek! Who's got you by the balls?" He set his
heavy frame on a grass tussock, wiped sweat from his
eyes, and waited for confession.

What he heard sent him off in a convulsion of
laughter. "A bloody marvel! Tough Thomas, the root-
and-run Carnival soldier, taken for slaughter by a girl
dropped out of the sky! This will rock the beerhouses
for a week."

"It had better not."

Johnno required considerable convincing that the
situation was more serious than anyone was likely to
realise without knowledge of each group's sexual biology, and that the intricacies of loyalties and responsibilities were potentially explosive. It did not
occur to him, any more than it could occur to Soldier,
that the man should take himself elsewhere and wait
out his torment at a distance. That course was not
available in a system of biological imperative; when
man and woman responded to each other the sequel
was inevitable, the cord between them more binding
than law, pledge or custom. Even communities in
mutual hostility would not think to hinder a mating
once the receptors had been overwhelmed and the
silent bond demonstrated.

The oral romances handed down in village gath-
erings had never postulated a barrier between lovers;
the notion was inconceivable. Yet here, in cold fact,
it existed.

Johnno, presented with a knot of impossibility,

was loyal but dumbfounded. Tommy must have his Anne but Tommy could not have his Anne. Johnno's competent brain was not geared to the resolution of paradox.

"You can't help," Soldier told him. "I just needed to explain it to you, to anyone. And to myself."

"Do you think the Searchers might kill you?"

"I don't know what their response might be." Johnno grimaced at the thought of weapons that shone and burned. "Worse," said Soldier, "they might harm Anne. We are not the same people with the same feelings."

He kept to himself the not unimaginable possibility that they might make of Anne a bait, a lure, a reward for his agreement not to pursue action against them. Such a conflict of loyalty and ungovernable need was beyond his ability to picture.

Johnno asked, "Can we fight them?"

"On their terms, no. That's why the ousting will be something new in the warfare of this age. There will be only one blow, ours, the last."

"Tommy, I can't help. If I could, I would."

"We'll see what comes of it when she and I meet."

The sexual imperative ruled out any possibility of matched lovers not meeting. The two men were preoccupied only with the dark unknown of consequences.

As he left Johnno, he looked across the saddle to see Allie's troopers climbing the approach to the drawbridge. The Searcher group, slower moving, would be still among the trees above the river.

At the drawbridge he briefed the troopers. They carried only cords and batons, which he ordered them to discard. "Manual arts will be sufficient to deal with Ordinands and Searchers and even those should not be necessary. You will report any friction between the two groups. You will intervene only in case of physical conflict and then deal no hurt, not so much as an open-handed slap, unless you are attacked with a weapon. There must be no cause for complaint by either party." He smiled at a sudden conceit. "Who knows but that you might be assaulting your great-grandfather many times removed."

It was a poor joke but it made his point as well as any amount of warning. It got the expected polite grin.

He entered the Library with the troopers; the vast interior, quiet at any time, echoed with emptiness.

The Tabulators waited at the crypt stairhead, impassive over surly resentment. They would behave as he bade them, fearing him a little and the absent Papa Melchizedech much more. He had only a general instruction for them: To give what assistance the Searchers required, with little idea of what that might be. They asked no questions and bore impatiently with his temporary authority; they did not think highly of the violent, materialistic soldiery.

He took a folding chair from the nearest room and returned to the drawbridge to wait for the Searcher party. They came soon, climbing raggedly; twenty-eight waking years of level sameness had robbed them of balance reflexes. They were clothed from head to toe against the sun and, he thought, probably sweating like horses. Nugan's explanation of skin cancers (probably the rare "skin evil") had meant little to him. The Stathos's Allie led, with blonde Sargesson striding beside him and straining not to seem close to exhaustion. The others were strung out behind—and the *rom* of Anne was unmistakable though faint.

Allie halted in front of his General and with a flicker of eyes and lips silently commented on the physical condition of his charges. Sargesson stumbled into the shade of the wall, dragged off his wide-brimmed hat, wiped his face and said, "Holy Jesus!" which Soldier had never heard as an epithet; there was more to Late English than the suave idioms of literature. The others grouped in shade on the drawbridge.

Anne came last, obviously blown but in better case than some of the men; youth, more volatile than its elders, had stood her in some stead. Intent on shade and relaxation, she did not at once see him.

Soldier observed her for the first time at near touching range. In his eyes she was tall for a woman; the men were taller and heavier than himself but not as strongly or as usefully made as any of the Genetics. Anne had her mother's expression but little of the colour of the Koori heritage; another strain had entered but she was still plainly Nugan's daughter. Nor did she share Nugan's slightly blocky robustness; she was slender, as a soldier's wife should be to carry on the Genetic. Her hair was a red-tinted light brown, exotic in his eyes because vanishingly rare in his time.

With careful control of face and body, and despite the immediate straining at his crotch, he stood up as she came by him, her hat pushed back and caught by a ribbon at her throat, framing her extraordinary hair. He put out a hand to take her elbow and at last she saw him. Her green-grey eyes widened, her lips parted in a smile and instantly the mating aura rose, defying weariness, and struck his vulnerability like a physical blow. This was the muted lure of a tired woman but for a moment he was scattered into the pieces of a man. His groin ached.

Not daring to return her smile for fear it would cry out his helplessness to the world, he drew her gently aside and said out of a dry throat, "Would you like . . . to be seated . . . for a while?"

Her smile broadened into the ghost of a laugh, both surprised and subtly conniving. "A gentleman! Mother says they're a dead breed." She dropped into the chair and laughed up at him. "You're Thomas. I've seen you on our screens."

He had to lick his lips to make his mouth speak. "And you are the Taylor's Anne, as your mother told me."

"Didn't I hear her! She was wild with me because I shouldn't have been there." Again she laughed as though this was all matter for amusement, but her sexual awareness was strong.

He could think of nothing to say and could stand no more of a closeness wherein he dared make no overt move. "I have duties. Please excuse me."

He went into the Library and round a corner, out of sight, to lean against a wall and draw deep breaths to settle body and mind. He beat his brain against a paradox: That her body said one thing and her voice another, and all his skill could not reconcile the two messages or understand how both might be genuine. Her *rom*, while not at its most powerful, was openly welcoming, yet her words were light commonplaces, offering nothing. With two people of the Genetics sexually "matched" there was no question of anything but fulfilment and those who witnessed the Matching—which happened often enough in public places—laughed and offered congratulations; it was not physically or psychologically possible for the pair to dissemble.

Yet for three days he had dissembled under the eyes of the Searchers because he could not let them discover the attachment until he knew what their reaction would be. So he had discovered that dissimulation was possible when the necessity was strong enough. Among the Genetics this was unknown because unnecessary; everyone within sensing nearness was aware of a Matching.

But—among these people of dulled, inoperative receptors, other manners and other procedures must apply. (In the name of the Net, how did their pairings ever find each other?) Certain sexual obscurities in the few of their puzzling novels that he had read began to unravel. He would have to behave with rigorous propriety (in their sense of the word) and it would be difficult.

How, then, could they two ever . . . ?

He returned outside to see if the Searchers were ready to enter the Library, while his mind and body wrestled intractably. It was a relief to see them vanish into the crypt. Only a faint residue of Anne hovered a while before dispersing in the draughts of the conditioners.

He went to the roof where the semaphore arms hung still and silent and Libary's telescope had that morning been removed for hiding away, and leaned on the parapet, gazing down to the black canopy where Nugan was, Nugan who could explain. But would she understand? Would that single friendly passage with her form an extra bond in his joining with her daughter, or would some undreamed of social complication turn her from friend to enemy?

He had been there for an hour, brooding rather than thinking, when Anne's aura rose close by.

She was at the top of the stairs and running towards him, *rom* swelling with every step. (Why, a part of him questioned, did it grow stronger when she was looking at him?) He thought she would throw herself into his arms but she stopped beyond his reach.

"I've been looking everywhere for you. I pretended I wanted to use the closet. I can't stay."

So she, too, recognised barriers to be overcome. He

was speechless, not knowing what gesture was required of him.

Anne looked rapidly round as if afraid they might be overheard and said, "You want me, don't you? I can see that you do!"

He nodded dumbly, his groin on fire.

"From our tents I can hear the axes down the hill. Can we meet there?"

He nodded again and heard his tongue utter a meaningless sound.

She said, "Wait for me there after dark. Not tonight because I have to think how. One night soon, very soon."

There was no mistaking her sincerity. The thrust of her head, the clasping of her hands, the haste of her words argued against dissembling.

He muttered, "I will wait. Every night."

She took three rapid paces, lifted her face and, like the fluttering of a moth, kissed his lips and was gone.

He did not see her again until the party gathered an hour before sundown to return to the encroachment. Sargesson, who seemed to be the leader, pronounced the Library a find, a cornucopia, a treasure house, a bottomless mine; already they had leads to much that had taken place after they left Earth and their computers were baying leads like hunting hounds. Their day had passed like a couple of hours, the Tabulators had been tirelessly useful and the whole project was a historian's ecstasy! He grabbed Soldier's hand and shook it violently—apparently a mark of endless approval—and led his band down the hill.

Anne, deliberately leaving herself last in the departing line, said with an unbelievable chasteness, "Good afternoon, General Thomas," and winked at him like a mischief-making brat.

He made no emotional sense of her behaviour, could only wait and hope.

5

ON THE FIRST NIGHT HE PATROLLED THE
tree line like a distracted animal, knowing that she
would not come yet hoping that in a miracle gift she
might. The hours dragged through an endless sexual
ache. He had never heard of the pain of uncertainty
once a Match occurred because he knew of no one
who had ever suffered it; he conceived his suffering
to be unique.

On the second night he slept a little, in moments
and often on his dragging feet, in sheer psychic exhaustion.

On the third night she came to him, and not an
hour too soon. His first lovemaking frightened her
with its violence until his intensity passed into her
also, heating and brightening her sense of adventure
in sallying from the cover of the canopy. What had
begun as an escapade became an experience drown-
ing her young fantasising in the reality of hungry
flesh.

When the encounter was exhausted and they lay
together on the soft mattress he had provided in a
bower of rustling shrubbery, she was frightened again
at a strength of desire she had not encountered before, and at an understanding, creeping slowly into
her, that he conceived of no going back from what
had begun.

Her sexual experience had opened in fumblings with the three teenage boys on the ship and graduated in two fly-by-night encounters with older men. Her desire for Soldier had been, in her thinking, just such another uprush of sex to be taken daringly on the run. The touch of the exotic had had its place in her desire for him, that and a simple pleasure, scarcely admitted to herself, in establishing a liaison that would raise the hackles of her elders and the admiration of her more cautious peers. She had intended a scalp-taking, a flirtation, certainly not a love affair, and she had fallen into an entanglement from which escape might come only with a severing cruelty.

She was not sure, yet, that she wanted escape. At any rate, not immediately. He would simmer down . . . He could not sustain such passion.

Other discoveries were taking place.

In one of them, Sargesson and his group had collated the results of three days of plundering the information lying fallow in the Library. At first they had dredged excitedly among the books, using hand-held microcopiers to transfer each one, page by page, to chips for entry into the computers. On the second morning they had found the cache of cassettes, tapes, wires, chips, and molecular blocks that had lain for centuries in sealed cases because the technology for reading them no longer existed. *Search* had beamed down battery-operated machines for playback and the hunt for history had begun in earnest.

The computers had ingested, conflated, and inserted the new facts into the gaps and loose ends of their own data, then sorted, rearranged and refined the mix into intelligible continua of history.

The beginning of an outline formed, of how the Last Culture had died and the new world risen from ruin. Quickly there was a basis on which to work.

In the Intelligence tent Sargesson had his first small audience of Brookes and Duval.

"You wouldn't believe!" he said, though his listeners were prepared to believe absolutely. "Can you imagine what six million books looks like, floor to ceiling the length and breadth of the building? And under that crypt there's basements full of stuff they haven't got round to sorting yet! That's where we found the recordings. The Ords didn't know what they were and didn't want them touched, but the General shut them up, quicksmart. He has some idea of what recording is about, seems he's read of it, and he said we were to have them. They didn't like it but they didn't argue, either; he says and they do. So Anne buzzed the ship for vocos and scribers and down they came. That was yesterday. We copied the stuff and fed the lot back to the main *Search* computer with an instruction of what we were after and back it came this morning."

Duval said, "For Christ's sake get on with it, Sargie. What have you got?"

"You wouldn't believe, I tell you!" Sargesson meant to have his moment. "Can you guess where this panpipes-in-Arcadia culture began?" Brookes sighed and Duval grunted threats under his breath. "Will you believe me if I tell you it all began with the building of *Search*?"

Brookes threw up his hands. "I promise to believe black's white if you'll only get on with saying so."

"All right, then: Remember back to 2095. *Kiev* was on its way with the Russian Orthodox Church singing hosannas and patting itself on the back and the Anglo Bloc trying to pretend it didn't care. Then that Holy Science of Human Destiny sect lifted up its Christian head and started howling that *Kiev* was a moral polluter and that the True Faith should be launched into heaven. That started the resurgence of religious cult-ing among the proles, and eventually the *Search* project arose out of all their noisemaking. It got so big that the Anglo Bloc took it over, eased out the psalmsingers and put in its own trained people—us."

Duval growled, "When do you get to the stuff we don't know?"

"Right now, but you have to see it whole. The Holy Science sect was genuine—up to a point, anyway—because at its core was a group of real scientists—mostly biologists and geneticists—dedicating their work to God. When *Search* was taken out of their hands, they started up a new line based on population and conservation: Mankind must reshape itself or perish. A hundred years of trying hadn't settled those problems but the Holy Scientists had some ideas about it—but not the sort of ideas you could let loose on the public—and we were in the sky before their ideas started to leak to the poor bastards who were going to be phased out. What they had was a big following of poverty-stricken proles who supported them with their widow's mites and barrel scrapings. They established laboratory-temple complexes all over the Anglo Bloc."

He paused expectantly and Brookes obliged. "I'd almost forgotten them. I never thought the Aitch Essess would come to anything. They were headed by that mad Brit playing New Jesus with his Wishart Futurist Complexes."

"That's right, sir—the General's Wizards."

Anne lay cradled in a bowl of stars and the sharp scents of the Australian bush, cradled too in excitement and surprise and triumph, all of it riding on an undertow of apprehension that a simple adventure had mutated into a tangle she could not grasp. The violence of Thomas's orgasm had at first stunned her, then carried her with him in a response that relegated her hole-in-corner shipboard experiences to memories of childhood. Her first reaction had been a blind startlement that maleness was a force beyond anything she had heard or dreamed of; she knew with unshakable certainty that no man in all the company of *Search* could have performed such a spasming eruption or roused her so utterly to answer his need and passion.

When at last he had relaxed into her arms she had stared into the night as she rocked and soothed him, with a feeling that defied all precedent in her limited knowledge: that once the moment of dominance was over, the man who had taken her with a ferocity of sexual power was all at once in her power, as a child to a mother, to shape and manage as she pleased.

She had seen and heard all the information Nugan had relayed to the ship and had thought, with the rest of them, that the gender relationships of this new Earth were curious, even barbaric in their implications. Now she saw that the dominance of the females was a reality, that the weapon of sex, far from being the possession only of fabulous Helens and Cleopatras, was here the strength of every woman. The male had the physique, the female the deciding power, so that two who "fitted" each other might indeed fuse into that "one personality" of the curdled romances of Old Earth. But she had no further idea of what she should expect of him or he of her.

She would have to learn.

She knew there would be Searcher trouble over this escapade (though the idea of "escapade" had become drowned in the torrent of fulfilment) but there was little even the Ship-Captain could do beyond frown and lecture. That was of little consequence. She had thrown her cap over the Moon and it had fallen back to her in the shape of copper gold Thomas who would never let her break away from him. Even when, in time, she wished to break away. There could be other long nights of learning and achieving—and even her mother had better get used to the idea.

In her arms Thomas stirred and said, "I am happy that you did not come to me virgin."

Her thinking hesitated while she construed his syntax. "What a funny thing to say." He had spoken so seriously, as if it mattered.

He raised his head to see her closely in the starlight. "Funny? It amuses you?"

She answered hurriedly, "I meant funny-peculiar."

There was a pause while he made sense of the loose expression. "It is not peculiar. Two seeking marriage should not come together in sexual ignorance."

She cried on a rising, incredulous note, "Marriage!"

Soldier read what he heard, what his hands felt of the uncontrolled reaction of her body, what his eyes made of her face in the glimmer of stars—and saw himself a puppet tumbling in an unimaginable pit with no possibility of rescue. He was indissolubly bound by his inbred imperative to one who, he saw with dread, was totally free, unbound by the Match and what it entailed, and with no conception of his engulfing emotional plight.

With a prescience of horror to come he saw, too, that between himself and Anne stretched more than a gap of centuries: they were alien species. He was trapped by the gene-magic of the Wizards.

Sargesson was enjoying his audience, winding up to his next spellbinding instalment, when Nugan Taylor put her head through the tent flap.

"Am I interrupting something? I'm looking for

Anne. I thought you might have her working here and I was going to bite a piece out of you."

Duval shook his head. "Haven't seen her since the Library crew came back. We aren't slave drivers, Nugan."

"So where the hell? It's going on eleven and she needs sleep if she's to do another shift with you tomorrow."

Sargesson saw that as a jest. "Goddlemighty, Nugan, she's got twice the bounce of any of the men. She'll be holding us up when we all fall down with the wearies."

"Just the same—"

"Just the same. sweetheart, spare a moment for what I'm telling here, and see how it ties in with what soldierboy and the old black bastard said to you."

She could not very well refuse a research request. She perched on the end of a bench and said, "All right, but make it quick."

"We know who the Wizards were—a religio-scientific bunch rising out of the Holy Science sect who kicked off the building of *Search*. They centered on a group of very classy gene topologists and molecular surgeons called the Wishart Futuristic Complex. Wizards, see?"

"Go on."

"Well, now, they started up a line of come-all-ye-faithful patter at a time when it seemed the gutter populations were ready to grab at anything that offered a glimmer of hope. More like romance really. Their message added up to: We've buggered our world and the nations can't even get together to talk sense about it; they're all at each other's throats and humanity is on its way out; so let's go out heads-up and proud—but leave a better race to take over when we've gone! And the starved proles gulped it down and got themselves a crusade. God and the Wisharts for sacrifice—or some such. Maybe Wisharts caught the mob when hysteria made self-immolation seem a fine finish, with the saving grace of leaving the world to a worthier folk. And Wishart Futurist, spreading its laboratories round the world, was going to produce the worthier folk. Make sense?"

"No, but something happened and it may as well have been this."

"The computers pieced this together from material in the Library but here they get a mite tentative. There's an ocean of stuff to look at still; we'll fill in the gaps as we find the filling. It seems that what the Wizards—call 'em that—had in mind was the creation of new human strains adapted to various kinds of country and climate, using native races as models and building special gene-lines into them to keep them at one with the land. Wasn't that what your Aborigines were on about? The-land-is-our-mother-and-we-live-in-harmony-with-her?"

"It wasn't a joke, it was bloody good sense."

"All right, all right; I grovel! The idea was to use well-adapted races like your Aboriginals, the Inuit, the American Indians, the Arabs, the Tamils, the black Congolese to form genetic groups adapted to forests or deserts or tropic islands or jungles or mountains or steppes or what have you—to do some gene manipulation on fairly large groups that showed the proper physical characteristics and get them to breed pure. And that's as far as we've got at the moment, but it fits with your information, doesn't it?"

Before she could answer, a duty messenger from the Surveillance Unit put her head through the tent entrance. "Mister Duval!"

Sargesson waved a hand at her. "Wait a minute. So that ties in with the tale of how the Forest and Desert Genetics came to be. Agree?"

Nugan said, "Of course it does," while the messenger spoke over her, "This is urgent, sir. Somebody has blinded two of the IF cameras by hanging coats over the lenses."

Duval snapped, "How long since?"

The woman swallowed nervously. "We're not exactly sure, sir."

Duval became dangerous. "Do you mean that nobody was checking the screens for movement?" The woman was silent and uneasy. "Your fault, was it? Were you the watch detail?"

"No, sir." She fumbled for words. "I think it was just that there hasn't been any movement, night after night . . . "

"And so there never bloody well would be! What have you got there?"

"The coats, sir. From the cameras. You'll want to check who they belong to."

Nugan stood, shaking and furious. "They're Anne's. She's gone out!"

Brookes asked calmly, "Where would she go, Nugan?"

"I don't know where but I can guess who to! I'll skin her alive—and him with her!"

"But who—who would be out there?"

She screamed at him, "The goddamned Thomas! Who else? I knew . . . I could tell . . . "

"Tell what?"

She sat down again, hard, swallowing rage as implications rose to appal her. She said, with the care of one treading thorns, "She saw him on the ship's screens. She asked about him because he's so different from the *Search* men. Then they saw each other when he came here to the tents. I twitted her about it and she passed it off, but I knew she was interested."

Brookes asked, "How did you know?"

"If you'd ever fathered a child, you wouldn't ask.

You know the shifts of their minds, and believe me all kids are shifty. You know when they're hiding things and I guessed she was having a teen crush on Thomas. That would pass, but it was him I didn't think about, that he'd know at once if she was attracted to him."

"How?"

"Pheromones. Haven't you studied my chips?"

He was taken aback. "I don't follow. Our people don't propagate those things."

Sargesson told him, "Yes, we do, sir. We don't notice, except subliminally, because our receptors have become recessive with lack of use in cheek-by-jowl settlements. These Genetic people smell us—I suppose that's the word—as easily as their own kind. They live in a much sharper sensory world."

Brookes had paid only passing attention to the sexual changes on Earth—interesting, good for a twist on some ancient jokes—but he was not slow now to see the snare. "If she was attracted, he'd know it!"

"Infallibly."

"And would take advantage of it?"

Nugan interrupted, "Only if he was interested or in need. Their idea of promiscuity is different from ours." Calmer now, she was thinking rapidly.

"So her slipping away by night may be just a teen-ager's adventure that could come to nothing?"

Sargesson objected that eighteen was pretty old for teenage adventuring. "Ten- and twelve-year-olds do that sort of thing when they're trying to assert themselves, to form their individuality."

"And when," Nugan asked him, "did any of our kids get a chance to assert anything more than a tantrum? They've grown up in what any psychologist would call a totally constrictive system with scarcely room to move, let alone think for themselves. We chose our life; they had it thrust on them. The urge to an act of free will must be stifling them."

Search people, with eyes on the stars, had forgotten growing up.

Duval was bemused. "It must have taken some courage, going out there alone."

Nugan mocked him. "More than you guess. Who else has poked a nose down the hill save with Thomas's permission?"

"We're taking it quietly until we establish some sort of relationship."

"That's one way of putting it. I say we can't stop huddling between walls after the walls have been removed."

Brookes came in smartly, "Don't bicker! We'll light up the hill and send out search parties to bring her back."

"No!" Nugan's thinking was ahead of his. "They won't find her if Thomas chooses to hide her. If she comes home during the night, well and good, and I'll deal with it as a parent and child affair. If not, I'll talk to Thomas in the morning."

"He won't show his face."

"He will. He'll be at the Library, supervising his responsibilities. He has a fanatical sense of duty; his life is governed by duty and receptors."

Her anger had ebbed, given way to hard-faced determination. Brookes had a different area of worry. "You don't think she is liable to come to harm?"

"With Thomas, no. And who else would she go to? She knows nobody else."

"I was thinking in terms of hostage taking."

She was almost contemptuous with her people who would not see the facts of their position. "What would they gain? They don't want bargains; they want us out."

Brookes inclined to ask, So why this Library permission? but said instead, "I can't accept such impulsiveness. She's almost adult."

Nugan laughed shortly, sharply. "She isn't. None of the kids are. What chance have they had to be young or anything else but hemmed in?"

Then at last she wept in worry and helpless guilt.

After the days of stress and waking, sleep crept over Soldier, dimming his vision of Anne's starlit face. "I am a soldier, lovely Anne, and have duties tomorrow." He cupped her chin in his palm, leaning close for the kiss. "I must sleep."

"Me too; I'll be a mess in the morning. But what does a General do all day?"

He roused himself. "Physically, little. I say to one, Go, and he goeth, and to another, Come, and he cometh."

"That sounds familiar."

"I quote one of your books of superstition. Matthew's book, I think."

She wanted to ask, Don't you believe in God? but thought better of it and found herself wondering how strong her own belief might be. There were times when "God" seemed a superstition, like unlucky thirteen or knives crossed on the mess table.

Soldier said, "My friend, Johnno, will bring food in the dawn."

"He's the big, strong one, isn't he? Mother sent up pictures of him."

"Yes. He will look after you through the day."

Anne wriggled free of his arm. "Oh, no, you don't understand. I go to work too, like you. I agreed to work in the crypt for ten days."

Duty and promises he understood and applauded, and that she should be a willing worker was what any man would approve in his woman, but here there could be complications outside his experience. "But surely they will know that you have been away from the tents. Will there not be—" He hesitated between "anger" and "punishment" and "retribution," recognised the limits of his knowledge and substituted, "—unpleasantness?"

"They won't like it. Old Brookes will pup."

"He will punish you?"

"Oh, Thomas, for what? There's no rule against leaving the tents or talking to Earth people or even sleeping with one. There are practically no rules because nobody knows what rules to make. They all stay in the tents because in their hearts they are afraid of the world they don't recognise as the one they left. Perhaps they'll come out now. Perhaps they just needed someone to show the way. I may have done some good."

He thought of Searcher parties descending on the village, noisy and gaping and offended by turned backs. It would happen, sooner or later.

"Mother will be the worst. She'll be furious. She won't worry about rules; if she wants to punish she'll make her own."

He said formally, "I am sure that Nugan is a good mother."

"Of course she is but she thinks I'm still a baby. Part of coming here was just to show her I'm grown up." Soldier was silent and she kissed him quickly. "Only a part, though; the big part was you."

The events of the night settled in her mind to make this retrospectively true; he loomed larger now in her thought than the exotic on-screen Thomas-image which had been the initial reason—attraction? urge? excuse?—for what presented itself now as romantic intrigue.

Soldier, seeing and hearing beyond the words and gesture, did not argue. In the Match, the female was unassailably in control in matters concerning herself—but in a true Match the woman knew both sides of the emotional symbiosis and what was due to her mate; Anne knew nothing. He said, "Nugan will prevent your coming here again."

The thought terrified him but she could not see the fear. "Just let her try! I'm a working detail now; I make my own decisions."

"I am afraid you will be kept from me."

She would never understand that the level words hid the cry of a man tearing himself apart at the behest of half-mythical, long-dead men of legendary power. She said, "I won't be able to come every night. I mean, I've got to get some sleep, Thomas. But I'll come as soon as I can. And I'll see you every day at the Library."

He knew she gave all she had to give, with no knowledge of a need beyond her giving.

In the early dawn Johnno appeared with dark bread, cheese, milk, and chicken flesh. When neither stirred to his footfall he thought, *Made a long night of it. She's got a nice face for such a thin piece, but—*

Waking them, he kept his own face politely averted from her while he spoke to Thomas, but the girl cried out, "You're Johnno," and more, in an English he could not follow. Thomas covered the breach of manners by introducing them formally, explaining that the Taylor's Anne had seen his picture as captured by Nugan's camera.

After that they seemed to have little to say to him or to each other; they behaved not at all like Matched lovers in their private Dreaming, more like troubled people whose minds were weighted with puzzlements. He had discussed Thomas's love with Bella, as Thomas had known he would, because there were no secrets in the Match, and she had been unexpectedly difficult.

"Loyalty!" she had insisted. "It is about loyalty. Is Thomas to fight against the Searchers and so against his own matchwoman?"

Johnno had already thought of that and decided that Thomas would find an answer. Thomas was not capable of disloyalty; that was for pirates and wood-robbers. He had pointed out to her that when transfer between communities was necessary the woman went with the man.

Now Bella showed herself more perceptive than he had thought her. "Does that woman know this? I have seen Nugan, who knows nothing of our need, and this one is her daughter, not a villager, not our kind. She is from the old people. It is the mating of a dog and a cat, who cannot live each other's lives. What will he want to do and what will she try to make him do and what will be the end of it?"

She had wanted to take the matter at once to the Top-Ma and he had had great trouble dissuading her. He had promised to thrash it out with Thomas.

Now he explained all this in a quick demotic which he knew the girl would not be able to follow.

Thomas nodded, appreciating the working of the village mind, and said only that he would take the matter to Libary himself later in the day. "And tell Bella there will be no disloyalty."

That was enough for Johnno, whose trust in him was absolute. But Libary . . . that old brute knew there are no absolutes in human behaviour.

6

NUGAN SAW ONLY THE USUAL TWO
sentries stationed at the portcullis. She had expected
that Thomas would be there, waiting for her. Surely
he knew she would come.

The anger that had driven her from the moment of
leaving the tents, after a blazing exchange with
Brookes, who had only reluctantly conceded her ma-
ternal right, swung at a fresh tangent. *Doesn't he want
to see me or doesn't he care a damn? Does he think
it's of no importance?* She knew, furiously, that she
was thinking in terms of her own time and culture
and that she had only a handful of bizarre facts about
the sexual conventions of this age; it could be that he
would simply resent her interference. So let him resent! Anne she could deal with; it was Thomas who
must be brought to reason. Her reason, not his.

She crossed the drawbridge in a dozen angry
strides and was halted by a soldier who simply stood
across her path, spread his arms, and used a word
whose implications had remained steady through the
years.

"Not!"

She resisted temptation to push past him with the
bland contempt of a termagant who would not be
stopped. He, with regard for duty and none for gender or chivalry, would probably seat her without dig-

269

nity on the planks. She dug into her small store of village demotic to demand with a full head of arrogance, "Bring Atkins the General to me! I am the Taylor's Nugan. He expects me."

The soldier, hawk-faced and slender but strong like his General, grinned at her and put two fingers in his mouth to blow a piercing triple of notes in a street urchin's whistle. His demotic was not too hard to interpret: "For a lady he will run to give service. Even an angry lady."

Outwardly she ignored the snigger; inwardly she murmured, *The bloody squire of dames, is he? A byword to his troops!*

He came immediately, crying, "Nugan, I am happy to see you. Come inside."

"Happy, are you?" she said. "Where's Anne?"

He took her arm and she shook him off. "She is in the crypt, at her work." Quietly he added, "Remember that the sentries have sharper senses than yours. They hear over a long distance."

Nugan dropped her voice. "I want to see her. Take me to the crypt."

"No. I have decreed a particular number in the crypt; I will not be seen to alter orders at a visitor's whim."

"I'll go down there and be damned to your orders."

"That you will not." This time his grip could not be shaken off. He guided her into Libary's empty office. "We will talk here; there is much I need to understand."

"That *you* need to understand!" Then she saw that he had forsaken his impassive mask; he was allowing her to see his feelings, and he was wretched. She recognised, with the beginning of an acute despair, that his view of the affair was far from her own and said, anxious to understand, "You were together all night, weren't you?"

He nodded, seeming surprised that she should ask. "And you used her for sex?"

"Used? Nugan, she came to me! She was not a virgin seeking experience."

"For God's sake, I know that."

"So she is not harmed by some rough boy's handling. You know that also."

Nugan said bitterly, "Don't remind me. Now you've had mother and daughter, are you satisfied?"

He did not hide amazement and anger and discarded all reserve. "Do you imagine I was playing a game, scoring points with practice and skill?"

"What then? How did you lure her away? And why?"

For a moment his face fell apart and she thought some frightened creature looked out at her. He recovered with visible effort to say, "Nugan, your Anne and I are in Match—bonded."

Her reflexive thought was, *But she's only a child*, followed at once by the realisation that she had not until this moment faced a monstrous fact, that she was considering the actions of an adult, a grown woman of marriageable age. She had thought from the first like a protective mother, seeing the girl's shipboard experiments as necessary incidents of growing up, but now recognising a menace to be fought.

She heard him say, "I have put it to you wrongly. It is I who am bonded; Anne is only in a transport of sexual triumph, but I am in Match! This is a thing that should not have been able to happen."

With a formless presentiment of horror behind the words Nugan watched lines of misery bite into his suddenly flexible, changing face, seeing tragedy with no idea of the nature of it, hearing words and making little of them.

"Nugan, you must help me. I am afraid."

And he was; his whole body spoke of it. The focus had shifted; a kiss-and-run adventure had assumed trappings of desperation with the man rather than with her daughter, and he was asking for her comprehension and solace. With the dregs of her impatience she said, "Thomas, you're talking riddles. Try to make sense. I'll listen because I need to know what has happened."

He spoke slowly, trying and failing to present the very core of a foreign culture in a manner assimilable by her kind. In a while she understood after a fashion, once the hard interface of incredulity had been passed. Then, like the breaking Soldier, she did not know what she could do. She could only express a comfortless wonderment in poor, unfit words: "It's so damned stupid that a passing love affair should make such an impossible tangle."

Soldier said—and had been saying it in a dozen changing ways in the past half hour—"You speak always of love, Nugan, yet I keep saying that love is not part of it." He felt that their minds chattered incomprehensibly one to the other without finding common understanding. "Each man, each woman has love affairs, passing affections or perhaps long affections, but these come to their ending and neither is harmed. Perhaps a small regret and a small transient loneliness—"

She interrupted, "That isn't love, Thomas, that's a sort of passion when the body looks for satisfaction."

"Other words for the same thing, Nugan. Or perhaps not. Your talk of love that lasts a lifetime I do not follow; it sounds like a slow dying without change or variety. No one on this Earth would want it. The Match is altogether another thing. It is forced by the science of the Wizards, or so we think; it is an inescapable bonding for the production of Genetic children and it is dictated by the woman. There is sexual need in it but not the love of free minds tasting life."

After a while Nugan said, "Anne can't stay here with you. She wouldn't want to. She hasn't the emotional maturity to form a true attachment; she has grown up where all experience is a rattling around in a tin can among people who don't know how to deal with children. I should never have borne a child into such conditions. But I didn't know much myself then, only thought I did." In his eyes she saw that this was almost unintelligible to him. "But what will happen to you?"

He said formally, as if closing a useless exchange, "I do not know. She is not a child of the Wizards; she has not the power to break the Match." His face returned wholly to the lacquered impassivity she was so accustomed to in him. "I will suffer. I do not know in what way."

When at last they parted she had in mind a nebulous project of consulting the ship's psychologists, though she suspected that the answers lay deep in the genes and the meddling of men long dead. She did not, for the present, try to see Anne, who would in time face altogether different questions of innocence and guilt.

Soldier watched her go. She had said she would not tell Anne the facts of her situation until they saw more clearly how it might be ended with least harm. He was unclear in his mind why he had chosen to confide in Nugan; he suspected, without following the suspicion to its lair, that the eternal strategist in him had seized the chance of a sympathetic hearing in the enemy camp.

At least one area of possible confusion had been closed off when Nugan had asked him if he still planned to force the Searchers off the planet and

Anne with them, and he had replied with a momentary reversion to the impassivity she was accustomed to, that he had not considered the question as it applied to Anne, but that the rest of them would certainly go when the time came.

She had said, with a mournful smile, that she had never expected to discover the classic conflict between love and duty enacted in real life.

For him such a conflict could not exist because the matters were distinct from each other. "Duty is inexorable; it guides all action. But the urging of the flesh is a necessity dictated by your Wizards seven centuries ago. It is a physical mechanism. It does not equate with your emotional descriptions."

When she had gone he called the Senior Trooper. "I am going to the village. Take charge until I return."

He started at a run.

Libary had taken up his temporary residence in the village meeting hall with a half dozen Ordinands and a great haul of documents which, he had assured Soldier with the distant frigidity of an emperor questioned by a slave, had no bearing on Searcher requirements.

In the street Soldier came on a disconsolate Bella who, instead of being at her work, was trudging away from the meeting hall and close to tears. "Thomas, you must speak to Johnno for me! Explain to him that I broke my word because the Top-Ma forced me."

There could be only one reference. "Concerning me and a Searcher woman?"

"Yes. Forgive me. I had to."

Well, sooner or later, and now sooner than later. "I know that Top-Ma; she'd soon have it out of you. But how did she suspect there was anything to tell?"

Bella shook her head, shivering a little because the betrayal was a serious breach of Match loyalty. "They always know. They know everything. Johnno will put me in Silence."

"No, no, he won't. I'll speak to him. Stop fretting; I'll make it right."

He packed her off back to work in a state of tremulous trust.

The scandalised Top-Ma's first report would have been to Libary and Soldier would receive a drought-dry welcome. Chance had it that as he entered the hall the Top-Ma was leaving it. She glared at him, looked away, and with set face tried to pass by.

"Top-Ma!"

She tried to avoid him but he crowded her to the wall though he had no social right to challenge when she had shown unwillingness. He swung in front of her. "Top-Ma!"

"This is not decent, General."

"It was not decent to threaten a girl with Silence because you suspected she carried a secret."

She slowed, stopped. "That is untrue. I saw she was unhappy in mind and did my plain duty."

As Bella had said, they always knew. The Top-Mas had their own methods of supervision, based on a body language reading as accurate as his own and a needle-sharp penetration of village psychology. "You threatened her with Silence, forcing her to break Match oath."

"Watch your own morality, General, before you question mine. You order your army, I guard my village. Now let me pass."

So she thought it only a moral matter, a little sexual titillation with the enemy, and would have run to Libary with complaint of possibly treasonous turpitude. It would be better now to have truth in the open.

He went directly to the main hall, where Libary sat enthroned on the dais while his Ordinand shorthand writers and assistants moved between tables loaded with surprising quantities of paperwork. His entrance brought a surly silence; they had not forgiven him this slum translation from the comforts of their own building and felt (what they would not have dared openly admit) that enforced cheek-by-jowling with the villagers was demeaning. Libary laid down a document and glared without welcome.

From the floor Thomas looked up to the black face. "Papa Melchizedech!" That set the tone; he meant business and meant that the old man should accept that he did.

"General!" Hard-mouthed, unforgiving.

"We have activities for private discussion."

Libary said, like a sentencing judge, "Privacy might be all we agree on. Come to my quarters." More order than invitation. He led through a door at the side of the dais and behind them an Ordinand giggled. All of them would be wishing the General taken down a peg; he might be powerful in his right but the Papa was mentor, nourisher, and most revered.

The quarters comprised only a single room containing a bed, a table, a chair, and shelves piled with documents. Soldier smiled privately while on a deeper level his heart wept, smiled for the reproachful pretence of enforced poverty, wept for the human weakness underlying the display. He said, "Such austerity does not become you," so neutrally as to leave Libary to read it as rebuke or disinterested comment.

"It serves. This is not a time for diversion."

"Quite so, sir."

"You agree? Is the Searcher woman, then, no diversion but a subtlety in your planning?"

"She has no part in my planning. Discussion of her can wait. It is time to discuss the means of eviction."

"So?"

"So please sit down and listen and save ill temper for a better purpose. You have no power to punish Desert Genetic save by indirection and connivance and I've no intention of seeing my efforts impeded by private angers."

The old man bowed his head in mock servility, seated himself at the table, folded his hands in front of him, and met the General's coldness with an equal glitter. "I do as told by the brat I reared."

Soldier refused baiting. "I have been pondering the phantom you raised with your attendant Readers."

"You saw nothing; you were not in the touching."

"The Taylor's Nugan described the black figure. It terrified her."

"Good. It was a message."

"And so understood, but it was not seen by the rest of the Searchers. Now that they are all together in a small area it should be possible to demonstrate . . . " He hesitated over the next words as Libary gave him a cat's grin, ready to pounce on error. " . . . that habitation of this world can be made unbearable for them."

"How so?"

"A demonstration could tell them once and for all that they are unwanted, that here they would be a community cut off from their kind as surely as in space."

"They have brains enough to know that already."

"Yet they have hope enough—or so I read them—to believe that with persistence they will find acceptance, that they will buy their entrance with gifts and willingness to learn our ways."

"They will not!"

That was not old man's defiance but a statement of determination. The question for Soldier was how far he could commit himself to revelation of his own conclusions drawn from the event on the roof. Well, win or lose . . . He said, "They do not understand that resistance would end in mental debility, perhaps madness."

Libary chuckled, a shade too carelessly. "That's a wild shot, Thomas."

"Thomas" at last; they were on proper terms. "Perhaps. I have given thought also to the social structure of this Earth and how easily it manages itself, setting Ordinands and Readers free to pursue such goals as they wish and discuss them only amongst themselves, with the unconcerned Genetics having no notice of what is being prepared under their noses."

Libary's brown eyes were wary. "What is being prepared, Thomas?"

"That I can't say. I say only that the Ordinands are fashioning for themselves a destiny in which the Genetics will have no part and that it is the Ordinands— or perhaps only the Librarians and Readers—who want the Earth free of strangers with knowledge enough to detect their aims and frustrate them. The Genetics, left to themselves, would welcome the strangers and their gifts."

"And be destroyed by them. History was not suffered only to be repeated."

"That I know. And so I will evict the Searchers."

Libary was not prepared to meet his General's eye; he shifted the papers on his table and covered dismay with gruffness: "I am happy I didn't rear a total idiot."

It was near enough to surrender. Soldier said, "I need to tap the power and knowledge of the Librarians to help me send *Search* back to its stars."

Libary said only, "You'd play with fire, but I'll listen."

* * *

If a soldier reared and drilled into his profession and view of the world, with only a pejorative knowledge of previous cultures to guide his thinking, could make the leap into suspicion and dissatisfaction, it was to be expected that Searcher minds with all the visions of history behind them should gnaw like rats at the structure of a culture they found highly anomalous.

While the General outlined his ideas to Libary and Nugan made her way slowly to the place she now knew was called by the local people "the encroachment," Jean Sengupta was hostess to an informal seminar in her tent.

Duval was present, with the intention of picking the brains of others while playing the amateur out of his academic depth. "What gets me is that nobody runs the show, no king, no president, no parliament, nobody laying down the law and keeping obstreperous buggers in line."

Miss Sengupta, familiar with his tactics, took the chance to expound basics. "On the contrary, Joel, there is a great deal of ruling and laying down of law, in the villages by oral tradition and supervision by the Ma women, in the armies by rigid internal discipline, and in the Libraries by something reminiscent of the monastic observance of vows."

"Sounds neat," Duval said, "but isn't. Three layers like castes with only limited social interaction but no overriding responsible body and no common code of behaviour! A planetary society can't work like that. All right, I know it does, but it can't."

"It does only because it can." Jean shuffled a pile of printouts in brown fingers. "Nugan provided enough relevant information to make the situation clear in outline, but it came in single comments and inferential statements that have been sorted and collated. I thought the villagers were the great problem until General Atkins revealed that malcontents are either dealt with in uncompromising manner, or make their way into unsettled areas to find what living they can, singly or in groups."

"Raid the crops and rustle the herds?"

"Living off the land may not be too stressful; there is plenty of wild country with kangaroo and rabbit and native plants. In our own time Aboriginals still did it. Food must be available because the military caste—I suppose one must call it that—keeps raiders out of the villages and communes."

"There are pirate catamarans in the oceans, too. But, about the soldiers, *quis custodiet?* Who or what keeps them in check?"

Jean had an idea but it needed corroboration. She said, "I don't know yet. If General Atkins comes here again, I shall try to question him. With Nugan he seemed always to answer a direct question."

"But did he always give a direct answer?"

She lifted a shoulder. "Who knows? He's nobody's fool. What stands out is that if anyone has authority in this area, it is he. But—and this is a monstrous but—there are indications that his authority can be exercised only when circumstances demand a central control. At other times, it seems, he has no intrinsic power."

Billy Grey, an agronomist/gene topologist, said he wouldn't risk telling soldier Thomas to go to hell on the chance of his authority being on an off day. "According to Nugan he's a killer."

"At need. He might content himself with breaking your teeth as a personal gesture against bad manners. He states a prejudice against killing."

Duval pointed out that the Mas seemed to have some authority.

"Some," Jean agreed, "but only within strict limits.

They supervise genetic suitability after a hit-or-miss fashion, but apparently with some success. A strange thing is that their errors seem to be off-loaded to the chain of Libraries spread over the globe."

"Only the suitable errors," Duval suggested. "What about the malformed and mentally retarded?"

"Nugan's pictures showed none. That is not conclusive but we may guess that a race with such a strict tradition of genetic purity deals unsentimentally with its misfits."

Billy Grey sketched a lurid vision of frozen-faced Papa Melchizedech tossing rejects into the Library furnace. Jean, suspecting he might be wrong only in the details, was not amused.

She went on quickly. "That leaves the special group of Ordinands, Readers and Librarians. It seems that the Librarian exercises a sort of rulership here but there's no evidence that his superiority is much more than the respect offered by scholars to a greater scholar. I thought at first that their celibacy had a religious provenance but now I think it is mainly philosophic, and that in many cases it could be a recognition of the person's unfitness to breed to genetic norms."

"As regards that," Duval interposed, "what do we have on this Carnival business? It seems to be a free-for-all romp and to hell with genetic purity."

"Our information there is incomplete and it may be only a letting off of sexual steam. I'm hoping that the Wishart records will make it plain."

"Wishart Laboratories have a lot to answer for."

"Yet it's a peaceful world by comparison with ours."

"And I see why: It's built on a microsociety scale. Big wars of conquest would be too damned hard to start in this dispersed setup. Just the same, there's surely one going on, only nobody's noticed. These

Ordinands and Readers and whatnot have it all their own way, with the Genetics kept in their places with no effort on the part of the Library hermits and nuns or whatever they think they are. It took our arrival to pose a problem the top dogs couldn't solve, so they handed it over to the General on a sort of temporary basis—to hell with peaceful philosophy, bring on the big stick. The army is called in to clean up the mess and then old Libary takes over again as by divine right. Or so I imagine. There's your social puzzle, Jean, with conquest already established."

Discussion became general and noisy.

Libary, who had reared a General as fine as any on the continent, struggled with an old man's pride in his handiwork while his persona as Papa Melchizedech recoiled from a proposition that seemed to him a debasement of the Net. To demonstrate to the enemy woman, Nugan, that great power could be called on had been agreed as a legitimate warning, but what this single-minded soldier asked for was far otherwise. All Libary's training, all the rigorous self-examination which recognised weakness of the flesh but insisted on ultimate purity of intention, rejected an action which might prostitute the Net and its Servants as abettors of mental damage, even insanity. There would be psychic aftershock and an incalculable setting back of the Plan while minds cleansed themselves of a deliberate, meditated sin against the Net. A whole generation of study and dedication could crumble into self-abasement.

He knew, however, that other Librarians might not see it so or, agreeing, might argue that the hiatus in advancement would be justified by the eviction of the diseased element from the past. They feared as much as he did the destructive influence of attractive but dangerous science, and the spread of alluring doctrines of freedom of action which had fragmented the Last Culture into a chaos of warring politics and ideologies. Above all, they feared the threat of Nugan's simple-minded offer of high speed, almost instantaneous, communication for the Genetics, a babble to be woven round the Earth. Ability to communicate at the press of a button had, in the Last Culture, made it possible for nations to meddle in each other's affairs as fast as words could fly, and so ensure that no peace or agreement existed anywhere at any time, that no action could be taken without parties an ocean distant spitting invective and objection, even dropping ready weapons of assault from orbit to murder the helpless and see to it that no balance of effort or goodwill should exist on the Earth.

The Last Culture had ended itself in an opulence of technology and an inability to understand that a halt should be called. That, at least, should not happen again.

Disturbed by the imaginative reach which had conceived such an assault, Libary protested, "Thomas, no such number of Readers and Librarians exists in Australia. They would have to be brought from the Islands and the Asian states and India. Such a concentration has never been convened."

Soldier had no interest in logistical objections; they could be overcome. "I ask can such a vision be created by such a concourse?"

"That? Yes." To Soldier he seemed distracted. "It has never been attempted; there was never reason for doing a thing only to show that it could be done."

"Then bring them from the Islands and China and India and any part of the world."

"Thomas, it is not merely the bringing. They must be fed, harboured, tutored. A thousand adepts in a circle of a kil diameter! The physical problems are immense."

Soldier had often been aware of Libary's sidling away from practical problems outside his experience, seeing impossibilities because his own reality was circumscribed, but where he had once found amusement he was now hard put to rein back an urge to bellow frustration.

"Bring them here! Only bring them! Send your messages, obtain their agreement! I will manage the rest of your difficulties."

"You?"

"With the armies of our regions. We cooperate when necessary as well as confront each other. Tell me what is wanted and I will provide fast transport the length and breadth of Australia; I will feed your adepts—and house and clothe them if I must. How long to bring them here?"

Libary capitulated. "If the semaphores are set to work tomorrow—"

"Tonight!"

"Tonight, Thomas, tonight. Allow eight days for all replies because not all adepts are at once available. They have duties. Allow two months for travel—"

"Too long. Fast catamarans with provisioning stops only, then horses or carriages overland or oared boats upriver. Allow five weeks."

"Thomas, these are not hard-bred Genetics!"

"Five weeks! They need only be a little seasick and boneshaken while others carry them. The eviction should take place on the night of Carnival, when spectacular miracles will pass unnoticed in the villages."

And so he had his way; the rest was mainly wording the messages to be semaphored across the Earth as soon as the teams could be assembled. They should meet on the Library roof at dusk; within two days the adepts in the northern islands should be reading the long and complex message. It would be an extended transmission, sectioned and farmed between all operating teams for simultaneous sending.

With his mind on logistics, a preliminary calculation of the needs of a thousand adepts and their attendants, Soldier was ready to return to camp. Libary detained him, speaking harshly now, conceiving himself on his own ground of authority.

"The woman, Thomas. Are you in liaison with this Searcher woman?"

Away from the *rom*, Soldier's busy mind had still not been free of her, in the nature of the Match could not be; part of him had been waiting for the question. "With Nugan's Anne? What of it?"

Libary stiffened to the resistance. "Is this one of your strategic games?"

"No game." He planted his bomb deliberately, in slow words: "We are Matched."

There could be no question of Libary's disbelieving him; a Match was beyond pretence, a physical manifestation not to be mimicked or hidden. Now he saw not only Soldier's predicament but another so unlikely that he had not considered it.

"Thomas, they must be besieged in their canopy village! Held there! They must not mix with villagers or soldiers. If there are Matchings, we will never be rid of them."

That said, his mind turned to Soldier's case, and his thought of disaster was plain before he could hide it.

Soldier, for once mistaking him, said grimly, "You wonder what power she will exercise over me to favour her people's desire for Earth. None! She does not know her power. She is not aware of the Matching; these people have not the perception. The gift of the Wizards was not passed to then."

"How is this possible? The woman chooses, makes the Match, takes and holds—"

"She made the choice; I do not know the means of it. She gives me no clue. It was not a transient wanting or some manner of Carnival release. She chose and the Match is unbreakable by me."

Libary muttered, "The Match is always unbreakable. She must remain when Search leaves. One woman will not destroy the Genetic."

"I have no certainty that she will wish to stay; it is not to be assumed blindly. But she is not aware of binding and she is not bound; she knows nothing of the permanence of the bond. *I* am bound."

Libary said from his masked face, "If she goes . . . " and floundered there because you do not tell a man his fate or the manner of it.

Soldier, guessing at reasons and thinking this was not the time to stare at the future, affected a carelessness that deceived neither of them, "Then she goes. Now I have work to do. We will meet on the Library roof, tonight."

He left quickly, not wishing to see an old man's struggle with dignity, love, and self-control.

Nugan, approaching the canopy, saw the bulk of the *Search* complement in the open, hatted and sleeved against the sun but venturing further down the hill than they had yet done, some with binoculars fixed on the Library, some moving to the blind side of the slope as though with caution they might discover the reason for the sound of axes and the occasional crash of timber.

Like prisoners distrustful of the open spaces outside safe walls. The ship years have regressed them to childhood fears of unknown places.

She knew what to expect of them and was ready for it. It came as soon as she was within calling distance: "Nugan, have they found Anne?"

She answered sturdily, conceding nothing, "Yes."

With the blunt syllable she hoped to shut off questions but someone, a woman anonymous in the huddle of a group, asked, "Was she with General Atkins?"

There could be no hope of secrecy. "Yes."

"What will you do?"

"I'll wipe your bloody mouth if I can locate you."

Some were shocked but a couple of the women smothered giggles and a man wolf whistled. For a moment it seemed there might be a noisy move against her, but years of social discipline were not overruled by a little air and sunlight. She reached the shelter of the canopy in an inquisitive silence.

She should have reported immediately to Brookes but went instead to her tent to catch her breath and change her sweat-soaked overalls. There she found the unexpected—Miss Sengupta, whom she knew only slightly, seated cross-legged on the floor, waiting for her.

Nugan paused in the tent opening, wanting no company, fumbling for an insult. All she managed was, "We're being very bloody oriental, aren't we?"

The Indian woman answered that her position was restful to those accustomed to it. "I have been waiting to ask if Anne is safe."

That was an improvement on open prurience. "She is safely with the Library detail, Miss Sengupta."

"So she is not held captive."

"No. Is that all?"

The slightly almond eyes, brown as Libary's, met Nugan's placidly. "May I ask, with respect, where she spent the night?"

Nugan said tiredly, "With General Atkins. It's common speculation and it's true. That's your cue to say, 'Like mother, like daughter—a pair of promiscuous sluts.' "

Miss Sengupta came to her feet with the effortless

lift of opening lazy tongs, smiling faintly and shaking her head. "You must not think like that. You kept your personal freedom of choice, which many others did only under wrap of whispers and secret meetings—as though secrets were possible in an anthill. Anne, like the other babies, had no true youth or mental adaptation to puberty in an ambience with little relation to real life. So she is an honourable, intelligent girl but not an experienced one."

Nugan recognised the overt stroking but responded to it, relaxing a little. "She's accumulating experience at great speed, with an expert."

"But will this be permitted to continue?"

Nettled, Nugan asked, "Did someone send you to question me?"

"I was not sent but I have held an impromptu seminar at which unanswerable questions were raised. It is possible that Anne may find answers to some of them."

Nugan sat on her bunk and slipped the overalls back from her shoulders. "If you think to use her as a spy, I won't permit it. The situation is unpleasant enough without slinking and subterfuge."

"I do not suggest that, only that she might obtain clues to some puzzling gaps in our understanding of how this culture operates. With its paradoxes it should not operate at all. Still, if you mean to terminate the contact, that is your right."

"I don't intend anything of the sort. For Thomas's sake it must continue. All I want to do is have Captain Brookes declare the matter out of bounds of all public discussion or questioning of Anne."

The brown face inclined to her in puzzlement. "You said, 'for Thomas's sake,' " and, doubtfully, "Of course he is your friend. The thing is complex."

"Complex enough to give your social sciences a jolt in the ribs. Since I've said that much, I'd better explain." She added meaningfully, "In confidence."

"That is understood."

The explanation took some time and at the end of it Miss Sengupta said happily, "Lysistrata!"

"What? Who?"

"The leader of some legendary Greek ladies who stopped a war by denying sexual relations to their husbands. That is at least part of the answer to the tranquillity of this unlikely culture. But what will become of your friend Thomas when Anne leaves?"

"Even he doesn't know that, but he is frightened out of his mind. He is a guinea pig in an uncontrolled experiment. And then there's Anne's problem."

"For her, what?"

"If she becomes pregnant, what manner of little brute will be growing in her?"

Miss Sengupta was improperly amused. "He—or she—might pass the gift of power to women."

Nugan took time to think of it. "The idea attracts until you look at what has come of it here. I think I'd lead the lynching party." Miss Sengupta's amusement became apprehensive. "You think I wouldn't? I suppose we'd have to try it first. It could become addictive."

Soon afterwards she took her information to Captain Brookes and with him decided how Anne's attachment should be handled under the social canopy.

When, late in the afternoon, Anne returned from the Library, she entered the tent she shared with her mother stone-faced and ready for fury, to receive instead a nod of greeting—and nothing more. Nugan was in fact unsure how to deal with an aspect of motherhood with no precedent to call on.

Anne shucked off her overall and asked, aiming for

a steady voice and achieving a tremulous stridency, "It's to be the silent treatment, is it?"

"No. I don't know that there's much to be said."

"I don't want to talk about it. Not yet anyway." She sat on her bunk, allowing her flesh to cool. "I walked down the tent rows and nobody took any notice of me. I'd thought there'd be—well, remarks."

"There would have been if Captain Brookes hadn't ordered that you be left alone, the subject not raised."

"Why? It can't be that important to him."

"It can. He wants to save you being driven out of your mind by innuendo and bitching."

Anne, unable to switch at once from defence to gratitude, muttered, "He needn't have bothered."

"Don't be so bloody meanspirited. He's trying to help you."

"Thinking about social discipline, more like it. I can look after myself. I showed them this morning."

"At the Library?"

"Yes. They tried to—I don't know, make me cry, I suppose—with double meanings. I told them I'd call Thomas down and see how brave they were with him."

Privately Nugan approved; she would have liked to have seen the faces. But it was not the moment for compliments. "Now you know the way they think. It's just a dirty joke. Have you wondered what I think?"

"Yes."

"Do you care?"

Anne was a long time deciding on a whispered, "Yes, Mother." Bending to take off her socks, she said shakily to the ground between her feet, "I'm going to see him, just the same."

"I'm sure you are."

The girl looked warily up at her. "You won't stop me?"

"No. That way I'd only get lies and subterfuge. You've done a damned stupid thing but you'll have to see it through. It's no good telling yourself how grown-up you are and how capable of managing your own life if you aren't prepared to follow through to discover the price of free will."

"What price? It's only an affair. Everybody has them. All over the ship they keep swapping partners and think we young people don't know about it."

Anne sought an alternative to truth. "Out there isn't the ship and there's always a price. One side or the other gets hurt, perhaps only a little, perhaps a lot." That must have sounded as vague to Anne as it did to herself. She snapped, "Just don't let yourself become pregnant. Those people's ideas aren't ours; there could be complications we know nothing of as yet." Anne shrugged. "And don't think automatically of abortion. For all we know they may regard it as murder. There were sects and groups in our time who did. Use contraception."

That gave Anne something concrete to think about, something she would have to ask Thomas. "I'll remember. I've had a long day, Mother; I'm going to bed."

In the dusk Soldier came up the hill, wondering at the numbers who stood about talking, walking in the cooling air but straying at most a hundred metres from their canopy. They showed little interest in exploring the world they had made such display of occupying. Could Nugan's account of the black demon have caused hesitation? He thought not; they would have dreamed a score of very technical explanations and dismissed it from their minds—just as he had dismissed the odd remark, which he had thought juvenile, that Anne had made when he joked gently that only she had had the courage to come out of the refuge: "They're not used to going anywhere; they don't know what to do." There might be truth in it.

With his receptors alert for Anne, he could not detect her; she must be inside, unaroused, her presence blurred in the impersonal sexual fog of a mass of people without *rom* control. He walked through the throng, looking directly at nobody, simply asserting his right to approach, and they moved out of his path, then stopped to watch him.

Under his nose, it seemed, a young voice chanted, " 'Tommy this an' Tommy that' " and then, in a cracking teenage yell, " 'an' Tommy *go away*!' "

He looked down at a boy, perhaps fourteen years old, who gazed up at him with an impertinent courage he thought safe to flourish in a crowd, though tension told Soldier he was ready to run. A man's hand fell on the boy's shoulder to pull him back but Soldier reached faster to sharply tweak his nose before young reflexes could dodge. "You lack manners with a stranger, small one. And it is you who will go away."

He kept on his way to the tent. A man's voice called contemptuously, "Do you really think you can chuck us off our own world, soldier-boy?"

Soldier could not distinguish him in the dusk. "I promise only what I will do."

That roused a murmur he did not try to distinguish. He sensed no lack of courage among them, rather an uncertainty of what a blind and undirected courage might achieve. They were, after all, superior tradesmen, not fighters. They were no doubt good enough people in their way, but their way was forgotten and unwanted.

Nearing the canopy's edge, he introduced himself to a man who stood alone, observing him stonily. "I am General Atkins. I ask that you inform your Captain Brookes that I am here and would like to speak with him."

The man stepped closer to say, "And I'm Jack McCann and I've got a message for you. Don't harm young Anne or I'll find a way to kill you."

"Harm? How can you think it? She is my—" He saw the hopelessness of explanation and said lamely, "I love her. Are you her father? No, the name is wrong . . . " He was mentally disarmed by the evocation of her name, unable to take command of the exchange.

"A friend to her and her mother," McCann said, "so take care, professional killer."

A good, lean man, Soldier thought; he would make a trooper. The good, lean man said coldly, "I'll get the Captain," and vanished down the lanes of tents. The threat had sounded genuine; there could be others before all was done.

He looked up at the canopy, that aberration in a season of hot sun. It appeared to be a thick-woven material whose nature defeated him—surely a black metal on the upper surface, coated over a heavy, coarse cloth. While he pondered uselessly, Brookes arrived.

The Captain had decided on full uniform, hastily donned; the damned Thomas was a sight too formal for his half-dressed habit. He saluted although in strict terms his command must outrank that of the small-time General; it was a matter of insisting on formal recognition.

Soldier made a fair experiment of returning the salute, saying, "I have a communication for you," while a part of his mind quested for Anne. Perhaps she slept.

"If you want to talk about Anne Taylor," Brookes told him, "that's a matter we have in hand here. Her mother has briefed me on your meeting last night. The girl will be protected."

"Against me?" He was incredulous.

Brookes gestured at the Searchers who watched from a distance. "Against unkind tongues."

"Ah. I had not thought so deeply. The customs are different. With us there would be no difficulty." With an effort he thrust Anne to the fringes of his mind. "Now, my communication."

Brookes lifted a hand to tap a finger on his pocket. "Recording you, General, for posterity; you are quite a memorable man. Your message?"

"In forty days will fall the day and night of Carnival. Nugan will explain the term to you. On that night of celebration you will leave the Earth and not return."

Brookes considered him through a short silence while thinking that this must be the most conversational statement of assault in history. At last he said, "You're very damned sure of yourself, feller."

"I state what I can and will do. No one will be physically harmed; the reactions of their minds I cannot guess. I suggest only that you take your people away without the need of coercion."

Brookes said wearily, "Oh, to hell with you."

Insulted, Soldier left without parting compliments.

7

DAYS PASSED WITHOUT INCIDENT UNTIL
Anne brought Soldier a message from Brookes, asking that four extra researchers be added to the number working in the crypt; so many avenues of interest
were opening up that a greater variety of specialists
was required.

"Tell him yes. A total of ten but no more. I can't
spare troopers to keep more under surveillance."

At a tangent Anne asked, "Why? Are they away
fighting?"

"Fighting is a small part of soldiering and there is
always work to be done." Indeed there was, patrolling the western tracks and supplying guards to the
gunpowder portages trudging out of the Western Region; word of the content of the loads would have
leaked through the countryside and the free-roving
bands would have predatory eyes on them.

Anne was not really interested in the troopers.
"You don't need to watch my people; they know how
precious the books are. Anyway, they make copies
on the spot."

"Lovers of fine books like to own them; there is a
temptation to be the sole owner of a precious work.
I have seen Librarians close to blows over a scrap, a
fragment, so the troopers are there on offchance."

He kissed her to end profitless talk and rouse her
to the point his urgency demanded.

*   *   *

The short conversation was prophetic. Three days later a trooper came at a fast trot to tell Soldier he was needed at the Library. A thief had been detected.

On arrival he saw that the prisoner was held by the portcullis sentries and that halfway across the drawbridge waited the man he recalled as Jack McCann.

Soldier approached him genially. "Are you waiting to kill me, Mister McCann, if I ill-treat your covetous shipmate?"

McCann returned him a frosty hint of a smile. "That wouldn't be my reason. I am here to record what passes between you. There may be differing concepts of justice."

On his forehead was set what Soldier thought of as a recording eye, similar to that Nugan had worn. He did not look for the listening ear; that tiny thing could be hidden under a fingernail.

"We will confer on differences. What has been stolen?"

"A holobook. One of your sentries has it."

He did not ask what the strange word meant; he would see for himself. What the sentry handed him was a tiny volume smaller than the palm of his hand. Its sixty-four stiff pages were brightly coloured pictures of scenes: Mountains, islands, seascapes, towns, steam that seemed to erupt in plumes from bubbling pools, animals in pasture lands, dark men with threateningly painted faces, women in skirts and dance postures, fern gullies, and timber forest scenes. People and ambience were strange to him. The pictures were in sharp colour printed on a paper whose surface seemed to blur and distort at different angles.

He looked at the thief, a young man (but they all seemed similarly young) obviously part-bred with some darker race than his dominant white, who faced

him steadily. Soldier read resignation rather than re-
morse, and an irritation at detection. "In the crypt are
many such books showing many countries." On the
cover, in faded gold leaf, was Ao-tea-roa. "This country I've not heard of."

The thief said stolidly, "It means Land of the Long
White Cloud; your maps probably say New Zealand."

Possibly, but many names had mutated or vanished. "Thank you. These books puzzle the Librarians. The pictures appear to move slightly or take on
depth or even turn a little aside."

McCann said, "It's a holobook. The pages can be
lifted out and placed in a, er—a projector, with special lights shone on it to create a hologram. That's a
picture in depth, in three dimensions. This little view
of a mountain can be enlarged and will seem miles
deep with the mountain far in the distance."

Soldier would have liked to see that. He said only,
"Has it special value for your research?"

McCann was silent. The thief said, "No."

"Then, why?"

"It is my homeland. If you have your way, I will
never see it again."

Soldier knew of no custom or local determination
that took account of the longing that spoke of pain
under the steady tone. The longing itself posed a difficulty; he tried to imagine himself leaving Earth,
never to return, and gave it up as requiring too much
of an effort of fantasy; countries where little changed
in a generation had no word for nostalgia.

"Love of a place! Mister McCann, in your conventions is that a reason for stealing?"

"Under present circumstances I would see it as an
extenuating factor. Extremely so."

"But not a total excuse?"

"Total, no. A punishment would be lenient. It is

not easy to say, 'Never again,' to every familiar thing."

"Not? And yet you said it seven centuries ago."

"And, as you see, we have come home."

Soldier turned the book over, trying to see it as a thing of emotional value. "All day you copy books on your tapes and wires. Why not this?"

The thief said, "You can't copy holographs on digital direct. It would just make a flat picture."

"What is your name?"

"Jones. Peter Jones."

He looked too exotic for such a plebeian name. "I shall inform Captain Brookes. Let him deal with you."

McCann interjected, "It can be copied on the big molecular reduction computer at the camp."

"So?"

"Let him copy it and return the book to you personally."

No end to pushing, Soldier noted; first leniency, now permission for special exemption. "How long might such copying take?"

"A few seconds for each page. It could be done tonight."

He turned to Jones. "Did you intend to return the book?"

"I don't know. I suppose so. I hadn't thought that far."

"And you a scientist, a man of logic?" Jones was silent. Soldier turned to McCann. "Let him copy it. I want the book in my hand tomorrow morning, undamaged. I make you responsible, Mister McCann."

Jones said, "I promise it will be here."

"Give it to the sentry now; he will return it to you this afternoon as you leave. In the villages theft is punished with a beating by the owner of the stolen article, with a limit of five blows. If you have seen pictures of our villagers you will know that that would mean a broken face. For a second theft, twenty blows. For a third, expulsion and exile."

Jones's cheeks tightened. McCann asked, "How about a kleptomaniac?"

"I don't know of such a mania."

"It means an irrational compulsion to steal."

"Compulsion? Meaning without profit motive? To simply see and desire and be unable to resist? Are there such people?"

"General, you'd have them smashed up and in exile before you got round to finding out."

Soldier tucked the thought away in his head for further consideration. "Sometimes in children . . . I will take it up with the Mas. There may be old observations, special knowledge, perhaps stories; there are stories with truths worth unravelling. What is your punishment for such?"

"None. We get the psychs to sort them out."

That took a deal of explaining; in the Libraries theories of psychology abounded but extended therapy was rare. For the present he saw the book handed to a sentry with an instruction to return it to Jones when he left at the end of the day, and congratulated himself that he had handled a delicate matter (in honesty, with McCann's help) for the best. Let Brookes discipline his own.

He called McCann back from the entry. "A word, please."

McCann returned, eyebrows raised as Soldier surveyed him from head to foot before saying, "I think you are no longer concerned for Anne's safety."

"I wait and see, General."

"I suppose that is wisdom of a kind but you are concerned for her. Surely you must be her father."

McCann's answer was stiff with resentment. "If so, her mother seems unaware."

Soldier exploded. "Your culture makes no sense!" Without being expert he had a competent grasp of the bloodline work of the Mas and would have claimed high accuracy for his summation of the ancestral traits he saw in Anne.

In the morning the book was returned, by Sargesson, with a note from Brookes, handwritten in a cursive script Soldier could not decipher. Sargesson read it to him: "General Atkins: Herewith the book of dissension, computer-copied and filed, with the thanks of all of us. Jones is barred from the Library. Your restraint from summary action is appreciated. Ship-Captain R. N. Brookes."

Summary action! What could he have done but frighten the man, and that only a little? The casualness of the note confused him. Did these people really not take their situation seriously?

He said, "Mister Sargesson, I have a question."

Sargesson found the formality amusing. "Ask away, General. No charge for information."

"Why do you stay here under your black roof? Why do you not leave?"

"We haven't seen enough of your planet yet, General."

This was mockery and Soldier became contemptuous of manners that lacked grace. "You sit on your hilltop. You see nothing."

Sargesson's smile remained. "Hasn't young Anne told you we're searching the planet?"

There was no understanding their ideas. He snapped, "She is not a village gossip and I do not use my matchmate as a betrayer of secrets."

Sargesson, taken aback, said uncertainly, "I suppose not. Man of honour and so on. You keep surprising us. There's no reason you shouldn't know we're surveying the countries and continents."

Soldier was incredulous. "You have made other landings?"

"No; it's done from the ship with miniature cameras—insect-sized—on monomagnetic beams. You've talked to McCann, I think; he's one of the operators. He'll be going back tomorrow for another tour of duty."

Insect-sized—and so virtually invisible. "Seeking a place that might accept you?"

"Somewhere to sit down and inconvenience nobody."

"There is no such place. Your position would always be known and hunted."

The smile returned. "We'd shake the Net and crease the pattern, would we?"

This was intolerable. "No. You would disturb the ecology, which would announce your presence with trumpets. As for the Net, you know less about that than I, who know too little to risk witticism on it."

He turned his back on the man who seemed unable to deal seriously.

Sargesson called after him, "Frightening a lone woman was easy. Frightening people who have rights is harder, Gameplayer."

8

FOR TWO NIGHTS ANNE DID NOT APPEAR and Soldier endured the savage discontent that fills absence with unstemmable longing. He stayed away from the Library, knowing that the *rom* she could not control would transform mental discomfort into torment of the flesh, unassuageable while he could not touch her; he feared for his control of reason.

He erected a small tent shelter at their trysting place and spent his nights there in muttered railing, incoherences that would have shocked his men's belief in his unshakable calm. He rehearsed whispered scenes wherein he abused and threatened her and broke her to his will and need, while writhing in the knowledge that no man could defeat his matchwoman. She had only to smile and beckon and cloud the air with lure . . .

On the third night rain pattered on the tent, thick, warm drops from low-lying clouds, heralding perhaps an electrical storm from the distant seacoast but not a breaking of the cyclic drought. He cursed the inconsistent weather, which would keep her from him for yet another unsleeping darkness . . .

. . . and she came, a little wet, frightened by lightning, and distrustful of the rain, events with no parallels on the ship. She clung to him, crying while he stripped away her damp overall and held her in his arms until her tears dried in his warmth and nearness.

The onset of love did not smother her complaint: "Oh, Tommy, I'm starting to hate this planet, the dust and heat and insects and now rain and lightning. I was sure it would strike me." The unsleeping tactician in him thought of the hundred others feeling likewise. Then she spoke the unbearable: "I want to live back on the ship where life doesn't keep on frightening everyone."

Self-absorption was commonplace aboard *Search*, where in-turning was the only retreat from too much company, but she was not quite proof against Soldier's desolate reaction; she was both touched and a little annoyed by his intensity. She stroked his hair, offering at least token comfort. "Never mind; there'll be heaps more girls after I've gone."

"No!" He was hard put to disguise rage and despair.

"But yes, dear. People don't love forever. They get used to each other and look about for new interests, new thrills. It's like that all the time on the ship."

In a frenzy of negation he tore at her nakedness, unable to hold back the plea that shamed him as he made it. "Stay on the Earth! I will make the world beautiful for you! Never leave me!"

Her experience of flirtation found his terrible earnestness edgily unreal and she offered a flirt's playful logic: "But you want us to go!"

"Let them all go but you! Stay with me!"

She thought, not for the first time, that his intensity was disarming but sometimes terrifying when he gabbled impossibilities; a demanding child not far below the surface of his manhood tried her patience. Still, he remained the most beautiful male she had ever seen, and bearing with strangeness was a small price for the eagerness and rapture. In the end she always responded with her body, holding the moment, letting tomorrow wait.

Later, when her *rom* had shrunk in lazy satisfaction, when the Moon had gone down and the scanty spitting of rain had passed, leaving a scent of newness in the parched grass, Anne told him, "They still say we won't go, Tommy."

Soldier murmured, "They learn nothing."

"They think old Libary will change his mind and find a place for us on some big island or somewhere away from other people." He knew quite well how they thought and that they did not understand that the decision did not lie with Libary or any one person. Then she said, "They don't talk about Postvorta any more."

"About what? What is Postvorta?"

"A star with planets. *Kiev* is there."

"That is the first ship?"

"Mm."

"So, after all, there is another world suitable for men." The words were out, past recall, and he suffered a twinge of guilt; honour as he conceived it, as well as his promise to Nugan, forbade pursuit of the subject.

"Oh, no, it sounds awful! It has its own people, savage things like men but not quite, more like walking plants. Most of it's in an ice age and they're being attacked all the time—or they were thirty-two years ago when they sent the message. That's how far away it is."

Rightly or wrongly he had obtained information of interest and he would seek out Nugan for further enquiry; she, if she felt an answer inadvisable, would send him roundly about his business.

He said, "I think you should not speak to me about that without first receiving permission from your Captain Brookes," but was unable to convince her of indiscretion. She could not see that it mattered.

He was prepared for Nugan's suspicion that he had employed sexual opportunity to quiz Anne for information; in order to convince her otherwise he had set aside his control of facial and bodily expression—no easy exercise, save in quick actorly flashes, for one trained to concealment.

"She spoke of disliking this Earth, Nugan, and felt that the alternative far away is little better. It was a remark in passing. I did not press her. I would not. Our confrontation with *Search* is without precedent and I must consider the propriety of my conduct at every turn."

"Propriety!" She did not know whether to laugh or hit him.

They sat together on the grass a hundred metres from the canopy's edge where, though he did not know it, directional microphones listened and recorded.

He protested, "There is a right behaviour, Nugan!"

In the end she believed him, in part because she wished to; their ability to trust each other for truth was the one unsoiled aspect of the clash of cultures.

Nugan said, "You can't blame her for hating the place. Weather came as a shock to one who had lived her life in a monitored climate."

"Do you hate it?"

"Me? I've seen too many weathers on too many worlds. This is better than most."

"So you would wish to stay?"

She hesitated over her reply, then settled for what in her mind she termed the party line: "Thomas, we will stay. You must accept that."

He read the tiny hiatus as a concession to correct Searcher thought, but gave only the expected answer, "There is no place for you on this Earth."

"There is a fine, empty desert in the west of the old United States in North America."

That was mere fishing for a response. "You would find desert weather equable but waterless."

"We can drill for water. We can also make adjustments to the weather once the small fliers are assembled for work in the upper atmosphere."

Soldier was silent a while, more awed than she imagined by the idea of commanding rain and wind. At last he said, "You may harness the hurricane and bring the ocean flooding in, still we will evict you from this Earth which has no place for you. We will reach you there as easily as here, or at the poles or in the mountains of Asia."

It was her turn to ponder a reply. "You trust your strength and we ours. We'll stay here, Thomas, if only because the Postvorta life is an inimical swarm. Even the *Kiev* landing crew have withdrawn."

He protested at once that she should not reveal the Searchers' private matters.

"How can it matter, Thomas? Anne told me of your scruples and I asked Brookes. He can't see that what happens thirty-two light-years away can affect us here."

Afterwards it seemed to him that his darkening mind had come alight at that moment. With no change of expression, he said, "So *Kiev* is voyaging again?"

"No. They are as disillusioned as we are with the hope of a new home. They have gone into cryo-suspension in orbit. Their message to Earth was a cry for help, for troops to guard their settlement from the savagery they don't know how to defend themselves against. The poor brutes don't know that only *Search* exists to hear their message. *Search* has no troops and would find a more present use for them if it had."

"Yet I saw you melt the ground."

"We Contact crews can protect ourselves against animals, that's about all. In a war I could kill one man while another with an arrow killed me from five times the distance. What sort of fighting is that? It's barely protection. We are scientists and artisans and farmers, not soldiers."

"Your people sent you like babies into the universe, unguarded and incompetent!"

"They saw it otherwise. If we found a superior culture it would aid us, if an inferior one it would be in awe of us. They did not conceive of something so alien that there could be neither aid nor awe. *Kiev*'s people retreated to their ship and called for a help that no longer exists."

Soldier saw, in a continuing intuitive burst, that the situation had altered in a fashion visible only to himself. Briefly his imagination encompassed the huge double trumpet, frozen and silent, circling an enemy world in endless loneliness and despair. "I think they must fight or spend their lives in the lanes of empty night."

"I suppose it could come to that."

He stood, brushing grass seeds from his uniform. "Meanwhile, nothing here is changed."

A faint light in her face died and he turned away. She called after his retreating back, "And what about Anne?"

He answered without turning, "When you go she will go with you."

Nugan watched as Soldier took a few steps before breaking into the run which seemed to be his normal pace when alone. She said to herself, but aloud, "And a bloody lot of good that did for the stay-put cause."

She had not heard Brookes's approach. He spoke behind her, "He seems unimpressed by our troubles." He detached the chip from his ear and tossed it pensively in the sunlight.

"Hard to say, sir. With us he always speaks as if we are overheard—and most times we are—but his parting line was genuine. We're going, and that's that."

"Shifting us will take more than a display of hypnotic tricks."

Say that again when you've seen them! She asked, "Do you really want to stay?"

"I don't know, Nugan. I feel guilty for giving in to pressure to come home, but the people who gave us our orders are forgotten dust and I can live with the guilt."

"We're not wanted here. Wherever we set down we will be hunted. It will be like living in a madhouse with armed maniacs and no warders."

"Perhaps," he suggested, "we could frighten them."

"With what, sir? Powered hand weapons that a longbow can outshoot? Bullets? There aren't enough guns aboard to fire a small salute. And don't think of bacteria; even the most rabid stay-puts wouldn't countenance plague warfare. Anyway, if we start killing, we're lost. They'd pick us off one by one and we wouldn't see what cover they shot from; in a month half of us would be dead. We aren't trained in organised violence and we're too small a force, just gnats for swatting."

Brookes took her elbow and walked her away from the canopy. "I've something private to say to you and I don't know who might be listening."

They continued downhill until the slope took them below the level of the microphones on the canopy uprights.

"I have received an application for scrutiny of DNA records."

Nugan was instantly aggressive. "Mine? No! I won't have it! The privacy rule doesn't allow it. Whose record besides mine?"

"Yours, Anne's, and one other. The privacy provision can be abrogated when the rights of others are involved."

She demanded fiercely, "Who's the other?"

"Drop Operator McCann. He made the request; you should be able to guess why."

"He's gone back to *Search*, hasn't he? I'll speak to him."

"I think you should allow the application."

"Why?"

"Because Anne has seconded it. So there are human rights at issue. Is he Anne's father?"

She turned her face from him. He waited patiently until she said harshly, defensively, "I don't know. Maybe. He's one of three and I don't know which. I don't want to know."

"Anne does. She likes the idea of McCann for a father."

"Because he once paddled her arse for her!" She found her eyes full of tears of frustration and cried out, "What the hell's got into him? He never cared before. And she didn't give a damn whose daughter she is."

"How do you know they didn't care? They respected your wish to keep your counsel and not start a gossip fest. As to what got into him, your Thomas did."

"Thomas!"

"The Top-Mas must be pretty accurate with their genealogy assessments, perhaps better than we realise, and Thomas seems to have picked up some of their technique. He's seen all three of you at close range and he picked McCann for Anne's father. He even had a little fit of ill temper when McCann told him he didn't know."

"That damned Thomas!"

"Something of a cultural polymath."

"And now Jack has his nose to the trail!"

"You don't favour him?"

Again he had to wait while she cast about in her feelings. "It mightn't be Jack. It might be the wrong one. We were ten years out and I was having a fling with the boys. If that sounds cheap, it's the only way to put it. Boredom, I suppose. The women treated me as a sexed-up tart and that made me worse. Just defiance. I got careless and I was drinking a bit, too. I

found I was pregnant and decided to bear the child.
More defiance." She turned to Brookes, her brow fur-
rowed with the effort at untrimmed truth. "I didn't
really want it. What I wanted was to flaunt freedom
of action in the faces of all the scandalised bitches,
and I did. You know what happened: I started a rush.
There were eight more kids in the next three years.
The parents were all happily stuck with each other
but I didn't want to know who was Anne's father because it might be the one I had learned to dislike and
despise, so I never checked the records. I didn't want
the wrong man pawing over Anne and making demands I'd have to put up with."

"But you've grown up now, Nugan, shipwise."

"I suppose so. Are you going to overrule me?"

"Unnecessary. I assumed the commander's privilege and made the identity check myself."

She faced him with fists clenched as if she might
fight off the facts. "Who? Not that bastard, Billy
Grey!"

"McCann. Your Thomas knows his genes without
the aid of an ID chart. Do I allow their application or
leave you to tell them?"

She said unwillingly, "Oh, I'll do it. Give me a day
or two to get my courage up. That bloody Thomas!"

She was angrily aware that Brookes thought it high
time she cleaned up that old corner of her life.

9

SOLDIER PASSED THE LOGGING CAMP where a fifteen-metre stripped trunk was being loaded onto a sledge for running down to the river. A sweating, yelling Johnno guided and bullied as the huge log was levered and manhandled onto the tray with its hundreds of small teak rollers.

He heard the first thunderous rumbling as the sledge began its jerking and erratic run, held from a careering breakaway by Flighty's stable of powerful dray horses and guided by men sweating on rope cables.

His own camp lay concealed in trees and fern forest in a low re-entrant half an hour distant. Once there, he called his Senior Patrol Sergeant and gave orders which that competent old sweat did his best to pretend were not outlandish and unprecedented. "You will take twenty men for close observation and a wing of gliderscouts as point observers." He handed the Sergeant a list of names. "I want each of these outlaws located and tailed for picking up when required. The tails must not be detected."

The Sergeant refrained from any frustrated observation about turning up a particular double handful of thieves in half a million hectares of hideout country.

"Set out after the midday meal. You have ten days

311

in which to locate them and report to me their where-
abouts."

Then he turned his steps to the village and Libary.
It was time the old man knew his General's mind.

The village was alive with strangers, many of them
black or nearly so. These, he guessed, would be the
first arrivals from Queensland and the so-called Sa-
cred Sand once known as the Northern Territory. The
north was the home of the greater part of the surviving pure-blood Aboriginal population and known for
the perpetuation of Songlines, Creation Tales and
The Dreaming; it was in the north that the ancient
indigenous culture was preserved. These thronging
visitors were the core of the Ordinand teachings in
Australia, people who lived "with the land" and preserved the beliefs and rituals of forty thousand years
of spiritual growth.

Spiritual growth? He saw little of spirituality in the
Genetic world; in a climate of easy guidance, simple
living, and small crises managed by an efficient soldiery, spirituality had lost its psychological necessity
and collapsed into a jigsaw of traditional tales and
local superstitions.

Had he, by bringing these *kurdaitcha* south,
opened floodgates of ancient teaching to wash over
the stolid Genetics and disturb them forevermore?
Hardly so; he believed that the Ordinands cared not
a curse for the Genetics, that this concourse of meta-
physicians meant only that their spiritual flaunting
was less a withdrawal from worldliness than a very
practical application of group powers he could not
yet pretend to understand. The old Aboriginal "religion" had been, he understood, based on the simple
necessities of living, of adapting to conditions and
passing knowledge from generation to generation by
way of tribal dances, songs, and stories. It was plain

to him now that the Ordinands' secretive creed was managed by very practical minds.

At the entrance to the assembly building he was stopped by a nervous young Ordinand shaking with his temerity. "Please, Atkins's Thomas, do not enter. The time is—is inconvenient."

"Why so?"

"Papa Melchizedech is in conclave with Elders."

Elders? Those semimythical inhabitants of the rarest regions of Librarian intellect? He had never seen an Elder and only half believed in their existence.

"Why, this is a rarity not to be missed."

The Ordinand gathered his courage. "No, sir! I am ordered—"

"I am the Area General; I give orders, I do not take them." He trod lightly on the man's toes, pushed him aside, and entered the conference room.

There was undoubtedly some form of Conclave in progress on the dais—Libary and three Elders in a tight circle of chairs, heads together—but on the floor the gaggles of clerks shuffled paper and snapped routinely at each other, until Soldier was seen and activity wound down to an uncertain halt. Libary turned his head, alerted by the quiet; the three Elders remained impassively still.

"Am I unwelcome? Inopportune?"

Libary said coldly, "Spare us sarcasm. We have been speaking of you." He raised his voice. "The clerks will leave the conference room until the afternoon." When the rustle of departure had died down, he asked baldly, "What do you want here, Thomas?"

"To tell you my mind and to ask a question."

"Your mind is known—in some degree. However, enlighten us further."

The Elders, Soldier thought, were as curious a group as he had encountered. They were either incredibly old or equally incredibly desiccated; they were of obvious Desert Genetic but thin beyond reason; the skin hung from their ribs in wrinkles; one of them seemed blind behind scummy eyelids. All wore thick grey beards and they slumped in their chairs without dignity, either too old or too unworldly to need it. They waited as though they did not care whether he spoke or not.

"Despite statements of immovability, the Searchers are uncertain of their future; that is why they remain in their area of encroachment and make no effort to visit the villages. They cannot risk a confrontation which would dash any hope of later assimilation. Also, they have no useful weapons with which to force themselves on us."

Libary said, "The Taylor's Nugan burned ground and grass with a finger."

"That was a defensive weapon for use against animals or close attack. It fires a bolt of power but it is not like the lasers recorded in the books of the Last Culture, able to kill or blind at a great distance. It is my opinion that *Search* carries no offensive armament; it is a settlers' transport, not a warship."

"Therefore?"

"Therefore I offer them what courtesies I can—"

"At the expense of myself and my Ordinands."

"A small sacrifice, I think, for keeping the Searchers quiet and inactive while we gather for action."

An Elder spoke, the blind man, his voice grinding with age; the words were barely intelligible, not only at some variance with the southern Angloo dialects but accented peculiarly high in the head, as though something cried out in a sandy waste. "Why do they not go? Why do they wait for the end?"

"They have nowhere to go."

"Nowhere? They tread stars and planets, yet have nowhere to go?"

"The planets of other stars are not like Earth. Men

cannot live in furnaces or ice deserts or oceans of acid. They have found only one world that might support them and that is the preserve of monsters—just as, seen from their point of view, is this one."

The sandy voice crackled at him. "Yet go they must."

"So I continually tell them."

"Yet you fraternise and take one as love-bitch."

"That term is unworthy. She and I are Matched."

"Let her break Match!"

"She cannot. She has not the power. She knows nothing of the work of the Wizards."

From the desert throat came a cackle of derision. Soldier did not at first understand that his plight was laughed at; this would have been unthinkable among the Genetics.

Libary cut into the exchange, plainly discomfited by the callousness. "The question, Thomas, is whether or not, in view of this Match, you plan in some fashion to save the Searchers from the trap you have yourself planned and set."

"We have had this talk before. I have told you they will go, and go they will."

"Yet they cannot understand this?"

"They hope for reprieve. They find it hard to come home from long voyaging to a slamming of doors. Hope dies even harder. Yet they will go."

"And your woman?"

"Will go with them. She is not bonded in our fashion and does not wish to remain here. She does not understand the meaning of the Match."

"You have not told her?"

"I am a General. I do not plead."

"And your future?"

"That I will discover in due time. Meanwhile I recognise that the Searchers could, under the impression that they bring gifts and miracles, destroy this world so laboriously built out of ruins, and so they must go. What will happen to me is a separate matter. I am a soldier first, a man second."

The desert voice creaked at him, "You'll die, lover!"

Libary cut across him. "So they will go. That is accepted. What then? Tell us your mind for the aftermath."

This was the moment he had known must come. He might prevaricate, even lie outright, but was unsure that he could carry it off; he had been trained to truth and contempt for falsehood. Besides, the ethic of community confrontation held that reasons and intentions should be stated before the engagement.

He said, "I will tell the Genetics to look to their slavery and their freedom, how they now give their muscle and time and devotion to providing food and clothing and labour for an Ordinand order of secrecy that plans for itself a glorious future which has no place in it for Foresters and Soldiers, Artisans and Sailmen, Craftsmen and Miners. I will tell them that they should share the knowledge of the Ordinands and that they should withhold their labour and good-will until the sharing is agreed."

In the silence he saw that Libary wept, sturdily upright and staring straight before him while tears crept from the corners of his eyes to stain his dark cheeks.

I have cracked his heart. Yet, what else could I have done? Truth is followed because once glimpsed it can never be put aside. So now I follow to the end.

The cracked desert chuckle of the blind man rattled in the quiet. "Hurry your telling, lover! Time grows short. The love-bitch returns to the stars and at once the insect begins biting at your brain. The mad preach neither long nor well."

His unasked question was answered; he had guessed at some such resolution and the prospect of

a failing mind was for him more horrible than any
threat of death.

He said, "You should teach that senile ape the
manners of men," and left them.

10

HE LIVED FOR FIVE DAYS IN THE NER-
vous tension of a silent screaming. It could not be
hidden; his normally still face receded further into
lined hardness, telling its tale of strain. Nobody
dared attempt comfort; the one who might have done,
Johnno, averted his face and pretended not to see his
friend when he passed the logging camp.

One morning Soldier stood behind him, speaking
quietly. "The village is under Ordinand suggestion
that I be treated with Silence because of what I
might—what I *will* say. I accept that you think first
of Bella. This trouble will pass and we will continue
companionship as if this time had never happened."

He left quickly because he knew Johnno capable of
tears and had been enough weeping these past
days.

No news came from the patrol he had sent into the
forest country. He had given the men a task without
precedent, the location and silent herding of individual outlaws, requiring more than common expertise.
He trusted his junior leaders, but in this case he had
given them a task whose end result was beyond plan-

ning but desperately necessary to his teeming, anguished mind.

Above all, Anne did not come to the bower. She sent no message by the Library teams and he could not display weakness by asking for her. Alone in the night he shook, physically shook, with an emotion that was neither fear nor desire so much as a sense of being progressively severed from the world. As well, he pictured the girl forgetting him as some new masculinity took her untrammelled fancy; he dreamed that this was the beginning of the Elder's promise that the insect would eat his brain. Anne could never know what forces of destruction her unfettered actions had let loose.

On the sixth night she came, in a shower of explanation and breathless apology, bringing "fabulous, fabulous news! I just forgot all about you and went up to orbit. I've been on *Search* with Jack." She saw the incomprehension and hurt in him and cried, "Oh, I know I should have told you but I didn't think, it was all so sudden. But how did you know?"

He said shakily, "I know nothing of this."

"But it was you that did it! Jack applied for examination of DNA records because you said he was my father. And so he is!"

It required sorting, Anne's account of her mother's indiscretions spilling out with a lack of proper gravity that he found shocking. He heard her out in a species of bedazzlement at her light treatment of unimaginable sexual freedoms, while his sinking heart saw that in no circumstance could he or any man be sure of holding her—or any man be sure of holding any woman of the Searchers. With such indiscipline, how could the race bear any but continual "misborn," with no place in a logical world?

At least she was with him for a while; his body

relaxed and the insect was denied entry.

Anne asked again, "But how did you know?" and he was forced to satisfy her by cramming a whole catalogue of knowledge into a simple statement of the sixteen major and forty minor points of genetic assessment. To her puzzled, "I look in the mirror and don't see all that much likeness," he answered that facial resemblance was not cardinal but only a superficial guide. He spoke rapidly of bone structure, telltale characteristics of hands and feet, hair distribution and fineness, skin texture, muscular flexure, and a dozen more "signatures"—all for examination as interlocking factors òf relationship between the three persons involved. "In predicting the makeup of unborn children our system is accurate three times in five, but having observed all three of you I could not err over a self-evident melding."

She said practically, "I must write all this down. The biologists will have forty fits."

But not now, Anne, not now! "Another time I will dictate the scale of comparisons to you." Then he turned her mind to more immediate needs.

In the morning, when he could manage the more formal courtesies, Soldier asked, "Are you happy to have your father known to you?"

"Of course. I'd pick him over any man on *Search*. It doesn't make any real difference but it's a nice feeling."

"And Nugan and he will live together now?"

Anne laughed into the sunrise. "They can't do that; Jack's married to someone else. She's pretty awful. And anyway, Mother doesn't want to be tied down. I can understand that; can't you?"

No, he couldn't, but he said tightly, "She must do as she feels right," while he thought, *What a cultural stew of unfeeling selfishness*.

"And there was something Jack said, not exactly a message for you but I ought to tell you. He used not to like you much."

"He was afraid I would harm you."

"Well, he knows better now. What he said was, 'The soldier-boy has come up trumps, so now I owe him one.'"

"One what?"

"A favour in return, silly."

He smiled as much at the phrasing as at the friendly thought, having no prescience that his life could balance on it.

11

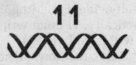

ON THE TENTH DAY THE PATROL leader sent word of having located nine of the named outlaws, the tenth being dead of a local quarrel. Soldier started off at once with a fresh group, assuring Anne that he would return in three days. She surprised herself by clinging to him in the romantically approved fashion of woman seeing her man off to the wars, and watched his departing back with a dismayed realisation that she neither wanted to part with him nor to spend her life on a rough-and-ready Earth that offended all her ideas of comfort and logical behaviour. She fled for comfort to Nugan, who tried unavailingly to talk sense to her without revealing the plight of her enslaved man, then to Jack, who scratched his head, made soothing noises, and achieved nothing.

Soldier returned a day late with his astonished and apprehensive prisoners under guard and his repressed need for Anne at exploding point. Yet, now that time was running out, their lovemaking became gentler, tinged with a preemptive sadness which neither could put into words—on one side a rather literary rapture of romantic parting covered a genuine but irresolvable emotion, on the other the pensive silence of the lover covered doubt in a desperate tactic in which he placed little faith.

On the night of Soldier's return, Sargesson held court for a small, selected audience: Brookes, Duval, Jean Sengupta (who had been most productive of suggestions bridging gaps in the research) and Nugan, whose special knowledge he needed for corroboration.

"We've got all these ancient tapes and chips sorted into order and have a pretty good idea of what the Wisharts did. You wouldn't believe—" Duval's snort cut his fancy back to basics. He continued hurriedly, "It all goes back to the Beltane business and the sterility virus the Anglophone Powers had produced with the idea of culling population down to safe reproductive limits—other people's populations, not their own. Beltane scuppered that plan but the hatred stirred when it was revealed set most of the planet readying for war, and that was when Wisharts decided to put finish to the whole sorry business and provide mankind with a fresh beginning. They recreated the sterility virus in lentiviral form and started in to redesign the race. Mad as hatters, I'd reckon, but clever scientists.

"First thing, of course, they produced a vaccine for the chosen who were to parent the new race. Races, plural, actually. Vaccine for themselves? Not a bit of it. They were good biologists who also reckoned themselves the Word of God; the whole thing was tied into religion, so they were bound to do The Right Thing, and in their crackpot way, they did. The Right Thing meant that those who didn't measure up to the genetic requirements decided by DNA inspection were to be phased out, including themselves if unfit, and the requirements were very bloody strict. What they proposed was the preservation of what they considered suitable physical types for coping with the strains of living in a world without a technological infrastructure, because they knew that as soon as numbers shrank below a certain point the technology couldn't survive. Nobody to service it and not many to use most of it and no distribution systems.

"So they looked for ideal types to survive in forests and deserts, on tropic islands, under extreme cold conditions, in mountain tracts, and so on. They settled on your Aboriginals, Nugan, as the ideal desert dwellers, Nuginians and mountain Japanese as hill people, Inuit for cold climates, and some Amerindian tribes as plainsmen. And so forth. Skin colour didn't count except when heavy melanin was a plus factor, so every racial type was represented in some fashion. Remember that Wishart Laboratories and their proselytising churches were spread worldwide, so they had easy access to every region and physical type.

"What they did was this: They made a huge survey of global genetic records on the pretext of producing a definitive study of human genetic statistics to settle the old questions of heredity and IQ, nature versus nurture and the like. They actually did the study and it's probably lying around in some library where nobody knows what it is, but it was only cover for locating and identifying the genetic ideals they wanted to preserve. They found a couple of million of their selected archetypes and vaccinated them against the lentivirus under the guise of proofing them against local epidemics and minor illnesses. You'd say it was as brazen as all get-out but it worked like a charm. Then, with all their Adams and Eves protected, they let loose the sterilising virus and, since it was a lentivirus with a delayed action up to twenty years, nobody realised the truth of the slowing birthrate until it was epidemically out of control. By then the destructive wars had split all research into underground fragments. When Wisharts themselves were bombed and burned almost out of existence there was simply no biological network remaining to recognise the virus or deal with it. Inside a century the world's population was down to bedrock; only the fertile selectees and their children remained.

"What were they like, culturally? Hunter-gatherers, perhaps, with a few farming communities on the plains. We can't tell because electronic recording had passed into history by then. The Collapse was over and the period old Libary's people call The Twilight had begun. There were probably handwritten records of a sort but the local library seems to have none."

Elsewhere on the hill Soldier put to Anne a question which had occupied him during his absence—since she lacked control of her *rom*, did she also lack other abilities? What he asked, with due care, was: "Do you control your fertility against me?"

"You mean, will I have your baby? No way, dear!" She explained birth control, not by psychophysiological means but by an injection once a month. Clumsy, he thought; the Last Culture had been in many ways primitive, denied essential capacities. "We don't want to start a child, Tommy, not the way things are. Not until we know our future."

He murmured savagely that they had no future and should make the most of the present. An unthinking movement brought his face into full moonlight and Anne cried, "What are you frightened of?"

He said quickly, "Of the present which is so short," and made physical fuss of her to bury the bad moment.

"The big Wishart problem," Sargesson continued, "had been how to prevent their ideal types interbreeding to spoil their separating-out of environmentals. With the luck of the meddling damned they discovered that pheromones can be structured to have high impact on their own genetic counterparts, and they decided to make such recognition inescapable. Along with the vaccine they injected males with a second, live virus which homed on the semen, specifically the Y chromosome. Its effect was to sensitise the almost dormant male pheromone receptors and render them violently reactive to female pheromones with close similarity to their own genetic pattern. So like was attracted to like and the system of localised Genetics was born. Purity was preserved—well, up to a point.

"It was complicated by all this rabid science being hopelessly mixed in with religious sectarianism and doubtful philosophies, with the clerical and dialectical branches inducting the proles into all manner of ecstatic beliefs. The big two were Conservation and Peaceful Co-existence. Conservation succeeded in the end because there weren't enough people around to damage the ecosphere. Peaceful Co-existence was tougher, but the general idea was that if women had an upper hand over the men, they would keep the world reasonably peaceful. So, the women's vaccination included a hormone-producing gene acting directly on the cortex, the control centre of the brain.

Its effect was to enable them to project or shut off their pheromones at will, as well as control their fertility.

"You can see how it worked: The female could look over the males and with an almost imperceptible release of pheromone pick out the best breeding partner among the affected males of her genetic pattern. She would release the full pheromone power on the chosen man and he was inescapably hooked because his receptors operate directly on the thalamus, like a powerful shot of an addictive drug. The best genealogy was preserved, in theory, though it seems to me that there was plenty of room for error and a big risk of inbreeding. The projection appeared to be that with a big gene pool and the usual generational variations and minor mutations, the thing would sort itself out in time, and apparently it did."

Nugan spoke for the first time: "It certainly did not. That's why the village Mas monitor the pairings and keep detailed records of genealogies and characteristics and guide matings very carefully."

Sargesson shot her a glance of irritation. He said, "Later, please, Nugan."

Brookes overruled him. "No, Sargie; now. Let her tell it. She's the one who's seen it all at firsthand."

Nugan explained. "Thomas told me that the female to male selection picks out the best of those presenting themselves but not necessarily the best available. The Mas often have to hunt out men from other villages. Even so, they get poor mixes about half the time and the babies are destroyed. The Mas separate the pair and seek out another male to match to the woman."

Jean Sengupta offered a single word: "Soulless!"

"Yes. Here, love has nothing to do with breeding. Mostly, the pairs do become mutually attached, but some separate once the breeding programme is completed and look for more socially compatible mates but don't breed with them."

They digested the variation on the sexual/social minuet with frowns and headshakes until Jean asked, "What happens to the fixated men when they separate? Continual stimulation of the thalamus is addictive."

Nugan nodded. "The withdrawal symptoms could be horrendous, but they have a system to deal with it. The woman withdraws her stimulation for longer and longer periods while the man is kept in a state of semisedation with herbal potions. Thomas told me this and he knows little about hormones and enzymes, but I must guess that the herbs have some suppressant effect to damp down the hormone production. After a while they bring in another woman—presumably a better choice by the local Ma—and gradually switch the man's receptor reaction from the old mate to the new one. The whole thing takes several months and for part of it the man has an unpleasant experience they call 'beetle-head'; he feels that an insect is burrowing at his brain and sometimes has to be strapped down for a day or two. What they call 'the Match' doesn't come apart easily—for the man."

Duval screwed his face up while Sargesson made furious notes on a pad. Duval said, "The girls have had their revenge, haven't they? No wonder they can wield social pressure. But it probably does help keep the peace."

Nugan told him, drily, "The Desert Genetic soldiers keep the peace; the villagers fight like hoodlums among themselves, women as well as men, but there are local rules and it isn't often that anyone is seriously hurt. Weapons are considered bad form outside the soldiery and the soldiers come down heavily on anyone using them."

Life on Earth seemed suddenly less paradisal. Jean asked, "What happens to the man if there is no managed period of withdrawal? If, for instance, the matchwoman is killed by accident?"

"I don't know. Thomas doesn't know, either, because such cases are very rare. Breeding pairs are surrounded with every possible guard against mischance and quarantined at the least sign of an outbreak of sickness. Sooner or later, though, it must happen and I think the 'beetle' would get the poor brute. The addiction is so powerful that 'cold turkey' doesn't begin to describe the cutoff. This is one area of Wishart meddling that got completely out of hand."

Duval happily thanked Mother Nature for their own hit-or-miss system.

"Which Thomas sees as barbarous," Nugan told him. "To him we are a genetic stew without direction or reason."

Jean said, tentatively, "About Thomas . . . he really does mean us to go, doesn't he?"

"He surely does."

"Then his attachment to Anne . . . ?"

"I've been wondering if anyone would think about poor bloody condemned-to-hell Thomas."

Sargesson snapped, "He's your friend, not ours."

Brookes signed to him to shut up. "Go on, Nugan."

"Thomas's attachment is essentially one-sided. Anne was fascinated by him as something new and different in male magnetism and at first sight of him in the flesh her pheromone level rose—and by all evil luck, on a thousand to one chance, they are a near enough genetic match to trap him helplessly. If that were not so, he would simply use her for pleasure and pass on, unaffected, but as it is the end may be tragic for him. The whole withdrawal procedure hangs on the woman being able to control her pheromone emission, to bring the man down like a junkie with ever smaller doses at longer intervals, but Anne hasn't the control gene. When we go—and I am sure we will go, no matter how you feel about it—the cut-off for him will be instantaneous and permanent. Thomas's guess is that he will go insane. He spoke of it to me as calmly as if it meant a bad headache, but he is terrified."

Sargesson said unpleasantly, "If he wasn't so keen on giving us the heave-ho, we might do something for him. He can always call off his dogs."

"If that's an invitation to blackmail, forget it. You don't understand his idea of duty. He sees us as a cancer threatening his people, and his lifework is protection of the people. That success may cost him his sanity or his life doesn't weigh against his dedicated duty."

"All right, so you have to respect him, but it all seems so unnecessary. A little gene surgery to cut off the hormone flow and maybe some work on the receptors to block the thalamic intake and he'd be as good as new."

"Offer it and he'll laugh at your impertinence. He's a soldier first, last, and always."

Brookes made an inarticulate, disgusted sound. "He acts and speaks like a monomaniac and there's no rationalising that kind. However, if he's so damned important and valuable, the Mas will do something for him."

"I don't think they can and if they can, they won't. I saw his friend, Johnno, yesterday on the Library track; I think he was looking for me. He told me that Thomas is under 'Silence.' That is a step short of social ostracism but I don't know what he has done and even Johnno can only say he seems to have talked out of turn, insulted the Elders or some such, but about what? His match with Anne is public knowledge and puts him under suspicion; the imposition of public Silence sounds like preparation for killing him when his immediate usefulness runs out."

Brookes threw up his hands. "For fraternising with the enemy? When he can't help himself? What a people! We might be well out of the place, even at Postvorta."

Duval spoke quietly. "I'm inclined to agree, but try telling that to the Wakings. They'll have to be dragged off the Earth screaming."

"And so they may be," Nugan told him. "Thomas doesn't talk for effect. I have a suspicion that he has tried to change the minds of the Ordinands and I may be responsible. We talked a lot about other forms of society and he wasn't slow to see advantages though he refused to discuss them. If that's so, once Anne is gone they'll let him rot alive—as a lesson to others who may contract intellectual illnesses."

"Why did this Johnno come to you, Nugan?"

"He's Thomas's close friend and he has a mind of his own. He seemed to think our Wizardries—that's his word for our science—could help."

Sargesson laughed. "Give succour and comfort to a manic obsessive whose one idea is to shove us back into space? Let him drop his plans first."

"I doubt that he could, even if he would. Johnno said the villages are crowded with high-degree Ordinands, so the thing probably has its own momentum. Remember that Thomas has promised that none of us will be harmed. Whatever plan is in the wind, it is already set up."

Duval pushed his head forward, searching. "Actually, he said none would be physically harmed. That must mean hypnotic attack by massed Ordinands. I think we can bear with that."

"Hypnosis? Then why did Libary give me the book on the morphic field, if not to frighten us off?"

"Do you believe in that stuff?"

"For want of any other idea I'm beginning to."

Sargesson said loudly, "Well, I'm buggered if I am."

Nugan shivered. "I was there. I saw."

12

DAY, NIGHT, DAY, NIGHT, TIME SLIPPED smoothly, swiftly toward the waiting uproar of Carnival and whatever other excitement might transpire amid the frenzy.

To the soldiers and villagers it seemed that the Searchers nested on their hilltop and made no attempt to explore; goods and "angels" moved between Earth and ship on an invisible line but no one ventured further than a short and nervous way beyond the Library.

To the Searchers it seemed that they lived in a ferment of plan, hope, fear, and anticipation. Deputations lectured Brookes on action he must take and he, knowing his and their limitations, denied them all; they bowed to his refusals because their ideas were nebulous and pettish. They dared not shed blood because that would block their acceptance irrevocably, showing them once and for all as neither peaceable nor honest; they could only wait and trust scientific sophistication to withstand the crudity of naive, hysterical attack.

A mental training system for resisting hypnosis—

a tried, proven, and very effective system—was practised by daily classes. Nugan attended as a silent par-
ticipant, unpopular and mostly ignored by the
Searchers who saw her as a dissident with peculiar
ideas of right and wrong. She hoped the system might
be useful but thought about the vague, repudiated
morphic field and wondered privately if hypnosis
was indeed involved.

All activity amounted to a tension of waiting.
*When they show their hand we'll take the necessary
action; they're only primitives with a trumped-up society that will fall apart as soon as intelligence is applied.*

General the Atkins's Thomas sat on the ground, his
nine Desert Genetic prisoners—men similar to himself in general physique but lacking one invisible and
disastrous faculty—seated around him. There were
no guards; these men would not try to escape now
that they knew they had not been brought in for ex-
ecution, and he wanted no listening troopers—yet.

He said bluntly, on the first of their conversations,
"You are called mental cripples."

They did not pretend hurt resentment; they were
accustomed to pitying contempt from even the outlaw criminals. The Yarra Valley General, though, had
a reputation for devious approaches to successful
projects. They reserved judgment.

Their lack was socially brutal. Birthing selection
for the Desert Genetic was less certain than for the
Foresters. The Mas shrugged irritable shoulders and
allowed that the Wizards had been careless or less
than wholly expert, but they had to watch Desert babies carefully for signs of the defect which did not
become apparent until puberty—a lack of *rom* receptors or a sense of smell. Those discovered were killed
or, if intellectually capable, steered into the colleges

of Ordinands, but there were always some, cunning and aware, who hid their disfunction until they could make their escape to the outlaw bands.

"You nine escaped," Soldier said, "because you have courage and good minds and a will to live—but not as Ordinands in the hermitage on the hill. Because you were born to be soldiers and athletes, you have survived. You have shown that you can live successfully outside the society of righteous rules and self-righteous judgments."

That brought their heads up; this was no talk to hear from a General.

"Why, then," Thomas asked, "should society not overcome its birth-fright to find a place for those who have much to contribute, given opportunity instead of condemnation?"

This was racial treason, but it fitted the half-formed longings of their lonely moments of introspection; there was stimulant shock in hearing it spoken by such a man. They did not accept the dangerous communication at once, but Thomas's reputation for honest dealing encouraged them; after some initial confusion they discussed it in terms of "rightness" and a misty concept of "fair play", for "justice" was a word with only restricted meaning in a society where behaviour was either right or wrong. Also, troopers had told them that the General was under Silence—a fact extraordinary in itself—for reasons unknown. Now they knew the reasons. The wonder was that he had been allowed to live.

In the end they shrugged and decided that discussion was fruitless; the communities had no use for them and they could live only by virtue of strong bodies, alert wits, and the existence of broad, unpopulated areas.

From Thomas's standpoint they were, if less than

bold in their attack on an ingrained repression, at least prepared mentally for new and strange suggestions from an able and friendly General.

He told them what he wanted of them.

Under the stars Anne said, "Today I was called your whore."

Soldier's ear heard her as only a little resentful and rather more excited at being a focus of attention. At eighteen she should have been emotionally better balanced, but he realised that in her ship she had experienced few of the formative problems and traumas of adolescence; her competent mind was hampered by stunted perceptions.

"I have read the word, Anne, but am unsure of its exact meaning. Is it pejorative?"

"It certainly is. It means a woman who has sex with any man who puts it to her."

"Why is that pejorative? All take pleasure where they find it; only the Match restricts." She did not want to hear of the Match; Brookes's influence had precluded any clear understanding of it and her mind filed it as some unpleasant practice of the villagers. He asked, "Why did they insult you?"

"They wanted something."

"The word was an attempt to soften your resistance with scorn?"

"Something like that." She fell silent, biting her upper lip as if unwilling to explain further. Soldier waited until she capitulated in the tone of one afraid of being thought foolish. "They said I could make you do anything I wanted."

"Make me?" She was manifestly uncomfortable. "Who said such a thing?"

"Some of the women. And Mister Sargesson, the biologist."

"He is a featherweight who thinks his beliefs are

truths. Did he say how you could make me?"

"By refusing to come here again if you didn't do what I wanted." Another silence stretched between them, her eyes searching the stars for comfort, his watching her face while he wondered if she understood the meaning of what had been told her. He thought not; she could not have concealed her knowledge. She asked, "You aren't that weak, are you, Tommy?"

"No, I am not. Shall I guess what you were to ask of me? That I call off my forces and allow your people to stay on Earth. Are they frightened?"

"A little bit, but mostly pretending it's all a big joke. You know, savages against a scientific culture. Some are curious what you'll do; some are contemptuous—or trying to be."

"Are they, indeed?"

"What will I tell them?"

"First, that my forces are of little importance; there will be no violence. Second, that the matter is not in my hands to help or hinder. Third, that if it were, I still would not interfere. And, last, that I have contempt for those who would use my love as a weapon of blackmail."

"I told them that last part. They only kept on saying, 'You tell him and we'll see.' They won't believe the rest; they won't want to."

He kissed her slowly, thoughtfully, repressing his fear.

After a while she said the painful thing she had been holding back, "This will have to be our last night, Tommy." She could not see the fear leap up. She was oblivious of his heightened heartbeat and the desperation struggling to reach his guarded eyes. "They won't let me come again; they'll be angry and they'll watch me."

"Would they harm you?"

She was unsure and behind the unsureness afraid. "Some of them might. They've left spiteful notes in our tent and twice someone has thrown stones at Mother and dodged out of sight. They blame her because she won't hate you."

Stress, he thought, *arouses the ugly child in the crowd mind*. He said steadily, "You must not come again. There are only three nights to Carnival and I will be with you, watching after you, at the end."

She saw that as chivalrous and romantic in an old-fashioned way and through the night she tried to comfort him, forecasting all the beautiful women he would love in years to come, remembering her only as the outlandish girl loved in outlandish meetings once upon a time.

She did not know she hurt him bitterly because under her chatter lay the shallowness of excitement and the power of her desire to leave this repulsive planet, this reality so at odds with the safe womb of *Search*.

Through the emotional turmoil he remembered the message she must carry for him. "Tell Captain Brookes that on the last night I will be there. He is a well-meaning man in his fashion and I may be of some assistance to him."

"Assistance, Tommy?"

"Yes. Tell him that."

In the morning he spoke again with his nine renegades and four of them rejected the chancy, dangerous offer he had made them. One had a woman with child in the forest and his place was by her. Soldier nodded; the Desert Genetic was reared in social duty and they understood each other. The other three preferred to remain with the outlaw brotherhood with all its hardships. "Better," they thought, "the fate you know . . . " He read them as fearing the unknown;

they had been trained as couriers, not as troopers, before they ran for their freedom. The five with military training opted to remain; they needed hope of a future and the General's reputation stood high.

One of the refusers asked slyly, "Have you told your troopers your dangerous ideas of the right to knowledge and the freedom to foment change?"

"I am under Silence; I don't disturb their peace by ranting at those who can't speak a word in return."

The renegade said, "In the forest we invent our own customs and restraints. We are deviants, thieves, and fornicators in continual Carnival; our restraints are as flexible as our daily circumstances. Your ideas don't surprise us as they will the villagers and troopers who follow custom without thinking about it. Still, they will listen and argue—and learn through argument."

"You would add subversion to your other troublemaking?"

"Why not? Who can put *us* under Silence?"

Soldier wrote them safe-conducts. "On the third morning you must be gone from this camp. You will not be pursued or harmed. As a courtesy, you should make me personal farewell as you leave. By then you might have something of interest to tell me."

The four laughed together as they left for the army lines, anticipating two days of devastatingly free speech under the written protection of the General.

"Now," Soldier said to the remaining five, "you have settled for an attempt which may or may not succeed, but I will do my best to bring it off."

That night the camp was in a state of muted uproar; several fights broke out. The ostracised General strolled between the rows of hut dwellings to be sure his renegades were not being beaten despite his written order, and found them busy with parties of rowdy, argumentative listeners. His troopers pretended, for the most part, not to see him but a few smiled quietly as he passed. Many of them, he gathered, were scandalised and shamed by the revelation of their General's offences against the norms of behaviour, but the quasi-intellectual loudmouths present in any large group were picking over the ideas with pretence of open-mindedness and some real pleasure in disruption.

In the morning a handful of troopers would be relaying the scandal to Johnno's timber-fellers—and the whole gaggle of Elders in Conclave could hardly put the army and all the Yarra Valley villages under Silence.

He did not imagine any great upsurge of questioning and demanding; he was planting a seed for flowering in its own time. He thought grimly that whether he died of the insect or by exasperated murder, he would be remembered.

On the morning of the day before Carnival, Soldier started for the village; there was a duty outstanding and he would not find a later opportunity to render it.

On the way he made his customary visit to the Library for his General's Inspection, which was unnecessary but expected of him and, under the Silence, only a gesture.

There he found Nugan waiting for him.

Before she could speak, he asked, "Have Sargesson's guttersnipes molested Anne?"

"They don't dare. Captain Brookes has turned some operatives into a policing team and given them permission to confine peacebreakers."

"He shows sense, but he will find that social restraints once installed cannot easily be withdrawn. What do you want, Nugan?"

She ignored the brusqueness; his circumstances were formidable. "I have a message: Our scientists know how your Wizards programmed the Genetics; there were laboratory records in the Library chips." He said nothing but his eyes fastened intently on her. She continued, nervously. "It didn't all work out as they intended. The Forest Genetic is far too muscle-bound and stocky for the ideal heavy labouring type they meant to produce—and the operation of pheromone detection, what you call the *rom*, had uncalculated consequences."

She stopped, searching his face. He asked, flatly, "So?"

"Thomas, I broke my word to you."

"You have told Anne?" His voice was dangerous.

"Heavens, no! Her conscience would never be rid of it. I told the Captain's council about the beetleheads."

"Why?"

"I wanted them to understand your situation."

He was puzzled. "To what purpose?"

"I was sick of hearing them blame you for every wrong thing; I wanted them to see that we have already loosed one curse by sheer happenstance."

Soldier smiled at last. "Nugan, under other fates we could be friends forever. They must hate you."

She brushed that aside. "They told me the surgeons can mend the effect of the broken Match. They know how it happens and it can be erased."

He sat down abruptly on the moat wall, head cocked, looking up at her. "Do you think this is true?"

"I'm sure of it."

He nodded to himself. "And the price?"

She spread her hands in helplessness. "I keep telling them that the situation is out of your hands but they still feel that you have only to give an order and the—evacuation—will be called off. You are the only authority they ever see in the flesh and I can't convince them that other powers are involved."

"It is sometimes difficult to understand, Nugan, that astute minds can be part of a self-deluding mass. If it were not for yourself and that Jack who says he owes me one, I would wonder if your culture was worth notice." He took Nugan's hands between his. "Or did you, in your secret heart, hope I could conjure up a miracle in return for the promise of life and sanity?"

She bent forward and kissed him, gently. "No, Thomas. I know you and your duty well enough. I have brought their message, no more than that."

Soldier stood. "I must leave you. I have told Anne I will be there to watch over her welfare at the end, so I will see you also tomorrow night."

"Consorting with the enemy to the end? Seeing us off in style? Jack will be here, too. He has made the drop in some fatherly fantasy of caring for his daughter, but I think he wants to see what happens."

"Strangely, you may think, so do I." He turned from her with a brief wave of the hand.

Ten metres away, he called over his shoulder, "Tell Captain Brookes I will bring a gift for him—not a victor's mockery but something for use at your distant star."

Brookes would have his message twice. That should be enough to engage the man's attention and gain him a hearing in the heart of the coming chaos.

A half hour later, in the village, he made no attempt to catch the eyes of those he knew; rather he observed the outland features of men and women in exotic dress who spoke in impenetrable tongues while they crowded the single long street. He had never seen Asiatics before, or even the nearer Nuginians, and could only guess their provenance from the recollection of travellers' tales and paintings occasionally studied. They packed the village and he knew that communes up and down the river were in similar state, their presence borne by the Genetics with public stoicism and private, caustic irritation.

He had demanded a thousand and they were here.

Without a pause for his tight-wound mind to reconsider, he turned into the meeting hall where Libary sat on the dais and clerical Ordinands murmured around the floor. No Elders were present; so much the better.

He stood in the centre of the hall to raise his voice, loud and clear and insulting: "Order your servants to be quiet! I have words for you, but they may hear them."

The place was instantly silent and still. Libary raised his head without haste and held Thomas's eye through a long beat of anger before he said, "I do not permit soldier-stratagems in my preserve and my Ordinands should not be subjected to insolence. We will speak in my quarters."

He left his desk and Thomas had no choice but to follow him, satisfied, however, that he had given clerical tongues some wagging matter; they would be shocked into greater chatter when the facts seeped through to them.

In the small, cluttered room Libary took stance in midfloor, taut and glaring, under attack. Thomas said, conversationally, "Tomorrow at evening the ousting of the Searchers begins. When they are gone, the ending of Thomas begins."

Libary did not speak but a singular motion shook him, a quivering of his whole body; for a moment it seemed that his frame wavered in the light of the single window. The anger died from his eyes and he reached for the desk to steady himself.

Thomas said, "I have some curiosity in the outcome. Does death by the insect's pecking come quickly?"

Libary's lips quivered, opened a little, and closed. He could not speak.

"Come, come, old man! You have your duty and I mine, so we can discuss damnation in the certainty of sharing it, you as executioner, I as victim. It is a settled procedure; emotion can be decently controlled."

Libary turned his back, perhaps to hide his shaking hands. He breathed deeply twice and spoke with a gasp: "Not quickly. Decay of the soul requires many weeks." He took another long breath. "As a strong man with a strong mind, you may not die."

"Not? Slobber and dribble out mindless years?"

Libary did not answer that but said, "I raised you to be a man with a questing mind but you have peered too closely at the future. The Silence is a necessary imposition but the girl, the Taylor's Anne, is not our doing."

Thomas told him with relentless cheerfulness, "At least I have tasted the great passion, but the price is high. You have done your duty as you saw it and I understand you better than you have understood me—Father."

The word struck home like an arrow, poison tipped. The old man shuddered.

"You don't deny fatherhood in this final meeting? Your scholarly order imposes harsh disciplines, I think, in its distillation of the pure, yearning spirit. Yearning for what? The ineffable?"

Unexpectedly, he was answered. "For the fulfilment of creation, the triumph of mind."

"Such self-loving nonsense! Domination finding a sweet-smelling name for itself! Soldiers are familiar with the excuse." With a change of tone, a drop into friendly gossip, he said, "The Searcher doctors know how to neutralise the insect."

Libary stiffened as if struck. He turned to face Thomas, head forward, seeking the unbelievable.

"They have made me an offer: I call off my dogs and they excise my beetle. Being an honest soldier rather than a devious Ordinand, I had to explain that those same dishonest Ordinands are not my dogs—alas for that—and so the eviction will proceed, with or without my contribution. They are still not convinced that you can shift them."

The old man's face faded to the hue of dried, yellowing paper as the blood drained from it. He whispered, "They will be," refusing the evidence of his son's monstrous dedication.

"I am sure of it. I designed the assault and I have never lost an engagement. But that's by the bye; I wish only to be sure that you understand where your rearing of an inquisitive intellect has led us both."

"Cruel!"

"I think I have earned a little satisfaction, Father. Who is—or was—my mother?"

Libary muttered, "The Top-Ma whom you challenged on your first visit here. Do not harass her."

"Why should I? She's an admirable woman within her limits, like yourself dedicated to necessity rather than humanity. She showed little interest in a not so negligible son. But then, it was a Carnival flutter, wasn't it? Nothing to be serious about. Well, Father, we shan't meet again so it is as well you should know that my subversive ideas—more subversive than you can guess—are in circulation and finding some timid acceptance. That will grow. Victoria will be contaminated in a month or two, Australia in a year. Not you or the whole clique of Elders will stop the tongues prattling because none of you will dare to put the armies under Silence, much less whole regions of chattering Genetics. That would be the end of your unspoken rule from the hilltop hermitages of ancient books and arcane shamanism. My insect and I leave the problem with you."

Libary put his hands to his head. Perhaps it ached or perhaps he hid tears.

"A last question, Father: When you were a human being, a mere member of Desert Genetic, still unconsecrated to ambition, was your name Atkins?"

The old man was silent.

"No? So Tommy Atkins, born to be a soldier, was a learned joke? 'And it's, Thank you, Mister Atkins, when the band begins to play.' Well, Tommy's done his job and you have done yours and the band is playing a fine coda for both of us."

When the old man collapsed, Soldier held him for a moment in his arms before he laid him on the bed, bent forward to kiss the black face, and left.

A good son might have been less cruel but I am only human, even where I love. I am Soldier, with death and the insect for company—and only Soldier's lust for life to cheat them both—perhaps, perhaps, perhaps . . .

13

THE FOUR WHO WERE RETURNING TO the forest, clad now in camouflage uniforms drawn for them from Store, made their farewells at dawn. The man whose wife was with child told Soldier that his attack on things-as-they-are had borne at least some fruit of argument, but: "Save in a few minds it remains an airy mental exercise. Overturning history is not simple while comfortable life beckons more than thorny questions."

Soldier nodded. "And you?"

"Oh, I'm an empty vessel for filling. Once I had fled from village law and custom, custom gave way to necessity, and the Ordinand version of wisdom faded. I'll argue your case where I find willing ears—and I speak for the four of us. Let troublemaking be our business!"

"You must keep on the move. You'll soon be pinpointed for death."

"What's new in that?"

The sly-eyed man, who had openly enjoyed his role as subversive element whether he believed his arguments or not, interposed sardonic warning: "We'll last longer than you, General. You'll be hunted as soon as tonight's work is over."

From behind Soldier one of the five who had elected to remain with him spoke sharply, "His own men won't hunt him willingly and anyone else must deal first with us."

That was warming; Soldier had been uncertain of their attitudes and the statement lifted his heart. He watched his four apostles move to the edge of the forest, wave to him, and become flickers of camouflage dying at once in tree and shadow.

He turned to the five. "I have orders to give to officers who are bound by Silence and so cannot question or make suggestions. Will you constitute yourselves Runners for me?"

The Caselli's Ramon, a redheaded outbreed with grotesquely contrasting dark Koori skin, answered for all of them, "You don't have to ask. We'll get used to taking orders if we live long enough."

"Thank you." He began to drill them in the precise, simple instructions to be passed. At the end, Ramon asked, "Will we be accepted as messengers? This is not friendly relaxation round a campfire."

"I think you will."

The Flynn's Rick-Jemmy, oldest of the five, asked, "But will they obey you?"

"They must. Silence shuts their mouths but does not absolve them of obedience." He grinned at them a little wolfishly. "The Silence tangles itself in paradox when not properly thought out beforehand."

As it turned out, the officers had reached that conclusion for themselves; the day moved smoothly to its fulfilment.

Later in the morning, the army of the Murray Valley General came marching out of the trees. With their arrival, preparation was almost complete; for each of the Ordinand adepts Soldier had now two armed troopers to stand behind him, sealing the Searchers in the heart of the circle.

An hour before sundown he trotted uphill to the black canopy, wearing uniform but carrying no weapons, his head and heart full of Anne as with a long, fine memory of something put aside. He had schooled himself to a dull, yearning grief while his will demanded total concentration on the work in hand. The man ached for the presence of the girl but the soldier needed her absence. A touch of her *rom* could bring him incompetent and undone.

The Ordinands were already gathering in groups on the slope of the hill. Was his father there yet? He did not want to know. He had wounds enough without opening that scar.

On the crown of the hill a few Searcher teenagers played a ball game with much throwing and running while the older people watched listlessly. They saw

him and became ostentatious in refusing to acknowledge him. Obstinacy was their only weapon; Soldier
could have shown them some quite ingenious offen-
sives available to people who thought with military
minds, but they had nothing in the way of communal
thinking to bind them for action. They were specialists, each enclosed in his or her discipline—in essence a mob. Intelligent, but a mob.

He waited in the ambit of the vid cameras until a
man came, one he recognised from the Library as Duval, a courteous man who asked nothing and offered
nothing and now stood mutely looking at him.

Soldier said, "Your Library Detail attended as
usual this morning."

Duval answered casually, completing the sentence.
"And will return at the normal time, a little before
dusk."

"They will find three thousand people, two-thirds
of them troopers, spread across the slope." Duval was
uneasy but silent. "They will not be prevented or harassed."

Duval kicked at a patch of dead grass. "Troopers?"

"A containing force, not permitted to attack."

"Who will guarantee that?"

"I. I will be here with you throughout the eviction."

Duval did not hide surprise. "That's a risk, General. Some overwrought evictee may kill you in the—
excitement. There are a few hand weapons here."

"In the gloves of the dropsuits? No matter. I imagine you are one who knows my situation with regard
to the Taylor's Anne. You will understand that con-
tinuance of my life no longer guides my decisions."
(That was close to a lie, but in ostracism he had begun
the manufacture of his own morality.)

Duval   flushed.   "Unfortunate . . . unfair . . . nobody's fault."

"The fault of our meddling Wizards, perhaps?" They exchanged wintry smiles. "I have an instruction for you."

"Instruction, General? That's an impertinence."

"So is your continued presence here. By sundown, all your people must be in the open, away from their tents, outside the canopy."

Duval abandoned courtesy. "The hell you say! Do you think they'll shift for you?"

"If they do not, I promise they will be most unpleasantly shifted."

"Troopers, General?"

"Not a hand may be laid on man or woman. That also I promise."

"Shifted by what, then?"

Soldier considered him sombrely. He thought Duval a man to be respected and that many of his people would be of his kind; they deserved some understanding of what they faced. "There will be realities because I deal only in realities; these will be my contribution to the planning. Papa Melchizedech has told me that each man and woman carries hell in the depths of the mind; of the reality of what he and his Readers plan I am less certain."

They had been given the book; if they had wisdom, they might observe the implications.

Duval thought, *The hypnosis bit; we're prepared for that.* He smiled. " 'A host of furious fancies?' Tom o'Bedlam marching with Tommy Atkins?"

Soldier shrugged, turned his back, and strode downhill. He had given as much as he deemed reasonable.

The Library Detail sweated its way up with an irate Sargesson in the lead, outraged and swearing. "The bloody hill is alive with soldiers and skinny, naked old buggers like a senility congress."

Duval, seated gnomelike on a tussock, nodded up at him. "You were not molested?"

"You'd have thought we weren't there. Some of them looked like Asiatics."

"I know. I've been down to see."

"So what's on?"

"How should I know?" He bent forward, abruptly alert. "What's that?"

A furry animal, point-nosed and long-tailed, pattered out of the grass between Sargesson's feet and stopped, nose quivering, examining the men, unafraid.

"A rat." Sargesson kicked clumsily, missed, and swore as it leapt away to vanish in the grass. "*Rattus rattus*, a sewer rat. One species time can't conquer."

Duval gazed after the animal, thinking that sewer rats were not found on bare hilltops or far from water; the country cousins were commonly smaller and— He dragged thought back to the moment. "Soldier Thomas has been here."

"So?"

"He says that if we know what's good for us, we'll all be out from under the canopy by sundown."

"Fuck soldier Thomas."

"Suit yourself; I only pass the message."

"I'm going to shower and change and write up my notes. Soldier Thomas can do a rain dance and invoke the spirits of his ancestors but I won't be watching."

One of the Detail asked, "What's to happen?"

Duval repeated wearily, "He didn't say. We're to be evicted, that's all."

Sargesson snorted. "Another *son et lumière*, as for Nugan? Spells and wicked enchantments!" He made to pass Duval, then stopped. "Those troops down there are armed with long poles. Why?"

"Crowd control, I'd say, in case we try to break out

of the magic circle. Those poles are called quarterstaves. Robin Hood stuff. They can deliver a smart bruise or crack your skull."

"Medieval junk!" He passed on.

The Detail, Duval noticed, were less openly contemptuous. Again he considered the rat, so far from its proper surroundings.

Nugan materialised in the sinking sunlight. "I've sent Anne back to *Search*."

"Wise. A distracted man may do something ill-considered."

She slapped at her face. "That's what I thought."

"Did something bite you?"

"Yes." She stared at the tiny, thin body and transparent wings plastered on her finger. "An insect of some sort."

He peered. "A mosquito. One of the old plague carriers. It shouldn't be here."

"Insects are survivors."

"I meant that mosquitoes are found only near stagnant water."

"Species change with time."

He was thinking that eviction might have begun without their noticing. "Let's look downhill."

Some three hundred metres down, a line of dark, naked men stretched across the slope and disappeared round its sides. They sat, cross-legged, two or three metres apart, faces turned uphill although the edge of the crest would prevent their seeing the canopy. Behind each naked man stood two camouflage-suited troopers, most of them armed with quarterstaves. The whole assembly was motionless and soundless.

Duval produced telelenses. "A few have longbows. Those things can fire an arrow better than half a K."

Nugan said, "The stillness is eerie. It must have

been like this before the old battles—everybody waiting."

Two rats, one brown, one grey, appeared as if from nowhere and scampered towards the canopy while something buzzed in the air above them. Duval slapped his hand and inspected the smear of blood. "Not waiting, Nugan. Let's get back to the crest."

As they turned, a dropsuited figure came clumping down to them, unhelmeted—McCann, asking, "Where's everybody?"

"Being brave in their tents. An act of defiance because Thomas warned them to be outside. Stupid."

"Maybe. I've brought down all the dropsuits we have, twenty-four of them, in case some get queasy and want to go up top. Do you know what I saw, coming down? That row of soldiers and Ordinands rings the whole hill. *Search* took a count and there's three thousand of them, all told, a circle a full K across. Nugan, here's your military mate."

A man had stepped through the line of Ordinands and now came steadily towards them. It was Soldier, clad only in shorts and shoes, weaponless and empty-handed.

McCann called out, "You've got a bloody nerve, coming into the enemy's nest!"

"Does it matter, Mister McCann? I am a dead man, whatever happens, and I promised I would be here. Where is Anne?"

Nugan answered him. "I sent her back to the ship."

"She went willingly?"

"At first, not. I persuaded her and I was pretty unpleasant about it. In the end she said, 'Perhaps it's as well it's over,' but she is regretful."

Soldier studied the ground. "That was best." She regretted, so it was not yet over.

The sun had dipped out of sight while they talked and the Yarra Valley was already dark. From the shadow marking the course of the river a low sound emerged and swelled, the sound of a crowd hailing the moment of celebration. From the deep shadow, fire shot into the air, red and yellow and green, streaking high to burst in coloured rain, in arches and fountains and umbrellas of brilliance spreading and drifting down into the roar of village humanity.

Soldier said, "Carnival begins. There is rejoicing down there, but not at your going. They have forgotten you—and me—already in the rage of unleashed licence."

McCann slapped his cheek. "I'm glad somebody's happy. What the hell bit me?" and Duval, staring over the canopy, asked, "What are those hang gliders doing?"

In the fading light the hang gliders came diving down towards the canopy, flattening out to skim across it and leave a trail of smoky dust that dissipated as it drifted down onto the black surface. There seemed an endless number of them diving, skimming, and disappearing down the further slope to catch an updraft and return to dive and dispense their dust again.

"What are they doing, Thomas?"

"Seeding the canopy with gunpowder. You are to have a fire."

Before a surprised Duval could ask more, from the depths of the canopy a woman's voice shrieked in hysterical terror and in moments the Searcher encroachment erupted in a panic uproar to drown the sound of Carnival.

14

SARGESSON MAY HAVE BEEN THE FIRST
visited by the fear, possibly because his arachnophobia rendered him helplessly susceptible, but it was
not he who screamed. His reaction to the spider was
a still, silent tension, a gut sickness and freezing of
thought, a disability with him from childhood that
no shame could cure.

He was under the shower, chewing on his contempt for the Ordinands, who threatened more than
they could deliver, when he saw the shadow on the
glassine curtain, predatory legs covering a span
wider than his hand, heavy bulb of body at rest in
murderous waiting.

He froze absolutely, arm upraised, soaping hand in
armpit, until his lungs could no longer function and
he gasped for air. He found at the bottom of revulsion
a tiny capacity to move, to retreat in little half paces
to the opening in the curtain, eyes on the monster,
sure that it watched him and would race around the
material to head him off. It shifted slightly, in a tentative, questing fashion and with a strangled sob he
backed out of the shower enclosure until the release
rail of the drying jet caught him behind the heel; he
sprawled full length and the activated heat shimmered in the air above him.

In terror of malevolent legs on his flesh he rolled

to his feet and ran for the door slit of the tent, to stop in agonised shock at sight of the thing poised at the apex of the slit, ready to spring if he passed beneath. No, it was another, larger than the first, jointed limbs rough with brown fur and flexed for the leap.

With an effort of will he looked back to the shower curtain, to see the first brute turn unhurriedly until it could see him. The other did not move; he was imprisoned between them.

He knew them for hunting spiders, commonplace in the gardens and forests. He knew, too, that they were the marauders who in winter squeezed through ventilators in search of warmth and skittered in random evil across walls and ceilings. He knew all he needed to know, that they were said to be harmless and more frightened than he, but were said also to deliver a gangrenous bite when cornered. Knowledge was meaningless against the fear. As a young man he had sat petrified while his mother swatted at the things with a flapping towel, and laughed at his paralysis and never understood it.

There was nothing he could do while the brown sentry guarded the escape, fangs oscillating gently in its waiting head. He might have been there indefinitely if someone listening from outside to the wasting water, had not shaken the tent walls and yelled, "Are you going to be there all night, Sargie?"

The shaking disturbed the larger brute. It raced upwards and across the flat ceiling panel with frightening speed and in blind desperation Sargesson dashed for the unguarded exit before the thing should drop to settle on his face.

A startled Peter Jones watched Sargesson run naked, towel forgotten, as if devils pursued. He called out and was not heeded, perhaps not heard. The man vanished among the tents.

Jones shook his head, puzzled but not disturbed.

He might have been thoroughly disturbed had he known that Sargesson raced for the dropsuit lockers and crammed his shaking body into the first to hand. But by then Jones had his own problem . . .

. . . naked, with only his towel wrapped round his hips, he stepped onto the draining-floor and at once saw the hunting spiders, huge brutes, larger than any he had ever encountered. He was not bothered by them but he knew now what ailed Sargesson. He had heard the man confess his arachnophobia with the half-rueful honesty of one who knows he will never face his fear in spiderless *Search*. This pair must have frightened the living bejesus out of him.

Jones could not empathise; as a ranger in the New Zealand forests he had been familiar with the things that leapt and bit and crawled. He had never . . . But he had, as a child . . . The memory returned with peculiar power, as if forced into his protesting brain, of the old holiday hotel room where to his terrified eyes the walls had seemed to writhe with their cover of cockroaches and in the darkness the bedbugs had bitten him until his father came to hush his screaming and . . .

. . . the spiders faded from sight, as if they did not belong in his vision. His mind clipped briefly on an idea—*Sargesson's spiders, not mine*—before it was wholly taken with the black mass of insects and the musty smell of them, clinging to the walls and crawling over his bed, seeking his unprotected face. It was the same room in the same hotel and on his flesh the bedbugs crawled and bit his legs and belly and arms, taking his blood, and in a resurgence of a three-year-old's horror he stepped back and out of the shower tent. The unforgotten room faded and the canvas returned.

Awareness of hallucination and of pressure from outside saved his sanity. *The General's bailiffs are at work! Unsettling if you let them get to you. Hypno-games but still only games.*

But how had that buried fear been detected and exhumed? He shivered in the suspicion that his memory had been rifled for his destruction. It had been so swift and subtle that the antihypnosis training had not been alerted.

Yet the bugs still bit. His legs and ribs were alive with them. Shuddering, he called up the antihypnosis mental routine . . .

. . . and still they crawled and bit. In an access of panic he slapped at the things to drive off the memory.

And saw blood where his hands squashed the feeding horrors.

Torn between reality and hallucination he examined his hands and saw the spattered body of a mosquito. His scrambled senses heard at last the humming of the swarm and he saw the things like a living fog in the light of the "street" standard. A cloud of them had settled on him, gorging blood until his skin burned and he ran like a frightened rabbit to escape them.

They did not seem to pursue him and in his tent he saw in disbelief the state of his skin, covered from ankles to chest with the swelling white mounds of their biting. In his feverish dressing he heard the rising hum of the swarm that sought him and he ran as Sargesson had run to escape the canopy, as if the night outside promised freedom from assault.

Ship-Captain Brookes was alone in the Data Correlation tent when the first horrified scream made prelude to pandemonium. Unlike many who had deliberately remained half-dressed and ostentatiously relaxed, as though simple defiance should be defence enough against the threats of semisavages, he was in full uniform. The concentration on computer printouts was his only pretence that his apprehension was not great; in his heart he believed that the General's bland mixture of threat and assurance covered ability to strike in undreamed of and terrible ways.

He suffered from two fatal disabilities never considered by those who had chosen him to head *Search*: he was an unimaginative man who could not conceive of action against formless fears, and he was an administrator rather than a leader. He felt powerless in a sea of unknowns.

So the scream froze him at the desk. He had to make an effort to stand and head for the tent doorway, telling himself that the moment had arrived with him all unready yet needing to be seen to act.

With his first pace away from the desk he stepped on something soft that wriggled and squealed, and he looked down on a monster of a rat writhing and trying to crawl away. In disgust he kicked it out of his path as a dozen more poured into the tent, black rats and grey rats and brown rats spreading across the floor. One climbed his leg as he watched in a moment of petrifaction before he was able to bring his hand down in a chop that broke its back.

Then they were everywhere, on the chairs and on the desk and the consoles, scattering papers and writing tools, slipping on metal surfaces and polished wood. They were no Libary figments; they were real and in hundreds. In horror he backed against the desk and one fastened little teeth in the ball of his thumb; in panic he clubbed it with his free fist and made for the doorway.

Something hit him sharply in the face, some little thing that stung like fire, and he saw the yellow-banded wasps, enraged at being unreasonably torn from their nests and murderously in need of an en-

emy to attack. The air was alive with them. As a teen-
ager he had once brushed against a papery nest and
the burning pain of the instant onslaught came alive
in memory. With no thought but escape he broke
from the tent and ran.

In the tent a half dozen wasps buzzed aimlessly,
lost and disoriented, while the rest of the apparent
swarm dissolved and vanished as the conjuring
memory fled. The rats, real and hungry and finding
no food, foraged through the tents, squealing and biting as sickened and frightened humans ploughed
through them in disorganised escape.

Others were visited by scorpions which vanished under treading feet, or by swarms of two-centimetre soldier ants which did not vanish but covered every
surface and corner in quest of sweetness, and
scorched like acid if incautiously touched. Down the
tent streets, hawks screeched and squawked in the
blind terror of finding themselves snatched away in
mid flight to emerge in inexplicable surroundings
where humans yelled and flailed at them. There was
no doubt of the reality of their blundering and smash-
ing into objects—or of the reality of the little fruit bats
entangling their musty bodies in heads of long hair.

It was Jean Sengupta's screaming that sparked the
flight to the outside air.

She was seated on her bed, reading, uneasy but
maintaining a precarious calm, when a flicker of
movement caught the corner of her eye. She leaned
to see what was at the entrance . . . and the half-
witted, predatory son of the sweetmeat seller pattered across the floor to fling himself on her and tear
at her clothes as he had torn at them in that horror of
her Indian childhood. He bit her again as he had bitten her then and when she screamed he hit her, rag-

ing at her hysterical attempts to fight and flee. He beat his knuckles on her mouth to silence her—

—and she had struggled from the bed to the floor before she discovered that nothing struck her, that her arms flailed through a phantom, and that her clothes still protected her shivering body although the thing gibbered in silent frenzy and flung its insubstantial form at her.

Not hypnosis. Not! muttered her terrified mind. Something worse and not harmless. She could not remain alone while such a visitation could be wished upon her.

In any case, her uninhibited screams had let slip panic in the area; the canopy was in uproar. She scarcely noticed the rats and mosquitoes as she snatched a dressing gown and fled for the security of open night.

15

THE SCREAMING DID NOT SURPRISE SOLdier, who had suggested the universal nature of the illusions infesting the tents, but the very real rats and mosquitoes puzzled him; there was a finer magicianship at work than his tentative presentation to Libary had dreamed of. This conflict of vision and reality should engender greater confusion than either alone.

Confusion there was. As if the scream had loosed a flood, the encroachment became a cauldron confining the sounds of outrage and fear, until the first fugitives reached the perimeter, yelling incoherence into the night. Some duty operator inside gathered scattering wits to switch on the perimeter lights before he ran with the rest before the tide of horrors.

One of the first to appear was Peter Jones, the part-Maori, in trousers and shoes, slapping his bitten skin as he struggled into a shirt, still running. In a moment the evacuation poured through all the open perimeter, a deranged flood running forty or fifty metres before discovering that nothing pursued them. Jones made straight for the small group at the edge of the crest, saw Soldier and yelled, "What are you up to, you bastard? Here to gloat?"

Soldier expected no less; what he did not expect was a seemingly instinctive movement of Duval, McCann, and Nugan to group protectively round him. More than ever he recognised unpenetrated bounds to his understanding of these quite alien minds. Jones, too, followed on unpredictably: he reached the group, panting and gasping, and appeared to make a physical effort to throw off panic and anger. After a moment he said with irritated rationality, "Are you out of your mind? This mob will take you apart. Kill you!"

Soldier smiled thinly. "They or others. Here or elsewhere. I thought you about to begin."

The noise under the canopy subsided slowly as the Searchers, few more than half-dressed, came into the friendly light, casting back for pursuers who did not follow.

Jones said, "For hate, you think? I was a park ranger, an ecology man, raised in duty. I only hate where it'll do some good."

I have found three to respect—Nugan, McCann, and now this one. Surely there are more. The thought did not embrace Anne, whom he knew for excitable and gauche and unbearably adolescent; respect had no place in the pitiless game of the *rom*, only endless desire.

McCann backed Jones. "Get out of the light, Thomas. We don't want to have to defend you."

At that he stepped back towards the edge of shadow and a little downhill. "You would do so?"

McCann sounded displeased with himself, growling, "Your blood wouldn't help anything."

Duval came in with authority, "We're not all too thick to see clearly, General. Some of us realise staying's impossible. The others have to be convinced."

"They will be. Who tries to remain will live in your ancient superstition's hell, day by day, wherever he hides."

"A hell-powerful argument is needed for people who have nowhere to go."

"Make the best of your star, Postvorta."

"Is that a victor's joke? Nugan has told you about that place; it is savage and relentless. *Search* is not a battleship and we are not soldiers."

"You can learn." That was more heartless and contemptuous than he had intended; he would have tried to soften it if Brookes, insanely punctilious in full uniform, had not come trotting in quest of Duval. He saw Soldier in the heart of a little circle, backlit by the arcs and spires of fireworks from the valley and lost a hard-held temper. Raging at a too-simple defeat and shamed by impotence to resist, he became impassioned at the sight of the near-naked man in a flower of Carnival light, as if the proceeding were some enchanted romance.

He breasted the enemy in a roar of anger. "Get out of here or I'll see you dead!"

Duval grabbed his Captain's arm, muttering urgently while Soldier protested, "I said I would be here to see you safely away, unhurt. That is a duty."

Brookes took grip on his useless rage. "You are bar-

baric. What you are doing will end in psychotic crip-
pling. Don't you call that hurt? Only a psychotic hate
could use such methods."

Soldier waved an arm at the slope below them.
"Down there they hate because your presence threat-
ens what they have created."

"And they retaliate with hallucination born out of
the deepest fears! Insanity as a weapon!"

"A calling-up of childhood terrors, Captain. Strong
minds will not bend far."

"The rats and ants, the hawks and mosquitoes, and
some other things were real."

Soldier felt uneasily that Libary and his Elders had
introduced elements not discussed with a General
under Silence. "To dangle you between reality and
magic. The beasts were not of my thinking; I had
planned only to drive you from your encroachment
with a small and mindless enemy your science could
not counter."

Duval said, "And old Libary one-upped you, eh?
Yet I think we can deal with this now we've seen it
in action."

"I think not, Mister Duval. The forces that commanded a harmless demonstration can also command more deadly beasts—and forest fires and
lightning and perhaps—" He shrugged, not knowing
where "perhaps" might lead; the Elders had built his
simple plan into something beyond his guessing.
"You have witnessed a threat; more malignant action
could follow."

Down the hill four lights like resin torches sprang
alive and lifted in short, simultaneous arcs, then flew
up and out across the stars, brilliantly white and red
and brighter than the fireworks below.

Duval made the connection. "The longbows! And
gunpowder!"

In rapid confirmation the snap of released strings reached them as the incendiary arrows whickered overhead and plunged down onto the canopy to create an inferno three hundred metres from side to side. The red flare was instantaneous across the whole expanse, to vanish at once in a pall of thick, black smoke rolling up and out over the edges of the canopy and down onto the astonished Searchers, to sting their eyes and lungs.

McCann chuckled. "Fireproof, Tommy! That one's a fizzle."

"So? Wait."

"For what, General Tommy?"

"I don't know, McCann's Jack. I had hoped to see your canopy collapse in fire. But Libary is not one to waste a gesture."

He was justified immediately. The smoke did not disperse but hung in a pall as if held in an invisible bowl, like thick liquid over the canopy. In a moment its darkness became pierced by small tongues of flame, red and yellow and blue, like distant watch fires in deep night.

Soldier's uneasiness became dread. Libary had given no promises. He wondered had the smoke indeed been rolled into a bank of darkness or had his mind been told to believe so? He felt no sense of persuasion, of being coerced into belief; he simply saw that what could not be, could be and was. To test whether others saw as he did, he said with as much of a touch of raillery as he could manage, "McCann's Jack, your fireproof canopy burns."

Duval's voice struck sharply: "It doesn't. It can't." Soldier watched him turn his back on the sight and stare downhill, shutting out the impossible—and turn back to discover that the effort at disbelief cancelled nothing.

Illusion or reality, the small coloured flames were

fed; they spread like fired grass over the surface.

Then, from no direction and from no freak of weather, came the cold—sudden, penetrating, and fierce.

The Searchers around the encroachment cried out at the strike and tried to gather their light clothing closer around them. The air was abruptly clouded with mosquitoes, already out of their proper habitat, fleeing the cold and beating downhill. After them came the rats, scuttling and leaping, careless of the humans, knowing no direction but downwards to a place of warmth.

Jones, kicking at one as it passed, said, "These are real. Sargie's spiders weren't. Memories of childhood weren't."

Soldier's voice seemed detached in the half dark. "Unreal things are created in the minds of those who fear them. I have always doubted the reality of Indra's Net but now I see that there is something that operates . . . or is operated. Misused? No wonder the Elders will have me dead." Then he bellowed in the voice of the parade ground master, "Stop them! Stop them!"

Rats, visions, and irrational cold had cracked the nerve of a few Searchers who started to move blindly downhill. They ran and staggered down the slope, first a struggling few, then a rush.

Soldier, after his first cry, made no move to interfere, but Jones and Duval tried to halt the firstcomers. Jones wrestled a writhing woman to the ground, to be bitten and screeched at while he held her under his weight; Duval, caught between two men, was kicked and trampled. McCann, in the dropsuit, could not move swiftly enough to intercept and Brookes watched in bemusement. Soldier shook his head gently. *This navigator and mathematician is not a man to make rapid decision and act on it. If Kiev is similar, any group of determined savages will deny them foothold.* He counted a dozen men and women who had not joined the stampede; there could be a nucleus of salvation among those.

The fugitives had vanished in the darkness. The sounds of flight changed suddenly to startled screams and desperate male yelling.

"Quarterstaves," Soldier said. "The troopers have orders to strike only on thigh, rump, and shoulder. There will be bruising but no breaking of bones."

Nugan cried out, "But you can kill with those things!"

"Those men are expert. The quarterstaff is the weapon of private quarrel; to kill with it is to be disgraced."

His eye was caught by brightness overhead. *Search*, larger and more brilliant than he had ever seen her seemed poised directly overhead, motionless in the sky. He asked Brookes, "Why is your ship so low? Do you mean to use weapons?"

"What weapons? We carry none. I have brought it down to take my people home—if that must be." Brookes came close to him. "Call off your dogs. Your battle is won."

Soldier regarded him sombrely. "You will not understand that the Ordinands are no dogs of mine. The plan will go on to its end. I can change nothing."

Five men came running easily uphill ahead of the limping, returning Searchers, men dressed in camouflage uniforms and carrying quarterstaves, each with also a two-metre bow slung at his back. Silently they ranged themselves beside Soldier.

Brookes stepped back. "What's this?"

"I think they fear for my safety." He spoke to them in village Angloo and was answered. "They think shamed men here may try to kill me."

Behind them came the Searchers, limping and

breathing hard, separating to go round the group, eyeing Soldier with hatred and the bodyguard with caution.

Soldier's attention was taken by a development higher up the slope. A figure had come into view, wearing a dropsuit with helmet retracted into the shoulder pack. Sargesson. He came slowly, deliberately.

Rick-Jemmy, the middle-aged survivor of half a fugitive lifetime in the forests, said, "This one has purpose, General."

"Do nothing."

"Nothing?"

"If I am hurt, protect me. Otherwise, nothing."

Nugan caught the gist of what had been said and turned to see what had caused it. "Thomas! The gloves!"

"I know it."

Sargesson, twenty metres away, called out, "What's wrong with you, McCann? Letting him get away with it, you traitorous bastard!"

Brookes bellowed at him to halt and Nugan ran towards him. With a half-lifted arm he burned the ground white between her feet and she halted, begging him to be reasonable, to wait and— He leaned his suited bulk on her and pushed her to the ground, leaving a clear line of sight between himself and Soldier. As he lifted the glove McCann, out to the side, snapped his own arm up and it seemed to Soldier that the buzzing of a swarm of bees enclosed Sargesson's suited figure. The armoured hand dropped and the man slowly after it, to shudder and twitch on the ground.

Jones and Duval were immediately on him, wrestling the gloves from the suit.

A trooper said, "I do not understand this. Why do they quarrel among themselves?"

"Because they are people, not troopers. Their world has no settled frame of behaviour." He shifted to Late English to call to McCann, "Is he harmed?"

"No. The vibrator shakes but doesn't break."

"My thanks—for the one you owed me."

McCann smiled briefly and lifted his hand in a half salute.

For Soldier it had been an anxious moment but he had counted the odds and taken the chance. *They are good people at heart. They pay their debts. But the greater risk is yet to come.*

Behind him his renegade troopers murmured to each other, trying to make sense of strange people. Down by the river the fireworks display had completed its welcome to sexual excess and the crowd noise had died down to a mumbling in the dark valley. Down there, the quieter business of the night had begun.

A fresh malice commenced. The heavy, lingering smoke of the gunpowder thickened and rolled impossibly back onto the canopy, to condense into a solid mass and rise towards the sky. Like little knives the cold bit more sharply. Soldier did not know what was planned now and feared that his assurances had been vain.

He addressed his five men. "You are inside a circle of power; you will see what you have not been prepared for seeing—illusions, unreal but terrible. Remember that they cannot harm you. Stay here with me; do not run. Close your eyes if you must, but stay."

Rick-Jemmy answered, "We don't fear ghosts."

"You speak too soon."

Because their lives and all their trust lay in him, they took him at his word and each prepared his heart against his mind's conception of the terrible.

On the ridge, eyes were fixed on the shaping

smoke. A sound of shock, between a gasp and a muted cry, came from the scattered Searchers when the perimeter lights went out as columns of impenetrable smoke rose over the standards and smothered them. Only the stars shone, and *Search*, like a lamp—and the faery watch fires.

Apprehension deepened in Soldier. That he knew it wished on him from without did not dim its presence and his acute hearing detected little sounds of premonition around the hill. He glanced behind to discover five pairs of eyes fixed on him, ready to endure while he endured.

Ten metres away, Sargesson drew sobbing breaths as he climbed slowly to his feet, examined his naked hands and looked around uselessly for his gloves. Then the fear and cold penetrated his angry brain and he sat down again on the dried-out grass, head in hands.

Now the watch fire flames covered the surface of the canopy, paused as if the fire readied itself, then deepened to a bed of scarlet above which the pillar of smoke deepened into a solid thing that extended rapidly upwards, sharpening its edges until it was a vast rectangle, a spotless domino a hundred metres high.

Its flat surface took on life, rippling and billowing as some small, wicked wind blew through it. *It is a doorway*, Soldier thought, and knew that the thought was not his own but an insertion, a command to wait on terror. All around him the hillside held its perturbed breath.

In the depths of the doorway a presence stirred, a tiny thing infinitely far away.

Nugan felt the plundering of her mind. The small illusions had been fed by universal fears drawn from the depths of human experience, but she knew, as surely as if fingers had opened her brain to seek and

bare the memory of guilt, that the secret consciousness of childhood had been ransacked for the Rainbow Serpent. Black Libary had sought her out, to use
against her the scrap of her history whose key she
had given him. Stripped suddenly of the barriers of
years and sophisticated knowledge, she cried out,
"Grandma! Hold me!" and fell on her knees, reaching
for the protecting arms of the old woman who had
told her little *nguyonawi* the tales of the Dreamtime.

In all the years since, she had not thought twice of
the Rainbow Serpent, the spirit presence in the day
of creation who protected the good and revenged herself on the wicked. Now Nugan had betrayed her people; she had brought the sky strangers to destroy the
land where the Dreamtime spirits still guarded their
children . . .

. . . and in the dawn of creation Ngalyod stirred.

Soldier heard Nugan cry out and saw her collapse.
He would have gone to her, but suddenly the hillside
was in motion, the Searchers milling in new panic at
the brilliance growing in the black portal. And, as
suddenly, a new thing enveloped them, a formless
guilt to shrink them together with the biting cold.

They became still and quiet, like prisoners in fear
of justice for an unknown crime.

It seemed to Soldier that like a star, and from the
unimaginable distance of a star, a creature approached the doorway to Earth. It was a thing of soft
colours that flowed and mingled—as if a rainbow
took on moving life. It swelled as it approached,
writhing as if swimming out of depths until he made
out, dimly, the shape of a reptilian head in a halo of
colour.

On the hillcrest, movement ceased. The Searchers
shivered in the unnatural cold and moved together
as unreasonable, unresolvable guilt sought company;

they watched what puzzled and alarmed yet had no meaning.

Nugan, kneeling alone, cried out a word Soldier did not catch. The rainbow creature swam closer and she cried out again, a word that sounded like "Nallod"—and he knew now what the Elders had brought out of darkness. Library educated, he recognised the powerful Rainbow Serpent, the fabled protecting mother drawn from the well of time to seek out enemies of her people. He thought: Part-bred Nugan remembered and was ransacked for a figure of fear.

In moments the monster swelled, still journeying, taking solid form as she came out of the ancestral past to a world where she was still not forgotten.

My little rebellion was not worth its punishment of Silence. They can shake every mind alive and terrify it into obedience.

In the quiet he heard Nugan weep and felt again that he should go to her, though his shaking, collapsing intelligence told him that nothing he did could help her or anyone. With the remnants of sense caught up in chattering cold and unassuageable guilt, he remembered that this display must have an end and that then his own game must begin. He glanced up to brilliant *Search*, thinking with the sharpness of deliberate structuring of his mind. *Our time is not over, Anne. There is still a hand to play. Wait!*

To that he must cling; the Match had its power and could not be wholly overridden by vengeful Elders.

He recognised beyond the doorway of smoke an immense rock python, jaws agape, bathed in the rainbow, rising and growing but not yet in the new world.

Behind him his five outlaws made small involuntary noises as their manhood shook before the terror.

Ngalyod came to the doorway and through it, rearing into the night a vast head and cavern mouth that might engulf a house, the python markings picked out in rainbow glow that flickered and flowed. Her head rose to the full height of the doorway and her forked tongue darted red spear thrusts as she looked down on the Searchers. Below her head, huge breasts announced her role as protector of her people; between narrow lids, golden eyes scanned the hilltop for those who menaced her children.

Soldier heard movement at his back and saw that the troopers had fallen to their knees and covered their faces. He needed intensely to do the same—but he was Soldier and General and dared not show weakness. Others might suffer the fears and fantasies of their rearing in the communes but the General must be steadfast. While he still could . . .

Anne! If I survive . . .

Astonishingly, he heard a man's voice, cracked, breaking. It was Sargesson, hysteria channelled into ragged screaming: "It's trickery! Fake! There's nothing there!"

But he had his back to the monster and his hands over his eyes.

The head of the breasted serpent turned to the sound, swayed gently in her robe of light, then struck downward like a bright comet to the Earth, jaws wide. Sargesson in his dropsuit vanished without sound. A few steps from his side Nugan screamed. The vast head swung to her like a rainbow pendulum and she was swallowed as though she had never been.

Ngalyod's head rose high again, yellow gaze scanning the shuddering crowd that dared not cry out or move.

Soldier's mind lost ability to resist, to pretend any longer that this was a dream forced on his unwilling brain. What was left of rationality whispered fearfully: *Now they have killed, and with it killed my promise to the Searchers, and I have nothing left.* Despite his assurance to Libary, he saw again the vision of *Search* searing the villages and the forest with its murdering white exhaust. He had warned, again and again, that there must be no death. *Now Anne is lost to me also.*

The hope of regaining her had never been more than a gambler's hazard; with Nugan and Sargesson the Elders had lost it for him forever.

The serpent flowed endlessly out of the depths of time, circling and settling until her coils covered the canopy resting on the bed of flame. As if the imponderable mass had at last become too great for it, the canopy subsided, forced flat with the ground, and the Searcher encroachment was utterly destroyed.

The bed of flame vanished.

With blinding speed Ngalyod whipped her head back into the portal and the immense coils unwound to follow her, to shrink and vanish in the Dreamtime like a thought that had faded before the mind could grasp it.

On the crest of the hill nothing remained but bare ground in the moonlight.

Then the perimeter lights flashed alive, the canopy brooded again over the hill and Sargesson and Nugan stirred out of vanishment to stagger to trembling feet.

Soldier turned to the troopers, who refused to meet his eyes as they rose to their feet. He said, "There's no shame to be suffered here," and embraced each man in turn. "You came into the circle to guard my life; you were not meant to endure the insanity of old and secret schemers. It is over. We can be men again."

16

SOLDIER COULD SEE NOTHING ON THE
dark slope, but acute hearing caught the faint sound
of muted speech and the rustle of parched grass as
three thousand defenders of their world retreated
into the night. The Ordinands would be drained and
silent; the troopers would descend in a sex-bent lo-
cust horde on the Yarra villages; Libary and his fold
would return to their desecrated Library and soon the
semaphores would begin victorious clacking across
the night. And the visiting Ordinands? To their village quarters, to writhe in their precious celibacy
while streets and fields rioted about them? He hoped
so.

The Searchers dispersed, some needing cajoling
and encouragement to return to the tents. He watched
Nugan support a staggering, soul-shocked Sargesson
back to the canopy. So much for the arrogant rage of
old science.

Duval said, "You've got what you wanted," his
voice weary rather than hostile. "Is it finished?"

"Yes. You will leave now?"

"At once, before a new hysteria begins. Harassment
like this, carried to its limit, would end in a colony
of lunatics."

Soldier shrugged. It was over. With care he might
now play his own game.

"Where is Captain Brookes?"

"Organising evacuation. It will take most of the night."

Soldier knew very well the administrative agility required for the movement of personnel and property without preparation. "I must speak with him before he leaves. I promised him a gift."

McCann was raucous. "A going-away present?"

"Is that the term? It is for use at his voyage's end."

Duval was snappish. "You're quite mad, Thomas. You're the last man he'll want to see any way but dead. He's humiliated and rabid."

"Why? I think he knew defeat was certain."

"That makes it acceptable?"

"No, but defeat is a soldier's learning process. Captain Brookes must win his next battle—on the planet by Postvorta."

Duval's governed temper threatened to break but McCann took his arm, asking, "What's the present, General Tommy?"

Soldier gestured. "These: Five highly trained fighting men to teach your peaceful settlers the sciences of self-preservation, defence, and aggression. For they are sciences."

Duval freed his arm with a jerk. "For Christ's sake, you impossible simpleton—" McCann shouted him down. "Be quiet! I never saw a battle but I did two years of military reserve training—square bashing, field movement, and stuff—and I know what he means. We should listen."

"Does he think he can turn scientists into an army?"

Soldier cut in rapidly, "Perhaps an army of settlers. In all your histories of America and Africa the settlers were farmers and traders who learned to hold their own."

Duval had calmed down. "Thomas, you mean well but you know nothing about the Postvorta planet; it's as far outside your experience as it is outside ours. Plants that tear themselves out of the ground to attack like beasts! Animals that are fungi and vines until they enclose and kill!"

"You have pictures of these strange actions? Pictures that move and show the nature of the enemy?"

"Hours of them."

"Why, then, the enemy can be studied and his ways understood."

"What's to be understood in a screaming wave that races up from underfoot?"

"Much, once you have faced other kinds of screaming, racing waves. Why were the pictures sent but to be studied? Your enemy sounds primitive and undisciplined; devising counter-tactics should be an elementary exercise, because there is always a pattern to be recognised and disrupted. These five are outlaws who have preserved their lives in the forests because they know the sciences of arms and have the agility of mind to turn knowledge into action. They will study your pictures and discover means to break the racing waves."

"Nobody's found any yet."

"Because you think like cloistered scientists rather than like soldiers or even settlers in a real world."

McCann studied the five outlaws. They faced him stolidly until Rick-Jemmy put out a hand to finger the dropsuit with puzzled curiosity and touched the metal glove. He said something McCann could not follow, but at a venture he pointed the glove down between his feet and in seconds showed the man a boiling puddle that hissed and sputtered. The others crowded to examine the glove, chattering.

Soldier explained, "They feel such a weapon should discourage any foe."

"It has limited range and focus. It's purely defensive."

"All weapons are defensive until you devise other uses."

"I'm willing to listen, Tommy." He urged Duval, "Give him a go, man! He kept his word to us about casualties. What have we to lose?"

"Time and efficiency are what. Some of those people have to be suited up like children into their baby clothes; they've had little practice with the things. The Captain will need both of us. Peter can stay and listen to Thomas. We'll come back later and see what's to be done. If anything."

He stumped off uphill. McCann stayed to pat the dismayed Soldier's arm. "Take it easy; the night is young and there's a lot to do. Talk to Peter; he could be more useful than you think. And he's on your side; he also feels he owes you one—" he grinned, "—for not hanging him out of hand."

He sketched a wave, and left.

Peter came diffidently forward. "Don't take Duval at face value. He's worried. Some of them would go off with unsealed suits if they weren't buttoned up and checked out. That's why Brookes brought the ship down; if anybody has suit trouble on the lift, they'll get there fast enough to do themselves no damage."

"I also am worried—" Soldier nodded at his five. "—about these. Can you be as useful as Mister McCann says?"

Jones sat down and patted the grass beside him. "Take the weight off, General. I'm the ship's cartographer, with nothing to map so far, but my other discipline is social conciliation, which was very important in my day. Duval wasn't wiping you cold; he just doesn't know what to do about your parting gift. We need to present it to a beaten and dispirited Captain in such fashion that he'll be prepared to risk the animosity of the Wakings which will be pretty hot. But it's a good idea.''

Soldier watched the man and listened to his tones, striving to read what hope lay in him. "You would have these men go with you?"

"It's worth a try. Besides, I don't fancy leaving them behind. They'd be killed, wouldn't they?"

"Yes, if caught. That they live is the mark of their expertise in hunting, fighting, hiding, and surviving."

"And we thought this was a peaceful world!"

The canopy went first. With magnetic seams released, the whole area rolled itself up like a hundred carpets, each balanced on a mooring mast. The monopole beams reached down and the outlaws exclaimed as the sections, each carrying its mooring mast, whipped into the sky.

Soldier said, "They don't believe in magic but are uneasy when they see it in action. And I cannot explain it to them."

"Difficult, but I can try." He soon found that mention of "old Wizard science" covered most technical gaps. The men really wanted assurance that what they saw was under human control.

The canopy went up and at once the containers came down where Searchers were bringing their belongings to the removal area. Beds, bedding, and tent furniture were lifted to *Search* in twenty tonne lots; the kitchen came rolling out on casters, clamped itself together in two square metal blocks and rose up like a featherweight; the system of water pipes rolled itself together like the fire hoses in the village street and leapt out of sight. The troopers applauded, children at a pantomime played for their pleasure for one night only.

When a sound like the muted roar of an ancient

stadium crowd floated up from the valley, Jones understood its meaning. "Two thousand troopers have just hit town. Your fellers will be wishing they were with them."

"These forest dwellers don't observe Carnival. They make Carnival where and when they find it."

From the depths of the tents men carried a metal box between them on slings. It was no more than a quarter of a cubic metre in volume but obviously very heavy.

"There goes the computer system and library."

"In that small space? Is that all?"

Jones did not feel up to explaining nanotechnology; life was too short.

For hours the evacuation proceeded.

Peter Jones asked, "How was it done?"

"I don't know how, Mister Jones. I can only guess by putting scraps of information together."

"Please guess."

"There is an old book called *Morphic Resonance*."

"Nugan had it copied for us. I've skimmed it."

"Without believing?"

"We call it pseudoscience, like the magic your troopers don't believe in."

"But there is an oral history of magic from the most ancient of times and a lurking readiness to believe."

"There always was, but if the morphic field exists, we should be able to detect it. There should be evidence of energy that instruments can register and measure."

"You speak as if it were light or heat. Perhaps it is a different manifestation, as gravity is different, requiring another instrument—perhaps, in this case, the brain. There—you asked me to guess."

"And the facts, General?"

"Ordinands sit in groups, naked, without instruments, and make contact with . . . something. Your own first experiments, some nine centuries ago, dealt with information passing mysteriously from humans to humans and from rats to rats without material intervention. The brain knows what it does but not how; it cannot see itself. I think the Ordinands have learned to see."

Jones was silent for a long while. "If that is the way of it, then all minds since humanity began should be preserved in the field."

"Animal minds also—in Indra's Net."

"That again!"

"Nugan saw Bella's wedding shawl with the symbols of the Net woven into it and she understood that the Net contains the souls not only of men and women but of all creatures. Instead of 'souls' let us say 'thoughts'—and Indra's Net becomes the morphic field. Perhaps the ancients of the eastern world knew more than you guess."

Peter was intrigued. "So thought speaks to thought—if you know the knack of thinking. Jean Sengupta fears rape, so her fear recreated rape. And Sargie's fear dredged up hunting spiders from the universal memory. Like that?"

"I think so, Mister Jones."

"Peter! Nobody on *Search* uses formal address—except to the Captain."

"Very well, Peter. I am Thomas." At last a stated acceptance! His game was beginning.

"Good. But how about the rats? They were real, not conjured up; so were the ants and mosquitoes."

"If a rat can learn from the field how to run a maze faster than the rats before it, cannot information be redirected to push its little brain into running to a certain place at a certain time? And were the little mosquitoes in some such manner transported? I do not know what is possible, but you will have seen that the dangerous things were visions; only the relatively harmless were real. It was my stance that no lives be taken."

Peter spread his hands. "All right, I'll accept your morphic field—until something more amenable to trial turns up."

What creatures of doubt we are, even in belief. Yet I believe that I will survive this crisis. He glanced up to bright *Search,* where Anne hovered beyond his reach, too far off for the power of the *rom* to touch him. And without it his life was over. *But because I also doubt, I am afraid.* Behind him the troopers talked quietly. *They must go to the stars; I offered them life and they must have it.*

His own life and sanity were another matter, not easily resolved. Born and reared to serve, he had lived in a profession where every move was predicated on the actions, loyalties, and ultimate welfare of others. Now at last he faced a purely personal problem for which no guiding social framework existed. For the first time he knew loneliness, like hanging, solitary, in darkness.

In the valley the revellers were less rowdy when, with the glimmer of dawn, the last load lifted to *Search.*

"Now the hardware is gone," Peter said, "the bodies will go up fast, two dozen at a lift. It's time I saw the Captain; Jack and Joel will have him softened up by now. Wait here."

He ran up towards the Searchers gathered in the dawn like murmuring shadows.

Soundlessly the first group was lifted.

Rick-Jemmy spoke for them all. "We are abandoned."

"Not so; we have the goodwill of honest men. Be

still now, and when the Captain comes give no sign of concern."

Four lifts of personnel went up and each time a load of dropsuits was returned for the next group. Then quietly, quietly it was full dawn and only nine figures remained. The suits came down with a faint swish in the clear air and wearers were checked into some of them. Only four went up.

The remainder burst into argument as if repression exploded out of them. One voice was Nugan's, expostulating, and Soldier found comfort in that, recognising the existence of a friend outside the social system. He was not quite alone, after all. Not yet.

When eventually they came down the hill, Soldier stood and his troopers followed suit.

Brookes opened with cold anger. "I meet with you against my will. I concede that you have kept your word and that no one has been physically harmed, but perhaps you don't consider hysteria and psychotic interlude as injury." Soldier repressed his opinion that the mental health and strength of his people was Brookes's neglected responsibility. "That aside, I'm told you wish to speak with me."

"I sent word, Captain, of a gift—not so much for yourself as for the people of *Search*."

"A handful of criminals, I'm told."

Behind Brookes, McCann put a warning finger to his lips and Peter winked as if to say, *It's all a front.* Soldier was in some degree aware of that; he read Brookes as harassed and pestered and determined to show himself a hard and dominant man, if only to bolster his slaughtered self-respect at the end of a disastrous night.

"The criminality is no fault of theirs, Captain. Has Mister Jones not explained their circumstances?"

Brookes swung on the New Zealander, ready for a victim. "You called them criminals."

"I said, sir, that their system regards them as criminals though ours would not."

"Did you? Well, what good are they? You, General Thomas! What use can these men be to anyone?"

"They can win you a place on the Postvorta planet."

"Something the first-class intellects and resources of ship *Kiev* could not do?"

Nugan lashed out in shrill frustration, "Something the brains and resources of *Search* couldn't do on their own planet."

Soldier expected outburst. *If one of mine said as much to me at such a pass . . .* Then he reflected that this man was not a serviceman but the leader of a civilised group of intellectual specialists. His authority expressed itself in rational explanation and decision among rational people—most of whom had long ceased to be civilly rational. Now, when he should discipline Nugan at once, he affected to pay no attention to her, but to concentrate on parading the patience with which he subdued his shaking temper. He asked grimly, "What have you in mind?"

Behind Soldier, Rick-Jemmy remarked in Angloo, with a still face, "The little fat one is no commander of men."

Soldier told Brookes, in the reasonable tone of one sure of his claim, "These men have the intelligence and experience to study your pictures of the savage enemy in action and discover how they move, how they fight, what factors govern their assault by day or night, what weaknesses exist in their mode of attack, and what weapons could be effectively used against them. They will see and understand small things your people will not see because they are not educated in such observation. They will see weaknesses where you see only brute strength, opportunity where you see only unstoppable numbers, possible victory where you see only refuge in flight. These are expert, brave, and proven survivors. They know conflict as action to be shaped and moulded to the will."

"The enemy on the Postvorta world are not men. Your rules will not apply."

"Were they giant apes or sea monsters or manlike things riding in your ancient metal tanks, the same ground rules will apply: Observe method, discover weakness, and exploit it." He paused before adding casually, "They may bring you weapons your powers have not dreamed of."

That was a little trip wire for Brookes and he stumbled unhesitatingly over it. "Weapons, General?" His tone said Soldier had overstepped common sense. "Show me!"

Soldier spoke a single word and held out his hand. Rick-Jemmy unwound a belt of thick cloth from his waist, opened it up, and very carefully lifted out a short metal baton. From its end he shook out a two-metre length of what might have been black cord, spreading his feet and making sure the cord did not touch him as it coiled on the ground, then placed the baton like a whip handle in Soldier's waiting palm.

"This, at full length, is a five-metre saw. It is fashioned of the hardest cutting material on Earth."

"Diamond, General?" The word was heavy with sarcasm.

"No."

Brookes frowned, suspecting trickery, more harassment. Soldier gestured and Rick-Jemmy held his quarterstaff out before him. With a light flick of the cord Soldier cut the staff in two. Rick-Jemmy held out the two pieces together. Then four. Then eight.

"No more. This tool is sharpened to an edge no

steel will take. If I missed the stroke, the man might lose his hand."

Frowning, Brookes reached for the thing.

"Take it by the handle only. Do not touch the saw; it will cut flesh like soft butter."

Gingerly Brookes examined it. "Who has a lens?" Duval provided one and the Captain lifted the saw to his eye, seeing clearly in the rising sun. "It's as fine as silk."

"And stronger than steel. It is called magnetite, made pliant and harder than any gemstone. Your Wizards made it. We like to think they made it for us, their children, storing them against the day when we would need them."

"As weapons? Did they design you to fight?"

"My Genetic was designed to cope with hot and arid conditions; suitability for combat was a by-product. The saw is a saw, not a weapon."

Nugan said excitedly, "The towers! I have always wondered how you brought them down to strip the metal."

"My clever Nugan! How did we do it?"

"You cut the concrete and steel at strategic points with the magnetite whips, then toppled them with huge blasts of gunpowder."

"Whips, Nugan? You peaceful people think always of weapons! Still, this could be a weapon though that was not its intended use. We have five of them here, stolen by my renegades; think, if you had a thousand like them, what a defensive fence you might build— one an enemy cannot handle to tear down! Can your ship's Wizards make such things, Captain Brookes?"

Brookes looked helplessly at Duval, who said, "If the lab can analyse it, the workshop can make it." He added, "That makes two gifts."

Despite himself Brookes flicked an eye to the troopers while Soldier thought, *Oh, cunning Duval.*

Brookes recovered belligerence with an effort, determinedly unimpressed. "So you've got something useful there. Anything else?"

"I have only these five men, and men are what count in conflict; weapons are secondary. These can teach your people how to work as groups wherein each knows exactly how competent the others are. In that fashion you conquer fear, and the enemy's despair is three-quarters of any victory. They can teach your Searchers how to use their bodies with economy and certainty, how to look and how to interpret what they see. Your man, Jones, knows the values I preach; he was once a park ranger with an eye for country and movement. And Mister McCann knows the basic elements of soldiering. Others will have talents you ignore but which may be seized on and developed. Perhaps, too, they will see in your everyday machines possible weapons, where you see only tools that clean and cook and perform small chores. If your people have heart, these five can win the Postvorta world for you."

A boast? Perhaps, but for any other than a fool he had surely offered enough.

Brookes handed back the saw. "Impressive, but there's poison in your gift. How do think my Searchers would react to a pack of violence-trained lechers interpreting every scent of a woman as a welcome to license? There would be chaos and very soon murder."

Soldier held the baton pointing down and waved it gently in his hand; the cord crept softly back into its nest. "These men have no *rom* sensitivity, Captain. That is the reason for their outlawry; their lives are sought because their sexual lack transgresses the Genetic requirement and could be passed on to another generation."

"You mean they're neutered?"

"No. I mean that they approach only those who welcome them and do not suffer the binding of Match."

Brookes turned on Peter. "You didn't tell me this."

"There's a lot I didn't tell you when you were too busy to listen to it all."

Brookes shouted, "But these are the enemy! Yet you want them, don't you, all of you! You think Postvorta's the last chance, that nothing further exists in the galaxy! Resistance among the Wakings would be tremendous, particularly from those who suffered here tonight." He waited for answer but no one spoke. He muttered, without conviction, "They can't even speak English."

Nugan said, "I can attend to that quickly. Angloo is close enough to our speech to make it easy for them."

"You too, eh? But what can be done with angry Wakings who will want the whole pack of them thrown out through the ports? This is the world that wouldn't let them come home!"

This was an argument Soldier had awaited with anxiety, yet it vanished almost at once. Peter said, "I can help there. Social conciliation is my alternate discipline."

Brookes snarled at him, "A damned lot of use you were when I had a mutiny on my hands!"

"With respect, sir, I was part of the dissent. I didn't want to help; I wanted to come home."

"So much for your judgment. And now you'll see me damned if I do and damned if I don't." He asked with an effort at sarcasm, "Do you all want this gift of outlaws, another culture's castoffs, aboard *Search*?"

Duval, as senior officer, bearded the weary lion. "We feel it would be a mistake to refuse a magnanimous offer."

"A winner can always be magnanimous with what his own don't want." He capitulated waspishly, minimally, without grace. "I'll take them aboard, General, and trust they are all you claim for them. I'll see they are treated well and given every opportunity to . . . to do whatever it is they have in them to do. Thank you for a gift we could not have anticipated." He fumbled for words, then said awkwardly, "You are a most unusual man."

Soldier made a half bow of recognition and spoke briefly to the troopers, who moved forward and ranged themselves behind the Searchers. Brookes scanned them keenly—one man on the edge of middle age, one blazing redhead, one almost pure-blooded Aboriginal, two nondescripts to be found on any street corner, all within two centimetres of a height and two kilos of weight and, except for colouring, as alike as brothers. There had to be something amiss with such genetic closeness. But he had made his decision and must live by it.

He said, "Well, that seems to be it, General. Thank you again if it turns out that you've saved us from wandering forever."

He turned uphill, wanting only to get away and find privacy and rest. His mind had been filled throughout the night with the frustrations of bulldozing undisciplined civilians into a coherent act of departure; through it he had been hounded, as he saw it, by Duval and McCann with argument, by an emotional Nugan with pleading, and finally by Peter Jones with torrents of information he could barely follow let alone ingest. Now he felt badgered into having taken aboard an activity which would plague his waking hours for all the long, journeying years. He felt also that some sort of gesture was required of him, some parting display of a panache he could not muster. *I am a navigator, not a stage manager.*

He halted to ask, "There isn't anything else, is there?" and at last became conscious of the loneliness of the slender figure a few paces below him on the hillside. The poor brute could be in for a rough time from his own people, but that was the ill fortune attendant on belonging to an alien culture.

Soldier answered him gravely, "I have nothing more to tell you. May you travel safely."

"Thank you, General."

He turned away again and McCann asked, "What about Thomas?"

Brookes's brain was slack with the excesses of the night. "What's that? Do you mean the girl? She'll have to get over it. For God's sake, I can't run everybody's personal problems as well as my own."

Nugan cried out at him, "Anne's not the point—it's Thomas. They'll hunt him down and kill him."

Brookes thought what it could have been disastrous to say: *I hope he drops dead and rots.* Then, as he made another attempt to leave, the troopers opened an outburst of jabbering in their incomprehensible dialect.

"What's up with them? Nugan, what are they saying?"

"That Thomas is their leader. That they had thought he was to come with them."

All Brookes's exasperation and self-pity and obstinacy burst out of him. "I won't do it! The Wakings wouldn't put up with it! He's the planning devil of everything that has happened to them! There'd be no peace on *Search* until both of us were dead. And who says he wants to come? He hasn't said so." Unnerved at finding himself forced into yet another corner, he yelled at Soldier, "What are you standing around for? It's over!"

Peter grabbed his arm. "Sir!"

Brookes shook him off. "You forget yourself!"

Peter persisted in a breathless murmur that Soldier could not quite make out, "Sir, he can't ask. He's the General, the commander, the word of life and death, the model for his men. In their ethic he can't beg in front of them; they'd never forgive him. Besides, the way he's been brought up to pride in duty, he won't even know how. He can't ask! *Can't!*"

Brookes said, so low he was scarcely audible, "Are you telling me *I* have to ask *him*?"

"Not ask, sir, invite. Give him the choice. We can't leave him to die when he did everything to preserve us."

Brookes turned to his people, stone-faced and unwilling. "Do you want him?"

Duval stepped forward. "He's part of our chance for a new world."

"This is another damned mutiny."

"It could be a crux of our history, sir."

Brookes eyed him with loathing. He faced Soldier for the last time, frustration choking him like unshed tears. His voice burned his throat.

"General Atkins, would you consider an invitation to come aboard *Search* as commander of your cadre of troopers?"

Soldier bowed from the waist, the most honourable compliment his military generation could offer.

"Captain Brookes, I shall be proud to accept such a post."

Perhaps the word should have been *grateful* or *relieved* or a phrase like *delivered from imminent hell,* but his head was feather light with anticipation that within the hour he would be again with Anne. He had trusted McCann and Duval and Jones, and across the gulf of years their humanity had matched all he had hoped; these could ask any service of him and have it.

And Anne, oh, Anne!

In the more rational area of his mind, the area that danced with triumph at the chance taken and won, he reached back in the military history he knew so well to say with one of his iron-nerved models, the General of Waterloo, that it had been "a damned close-run thing."

And now, Anne, the stars!

A thousand years passed before he returned, an old man, homing.

part IV

STAR SOLDIER

1

THE SHIP HOVERING OVER THE YARRA
Valley was no clumsy *Search* or *Kiev* but a miniature,
a slender tube of living quarters and cryogenic dormitory formed round the central jet system. The great
trumpet-bells of monopolar magnets gathering fuel
from the dust of space were gone from fore and aft.
New systems reached million-K claws into space to
draw solid particles into the accelerator throat, systems that Soldier, more conversant with moralities
than with mechanics, neither understood nor wished
to.

Jack McCann claimed understanding of these miracles of the new breed of physicists, but Jack was an
old man, older than Soldier by a few unimportant
years and showing it in falterings of memory and purpose and comprehension. That his receptiveness to
juvenation treatments was failing did not affect his
operational expertise; his dropping was ingrained,
automatic as breathing.

"That damned Library is still there. Want to drop
on the roof?"

"No, Jack. On the hill where Ngalyod chased us off
the planet."

"Nothing there but grass."

"Good enough. I can look around before I find the
people—or they find me."

"There's no people, Tommy, here or anywhere on the planet."

"They are somewhere. It is not a destroyed world."

Jack's probes had flitted through the ruins of cities and found only emptiness, but it had never been worthwhile to argue with Thomas; he wanted people here, and would believe in them until truth poleaxed him.

Soldier whistled a staccato code and the bundle at his feet unrolled itself to spread across the floor of the Drop Chamber, adjusting its shape until it became an eight-petalled lotus five metres across, green-fleshed, yellow-veined, pulsating faintly. He removed his boots and unbuttoned his tunic.

Jack said, "It's cold down there—seventeen degrees. In an Australian summer!"

"I can bear the chill for a while. Whitwhit can warm me if need be."

At the sound of its name the lotus shape shivered slightly (whether in pleasure or simple readiness they were still unsure) and lifted the edges of its petals as if in greeting. Soldier stripped and stepped onto the flattened hump at its centre. Nakedness revealed him as a slender millenarian, grown grey and stringy with age, and showing his Aboriginal heritage more plainly where his face was lined and loosened.

The lotus lifted up its leaves to enclose him in a seamless bud and extruded thick stumps of its core to form elephantine limbs on which it padded to the air lock.

Sixty seconds later, General the Atkins's Thomas was plummeting home.

2

THE LOTUS LANDED VERTICALLY, WITH-
out shock. Soldier (the name had never left him)
whistled for vision. Inside the thing's structure (ani-
mallike and plantlike but in fact something that was
neither) a rapid flow of messenger proteins and en-
zymelike cell-operators took place; the green tissue
cleared to glassy clarity save for fine yellow veins
branching and pulsating. He looked out through a
light golden mesh.

He saw only grass and, on the neighbouring hill,
the Library. It was in ruin, shabby and crumbling,
radiating emptiness as a thing deserted and forgotten.
He turned slowly, seeing that the eucalypts on the
lower slopes had gone. Seventeen degrees too cold
for them? There would be snow here in winter as the
ice advanced from the pole.

He turned to the front again and saw, with shock,
that a . . . person . . . had appeared as if from nowhere. He had been sure there was nobody within a
kil of him.

The . . . person . . . seemed curiously indetermi-
nate; his—or her, or its—face was unformed and flu-
idly moving, as if seeking shape, and the limbs
swelled and narrowed, even lengthened a little as he
watched. It displayed no sex.

It opened a mouth where no lips had been and

spoke hoarsely, as if attempting speech after long silence: "Come out of there, Tommy."

Soldier's flesh crawled.

As if a decision was made and implemented, the thing shuddered over its whole vague shape—and was Johnno.

It smiled in welcome—and was not quite Johnno. With a rueful shake of the head it tried again—and was Johnno to the life. It said, "You've waited long enough to return," and now the voice was rightly pitched but the words wrong; Johnno would have been much more animated.

Soldier took strong grasp on his sickened reason. On other worlds he had encountered entities as disgusting.

Is this the end of the Ordinand dream, the shuffling on and off of flesh, the sinking of identity?

He considered the simulacrum and his own position. The thing, conjured from nothing, had made no effort to deceive, to seem other than a pretence; it had even mocked its first failure. So, it was a channel, a means of communication. But with whom? Or, perhaps, with what? Change he had expected but nothing so fanciful or disorganising. Terranova's scientists had thought deeply over Indra's Net and the morphic field and had warned him of unpredictable possibilities in the biomass, but they had not guessed at anything like this.

Humanity was not entirely gone from Earth; he had been recognised and familiarly addressed. Yet his decision to come uncovered and unarmed, demonstrating goodwill, might have been a tactical error. The Johnno-thing's friendliness could be a trap designed to lull. But, if so, why?

A possible threat to his life did not greatly disturb him; he had seen and done enough for a single existence and the return to Earth had been, deep in his

mind, a return to origins, an act of farewell. Whatever
happened to him, Whitwhit and Jack would between
them have a total record of what took place, more
complete than one man's senses could provide.

He whistled and the lotus unfolded; he stood quietly in its centre while the Johnno-thing held out
friendly arms. He had no intention of embracing it.
He asked, "What are you? A palimpsest?"

It nodded approval. "No and yes. For the moment
I'm Johnno, written over an ancient armature of flesh.
I'm still gathering the memories. There is so much to
be plucked from the field, assembled and ordered."

Soldier said slowly, "I don't approve of old affection offered as a lie." Indeed his stomach was in revolt.

Instantly the thing lost shape and identity. Its features ran like thick liquid; the heavy muscles shrank
and the slightly bowed legs straightened and
thinned; its colour deepened.

Presciently, Soldier rejected it. "Not you, either."

The half-formed Libary hissed at him, "Deny your
father as you denied your world? Traitor to your
race!"

"That's foolishness."

"So? Then what is this?" It pointed a black index
finger and white light shone from its tip to strike the
ground between two of Whitwhit's petals. The soil
smoked, bubbled, blazed blue-white, and the lotus
curled its body aside, trembling and frightened.

Soldier whistled urgently: *Not to fear! Not hurt
you!* To the Libary-pretence he said, "The action is
remembered and the message taken. If there is to be
speech, find a more suitable speaker."

He supposed, as it began to change, that this prod-
ding must have a purpose. But who or what was the
puppet master? And who the next puppet?

At first he could make nothing of the slender,

lightly brown figure forming itself, but as the Genetic shape solidified he thought, *One of my troopers.* Then, as recognition dawned: *This one I cannot refuse!*

The two Soldiers, the old and the young, scanned each other closely and laughed together. Old Soldier said, "I have been welcomed and I have been warned off. What now?"

"Gossip, venerable Soldier Tommy! Did you capture your Postvorta world?"

"A debriefing session? We took enough for living space."

"Conquistador!" It smiled slyly. "An ecology imperilled, an alien culture shattered?"

"Not at all. The silicon folk recognised intellect in us before we realised the existence of an intelligence embracing parameters and ideals quite inexplicable to us. Much of what seemed murderous hostility was a despairing effort at communication. As for the fighting, it was grim but not irredeemably destructive."

"Soldier Thomas, I am you as at the moment of your leaving Earth; contact was lost when your mind passed beyond the matrix. I know nothing of silicon folk."

Much became plain. But appearance from nowhere remained a mystery. "You will know that we are chemically, biologically, carbon-based structures. The Terranovan biochemistry is silicon-based."

The simulacrum frowned and Soldier recognised his young self in a moment of concentration, seeking an exact expression or a suitable tactic. Its brow cleared; it nodded. "The chemical possibility had been recognised by the Last Culture."

"Why the hiatus, mimic? Were you searching the files for old knowledge?"

"Your old wits are still quick. The morphic field contains the knowledge of every creature that ever thought on this planet. It takes time to winnow one grain of fact from many trillions of grains. And the field enfolds and interpenetrates the planet. It is huge; the transfer of information requires noticeable time." It smiled briefly. "This is reality, not metaphysics. The laws of energy transfer hold."

The theorists on Terranova would be in ecstasy over this. "So you hang in Indra's Net, each at his point of the mesh, awaiting eternity?"

"Jester! That is metaphor. The field is real, detectable by the machineries of mind."

"Connected with the flesh, however. Enough to forge a figure for a returning voyager."

It regarded him thoughtfully. "If I say that the field and the material Earth are interwoven, each an extension of the other, will that have meaning for you?"

"I think you speak of Gaia."

"Near enough; it will do. Tell me something of yourself."

"Your field can't read my mind?"

"As an open book? No. Or not yet. The total of your life's knowledge was absorbed as you entered the field but it must be deployed—tabulated, if the simile helps you—not simply added to the sum of the twenty-eight-year-old who lived on Earth. I repeat that the field is subject to physical laws. So, what you tell me will act as nodes of reference to simplify absorption of the whole."

A shocking possibility occurred to Soldier. "I do not wish to be trapped here. Your Gaia holds nothing I want."

"Why should it? You have your own Gaia to be rejoined on Terranova. Does that surprise you? We did not create Gaia, we joined it. With the emergence of intelligence the field is formed; where life is, there is the field—even a tiny one like a quantum fog around your sleek little ship up there."

Soldier smiled at a thought. "I have been on many worlds."

"And left your trace on the field of each."

"Some were lifeless."

"No longer, Old Soldier. Your lonely spark is there, tenuous but waiting for other life to add to it."

Soldier shuddered at the thought of his mind sprinkled like a dreaming mist across worlds and light-years. He saw himself, momentarily, as a child racing over the stepping-stones of stars, leaving meaningless footprints on lonely silent worlds.

He said, "I will have to confess on Terranova that my poor little rebellion achieved nothing all those years ago."

"It brought Gaia. It opened the selfish minds of the Ordinands to the necessity of gathering all life into their intellectual scheming, not only the self-chosen. You brought Gaia that much nearer, playing your part in the awakening."

So I am a pivot of history! The distinction doesn't charm me. But it will be all one in a million years.

The simulacrum was insisting, "Tell me of yourself. What of Anne?"

He was astonished. "Do you care for her still?"

It explained patiently, "I am not you, the caring Thomas; that man is part of the matrix. His old emotions are only memories of fact, not persisting feelings. It is about you that I ask, using Anne as a key to recollection."

Soldier saw himself more clearly now. He was a vessel discharging its contents into a hastily created recording instrument, offering trifles of fact to a . . . mind? intellect? data base? . . . enclosing not only the physical Earth but its millions of years of history since the first mind thought, I am. It was an overwhelming perception, one to become lost in. He fastened his mind on Anne.

"She was a young girl with an inadequate social background and little emotional schooling. I was an excitement, an explosion, a novelty. She tired of me and settled at last with one of my troopers. I forget which."

"And your beetle?"

"The Search biologists scotched that before it bit."

"And you learned the ancient way of love?"

"Slowly. The scream of a woman signalled the panic rush of Searchers from their canopy on that final night. She was Jean Sengupta, a dark Hindustani woman. She bore me two sons before we reached Terranova. She died in a skirmish early in our time there. I did not contract another close alliance; in a people whose sexual play is a commonplace, bonds are not essential. Is that what you want? And does it matter?"

The thing repeated, like a patient tutor, "It forms a node around which your impressed thought clusters. What is your physiological age?"

"In waking years? About two and a half centuries; I do not keep annual count. Much . . . most of my existence has been spent in cryo-sleep between stars."

"An explorer?"

"The mores and beliefs of the Last Culture did not attract me; I found myself becoming contemptuous of the Searchers and impatient with the religious primness of the *Kiev* people. Since arrogance is a poor attitude in a leader—I was for a short while master of the planet—I finished the work for which I had been enlisted and became an investigator of the nearer stars. I have dropped on forty planets."

The simulacrum rapped, "Life! Is there life?"

Soldier smiled at it. "So your matrix is capable of excitement! Is Gaia lonely for company? There's little of it out there and what there is may require study to recognise it. There is a planet on which pools of oil exhibit communal behaviour, forming groups in flowers shaped like trays of shallow cups. There's another where something we could not find moved stones and mounds of earth to form geometric patterns. It tried to bury my partner under rubble. You will recall the McCann's Jack?"

"The matrix forgets nothing. Only the volume of data inhibits immediate access." It surveyed Soldier abstractedly, as if it tired of him, and said, "You should leave now."

"So soon, my image?"

"What is there here for you?"

"Nothing. Man has moved on and left behind him a spirit world. I am cured."

The image asked, "Of what?"

"Surely that knowledge will be recoverable."

It insisted, "Of what, Old Soldier?"

"Of the mysterious disease I could not understand in Nugan and Jack—homesickness. I contracted it at last and made a final voyage—to discover that in time and mutability there is no home to visit. You, having never left Earth, could not know the ailment."

"Filed for reference, Old Soldier. Now go; you have served your purpose."

"Meaning that I have served yours."

The image did not answer but began to lose rigidity and shape. Soldier watched curiously as it flowed like a melting snowman, collapsing into a mound, changing colour and texture, becoming a small grassy hillock that had not been there before.

So men have become one with their world. They must have moved rapidly to absorption once the mental key was turned. A consummation I am happy to have avoided; being ancient and decrepit Soldier is still more satisfactory than the life of a neurone pathway. Or so I think. But, perhaps there are ethereal compensations.

A clutch of yellow dandelions rose in the grass, the

flowers like tiny faces watching him. Mockery? A salute? Smiling at his fancy, he bowed to them. Solemnly the flowers nodded back.

He whistled, and Whitwhit closed round him.

"Lift me home, Jack."

He would never know it, but he took Earth with him.

3

FROM THE EARTH-FIELD A TENDRIL OF power, infinitely fine, clung to the morphic bubble of Soldier's consciousness, drawn out like a thread from a cocoon, until it met and merged with the tiny field created by the crew of the ship.

The intellect that was Earth prepared for its leap to the stars, for its destiny.

The link, stretching unseen behind the homing ship, would never be broken. It would follow the bubble of consciousness to Terranova and become one with the planet's field, taking into itself the nature and history of intellects vastly other than its own, feeding the wonder and ecstasy throughout its expanding mind. It would follow explorers to the stars and their planets and, over the unending years, to all the sentient worlds of the galaxy. And, perhaps, beyond . . .

Gaia hungered after her children and would be with them always, until they learned their last longing and abandoned the flesh and came home at last.

flowers who they knew smelling him. Blushing? ...
i.e., Willing at him, Emily, he kneeled to them, but
only the flowers nodded back.

The affliction and When it slosed reach him ...
of the bone, fell ...

He would not to know it, she knows, Earth with
him.

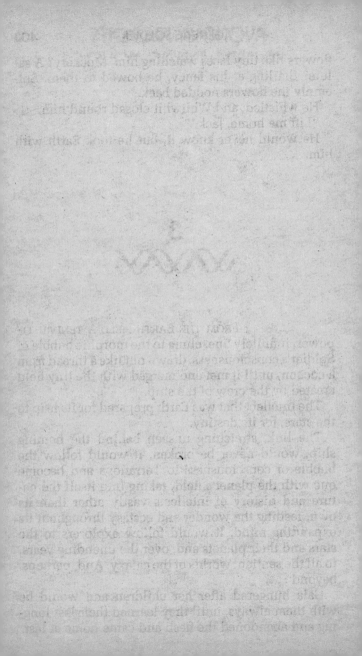

I... Soon the Earth slowly spun in its
power, finally stretching to the normal invisible c...
Slowly a smooth sleeve drawn outlike a thread that
a cocoon, until it met and merged with the tiny cold
sparks in the crew of the ship.

The beauty that was Earth prepared for herself for
the time for it, destiny.

...back, preparing to snap healed the beauty
ships world. Long, he wished, it would follow the
fabric of consciousness. Tomorrow's age become
age with the pleasant field, releasing their itself the returned history of children's realty, other than their
return, testing the wonder and acting throughout the
organisms, mind. It would follow explorers to the
stars and far-flung lands and over the unending years
to all the earthen worlds of the galaxy. And now on
beyond ...

Safe blissward after her children and would be
with them always, until they learned finished things.
The sun abandoned the field and came some at last.

AVONOVA PRESENTS
AWARD-WINNING NOVELS
FROM MASTERS OF SCIENCE FICTION

WULFSYARN
by Phillip Mann   71717-4/ $4.99 US

MIRROR TO THE SKY
by Mark S. Geston   71703-4/ $4.99 US/ $5.99 Can

THE DESTINY MAKERS
by George Turner   71887-1/ $4.99 US/ $5.99 Can

A DEEPER SEA
by Alexander Jablokov   71709-3/ $4.99 US/ $5.99 Can

BEGGARS IN SPAIN
by Nancy Kress   71877-4/ $4.99 US/ $5.99 Can

FLYING TO VALHALLA
by Charles Pellegrino   71881-2/ $4.99 US/ $5.99 Can

ETERNAL LIGHT
by Paul J. McAuley   76623-X/ $4.99 US/ $5.99 Can